WISHFUL THINKING

Published 2015
Printed in the United States of America
ISBN: 978-1-63152-976-4
Library of Congress Control Number: 2014951205

Book design by Stacey Aaronson

For information, address:
She Writes Press
1563 Solano Ave #546
Berkeley, CA 94707
www.shewritespress.com

She Writes Press is a division of Spark Point Studio, LLC.

WISHFUL THINKING

A Novel

BY KAMY WICOFF

SHE WRITES PRESS

To Max and Jed. Duh.

J ENNIFER SHARPE HAD ALWAYS dreamed of being two
people. She had dreamed of being two people when she
was a little girl and wanted to be both a stay-at-home
mom and the president of the United States when she grew up.
She had felt like two people in junior high, when adolescent-
girl hormones could send her from the top of the world to the
bottom in ten seconds flat. But she had never needed to be two
people, or even three, as badly as she did when she woke up
one day (or so it seemed) to find herself a thirty-nine-year-old
divorced mother of two with a laughable amount of child
support, a high-stress, full-time job that didn't pay enough to
cover the child care it required, and a cat that constantly threw
up on the couch.

It was hard to understand how this had happened.

Jennifer tried to understand it as she prepared dinner (it
was a stretch to call boiling pasta and heating up chicken
nuggets *cooking*) while coaching her older son, Julien, through
his math homework while his little brother, Jack, repeatedly

hit him over the head with an inflatable hammer until she grabbed it, put it up on the highest bookshelf, and sent him to his room wailing. She tried to understand it after the boys fell asleep—sometimes as late as ten o'clock when they were particularly reluctant for the day to end and, in truth, she didn't want them to go to bed, either, because her evening time with them was so precious—poured herself a glass of wine, cleaned up cat vomit, and answered e-mail until crawling into bed to read for ten minutes of "me" time. She tried to understand it when she had to drop her boys off with her out-of-work-actor ex-husband every Saturday for his one night a week with them—a night that, even after a year, she still felt he didn't deserve, since for the first two years after the divorce he'd sometimes gone months without seeing them— and observed that he had gotten a very obvious eye lift, which was apparently more important to him than contributing to Julien's guitar lessons. And she tried to understand it when she arrived for her job as executive vice president for community programs and development at the New York City Housing Authority each morning and confronted a mountain of paperwork only an eighteen-armed, multi-brained superhero could ever make disappear. Fourteen years before, she had been an attractive, accomplished, fresh-faced business school graduate with a hot boyfriend who was starring in a TV pilot. Now she was struggling to keep her bathtub clean.

Somewhere there is a woman, Jennifer had written in a recent e-mail to her best friend, Vinita, also a working— though semi-happily married—mother of three, *who, at thirty-nine, has multiple children who play multiple instruments and multiple sports and excel in multiple subjects, who also runs multiple businesses, sits on multiple charitable boards, and can do multiple sit-ups.* Thinking of the slew of books and articles she could never stop herself from reading by women who had it all, humble-bragging about the difficulties of having it all, she'd ruefully gone on: *I, on the other hand, can only do one sit-up and hold down one job (just barely), and yesterday I tried to register Jack, who plays zero sports, for winter soccer, only to be told I was multiple months too late.* Vinita, whom Jennifer had known since college, had written back immediately: *Show me that woman,* she replied, *and I will give her multiple kicks to the ass.*

Jennifer had appreciated the sisterly support. But part of her had had a hard time laughing about it. This woman was out there. How did Jennifer know it? Because every day, as she vainly attempted to keep up with her, Jennifer was pretty sure she was the one whose ass was getting a kicking.

Tuesday, September 24, began like any other day in Jennifer's life since she and Norman had split up. At 6:45 a.m., her Mr. Coffee programmable coffeemaker, the reigning love of her life, began to burble, emitting piquant caffeinated smells from its perch on a barstool next to the sofa bed she slept on that, when fully deployed, occupied 75 percent of the living room of her apartment. With a groan and a stretch, Jennifer swiveled into an upright position, stood up, and made her way down the hallway to the bathroom, where she stripped off her favorite Beatles *Revolver* T-shirt and pajama bottoms and stepped into the shower. The water pressure was low again, and the shampoo in her hair dripped down her face at the pace of sludge as she stood beneath the trickle flowing weakly from the nozzle. Just as she was beginning to come to, she heard the tap of little-boy feet and smiled. Julien.

"Hey, Mom," he said from outside the shower curtain in his eight-going-on-fourteen, offhandedly cool manner. *Whatever happened to "Mommy"?* she thought. "Can I play a game on your phone?"

"Julien," she said, pulling the curtain back sharply and sticking her head out, shampoo foam still clinging to her nose, "this cannot be an every-morning thing! If you play, your brother is going to want to play, and you know it's impossible to get him out of the house in the mornings anyway—"

"But, Mom, I already practiced guitar for twenty minutes and Jack is still asleep and yesterday you said I could if I practiced guitar and did all of my homework but then you came home late again so I haven't played on your phone for, like, two whole days! Please! *Please?*" Julien's speech had almost instantly taken on the pressurized whine that made Jennifer's teeth ache with irritation. But her chest had tightened sharply when she'd heard Julien say he'd been up even earlier than she had, practicing. She worried about his intensity, his inability to relax sometimes, to give himself a break. She'd been the same way when she was a little girl and wasn't much better about it now.

"I practiced for thirty minutes yesterday," he said, switching from entreaty to reproach. "Are you *sure* you can't come to my recital?"

Jennifer shook her head sadly. Julien's guitar recital was at four o'clock that afternoon. Four o'clock on a weekday. How was any working parent supposed to swing that? She wanted to say as much, but Julien would have protested, because while she'd always been a working mom, until a few months ago she'd been a working mom who could attend afternoon guitar recitals. In fact, her old boss at the New York City Housing Authority had recruited her from a much more lucrative career in management consulting largely by promising her precisely that kind of flexibility. But NYCHA had recently been taken over by a new chairman, handpicked by the mayor as part of his plan to impose a "private-sector work ethic" onto every branch of city government. Which meant that for months now, leaving work for things like music recitals and even Jack's speech-therapy appointments had been next to impossible.

"Please can I play on your phone, Mommy?" Julien asked again, smiling at her hopefully. *Mommy.* That did it.

"Okay," she said. As his lean, shirtless, little-boy body zipped out the door, she called after him, "But only for ten minutes!"

Alone again in the underwhelming shower, Jennifer looked a little longingly at the space where he'd stood. Then she pulled the curtain closed and began to scrub at the lingering suds in her hair. It was time to wake up for real and tackle the day.

Each morning in the shower, Jennifer composed two mental to-do lists, one for work and one for home. These lists corresponded to her two jobs, first as a city employee and second as personal assistant, cruise director, and waitress (or so motherhood seemed, at times) to young masters Julien and Jack Bideau. Some part of her felt she had the order wrong—shouldn't her *first* checklist be her mommy to-dos and her second checklist be her work to-dos? But the reality was that while work demanded her full attention in order for her to stay employed, playdates, field trips, and pizza days were things she worked hard to stay abreast of but often just plain screwed up, and there was no boss to reprimand her when she did. Jennifer wished her longtime babysitter, Melissa, would make the home to-do list her own, fulfilling a dearly held fantasy Jennifer had of a babysitter who ran her household with the military precision of a housekeeper from a *Masterpiece Theatre* series. But Melissa was a well-meaning twenty-something who had come to work for Jennifer because she lacked direction in life, and she never even did the dishes.

As she began to compile her lists, Jennifer's brain soon

began to scramble. Did the boys have playdates? Did Melissa have to leave early today? What was her first meeting at work? Who was she supposed to call, what was she supposed to order online (a new pair of soccer cleats, supplies for a school project, groceries?), who had she said she would have lunch with, and what time was the spin class she wanted to at least pretend to intend to attend? Jennifer turned off the shower and stepped onto the bath mat. There was only one remedy for the all-too-familiar anxiety that had overtaken her, as it did most mornings: her phone. Or, more specifically, the calendar on her phone, which, with its assiduously kept lists and color-coded entries, was the scaffolding that supported the fragile, absurdly complex, always-near-collapse structure that was her life.

"Julien!" she shouted, mentally adding *wash the towels* to her "home" list as she pulled a damp, faintly sour one from the rack. "I need my phone!"

"I can't find it!" he yelled back.

Towel wrapped around her head, body still dripping, Jennifer froze like an animal, her ears pricked up, her mind racing. Julien couldn't find her phone? Julien could always find her phone. She always kept her phone on the end table next to the couch. She always looked at it before she went to sleep. But last night she had fallen asleep with the television on after having finished half—okay, three-quarters—of a bottle of wine. (She'd decided to have more "me" time, as though becoming steadily less conscious while watching *Gilmore Girls* on Netflix was treating herself somehow.) Her phone was her life. Her life was in her phone. How could she not know if it was there?

Jennifer dressed quickly and walked into the living room. She found Julien determinedly searching the crevices of the creaking sofa bed. She began searching, too, starting with her briefcase and moving on to every counter and surface she could imagine leaving her phone on, but came up empty every time. She soon confirmed that it was in none of the usual places in the boys' room (under the bunk beds, next to Julien's clock radio) or her bathroom (back of the toilet, next to her toothbrush), either. As she reentered the living room empty-handed, Jennifer's heart sank. When was the last time she'd had it? She'd gotten home late the night before and had had to rush through the evening routine with the boys, so she hadn't checked her phone then. Vinita had called her on her landline. And after she'd hung up with Vinita, there'd been the wine, the TV, and the sleep. It wasn't at work, she knew, because she'd texted Melissa from the cab she'd taken in her rush to get home.

It was gone. She was sure of it. She'd lost her phone once before—about as expensive a mistake as you could make, aside from dropping a diamond ring down a grate—and even with the free upgrade she'd had coming, it had cost her $300 to replace. She didn't want to think about what it was going to cost her to replace it now.

Julien was tugging at her sleeve. Crouching down, she took him by the shoulders and looked him in the eye. "I must have dropped it somewhere," she told him. He let out a cry. "It's a phone!" she said, attempting to be the grown-up, though she couldn't help adding, "And losing it is much worse for me than it is for you."

Julien raised his eyebrows skeptically, like, *Really?* She raised her eyebrows back at him. *Really.* "Sorry, Mom," he said. "Can I have gum on the way to school?"

"No," she answered. Jennifer sat back on her heels. The battery on her dirt-cheap cordless landline was dead (she'd left it off the charger, naturally, after hanging up with Vinita), so she couldn't even try calling her phone until she got to work. She sighed. But part of her wondered, would a morning without her phone be so bad? Yes her phone kept her life together. But sometimes its chimes, pings and never-ending emails weighed on her like a digital ball and chain.

Suddenly, Julien pointed to her laptop on the kitchen table. "Did you try that thing?" he asked.

"What thing?"

"That thing we installed last time. Find My Phone."

Find My Phone! How could she have been so stupid? Jennifer got quickly to her feet, trying not to be too hopeful but hopeful all the same, ran over to the table, sat down, and booted up her laptop.

She typed the URL and logged in. Julien stood expectantly at her side. A big green button appeared: FIND MY PHONE. Most likely her phone was somewhere in Queens, being prepped for sale on Canal Street, she thought, having been hocked by her opportunistic cab driver. (*Bastard!*) But it was worth a try. She clicked. She watched the wheel spin. LOCATING . . .

A map appeared, and on it a blue dot. Jennifer did a double take. The dot was at 270 West Eleventh Street. "That's our address!" Julien cried. "It's here!"

Could it be? She had looked everywhere, and she could find a Lego head in a box of Playmobil. Maybe she had dropped it in the lobby?

Just then Jack came stumbling in, half crying. "Mama," he said, climbing into her lap and rubbing his eyes. "Do I have school today?" Jack asked this every morning. Unlike his older brother, who had celebrated the first time he'd had "real" homework (though he was now considerably less enamored), Jack liked to cuddle, sleep in, and wear pajamas to the park. "Yes, darling," she said. Glancing at the time on her computer, she saw that it was already seven fifteen. To get both boys to their respective schools and her to work on time, they had to be out the door by 7:40 sharp—a departure time that was quickly receding from the realm of possibility.

"Play the sound, Mom," Julien said, reaching over her to the trackpad. He clicked the button that read PLAY SOUND. "Do you hear anything?" he asked. She didn't.

"Do you want to play a game?" Jennifer asked Jack, nudging him off her lap. "We need to listen for a sound coming from Mommy's phone so we can find it!"

"You wost your phone *again*!" Jack cried.

"*Lost*," Jennifer corrected him, deliberately pronouncing the *L*. Correcting Jack's speech, which she, Jack's speech therapist, and his preschool teacher worried over constantly these days, had become so automatic she probably would have done it even if he were saying, "Wook out!" as a steel beam fell on her head.

"Lllost," Jack repeated, pressing his tongue dutifully against the top of his palate.

"Shhh," Julien said impatiently. "Be quiet." Julien began canvassing the living room, tiptoeing around it like Elmer Fudd in hunting season. Jack followed suit. Jennifer walked down the hallway into the boys' room but heard nothing but the sound of her children, fighting in the living room over who would get to play on it first once the phone was found. They were making such a racket she couldn't hear herself think, let alone hear her phone if it were bleating for help.

"Enough!" Jennifer barked, walking back into the living room. "Jack, get dressed! Julien, pack up your homework!"

The boys skedaddled posthaste. The room was quiet at last. Alone, Jennifer held her breath and listened. This time she heard something. Faint but distinct, it was a reverberating chime, like a prolonged submarine ping. Following the sound of it, she found herself hunching down in front of her own front door. The muffled ping was coming from the other side.

Jennifer fumbled with the locks, then flung the door open

and looked down. To her astonishment, a heavy, cream-colored envelope lay at her feet. *FOR MS. JENNIFER SHARPE, 270 West 11th Street, Apt. 19A, New York, New York, 10014.* There was no postmark and no return address. Jennifer bent down and picked up the envelope. The lettering was extravagant, like a wedding invitation, though on closer inspection she could see it wasn't handwritten but had been printed somehow. She turned the envelope over and opened it, careful not to let the elegant object tear. Its interior was lined with what looked like gold leaf. Her phone, its chiming beacon still sounding, was tucked inside.

It was all Jennifer could do not to kiss it. Sliding her thumb across her phone's smooth face, she silenced the chiming sound and allowed herself a moment of delicious relief, which was immediately interrupted by the boys, who'd heard the pinging and come barreling down the hall, lunging over each other for the phone. Jennifer was about to tell them to shut up and put their shoes on (though not in so many words), when she saw something strange on her home screen: an envelope, the same creamy color as the envelope her phone had been in moments before, addressed in the same elaborate, formal font, to her.

By now the boys were practically climbing up her legs. "Quiet!" she said. It was like screaming into the wind. "*Quiet!*" she roared. Startled, the boys exchanged a glance.

"What is it, Mama?" asked Jack, who had not made it past striped socks and a *Green Lantern* T-shirt in his interrupted efforts to get dressed.

Jennifer, not answering, tapped the envelope once with her thumb. It opened, and a piece of stationery glided out. She had just begun to register that a message was written on it when, at a volume Jennifer had not thought her phone capable of, a clear, ringing female voice filled the room. "Dear Ms.

Sharpe," it began. The boys' eyes went wide. "As you have undoubtedly deduced, your phone came to be in my possession last night. I am sorry not to have returned it to you immediately, but the hour was very late." Jennifer turned her phone over and around, as though its exterior might provide some clue to the adventures it had been through during the night. Her boys stared too. The voice, sonorous and precise, had established a commanding presence in their little living room.

"I have taken a small liberty, however," the voice continued. "I am an inventor, of sorts, and I have been working on an application designed, I now realize, precisely for a person such as you. Last night, in a fit of inspiration, I installed this application on your phone." Upon hearing this, Jennifer held her phone away from her body. The boys took several steps back as well.

"It really is quite a miraculous application; I'm sure you will agree! A word of warning, however. If you choose to use it, please contact me first. It is a very powerful technology and requires some instruction if it is to be used safely. Again, please accept my apologies for any inconvenience this may have caused. I hope to hear from you soon. Ta-ta for now! Sincerely, Dr. Diane Sexton." The message ceased its methodical scroll, slipped back into its envelope, and vanished.

"Whoa," Julien said.

"Double whoa," Jennifer agreed. Then she looked at the time: 7:29. *Seven twenty-nine!*

Snapping out of the spell that had temporarily ensnared them, Jennifer knelt to activate her two still-somewhat-stupefied sons. "Seven twenty-nine!" she cried. "Julien, put on your shoes! Jack, pants, now!"

The boys scattered with shouts of assent, though Jennifer knew she'd soon be in Jack's room, ensuring the execution of the pants portion of his ensemble. Jennifer quickly crossed to the kitchen and threw turkey slices, an applesauce, and a squeezie yogurt into Jack's Scooby-Doo lunch box (Julien ate lunch at school), then grabbed two breakfast bars for the boys to eat on the train. Gathering her own things, she ran through her mental checklist, grabbing each item as she thought of it: laptop, notebook, lipstick, wallet, keys, phone. *Phone.*

She smiled. *How lucky to have it back,* she thought, as she slipped its slim frame into her coat pocket, the feel of it in her hand as gratifying as a shot of dopamine. The circumstances of its return could hardly have been stranger, to be sure. But it had been returned to her, and for now that was all she needed to know.

two | WORK

THE BOYS GOT TO school on time, but not early enough for Jennifer to get to work when she was supposed to, which, in the new regime, was punishable by public humiliation by staff meeting. And so she was running through a fine fall mist, laptop bag slapping awkwardly against her left hip, the band that held her thick, shoulder-length brown hair sliding steadily downward toward the tip of her ponytail as her chunky heels clomped along the concrete.

This happened more often than she liked to admit: not "running" to an appointment or to work or to the boys' schools in the metaphorical sense, but *literally* running, without a moment to spare. In the not-so-distant past, the only time Jennifer had run anywhere had been when she was training for a marathon. (Had that really been her, in a pre-baby, pre-divorce life, sailing through Central Park in a jog bra with the slightest hint of a six-pack?) Arriving at the offices of the New York City Housing Authority at 250 Broadway, Jennifer stopped to catch her breath at last and, producing a Kleenex, dabbed at the sweat stippling her forehead. As she stepped into the hustle and bustle of the building's vast lobby, however, taking her place among the ranks of neatly dressed adults holding cups of coffee and swiping ID badges one after the next at the turnstiles next to the elevator banks, nary a child or sippy cup in sight, her frantic dash gave way to a sense of purposeful calm. In the morning, work was a refuge. By the end of the day, she longed for home.

Riding up the elevator to her office on the twentieth floor, Jennifer shifted her focus entirely to her job, which, for all its headaches and despite her new boss, she loved. She had a boggling number of things to do, *but it's morning!* she reminded herself. Anything was possible.

Then the elevator doors opened and Jennifer saw her eager, easily flustered, and very young assistant, Tim, standing there, evidently waiting for her. This had never happened before. She was a city employee, not Anna Wintour. But there he was, holding his phone and gesturing at her with it in a faintly accusatory way.

"Is your phone on?" he asked.

"Of course it is . . . oh, *Fahrvergnügen!*" she exclaimed, pulling a face and *grr*-ing with frustration. Tim made a face, too, though it was more of an eye roll. (He had never gotten used to the array of curse-word substitutes she had adopted since she'd had children.) She pulled out her phone and found it was set to silent—she must have forgotten to switch the sound back on after her last meeting yesterday. There were at least six messages from Tim from the last half hour, stacked up like little green planks eating up the surface of the screen.

"Bill is waiting for you," Tim said as they began to walk toward her office. "He says he e-mailed you last night? There's somebody here; she's been here since eight thirty."

"Who?" Jennifer asked.

Tim pulled up an e-mail on his phone. "Alicia Richardson?"

"Alicia Richardson? What's she doing here?" Jennifer hadn't seen Alicia Richardson in years. A former high school principal who had turned around one of the worst-performing schools in Brooklyn, Alicia had been running education programming for the department when Jennifer came on board. The two of them had overlapped only briefly, but it had been long enough for Alicia to make clear just how unimpressed she was with Jennifer's credentials. "That MBA," Alicia had once acidly informed her, "is about as relevant to what we're doing here as an astronaut suit." Alicia had left soon after to become a superintendent at a district in Brooklyn.

Once in Jennifer's modest office, which had just enough room for her desk and a single chair for visitors sandwiched between the wall and a bookcase, Tim managed to sit down across from her, long legs bent, knees grazing the edge of Jennifer's desk. Jennifer woke up her computer and began scanning her inbox for Bill's e-mail.

"Don't forget to punch in," Tim said with singsong sarcasm.

"Oh, for Pete's sake!" Jennifer said, minimizing her e-mail and opening up the Employee Time Clock application Bill had imposed upon them during his first week as department head. A window popped up. *You're late*, it read. "I know," she muttered. Then another message popped up. An IM from Bill. *Please join me in my office. Meeting with Alicia Richardson as per my e-mail last night.*

Barely suppressing a groan, Jennifer grabbed a legal pad and a pen and stood up. Tim stood too. "Remember how it used to be?" he asked, following her out into the hallway, his wide, bony shoulders slumping. "When it was just you and me, and I didn't have to pick up anybody's dry cleaning?"

Jennifer, despite her rush, stopped and put a hand on Tim's arm. She knew that in many ways he'd gotten the rawest deal when Bill had taken over, having gone from being Jennifer's assistant—doing grunt work, yes, but plenty of meaningful work too—to being Jennifer's and Bill's, which had turned out to mean mostly Bill's, whose "private-sector work ethic" had come complete with the expectation that his underlings would serve him in the style to which he had become accustomed.

"It's going to get better," she reassured him, squeezing his elbow and feeling, as she often did, as though he were one of her boys too. But as she went walk-running down the hallway, late for a meeting she hadn't even known was happening until ten minutes ago, Jennifer knew he didn't believe it.

Why should he, when she didn't either?

BILL TRUITT HAD NOT been on the job long, but his office, with its cool gray carpet, big glass desk, and fragrant, hotel-size arrangement of lilies, was much more like the offices of the powerful men Jennifer remembered from her years as a management consultant than the dingy government offices she'd grown used to. (She couldn't imagine how he'd purged that old-government-office-building smell so fast. Maybe it was the lilies.) On the walls hung what Jennifer and Tim privately referred to as Bill's Wall of Fame: photos of him with a who's who of wealthy New York, many of the photos prominently featuring Mayor Fitch. They were an odd couple, Bill, the African American former all-American football player and New York real estate heir, and Mayor Fitch, the fair-skinned, thin-lipped managerial numbers type who never got a tan and played golf only because he had to. Being fellow members of the .01 percent, however, with multiple homes, wives with staffs, and children in the Ivy Leagues, had apparently closed some of the gaps that undoubtedly still existed between them.

After a light tap, Jennifer pushed the door open, and as she walked in, Alicia Richardson stood to greet her. Jennifer had almost forgotten how elegant and striking Alicia was. Her light brown curls were close-cropped as perfectly as Viola Davis's at the Oscars, and she was wearing one of her signature cream-colored suits, its ivory sheen offsetting her mocha-colored skin. Alicia had always made Jennifer feel like she was wearing mom jeans to a cocktail party. Their eyes met, and despite herself Jennifer felt her body zip up and stiffen. Alicia, however, didn't blink. She even looked somewhat smug. Which was alarming.

"Jennifer," Alicia said, offering her hand and smiling. "It's good to see you again."

The three of them exchanged the necessary pleasantries and then sat down. Outside the window, the 110-story building that Bill's company, Bill Truitt Enterprises, had completed just before his appointment as NYCHA's head dominated the skyline. Bill had proudly pointed it out to Jennifer during their first meeting at his office, but despite the macho posturing (what better than a 110-story dick planted right outside the window to set the proper tone with new employees?), that meeting had been a good one. For a few weeks after his appointment, in fact, Jennifer had thought Bill Truitt was the best thing that had ever happened to her. Almost every day now, she tried to remind herself of this fact: that Bill Truitt—along with a portion of the $300 million of federal stimulus money the new mayor had used his business contacts to extract from a Republican-controlled Congress for

NYCHA—was responsible for reviving the project dearest to her heart, one she'd invested so much in that it had almost been like a third baby: a new kind of community center she called It Takes a Village.

The concept for It Takes a Village was simple. When she'd first begun working at NYCHA, Jennifer had observed (as many had before her) that one of the biggest problems low-income-housing residents had in getting ahead, or even just in managing their lives, was wasted time. There was no central place where they could get job training and pay the rent; pick up assistance checks and get child care; get matched with the best-suited nonprofit resources for their needs and meet with their social worker too. Everything was scattered, and every-thing took forever. From this problem the solution of It Takes a Village was born: a community center that would house under one roof outposts for all the agencies, services, and resources residents needed, government and nongovern-ment alike. After years of work, both designing the center and lining up the necessary support from private foundations and government agencies, Jennifer had finally completed a request for proposal for contractors to bid on building the flagship site. Just as the RFP was about to go out, however, the economy crashed. Jennifer still remembered standing in her office when the news of a citywide freeze on new projects came down, and the feeling of her heart breaking. The funding drought after that had been so severe that Jennifer had ceased to consider It Takes a Village a dream deferred. Instead it had been a dream DOA.

That was, until Bill Truitt, builder of big things, came on board and Jennifer decided to take a chance and show him the old RFP. To her delight, he loved it. It Takes a Village, with its proposed partnerships between government agencies and private foundations, and its artist's renderings of what the center might look like, combined his twin loves of building and social entrepreneurship. It would, he said, be his legacy. Bill's ties to the mayor made securing a portion of the federal stimulus funds easy, though Bill had made it clear that would be the only easy thing about it. "This federal money shouldn't be making anybody feel that things are going to get cushy now," Bill had told her and Tim sternly, as if they were a couple of lazy babies. "The city is still broke, and all of us have to do more with less. That means longer hours, more efficiency, and more accountability in this office for your time. Having worked in the private sector, Jennifer, you know what I mean."

She did. But it was one thing to put in an eighty-hour workweek for a job that paid better than most; it was another to do it for a job that paid considerably less. The prospect of finally seeing the center built, after so many years of waiting, had kept her going thus far, but she still hadn't been working the hours Bill expected, something the tattletale Employee Time Clock never let her forget.

Sitting down, Jennifer noticed that Alicia was holding a copy of the original proposal for It Takes a Village in her hands. Jennifer's stomach clenched. She was about to ask to what she owed the pleasure, when Bill turned toward his wall, took a photo down from it, and, giving Alicia a wink, pushed it across his desk, gesturing for Jennifer to look. It was picture of a very young Alicia, in a cap and gown, standing next to a very old Bill, with salt-and-pepper hair.

"My father, Bill Senior," Bill said, "with one of the first graduates of the BTE for Good Foundation's scholarship program, Alicia L. Richardson." Jennifer peered at the photo with as much cheerful interest as she could muster. "You two already know each other, right?" Bill asked as he hung the photo back up on the wall.

"Yes," Jennifer said. "Alicia was here when I started seven years ago. How inspiring about your father, and about the scholarship. Wow!"

Bill smiled. Alicia smiled. Jennifer smiled. She wished she'd had time to read that e-mail. "So, Jennifer," Bill began, leaning back in the black, throne-like Eames office chair he had purchased to replace his subpar city-issued seat. "You know I hold you in the highest regard. It Takes a Village is the most exciting thing happening at NYCHA right now, and we have you to thank for it. But frankly, things just aren't moving fast enough."

"We are right on schedule," Jennifer said, "according to the plan you and I formulated when—"

Bill cut her off with a wave of his hand. "I want to open the flagship center one year from now. Two years is too long. We should be breaking ground soon, not having another damn residents' meeting." Jennifer was about to object, when Bill sat up and placed both elbows on his desk, clasping his hands in front of him. "I've built shopping malls in less time than we've allotted to build this center. I'm not saying it's your fault. I think you need some additional help. Which is why Alicia is here. Alicia has been the superintendent over at District Thirteen for several years now, which of course is the district where the center will be built. She grew up in the Marcy Houses. Grew up there and got out! She knows the community, and she's a leader."

Jennifer tried not to blanch. What was Bill saying? Was he going to put Alicia in charge of It Takes a Village? From the way Alicia was nodding and smiling, clucking modestly as Bill sang her praises, it appeared he was about to do exactly that.

"I think what Bill is trying to say, Jennifer," Alicia said, turning to her and speaking in the firm but friendly tones of the high school principal she had once been, "is that since

Binnie Freeman left, you haven't had someone in the department with a history and track record with the community, something I can bring to the table as the public face of the project." It was true that Jennifer was an outsider, with her white suburban upbringing and her formerly white-shoe career. Binnie, her former boss and mentor, had been the one with a history with the community. But she had been with the department seven years now, and It Takes a Village was *hers*, body and soul. The idea of being demoted to some kind of behind-the-scenes brain-on-a-stick, good for nothing but number crunching and spreadsheets while none other than Alicia Richardson took the credit for her hard work, was devastating. "To begin with—and Bill agrees with me on this—we ought to change the name. I came up with One Stop."

"Doesn't that take some of the poetry out of it?" Jennifer asked.

"It helps if the residents understand what it *is*," Alicia responded. Jennifer somehow managed a tight-lipped smile before turning back to Bill. When she did, however, she was surprised to discover that he was now fixing Alicia with the same sober, tough-love expression he'd trained on Jennifer just moments ago.

"When we first discussed this a few weeks ago, Alicia, we talked about your coming on as the head of this project." Alicia nodded. "But since then," he continued, "I've reconsidered." Jennifer now had the pleasure of watching the smugness drain right out of Alicia's face. "After careful review, I've decided that the best thing would be for you and Jennifer to serve as co-heads of One Stop. You will manage the residents and community partnerships, and Jennifer will head strategy and interagency planning."

There was a pause you could have parked a car in. Then Alicia and Jennifer both began to talk at once.

"Hold on a minute, now," Bill said. "You don't even know the whole offer yet!" Opening a file drawer, he produced two sets of blue-backed contracts. "I thought you might not like the cohead idea, Alicia. And, Jennifer, to be honest, I've been concerned about your level of commitment. So I decided to do a little innovating of my own. To sweeten the pot for both of you." Bill passed a contract to each of them.

"Because this is a public-private partnership," he continued, "it's possible for me to allocate some additional cash to staff costs from the private-foundation side. If you can meet the milestones set out here over the next twelve months," he said, "you'll be given a cash bonus of five thousand dollars *per quarter*, provided by BTE for Good." Bill sat back again, clearly relishing having leaped from the Grinch to Santa Claus in a single bound.

Jennifer couldn't believe her ears. A $20,000 bonus in a single year? With that, she could put something away for the boys' college fund. She could pay off her credit card bills. She could even, she thought, take her sons on a real vacation. (Or maybe just pay off her credit card bills.) With what was effectively a $20,000 raise, she could breathe a little easier— financially, anyway—for the first time since she and Norman had split.

"It isn't charity," Bill added. "If you fail to meet your quarterly milestones, you'll be let go. Simple as that."

Alicia was looking over the contract, brows knit. Jennifer began to scan hers too. Twenty thousand dollars was a lot of money, but at a glance, Jennifer could see that if she accepted these terms, she'd pay for every penny.

"This is a lot to take in," Jennifer said, looking up at Bill. "I'm sure Alicia will also need some time to review it."

Alicia nodded once, already standing.

"Of course," Bill said, standing too. "But I think you'll find it a very attractive proposal. An offer you can't refuse, as they say." *As who says?* Jennifer wanted to ask. *Mob bosses?* Coming around his desk, Bill joined the two of them, picking up the copy of the proposal for It Takes a Village—now called One Stop, apparently—that he kept on his desk.

"You know, Jennifer," he said, "we never really talked about why I took this job. About why I'm taking time out from projects like that"—again with the goddamn skyscraper—"to work on a project like this." Bill tapped the proposal's cover. "Alicia knows," he said, nodding toward her. Bill opened up the proposal to a dog-eared page: a photograph of Coco, a young single mother from the Whitman Houses, on a stoop with her three sons. Jennifer loved Coco. From the look on Bill's face as he gazed at the photograph, Bill did too.

"I'm doing this for her," Bill said. "No man in this picture. Just a single African American mom, buried in paperwork and government bureaucracy every time she tries to change her life, or even just get what she needs, stuck in a system that isn't an opportunity but a trap." Looking up, Bill met Jennifer's eyes. Jennifer saw true feeling there, but she also saw a flash of the politician she suspected Bill aspired to be. "That was my grandmother, in public housing in 1950's Chicago. And that," he said, pointing to one of the little boys, "was my dad."

At that, Alicia managed to look at Bill with some of her previous warmth. "Your father was a great man," she said. Jennifer murmured her assent, though all she knew about Bill Truitt Sr. was that he was responsible for building the real estate company Bill Jr. had inherited, and that Bill, who had grown up summering in the Hamptons, knew about as much about growing up in the projects as she did. Bill, however, clearly pleased with his performance, set the proposal back down on his desk, solemnly thanked them both, and walked them to the door.

His proposition was straightforward, Jennifer thought. That was for sure. If she met the milestones, she'd put an extra $20,000 in the bank. If she didn't, she'd be fired. High risk, high reward: a familiar tenet of the business world. As she shook Bill's hand, however, and observed the thick, diamond-encrusted watch that always hung heavily from his wrist—a watch that cost more than she would earn that year by working herself to death—she couldn't help thinking, *Though while some of us are risking our rent, some of us aren't even risking our Rolex.*

three | WISHFUL
THINKING

BACK IN HER OFFICE, Jennifer closed the door behind her and sat down, already weary. She had two hours to prepare for a noon meeting she should have spent twice as much time getting ready for. It would take her all day to answer the e-mails that had come in just since the night before. Placing the contract from Bill on her desk, she sighed. Melissa, her babysitter and life linchpin for so many years now, had recently done something about her lack-of-direction problem and enrolled in night school, and had suggested wanting to reduce her hours, a request Jennifer had already been unable to imagine accommodating. How could she work harder than she'd been working already? She couldn't rely on Norman for anything more than his one day a week. And she had no family to call upon—not anymore.

A little more than a year ago, Jennifer had lost her mother to cancer. That was the blow she still couldn't bear, the aching sadness and fear that woke her up in the night, the thing she

never would have believed could happen. When she and
Norman had split, her mother had begun traveling to the city
every weekend from Rockland County, where Jennifer had
grown up, to help her with the boys. For her mother, who had
battled depression on and off her entire life, and whose
marriage to Jennifer's father had never been much more than
tolerable, the boys were just the right kind of medicine. For
Jennifer, having her mother's help had felt like the difference
between sinking and swimming. This had been especially true
during the first two years after the divorce, when Norman had
routinely disappeared at a moment's notice, pursuing second-
rate acting gigs or attending singles' meditation retreats to help
him "heal." Having her mother around had meant that if
Jennifer needed to go to a work conference or even get away
for a few days at a spa with Vinita, the boys would be not only
taken care of but also as happy as they were when they were
with her. Having her mother around had meant that there was
someone in the world she didn't have to pay to take care of,
much less love, her children. And having her mother around
had meant she wasn't alone. When her mother had died, it had
been hard to feel anything but, and Norman's reappearance a
year ago as Saturday-night dad had done little to make her feel
less so. To make matters worse, within months of her
mother's death her father had moved to Arizona with the
hospice nurse who had cared for her mother when Jennifer
couldn't manage it anymore. Jennifer had never been close to
her father, but she'd hoped that in the wake of her mother's
loss, her dad might stay close to her and the boys. Instead he'd
gone west, and she'd been left feeling as if she had lost not just
one parent, but two.

It takes a village, she thought. She could fit her village into
a telephone booth. Her mind flashed to Julien's face that
morning when she'd told him she couldn't come to his guitar

recital. She'd hated having to tell him, again, that she couldn't be there; she hated saying Mommy can't come, Mommy has to work, Mommy wishes she could, but she can't.

Jennifer gave her head a little shake and pinched herself. "Stop it!" she said out loud. She needed a laugh. Jennifer began to compose an e-mail to Vinita. She counted her lucky stars every day that the two of them had ended up living in the same neighborhood in New York (their kids even went to the same public school), though with Vinita raising three daughters under the age of ten and running her pediatrics practice in the West Village, too, the two women provided each other with moral support more than anything.

Somewhere there is a woman, Jennifer typed, *who woke up this morning before her children did, practiced ashtanga yoga while standing on her head in a sweat lodge, showered and shaved her legs, prepared gluten-free pumpkin pancakes to usher in the fall season, and got her children and herself to school and to work on time. I, on the other hand, woke up in a sofa bed with an empty bottle of white wine rolling around under it, fed my kids breakfast bars on the train, and got to work so late I almost missed a meeting I didn't even know was happening.*

That, of course, was the least of her morning's drama. Jennifer thought about losing her phone, the bizarre way she'd gotten it back, and the message from the woman who had returned it to her. *In addition to the usual failures,* she typed, *which include the fact that I am missing Julien's guitar recital today (again), I lost my phone last night and got it back with a weird message about some kind of miracle app.* Jennifer paused, eyeing her phone on her desk. *Call me?*

She hit SEND. She picked up her phone. *An app,* the voice had said. She should look for it. If nothing else, it would be a diverting way to procrastinate. She'd just begun scrolling through the apps on her phone, however, when there was a knock at her door. Tim.

"How'd it go?" he asked, poking his head in.

"Alicia Richardson may be working here soon," Jennifer said, "though it isn't for sure yet."

"Am I going to have to be her assistant too?" Tim asked, his voice rising. "Remember what Bill said when he started? That I was going to have to 'expand' to assist you both? I can't just keep 'expanding'! I'm a human being, not a rubber band!"

Jennifer chose not to respond, and Tim, chastened, switched back to business mode. "I came to check in with you about your schedule," he said. "What do you have today?"

"Let me look," Jennifer answered. She launched her calendar on her phone. And when she did, an unfamiliar screen appeared, filling the surface of her phone with a dark blue, velvety, starry sky. Jennifer blinked, caught in a cognitive double take. *Is this it?* she wondered. As well trained and habituated as a hamster when it came to navigating new apps, she was about to tap her screen, when, against the midnight-blue background, a sparkling wand appeared. Bright and white, it was very like the wand that the plump, grand-motherly fairy godmother in *Cinderella* wielded. Mesmerized, Jennifer stared as the wand began to move. Gracefully, at an almost leisurely pace, it spelled out the words *Wishful Thinking*. Below them materialized the most alluring tagline Jennifer had ever seen in her life: *An App for Women Who Need to Be in More Than One Place at the Same Time.*

This was it, Jennifer thought. Wishful Thinking was the miraculous app Dr. Diane Sexton had taken the liberty of installing on her phone.

She was about to flip it around, show the screen to Tim, and relate the whole story. But something stopped her.

"Give me a minute?" she asked, looking up at him. Nodding, Tim left. Alone again, Jennifer bit her lip and tentatively touched the wand hovering on her velvety-blue screen. Like a shot, her tiny office was filled with the ringing, resonant voice she'd heard earlier that morning.

"Have you ever needed to be in more than one place at the same time?" the voice asked. *Obviously!* Jennifer thought as she cranked down the volume, praying Tim hadn't heard. "With Wishful Thinking, you can be. Simply enter the time, date, place, and Google Maps coordinates for the second appointment you wish to keep the place you *wish* you could be—and through the magic of Wishful Thinking, you will be able to be in both places at once." Then, on the screen, the word *warning* appeared. "This app utilizes a powerful technology," the voice continued sternly. "Prior to use, please contact me, Dr. Diane Sexton, for further instructions."

Dr. Diane Sexton's name was hyperlinked. Jennifer's finger was poised above it. Should she contact this woman? Or should she wipe the entire thing from her phone? Clearly, this was crazy. Dr. Diane Sexton was clearly crazy. *Clearly* (she found herself wanting to use the word *clearly* as often as possible), this was a lifestyle app, a game for desperately overtired and gullible women like her, and as soon as she typed *Guitar recital, the West End School for Music and Art, 4:00 p.m.*, she would be delivered ads for children's guitar lessons and the latest Dan Zanes album and invited to share her Wishful Thinking calendar with friends on Facebook, where they could all "wish" to be together in a virtual coffee shop and max out their credit cards buying imaginary lattes.

Which made it hard to understand why on earth she would e-mail a perfect stranger for "further instructions." She had no idea who this woman was or what she was after. Typing a Wishful Thinking calendar entry, however, was tempting. An app that let a woman be in two places at the same time? It was mommy porn, to be sure. But she couldn't see the harm in fantasizing.

A small white arrow pulsed in and out of view in the lower right-hand corner of the screen. She swiped it.

A window appeared: CREATE AN EVENT.

Guitar Recital, she typed. *West End School for Music and Art, 55 Bethune Street, Tuesday, September 22, 4:00 p.m. to 5:00 p.m.* After saying yes to the app's request to use her current location and confirming the Google Maps coordinates for the West End School, she hit ENTER, and that was that. Her old, familiar calendar returned to the screen, with its legion of entries already eating up every minute of the day—but now with one intriguing addition: the midnight-blue Wishful Thinking entry pulsing subtly in and out of view, like a tactful dinner hostess hovering over the table without quite taking a seat.

Despite herself, Jennifer smiled. *Guitar recital, 4:00 p.m.* She knew it was impossible. But even though it was only wishful thinking, typing the details of Julien's recital so confidently into her calendar had given her a distinct feeling of happiness. Closing her eyes for a moment, she imagined it: that she really could be in two places at the same time, both front and center at Julien's concert *and* at the staff meeting scheduled for four o'clock that day, missing neither an occasion nor a beat. And for that fleeting feeling of transport, Jennifer permitted herself a moment of gratitude to the clearly crazy Dr. Diane Sexton.

IT WAS A LITTLE bit before four when, after an exhausting two-hour meeting, the majority of which involved Jennifer's refereeing between an officer from the Administration for Children's Services and a group of angry parents from the Walt Whitman Houses, Jennifer told Tim she was going downstairs to get a coffee. He reminded her—unnecessarily, as the Employee Time Clock periodically flashed reminders of department meetings—that the staff meeting had been pushed back to four thirty, then asked her to get him a skinny pumpkin-spice latte. Rather than immediately taking the elevator down, however, Jennifer walked to the stairwell. She was going to get coffee, but she needed to make a pit stop first. She was headed to her secret bathroom.

The secret bathroom was on the eighteenth floor. Two months ago, the tenant—a private company that did something in insurance—had filed bankruptcy and departed ignominiously, vacating the entire floor's office space in less than a week. Jennifer still remembered watching as its employees glumly filled elevator after elevator, boxes and picture frames in hand. The first time she and Tim decided to walk down and see what it looked like, both of them found the vast, empty space depressing. But then Jennifer discovered something. While the offices on the eighteenth floor had been padlocked and papered over with threatening signs from creditors, the women's bathroom had been left wide open and, better yet, relatively well kept. It had only taken a few goings-over with cleaning supplies brought from home for Jennifer, who hated to use the NYCHA bathrooms, where a private moment could turn into a chatty meet-and-greet and her colleagues routinely engaged in cross-stall conversation, to turn the secret bathroom into a sanctuary. Only Tim, who had been with her when she found it, and who she felt should know her whereabouts in the event of an emergency, knew of its existence.

And so, at 3:54 p.m., Jennifer was in the secret bathroom, doing her business. She was idly scrolling through *New York Times* articles on her phone when, noting that 4:00 p.m. was approaching, she decided to take a second look at her Wishful Thinking appointment.

It was easy to spot, in what she was coming to recognize as the app's trademark midnight blue: *Guitar Recital, West End School for Music and Art, 55 Bethune Street, Tuesday, September 22,*

4:00 p.m. to 5:00 p.m. As before, it seemed to float above the screen like a mist, utterly distinct from the solid, color-coded calendar entries she was so used to seeing there: orange for work, green for home, baby blue for the boys' school schedules, and on and on. As she turned her phone this way and that, the Wishful Thinking entry, Jennifer thought, was *shimmering*—that was the only word to describe it. Trying to understand how this effect was achieved, she brought her face closer and closer to the screen, eventually drawing so close her nose was practically touching its surface, when suddenly an earsplitting *PING!* nearly sent her down the plumbing.

In a jam in every way, Jennifer did not even attempt to get off the toilet. To her surprise, in fact, she found that she was shaking. Surely she didn't believe there was something to this craziness—that the app, after all, might be real. Taking a deep breath, she willed herself to look back down at her phone. And then she laughed. It was not a teleport or a wrinkle in time or even a message from Wishful Thinking that had caused her to startle like that. It was a plain old text message from Vinita. Ten years ago, text messages had seemed like magic. Now the familiar green thought bubble was as reassuring to her as buckwheat pancakes.

Hey J, the text began, *got your email. Will def call later. Do NOT stress about recital. Yoga chick spent an hour this AM shitting out excess kale. xoxox, V.* The text was punctuated by a very funny-looking emoticon of a tiny pink creature break-dancing, from a Japanese app Vinita was currently obsessed with.

Jennifer was typing *yes call later* when out rang another *PING!* This time she didn't flinch. But this time her whole screen went midnight blue.

She froze. Slowly retracting her thumbs from text position, she cradled the phone in both hands. Then she watched, transfixed, as the gleaming white wand appeared. It hovered a moment on the screen and then, with the subtlest flick, freed itself of the constraints of two dimensions and rose out of her screen to hover above it in midair. Jennifer, suit pants still around her ankles, emitted the tiniest of gasps. *The wand was in 3-D.* She couldn't help thinking that it was reveling in her amazement, pausing to twirl around. At last it tipped back slightly and then snapped forward, pricking the surface of her phone and sending its surface rippling. As the screen settled, these words emerged: *Reminder: Guitar Recital, West End School for Music and Art, 55 Bethune Street, Tuesday, September 22, 4:00 p.m. to 5:00 p.m.*

As clearly crazy as Dr. Diane Sexton was, Jennifer thought, she had to admire her style. *Guitar Recital.* She closed her eyes, and for a moment she was there, basking in the glow of her beautiful little boy. Once again, with its tasteful reminder—in 3-D, no less!—Wishful Thinking had briefly transported her from the city offices she'd ducked out of, with their stale smell of cheap mustard and decades-old carpet, to the place she dearly wished to be.

Remember! the reminder continued, the wand straightening up suddenly and assuming a crisp, authoritative air as it tapped each word of warning. *At the appointed hour, find a place where you can travel unobserved. You must be physically in contact with your phone at both the beginning and the end of the appointment time. When your appointment has concluded, you will be transported back to the place and time where you began it. For further instructions, please contact <u>Dr. Diane Sexton</u>. Safe travels!*

With that, the wand disappeared with a faint *pop.*

The spell broken, Jennifer let out an irritated sigh. A harrumph, more like it. *Safe travels?* Jennifer thought as she pulled up her pants. *This lady really is batty.*

At 3:58, however, Jennifer was standing with one hand on the bathroom door, staring at her phone.

She really should get going if she wanted to get coffee before the staff meeting, she thought. But still she stood unmoving. Was it possible? Could she "travel" to the West End School, go to Julien's recital, then "travel" back to four o'clock in the secret bathroom, and no one would be the wiser?

Three fifty-nine.

Only one more minute. She was certainly unobserved. The staff meeting wasn't for another half an hour. Her hand was on her phone.

Why not wait?

Then Jennifer did something silly. Clicking her heels together lightly, she shut her eyes like Dorothy and whispered a single word: "Julien."

"Julien, Julien, Julien."

Four o'clock.

Hand on her phone, Jennifer felt a jolt. A powerful jolt. And in an instant, a flash of heat emanated from where her fingertips touched her phone. For a moment her skin seemed to adhere to the surface of the now-superheated screen, as though the pads of her fingertips were welded there, but in the split second it took her mind to register the heat and send her hand the signal to pull away, the current spread and shot through the rest of her body. She was melting. Watching as her phone gave rise to a portal, a whirling tunnel materializing before her eyes like the narrow end of a tornado, Jennifer wanted to scream. But while her mind was one big, guttural cry for help, her mouth could not make a sound. Her hand and her phone were one now, and, even stranger, this was becoming true of the rest of her body too. It was as though she were being collapsed and drawn into a tiny point, sucked into a hole that was expanding, opening to take her in . . . and the hole was her phone. Her magical, marvelous smartphone, which, she thought, just as everything went black, was about to do her in completely.

* * *

IT STOPPED AS QUICKLY as it had begun.

Jennifer blinked. It was dark. The dark was so complete at first that she wondered, for a minute, if she had gotten lost somewhere in space. Her heart was ramming in her chest, and her armpits and the middle of her back were dripping with sweat. Her fingers were clenched so tightly around her phone, she was amazed that neither it nor her fingers had cracked in two. Despite the phone-related trauma she had just been put through, however, she was comforted to feel the device intact in her hand. For years she had reached instinctively for her phone whenever she felt scared, threatened, or lonely, searching it for the distraction, the connection, or the message that would calm her. The fact that her phone might now be the threat didn't seem to matter. Or perhaps that was more than she was ready to think about.

The roaring in her ears was gradually beginning to subside. Jennifer, however, remained paralyzed.

PING!

Yelping with fear, she hurled the phone from her body, stumbling slightly and banging into something when she did, causing multiple objects to fall to the floor with a clatter.

Oh my God, she thought, *what have I done?* Shaking, she got down on her knees and began to search madly in the dark, groping desperately until she heard the *ping* again. Then she saw it: a faint glow emanating from under a set of what were apparently metal shelves. Reaching underneath them, she managed to make contact with her fingertips and drag her phone toward her, scraping a bit of skin off the top of her right hand as she did. Exhausted and shaking, she raised her phone hand—she was beginning to think of it as such—level with her face. And there it was, in that distinctive Wishful Thinking script: *Guitar Recital, West End School for Music and Art, 55 Bethune Street, Tuesday, September 22, 4:00 p.m. to 5:00 p.m. Arrived.*

Arrived?

The cool light from her awakened phone began to awaken her senses too. Slowly she started to look around. She was able to make out the outline of a door in front of her, fluorescent light visible around its edges, and there was something plastic and yellow next to her that moved a bit when she nudged it. A mop bucket? She put her phone in flashlight mode, swung it around to her left, and saw brooms and shelves full of cleaning equipment—some of which was now on the floor.

She was not in outer space. She was in a broom closet.

She stood up. Reaching out, she placed her hand on the cold metal door in front of her. Should she open it? She was in a broom closet, yes, but she could be anywhere. She was probably in a broom closet on the abandoned eighteenth floor of 250 Broadway, having temporarily lost her mind, blacked out, and stumbled into one somehow. Could she have made her way from the bathroom to a broom closet without even being aware? Was the door locked, she wondered, or would she be trapped until it occurred to Tim to look for her here on the secret-bathroom floor—if it ever occurred to him? Her clock read 4:01 p.m. She'd already been gone at least ten minutes. Nobody would miss her, most likely, until the staff meeting. She had to find out where she was.

Jennifer turned the knob slowly, carefully, to the right, opening the door a tiny crack.

That was when she heard it: Julien's voice, as clear as day.

"I wish Mommy were here," he said.

"Mommy works very hard to take care of you, Julien," a male voice replied, "and I know she would have been here if she could have." Norman? Jennifer felt almost as shocked to hear Norman talk about her like that as she did to have been sucked into her smartphone and spit out halfway across town. The voices faded. Could it be? Was it possible that she was at the West End School for Music and Art, just as the app had said she would be?

Peeking out of the closet to make sure the coast was clear, she saw them: Julien, Jack, Norman, and Melissa, filing into the recital hall.

She did not know how she'd gotten there, and she couldn't imagine how she would get back—not to mention what was happening right now, at 4:00 p.m., in the building where she had just been standing. But she could still see the top of her son's head as a stream of parents and children pushed past her, and, knowing he was so near, she didn't care. Something miraculous had happened, and she, Jennifer Sharpe, was going to make the most of it.

"Julien!" she called, her whole body still reverberating with shock but quivering with a kind of triumph too. "I'm here!"

four | IT WORKS;
IT REALLY WORKS

AT THE SOUND OF her voice, Julien whirled around and
then came running. She bent forward, weight on her
front leg, and pulled him upward as he leaped into
her arms, nuzzling her nose into his neck. At eight he was
heavy now, but this was a way of greeting each other they'd
perfected during the years when Norman had made only the
occasional appearance in their lives. Now, however, she was
faced with Norman, who was here, looking at her with a
mixture of surprise and, she thought, quizzical irritation.

"I thought you couldn't make it!" said Melissa, smiling
warmly at her.

"I changed some things around," she said, putting Julien
down. She kissed Melissa hello as Jack wrapped himself
around her legs, nestling his face into her stomach. "This was
more important!" She was a little startled by how easily she
lied—not only lied, but milked the lie for mommy points.

"It's great that you're here," Norman said. He tried to meet
her eyes, but she quickly looked away.

"Let's go!" she enjoined. Motioning to the four of them to file ahead of her, she hung back a bit, surveying her body to make sure everything was still put together right. So far so good: no signs of scrambled parts or teleportation skid marks.

Was she in two places at the same time, she wondered, as the app had said she would be—here and at the office? She couldn't be, she told herself. Clearly she couldn't! But as soon as she had soaked in Julien's delight and Jack's kisses (delivered with a faceful of chocolate from a cookie Melissa had brought along—*Too many sweets!* Jennifer thought), sent Julien backstage, and taken her seat in the front row with Jack in her lap and a program in her hand, her heart, the one that had miraculously continued beating as she had traveled through space via phone, began to pound anew.

I'll text Tim, she thought. *Or, no, I'll call Vinita.* She took out her phone, and a message appeared, in midnight blue.

While on a Wishful Thinking appointment, it read, as polite and civilized as ever, *the receipt or transmission of data is strictly prohibited. Your phone is currently in airplane mode and will remain so until your Wishful Thinking appointment is over.*

Why wouldn't she be allowed to use her phone while on a Wishful Thinking appointment? She could think of some good reasons—but only if she really was at her office right now, and at the West End School at the same time.

Norman leaned over and touched her arm. The sudden sensation of his hand on her skin caused her to jerk backward so abruptly, Jack almost tumbled out of her lap.

"Easy there," he said. "I was just going to ask if it was hard to get away from work. You've been so busy lately."

"A little. Not really," she added, backtracking. "How great that *you* could be here!" she said, hoping to distract Norman from searching her face too carefully—not that he would be able to read anything there. For an actor, Norman was remarkably inept at reading other people's nonverbal cues. "I was here the last time," he said. He looked at Jennifer's hand. "What happened?" he asked. "Fisticuffs at the office?"

Before she could answer, however, something over her shoulder caught his attention. She recognized an eager look she knew too well.

"Hey, did you see Scott Spencer is here?" Norman asked, rising from his seat and dusting the cookie crumbs from his pants. "He was in that show *Notorious Minds*? I have a pilot idea I've been wanting to pitch him." Jennifer remembered another way she depended heavily on her phone—she pretended to study it at moments like this, when Norman was trying to impress her. She stared at her wounded hand instead. "Jennifer, did you hear me? I'm going to go talk to Scott Spencer about a pilot." Nodding, she smiled. Running a hand through his thick, dark hair, still his greatest asset, Norman headed toward Scott, who immediately took out his phone and started typing on it, apparently employing a similar defense against Norman's advances. Jennifer sighed. Now Norman would be a kiss-ass, Scott would blow Norman off, and Norman would think it had gone well. Even worse, Scott would probably steal his idea, as Norman actually was a talented writer. Norman was a starfucker who got fucked by stars.

Melissa and Jennifer exchanged a knowing look. After all their years together, Melissa knew Norman almost as well as Jennifer did. It was hard to believe Melissa was in her late twenties now. Jennifer had found her nearly six years before through a West Village mommy message board, a girl from Long Island with four older brothers who showed up for her interview wearing too much perfume, tight-fitting sweats that rode dangerously low on her hips, and a glaring addiction to tanning booths. Julien had immediately fallen for her, and she for him.

Jennifer looked at a clock on the wall. It was already ten after four, and there were no signs of the recital starting. "How long will this take?" Jennifer asked Melissa. "I mean, what time will he go on?"

"Just a sec," Melissa said. She was texting somebody on her phone. Jennifer stared at it hungrily. She had an overpowering urge to ask if she could borrow it to call Vinita, but she resisted. If she wasn't supposed to use her phone, maybe she wasn't supposed to use other people's phones, either.

Melissa put away her phone and took out the program. "So what time?" Jennifer asked her again, anxiously. Jack had begun covering Jennifer's scratched hand in chocolaty kisses. "He's playing close to the end," Melissa replied, yawning. "Maybe five or five fifteen?"

Jennifer jerked her hand away from Jack, who wailed. "What?" she cried. "I mean, I thought the whole thing was over by five. I have to get back to the office." She had formulated a plan: listen to Julien play, then run like hell back to work. The West End School wasn't that far from 250 Broadway—fifteen minutes by cab, if traffic was light on the West Side Highway. If she hurried, she thought, she might even make the four thirty meeting, or at least be only a few minutes late. She certainly wasn't going to wait around until 5:00 p.m. and hope the app would work a second time and transport her back to 4:00 p.m. at her office. It was much too big a risk.

She nudged Jack off her lap and placed him in Melissa's.

"But Mama's hand is hurt!" Jack protested. Instinctively she reached for her phone and handed it to him. "Play Angry Birds," she said. "I'm going to find Julien's teacher." Appeased, Jack reached for her phone. "No, wait!" she yelled, grabbing it back as though he'd just picked up a hand grenade on the street. This time several people stared, including Norman, who had returned from his "meeting" with Scott Spencer after all of thirty seconds. "I need to keep it with me, actually," she said, as coolly as she could. "Norman, can he play on yours?"

"I don't have Angry Birds," he said. "You know I don't believe in it."

Jennifer wanted to ask him how it was possible to "believe" or not believe in Angry Birds, while having her usual nagging doubts about whether her dependence on Angry Birds in situations like this made her a bad mother. But now was hardly the time.

"Melissa?" she asked, trying not to sound desperate.

"I have it," she said cheerily, handing her phone to Jack. "I even have the one that's in outer space!" As Jack settled in to play, Jennifer headed backstage.

"BACKSTAGE" WAS REALLY JUST one of the larger practice rooms in the school. Once there, she navigated her way through at least thirty-five kids running around the room, abusing their instruments, until at last she spotted Owen, Julien's guitar instructor. Wanting to avoid Julien, who she was sure would immediately suspect something if he saw her there, she managed to attract Owen's attention and beckoned him to a quiet corner of the room.

Owen walked up to her and smiled. "What's up?" he asked in his easygoing, not-from–New York manner. Where *was* he from? she wondered. She'd never asked.

"I'm so sorry to do this," she said quickly, "but I made some very difficult arrangements to be here, and I thought it was going to end right at five, you know, on the dot, and I told my colleagues I could be back in my office by then, or maybe even a little sooner, and so I was just wondering, is there any possible way that Julien could play a little bit earlier? Like, first?"

Owen paused, knitting his brow a bit.

"Jennifer, right?" he said. *Oh God,* she thought. *This is going to go badly. The obnoxious, absent working mom who thinks the world revolves around her and her schedule, barging in right before the recital starts and asking for favors.*

Hoping to impress her humble desperation upon him, she sought to meet his gaze, but he was distracted for a moment by some horseplay between a violinist and a portly kid with a trombone. Owen was tall—she had not processed just how tall until now, as she was forced to tip her head back slightly in order to look at him pleadingly. He also had long, straight, light brown bangs that fell into his eyes—bangs on a man in his mid-forties, and he could pull it off. She was staring at them stupidly when he returned his focus to her and placed one huge, callused hand on her shoulder. Their eyes locked for a minute. That was when she felt it. *Kapow!* The unmistakable pop of sexual attraction, like a string attached to her crotch that had just been given a delicious yank.

Whoa! she thought. She hadn't felt that in a long time. So long that the feeling was as startling as it was pleasurable.

"Please?" she repeated, as steadily as possible.

"I'll move him up on the program," he said, giving her shoulder a gentle squeeze and then pulling his hand away. If he felt it, too, she thought, he showed no sign. "I'm not sure he'll be first, but he'll be close."

"Thank you!" she said brightly. "And I'll come to his next lesson, really! It's been too long!" Owen, taking it all in stride, shot her a smile that sent another shudder through her. She turned away, hoping he hadn't seen her blush.

IT TOOK ALL OF Jennifer's willpower—and then some—to stay seated and silent when Julien did not go first. Or second.

Or third. But after the third rendition of "Smoke on the Water" (which was interpreted, painfully slowly, by three first-graders in a row), and just as Jennifer was contemplating heading for the door, Owen loped up onto the stage, followed by Julien.

"Slight change in the program, folks," he said. (*Folks? Really, where *was* this guy from?*) "Julien Bideau will be playing next. He's playing 'Here Comes the Sun,' and I think," Owen continued, finding Jennifer in the audience and looking right at her, "this one is for Mom." And then he winked. Norman didn't notice the wink, of course. He was too busy training his Hubble space telescope–size camera on Julien. But Melissa turned her head toward Jennifer and raised her eyebrows questioningly. Jennifer threw her hands up—*Beats me*—but she couldn't help smiling. She made eye contact with Owen and gave him a little wave. Ducking his head slightly, he made a gesture with his hand like a gentleman doffing his cap, as though to say, *It was nothing.*

But it was not nothing. Julien looked so self-assured as he pushed his long hair out of his eyes—hair he had insisted on growing out the moment he'd hung his first John Lennon circa-1970 picture on his wall—and as he perched himself on the stool, his sneaker-clad feet swinging in midair, and started to play, she felt as giddy and important as a rock star's girlfriend seated in the very front row. (She wanted to cheer like one but managed to restrain herself.) For his part, Julien played as though he were playing only for her. More than once as he plucked and strummed, he actually managed to look up, find her eyes, and smile.

It was over by 4:23. The instant the applause began, Jennifer, clapping as she stood, waved good-bye to Julien, hugged Jack, nodded to Norman, and gave Melissa a kiss, then climbed over the legs of several annoyed parents and headed for the door.

She was outside again. It was a sunny, chilly autumn afternoon, and for a moment she stood stock-still, suddenly sober after drinking Julien in in the darkened auditorium, her phone gripped in one hand. It was 4:24 p.m. now. Was her plan to rush back to the office the right one? It was too late to be on time, and after that morning's humiliation, being late a second time in one day was going to be hard to explain. But the idea of buying a latte and hanging out at Starbucks, waiting until 5:00 p.m. to be transported back to work at 4:00 p.m., was intolerable. The urge to do something, *anything*, was overpowering.

"Taxi!" she cried, sticking out her arm. It was time for the drivers' shift change, however, and every taxi that passed was unavailable. Precious minutes ticked by. Finally, a taxi stopped. It was 4:27. Jennifer hauled the door open, gave the driver the address, and slid inside.

She was going to be late for the staff meeting, yes. But not crazy late. Not where-have-you-been-you're-fired late. Was it possible, she let herself wonder for the first time, that this was all going to be okay?

Not if the traffic gods had anything to say about it. The West Side Highway moved slowly, and downtown was snarled with double-parked delivery trucks. It was already four forty-five when the cab reached the light at the corner of Duane and Broadway, just a few blocks north of NYCHA's offices. Jennifer's anxiety was so acute by then that she even craned her neck out the window to yell at a livery cab that was blocking the intersection. As they finally passed through the light, however, and Jennifer began to breathe a small sigh of relief, her phone suddenly delivered a moderate but painful electric shock to her hand. She dropped it like a hotcake, cursing. The phone, for its part, began to blare from the floor of the cab, emitting a pulsing, shrieking *eeek* like a smoke alarm, so loud Jennifer could feel her eardrums shrivel. Whirling around, the driver screamed at her, "Turn that thing off!"

"Just a minute!" Jennifer called over the din, groping for the phone. "I'm trying!"

Phone in hand at last, Jennifer looked at the screen. She saw one word flashing there, and it was not in midnight blue.

STOP!

STOP!

STOP!

Stop? *Stop?* "Stop!" Jennifer cried.

The taxi driver cut the wheel so hard they almost turned over a hot-dog cart. Jennifer was thrown toward the center divider of the cab. "Get that thing out of here!" he yelled as soon as they came to a halt. Nodding, Jennifer reached into her bag for her wallet. "Forget it!" the driver said, which, Jennifer couldn't help thinking, gave some idea just how god-awful the noise was. Shoving the phone under her armpit, Jennifer opened the door and jumped out. Producing it again on the sidewalk, Jennifer ignored the angry pedestrians who colorfully cursed at her, many physically recoiling from the unbearable sound as they passed. She jabbed at the screen. At last the *STOP!* sign disappeared and was replaced by a warning.

WHEN USING WISHFUL THINKING, YOU MUST MAINTAIN A DISTANCE OF FIVE HUNDRED YARDS FROM THE ORIGIN OF YOUR WISHFUL THINKING APPOINTMENT. REPEAT: YOU CANNOT GO WITHIN FIVE HUNDRED YARDS OF 250 BROADWAY, 18TH FLOOR, OR A CAUSALITY VIOLATION MAY OCCUR.

"Five hundred yards?" she yelled at the phone, as she began to run back in the direction from which she'd come. "How far is five hundred yards? One hundred yards is a football field . . .

How many football fields are in a city block? How am I supposed to know that! I can't use the Internet, remember?" Holding her phone up to her face as she ran, shoving past people and jaywalking as she headed away from her office and back toward Broadway and Duane, where the barrier had ostensibly been crossed, she couldn't help addressing the only person she knew to be responsible for what was happening. "Dr. Sexton!" she yelled at her phone. "Are you there?"

Unsurprisingly, no response was forthcoming.

At last she crossed back over Duane Street, and as soon as she did, the sound ceased as abruptly as it had begun. Jennifer stopped, bending over to catch her breath. She let her body unclench, her ears luxuriating in the familiar street noises of Manhattan, which, in contrast with the horrible sound, were as soothing as a warm bath. Standing, she looked around. "Five hundred yards," she muttered to herself, "is about as far as I can sprint without collapsing."

She had been so close to her office. Was it really possible her phone could not travel there? Wary, she held her phone away from her body and retraced her steps, slowly, cautiously, back to the point where her phone had ceased its blaring. As soon as she was about to cross Duane heading north on Broadway, however, the sound kicked in again and Jennifer was forced to yank her phone back across the invisible threshold.

Her phone could not break the barrier, she thought. But could she?

Jennifer stretched her phone-free hand out in the direction of the curb. Her fingertips crossed the invisible line. Nothing. Emboldened, she stepped closer, inching more and more of her body into the space on the other side. Still nothing. And then she couldn't help herself. She pulled her phone across too. The alarm was instantly triggered.

Wincing, Jennifer jumped back onto the curb.

Evidently *she* could go back to her office, but she would have to leave her phone behind. Could she hide it somewhere? Ditch it on the street?

Neither. She couldn't shake the frightening idea that her body and mind had been melded to her phone somehow, were even being carried inside it. If she parted with it, she thought, she might go up in computer smoke, her body blown to bytes.

Besides, it was 4:53 p.m. Even if she ran back now, she would be thirty minutes late for her meeting. But what if, at five o'clock, her phone delivered her back to the secret bathroom stall at 4:00 p.m. sharp? She could still get the coffee and make it on time—early, even. It had worked before. Why wouldn't it work again? It was worth a try.

She remembered the app's first instruction: *find a place where you can travel without being observed by anybody else.* The secret bathroom had been perfect. But now she was in New York, on Broadway, at rush hour.

Moving down the block, beginning to despair, she heard another *PING!* It was 4:55. Her screen went midnight blue.

The wand appeared—jaunty, and, she recalled, about to go 3-D. Cupping her hand over her phone, Jennifer attempted to squash the wand, whispering, "Ixnay on the three-D-ay!" When she ducked around a corner and removed her hand, however, she found the wand hovering in midair anyway, as pleased with itself as ever. It tipped back slightly, then snapped forward and pricked the surface of her phone. *Reminder: Return journey to 250 Broadway, 18th floor, Tuesday, September 22, 4:00 p.m. Please proceed to a place where you can travel unobserved.*

"Unobserved—I *know*," she said to her phone, wishing again that it would answer her. "But where?"

And then she saw it, two blocks away, in a small city square that had gone from a crack den to a public garden in the

Giuliani years: an APT, also known as an automatic public toilet. Jennifer had never been so happy to see such an unappealing sight.

Jennifer knew about APTs because, early in her tenure at NYCHA, she had actually had to attend a ribbon cutting for one. The previous mayor had loved them. Designed by a hip architecture firm, the units sported an ultramodern steel-and-glass motif—which made them particularly well suited to host time travel, she thought, at least from a design perspective. More important, for twenty-five cents, an APT gave you up to twenty minutes alone. Once the twenty minutes were up, an "acoustic alarm" sounded and flashing red lights went off for three minutes, a powerful deterrent to anyone considering taking up residence there. The door then closed again in order for the unit to self-clean. Which meant that—provided she could go in without being seen—the bathroom would reopen its door and take care of itself after she'd gone.

At 4:58, Jennifer reached the unit and found it blessedly empty. She took out her wallet and pulled out a quarter. For a moment she paused to marvel at the fact that her purse had traveled with her, too, something she hadn't given much thought to until now. The fact that she had a quarter, when she rarely used cash anymore, seemed almost equally miraculous.

Once Jennifer was inside, it took a full twenty seconds for the doors to close—she'd forgotten about that. But by 4:59, she was safely ensconced in the APT, another sort-of-secret bathroom, though not nearly as nice as the one on the eighteenth floor. (Despite the best efforts of the Little APT That Could Clean Itself, wads of soiled toilet paper littered the floor.) Defending herself against the stench and trying not to gag, Jennifer bent one arm across her face and wedged her nose into the crook of her elbow. With the other hand, she gripped her phone tight.

The phone struck five. Jennifer felt a powerful jolt.

"Here we go," she managed to say as the crackling tornado yawned open to envelop her.

And off she went.

five | SUPERWOMAN MAKES
A LANDING

IT WAS JUST LIKE the last time—the same superheated sensation, as though her fingertips were fusing with her phone; the same feeling of being scrambled and squeezed to the size of an atom and then being pumped full of weight and mass again, like a tiny balloon dunked into Niagara Falls. But this time, when she found herself once again in her secret bathroom, standing in front of the sink with one hand on the door handle, exactly as she'd been when she left it, Jennifer did not panic or curse. Instead, she laughed.

Except she didn't just laugh. She laughed like crazy, or like she'd gone crazy—she laughed so hard she cried. Tears fell from her eyes and made a mess of her mascara. Her stomach muscles cramped with hilarity. She laughed so hard she hardly recognized herself, goofy and gasping for breath. It had been years since she'd laughed like that, and she let it wash over her and run through her with pleasure. Laughing like that, she felt as alive and free as she had when she was a little girl and would jump so high on her next-door neighbors' trampoline she could pull handfuls of leaves off their sycamore tree's branches.

After a minute or two of this, however, she glanced at the mirror and, seeing the damage she was doing to her appearance, forced herself to take several long, deep breaths. Then, still giddy but with some measure of self-control, she looked at the clock on her phone: 4:02 p.m.

"Four oh two," she said aloud. It was astonishing, and confirmation of what she already knew. Wishful Thinking had worked again. She'd gone from 5:00 p.m. to 4:00 p.m. She had traveled backward through time.

And now it was 4:02! Which meant that she had time. Time to clean up her smudged makeup. Time to get Tim his skinny pumpkin-spice latte, even if the afternoon coffee-break line was long. Time to get to the staff meeting with time to spare. And she had gone to her son's guitar recital without Bill Truitt or his Employee Time Clock having the slightest idea she'd ever left the building.

Was she really at the West End School right now, too, trying to get her bearings in a broom closet?

And then she saw it. The scratch on her right hand, and next to it the faintest trace of a chocolaty kiss.

Smiling, Jennifer took out her lipstick and, as she applied it, began to hum. *Somewhere there is a woman,* she thought, *who went to her son's guitar recital in the middle of a workday without missing a meeting, and who will never have to miss anything, anywhere, ever again.*

I am that woman, she thought. *I am a time traveler. Forget the time traveler's wife.*

JENNIFER TOOK HER SEAT in the conference room five minutes early, coffee cup placed neatly above the upper-right-hand corner of her legal pad, photocopies of the meeting's agenda in hand, collated and ready for distribution. All she needed was a couple of freshly sharpened number 2 pencils, and she would have rivaled the overachieving overpreparedness of her sixteen-year-old self, seated in the first row of trigonometry class.

Only a few agenda items into the meeting, however, Jennifer's time-traveler euphoria was gone, replaced by medium- to low-grade time-travel panic. What had she been thinking, cavalierly ignoring Dr. Sexton's instruction that she contact her before using the app? Could she safely go home to her children without knowing what she had just put her body through? What if her phone was dangerous somehow? In the sobering light of the conference room, the question she asked herself most was: How could she have been so reckless? The first time was understandable. She hadn't believed the app was real. But to put herself through it a second time without having any idea how it worked or what it was had been crazy.

Vinita, Jennifer thought. *I have to talk to Vinita.*

Possessed by this new resolve, Jennifer began hurrying the agenda along—so much so that Bill asked her sharply if there was someplace else she needed to be.

"Doctor's appointment," she found herself saying. "I made it for the end of the day, but five thirty was the latest I could get." Bill frowned and Tim raised his eyebrows. It was 5:20. "So if we could wrap this up?" she asked. "I'd be very grateful. I'm already going to be late."

She felt bad lying to Tim (though not to Bill), but it was only partly a lie. Vinita was a doctor, and she needed to see her badly.

Back in her office, Jennifer opened the Employee Time Clock and logged out. A window popped up. *You're leaving early,* it read. Six o'clock was her official quitting time, though she knew Bill thought she should stay later.

"And I went out for a whole hour this afternoon," Jennifer replied, sticking her tongue out. "So there, dummy."

As she rode down the twenty floors to the lobby, squeezed in between a man whose suit jacket smelled like a dirty sock sautéed in curry sauce and a woman reeking of tobacco, Jennifer felt woozier and woozier. Trapped in the stale air of the subway platform a few minutes later, she leaned against a column and fanned her face. Jennifer had always had a sensitive stomach, and suddenly she knew she had to find the nearest garbage can. She lurched toward one, barely making it before emptying her stomach into its overstuffed insides. A man offered his handkerchief to wipe her mouth with, but the sight of it—yellowing, wrinkled, damp—only made her want to throw up again.

Isn't nausea a symptom of being exposed to radioactivity? she worried. *What was that blue light, anyway?*

After what seemed like an eternity on the train but was really less than ten minutes, Jennifer emerged from the subway at Christopher Street and called Vinita.

It was 5:35. Jennifer was put on hold. She could hear a small child screaming in the background, most likely a toddler who had just gotten a shot. Vinita took two afternoons off every week to be with her girls, so her workdays were long, with her office hours often extending until 7:00 p.m. Jennifer never ceased to be amazed by her friend's calm in the presence of other people's sick children—or, more specifically, her calm in the presence of sick children's parents, who were by far her most difficult patients.

"Hey, you," Vinita said when she picked up. "It's a total nightmare here; pneumonia's going around, some Charles Dickens type of shit. Can I call you tonight?"

"Something *really* weird happened to me, Vee," Jennifer said. She was still shaking a little from being sick on the subway. "The weirdest thing that has ever happened to me in my life. Can I come by the office?"

"Where are you?" Vinita asked, switching crisply to what they both referred to as her "doctor voice." Jennifer must have sounded worse than she knew.

"Christopher Street. I'm afraid to go home. I need you to check me out. Physically. Just to see if I'm okay."

"What do you mean?" Vinita asked. "Are you hurt?"

"I don't think so," Jennifer said, turning in the direction of Vinita's office. "I promise I'll tell you everything when I get there, okay?"

"Melissa's with the boys?" Vinita asked. *Melissa!* Jennifer thought, her heart sinking. Melissa had reminded her yesterday that she needed to leave right at six for school tonight. But Jennifer couldn't go home yet.

"She can stay a little bit late," Jennifer lied again, hating herself for it.

"Okay," Vinita said, "come now. I'll make it work."

Heading toward Vinita's office, Jennifer breathed a sigh of relief. Just the sound of Vinita's voice reassured her. From the day they had first met, as freshman roommates at Amherst, Vinita had been the reassurer in Jennifer's life. Vinita was the smartest, most competent, and most no-nonsense person Jennifer had ever known, a perfect foil to Jennifer's often impulsive, sometimes forgetful, and passionate personality. Vinita had known what to do (or at least whom to ask) when you were nineteen and got vaginal warts. Vinita would know what to do now.

A few minutes later, Jennifer walked into Vinita's cheerful, pale-yellow waiting room. It was the usual chaotic scene, crammed with coughing kids, stoic nannies, distracted parents, and a lot of beat-up books and plastic toys. Choosing a seat as far removed from everyone as possible, Jennifer tucked herself in behind a plastic toy refrigerator she knew well. It had been one of Jennifer's contributions to Vinita's waiting room—her mother had given it to Julien years ago. Her mother had always insisted on giving both her boys what she called "gender neutral" toys, though generally they were "gender statements" for boys, from Barbies to baby strollers. Julien had never warmed to most of them, but Jack still sometimes pushed his baby doll around in its plastic pram. The refrigerator had been a hit with both boys, but it was too big for her apartment.

Jennifer was about to push a familiar button on the refrigerator, when she thought, *Pneumonia* and pulled back her hand. She took out her phone and texted Melissa. *Running a little bit late at the office,* she wrote guiltily. *Will get there as soon as I can and put you in a cab!*

Just then Vinita appeared, and, as always, Jennifer couldn't help marveling at the sight of her. Even with a pneumonia strain ripping through her clientele, Vee looked more like a star of *Grey's Anatomy* than a harried pediatrician, her shiny black high-heeled boots accenting her white lab coat, her dark hair swept back into a neat French twist, her plum-colored lipstick complementing her light brown skin. (Vinita was Indian, by way of New Jersey, where her parents had immigrated in the sixties from New Delhi.) Vinita would have looked put-together in a Civil War tent, Jennifer thought. Suddenly she wondered what a sight she must be. She had just puked on a subway platform, after all.

"You look like shit," Vinita said, after closing the door to the exam room behind them. This time Jennifer didn't laugh. Instead her face—her whole body—crumpled into a sob.

"Oh, sweetie, I'm sorry!" Vinita said, hugging her, then pulling away to search her face. "You're scaring me. What happened?" Jennifer shook her head and took a deep breath, stopping her tears. Vinita locked the door with one hand while using her other to find Jennifer's wrist and check her pulse. "Do you want me to give you something to calm you down?" Vinita asked.

"No," Jennifer said. Having been sucked up by her smartphone earlier that afternoon, she thought it seemed inadvisable—at least until Vinita had checked her out—to add even the most anodyne of mood-altering medications to the mix. "I'm sorry I'm scaring you. But can you give me a quick checkup? You know, vital signs and all that? Then I'll tell you everything."

Vinita motioned to Jennifer to get onto the examining table. There was a loud crinkle as Jennifer's butt hit the Elmo-printed paper. The two of them then sat in silence as Vinita did one of the things she did best: examining a nervous and emotionally fragile patient. She palpated. She peered. She listened, looked, and measured. She pulled back.

"Your eyes are a bit dilated," she pronounced. "And you have this look—it's funny, because you don't have a fever, but you have the look of someone with a high temp, a little glittery and feverish in the eyes. And you're flushed. And you have a little vomit on your sleeve. You threw up?"

Jennifer nodded, looking at her sleeve and making a face.

"Since you still haven't told me what's going on, I might be missing something. But in my professional opinion, physically, anyway . . . you're absolutely fine."

"Thank God," Jennifer said. "Now let me tell you what happened."

And so she did. The missing phone. The mysterious envelope. The app, and Jennifer's certainty that it was a gimmick to exploit pathetic mothers on the verge of a nervous breakdown. Booking an appointment anyway and getting sucked into the tunnel of blue light. Landing in the supply closet. The recital, the return trip to the office, and what happened then. Vinita listened with her head cocked back slightly. She looked deeply concerned, which sent a fresh wave of panic over Jennifer.

"Are you thinking what I'm thinking?" Jennifer asked. "That maybe I was exposed to something? Radioactivity, maybe? What would it be? I have no idea how it works. . . ."

Vinita didn't reply. "Can you show it to me?" she finally asked quietly. "The app?"

Jennifer took out her phone and woke it up. She launched her calendar, but Wishful Thinking did not appear. She went to CREATE AN EVENT, but when she scrolled down the list of available calendars, there was no sign of Wishful Thinking there, either. She did a double take. She looked again. There was her home calendar. There were the boys' school calendars. There was her work calendar. But the Wishful Thinking calendar, and the entry for the guitar recital?

Gone.

There was nothing on her phone, in fact, even approaching midnight blue.

"What the . . . ?" Frantically, she scrolled through every screen. She turned it off and on. She shook it like a Polaroid picture. It was no good. The app had disappeared—*poof*—for real.

Out of options, Jennifer looked at Vinita, who had waited patiently through her search, even as her intercom was buzzing with constant requests for her attention.

"I don't understand," Jennifer managed, as a sickening fear took hold of her. Images and sensations flooded through her: the sound of Julien's guitar, the feel of Owen's hand on her shoulder, Jack's chocolaty kisses. "It was real."

"I'm sure it seemed very real," Vinita said carefully. "But extreme stress can bring on all kinds of mental symptoms—"

"No!" Jennifer cut her off. *"No."* Reaching over to her right hand, she ripped off the Band-Aid she'd applied before the staff meeting with a yank and pointed at the messy scrape. "I cut my hand," she said. "Scraped some skin off when I was reaching for my phone in the broom closet. Look!"

Vinita did not look as long as Jennifer thought she should have. "Or you scraped it when you passed out in the bathroom," she said.

"On what?" Jennifer demanded. "The toilet bowl?"

The intercom cut in again, disrupting their standoff. "Dr. Kapoor, please pick up. Emergency on line one."

"I'll be right back," Vinita said. "Don't go anywhere."

Left alone, Jennifer searched her phone again and wondered, was Vinita right? Had it all been a dream? Had she passed out in the bathroom, her desire for the app so great it had knocked her out like some kind of mommy roofie?

A few minutes later, Vinita walked back into the room and closed the door behind her. "Sorry," she said. "Julie's off, and all these walk-ins, and naturally the computers are down." She stepped toward Jennifer and took her hand. This was an unusual thing for Vinita to do. As a rule she was not the touchy-feely type. Perhaps for that reason, Jennifer did not find it reassuring at all. "I think I know what might have happened today," she began.

"I don't," Jennifer said quickly.

Vinita ignored her. "I think what happened today was what's called a dissociative episode," she said, "brought on by extreme stress. I'd have to run some tests—an EEG, an MRI— and refer you to a psychiatrist, of course. But that's what I think."

Jennifer was silent.

"A dissociative episode is a kind of . . . break," Vinita went on. "A mental break, where you can experience powerful hallucinations, like a waking dream."

Jennifer pulled her hand away from her friend's.

"Think about it," said Vinita gently but firmly. "All the things you've been dealing with." Jennifer winced. "Jack's speech issues. You get no support from Norman. You're under tremendous pressure at work. And your mom." This last she delivered with special care, trying to go easy. "Losing your mom."

My mom, Jennifer thought, *would have believed me.*

But would she have? Either Jennifer had come into possession of a time-travel app nobody on the planet had ever heard of, installed on her phone by a woman she'd never met, or she had had a dissociative episode. It wasn't hard to see which was the more likely explanation. It had occurred to her to call Julien, to ask him if she'd been at his recital or not. But suddenly the idea just seemed nuts. She looked at the clock.

"It's ten after six," Jennifer said. "I gotta go." Vinita's office was so close to her apartment that if she hurried, there was still a chance she'd be only fifteen minutes late.

She slid off the table. Vinita pressed two prescriptions, one for the EEG and another for the MRI, into her hand. "You should get these tests done as soon as possible," she said. Jennifer nodded. "I'm here for you, okay?" Vinita said. "Can we see each other in the next couple of days?"

Jennifer nodded again. "Love you," she said, trying to sound normal.

"Love you too," Vinita answered.

It was time to run again. It was time to go home.

six | HOME

J ENNIFER GOT HOME AS fast as she could. At 6:20 p.m., however, after walk-running down the hallway and unlocking her door, preparing to usher Melissa out with cash for a cab, she opened it to find a very unpleasant surprise: Norman, right there in her living room.

He was playing some kind of tickling-wrestling-punching game with the boys on her couch. The cat was sitting at a decidedly disapproving distance on the windowsill. What was Norman doing there? Aside from Saturdays, he was generally not seen or heard from except at the occasional school function, Julien's winter soccer games (maybe Norman should find a way to get Jack a spot, she thought), and, lately, at Julien's music recitals. She couldn't remember the last time she'd laid eyes on him in her house on a weeknight. Couch cushions were everywhere. Plates of half-eaten spaghetti were on the table. She guessed Julien had not done his homework and Jack had not done his speech exercises. Not that Norman would have any clue about those.

Where in the world was Melissa?

"What are you doing here?" she asked as she attempted to hang her bag on one of the hooks by the door and was hit by an avalanche of jackets and backpacks.

"Hello to you too," Norman said jocosely, continuing to wrestle with the boys, making a show of his hair-tousling, wet willy–dispensing manliness, performing, as usual, for her, for the boys, for himself. It irritated her to no end, not least because Norman acted more like a rascally uncle than like a father and would soon walk out the door and leave her with a hyperactive duo not remotely ready for bed. If she was honest, however, watching him filled her with jealousy, too, seeing Julien and Jack delight in a kind of roughhousing she could never get quite right. Eventually Norman told them to stop, though they didn't listen. He was deflecting running charges from one and then the other when he answered her.

"Melissa texted to say you were running late and that she really needed to go to class, so I thought I'd come by."

"Oh, damn! Night school. I forgot," Jennifer said, lying again. Since when, she wondered, did Melissa look to Norman for help? "Maybe next time you or Melissa could ask me first?" she said. "I'd like to know when you are going to be in my apartment." She looked around as she said it, as though there could be something incriminating there. But her life was so dull, the most embarrassing thing in the room was a stack of fifteen rice-pudding containers crusting over next to the TV.

"Boys, Daddy has to leave . . . ," Jennifer began.

"Daddy, don't weave!" Jack cried, jumping onto the couch.

"*Leave*," she and Norman both corrected.

"Jinx!" Julien called.

"Baths and pajamas!" she said, glaring at them both.

"You can't talk, Mommy; you're jinxed!" Julien shot back. In response, Jennifer took him by the arm, swiveled him around, and gave him a little shove down the hall. Jack reluctantly followed.

"Wait," Jennifer said. "Say bye to Daddy before he goes." The boys whirled around and rushed Norman, wrapping their arms around his legs. He gave them each a kiss on the top of the head.

"See you Saturday, you little monsters," Norman added with a playful growl. Growling too, the boys retreated down the hallway.

"I'm glad Melissa got off okay," Jennifer said to Norman. It had been good of him; she could at least acknowledge that. "Thank you." She slipped off her shoes. "See you Saturday?"

"Actually," Norman said, "there's something I need to talk to you about."

"What's up?" she said, walking over to the fridge and taking out a bottle of wine. She gestured to it. Norman shook his head.

"I got bunk beds," Norman said.

"Really?" she said. The second surprise from Norman that day.

"And I got a teaching job," he added. At this, Jennifer sat down. "Really?" she asked. The third surprise, and by far the biggest of them all. "What happened to 'teaching would mean the end of my acting career'?"

Norman sat down too.

"Well," he said, fiddling with a napkin ring on the table. "Things change. A spot opened up. Poetry and Poetics. Fourth grade."

"At St. John's?"

"Yep," he said. Only St. John's, one of the most artsy, elite, progressive schools in the city, would teach a class called Poetry and Poetics to fourth graders. St. John's also happened to be Norman's alma mater. Naturally, they couldn't afford to send their own children there. And naturally, when they'd needed it most, Norman had refused to apply to St. John's for a job. But it was better late than never.

Then Norman smiled. *Could it be?* she thought, hardly daring to hope. *Child support?*

"I'll be able to increase my child support payments now," he said. "I'm really happy about that." If Norman was happy, Jennifer was ecstatic. This would be the first steady job that Norman had had—and the first steady stream of support he could offer her—in years. Just as she was about to smile back at him, however, she saw it. A look. An evasive, uncomfortable look she knew all too well. He was screwing up the courage to ask her something—something she was not going to like.

"But I also want more time with the kids."

That was easy. "No," she said.

"Yes," he said, sitting up in his chair a bit. "Jennifer. You know and I know that the custody schedule we have now is completely unfair."

Jennifer tried to control herself, to fight back the bile that had instantly leaped up in her throat. "You know and I know?" she repeated. "Completely unfair?" Norman nodded. She looked right into his eyes. "No," she said firmly. "It isn't."

"I want fifty percent," Norman said.

"What?" she cried. "Are you out of your mind? You have them one night a week, Norman! And half the time you aren't even around for that!"

"You need to update your information," he said coolly, working hard, she knew, to fight his instinct to shut down in the face of conflict. "If you were paying attention, you'd have noticed that that hasn't been true for a long time."

Jennifer dug her nails into her palm. Was this what he had been up to? Showing up for Julien's recitals, covering for Melissa, and, yes, now that she thought of it, not missing a

Saturday in a long time? *How long?* she thought, struggling to remember.

"I haven't missed a Saturday in eight months," he said. *Eight months?* Could that be?

"So what?" she shot back. "You think you can disappear for *two years* and then, after a year of Saturday nights, demand equal time with me? Now that the hard part is over, with the bottles and the Cheerios and the strollers and the baby-proofing and the diapers? Do you remember where you were when Julien had hives for an entire summer and none of the specialists could figure out what was wrong with him?" Norman was clenching the napkin ring with such furious concentration now that Jennifer was sure he'd crack it. "Summer-stock theater! Do you remember where you were when Jack had a hundred and four fever and was throwing up so much I had to bottle-feed him Gatorade?" At this, he visibly flinched. "I don't! But it wasn't here!"

"We were divorced," Norman said. "It wouldn't have been here."

"This is a total nonstarter, Norman. You hear me? *Total.*"

"Jennifer," Norman said. "The boys. Keep your voice down."

Jennifer could hear Julien running the bath and Jack singing loudly along with a Beatles song in their room. It was not for their sake that Norman wanted her to shut up.

"*You* left *me*," he said. "Do you have any idea how devastating that was? What it did to my self-confidence? I'm sorry I checked out for a while. But I needed time, and now—"

"Yes, I left you," she cut him off. "But *you* left *them.*"

Norman could not conceal, or did not want to conceal, the hurt on his face.

"I'm their *father*," he said, with a choked, gulping, melodramatic *How could you say that to me?* delivery that hardened her heart completely.

"And you are welcome to see them," she said. "Anytime. Here. Where they live. *At home.*"

For a minute they sat there in silence. Jennifer was shaking. It took her a minute to notice that Norman's hands were trembling too. Taking a moment to steady them, he then reached into his back pocket and took out a folded-up piece of paper.

"I didn't want to do this," he said.

"What?" she asked, her voice rising. What was he pulling out? An order from a judge? It couldn't be. They had never used lawyers, just a mediator. There had been so little to fight over.

But it was not a legal document. Instead it was several pieces of lined notebook paper, and on each of them was a long list of dates, followed by notes in Norman's cramped, grade-school handwriting. "I thought you might react that way," he said. "Because you have such a strong picture in your head of what I'm like as a father, and what you're like as a mother, that you don't really see what's happening." She leaned over the table, fighting the impulse to grab the paper out of his hand.

"It's a log," he said, "of how often, when the boys are staying at your place, they are with you, and how often they are with Melissa."

"Melissa?" she said. "What does this have to do with Melissa?"

"I don't have to share custody with a babysitter, Jennifer," Norman said angrily. "And I've noted something else here. Do you know how many school events you've missed in the last few months? How many of Jack's speech appointments you've rescheduled? The therapist's office called me. He's weeks behind."

Jennifer's heart sank. Suddenly she felt completely sad, and ashamed. The last few months she had had to cancel several of

Jack's speech appointments, it was true. It had been impossible to get out of work. But she had always rescheduled . . . only to cancel again. She knew she had been falling far short of perfect lately in the mom department. But she had worked so hard for so many years to do it all. She hadn't just given birth to her boys. She had earned them. And Norman hadn't.

"So you've been spying on me?" she said. "You've got to be freaking kidding me, Norman."

"You used to be so good at swearing," he said with an awkward chuckle, as though this would somehow clear the air.

"Yeah?" she said, her anger emboldening her. "Give me that little log." She snatched it out of his hands and crumpled it. "Fuck you, Norman. *Fuck you.*"

"That's really nice, Jennifer," he said. She felt embarrassed. She uncrumpled the paper and offered it back to him. He shook his head. "You can keep that copy," he said. Sighing, he stood. "I just wish you could think of them and what *they* need."

It was pointless to respond to that. If she had learned anything from her divorce, it was that two people who had once shared a story of their lives could suddenly and irrevocably break with it, and where there had once been one story, two different stories, with two different sets of irrefutable facts, took its place. Norman thought Jennifer was selfish; he'd said it over and over again when she'd left him. Jennifer thought only a total narcissist could interpret her actions, and her life, through such a narrow lens. And there they stood. On two sides of a narrative chasm neither could cross.

"So what are you going to do?" she asked. She was beginning to look through the crinkled paper in her hand. The log was detailed. Worst of all, it was accurate. Days she'd worked late, things she'd canceled, meetings she'd missed. Her job already required her to make the fact that she was a single mother all but invisible to Bill, and that was hard enough. But if she agreed to meet the milestones he'd set out in order to get the bonus (and, possibly, in order to keep her job at all), she wouldn't just need to pretend not to have children; she would need to pretend to have a wife—the kind of wife even husbands didn't have anymore. For three years now, Melissa had been the closest thing to a wife she'd had, though the kind who didn't cook and never did the laundry. And now even her dependence on Melissa was being used against her.

Melissa.

How did Norman put this together? she wondered. There was only one possible answer. He'd had help from the person she trusted the most. Could Melissa really have done that to her, after all they had been through together?

"Do you know that when you showed up at the recital today," Norman said, "it was the first time you'd made it to something like that since you got that new boss?"

Jennifer was about to answer him, when she froze. *When you showed up at the recital today?*

"You don't have to do it all by yourself, you know," Norman went on, though Jennifer was only half listening now. "Be everywhere all the time. Do everything for everybody. You just have to let people help. Let *me* help." Then, gesturing with one hand to her tiny, messy apartment, he added, "And really, Jen. Would a little help be so bad?"

Jen. Only Norman called her that. Before she could answer him, he'd gotten up from the table, opened the door, closed it behind him, and was gone, without another word between them. She'd hardly been able to concentrate anyway. She had showed up at the recital. The app was real, and she had to get it back.

* * *

AFTER PUTTING THE BOYS to bed, Jennifer pulled out her springy lump of a sofa bed and booted up her laptop, her heart racing. She hadn't had a minute to herself since Norman had confirmed her presence at the recital (as Julien and Jack also had, after he left), but as soon as she did, something told her not to call Vinita—not yet. She decided to track down Dr. Diane Sexton instead. If Dr. Sexton was real, she reasoned, she must exist online. *Find Dr. Sexton,* she thought, *and I will find the app. Find the app,* she prayed, *and I will be saved.*

Finding Dr. Sexton online, however, was not as simple as Jennifer had assumed it would be. For a physicist of her apparent abilities, in fact, the search results were weirdly few. She had graduated from the PhD physics program at Caltech with honors in 1971. For many years she had been affiliated with the Institute for Strings, Cosmology, and Astroparticle Physics at Columbia. She had been only an adjunct there, however, and a year ago her association with the institute had ended. Her list of journal articles and publications was short and not very prestigious, at least as far as Jennifer could tell. The only explanation she could imagine for this was that Dr. Sexton's work existed somewhere outside the physics establishment, which wasn't entirely implausible: as Jennifer learned from her new physics boyfriend, Neil deGrasse Tyson, whom she'd watched on YouTube after searching *time travel physics real?*, the inventors of no less than the big bang theory and plate tectonics had been treated like quacks for decades. But it was more than a little unsettling, and enormously frustrating, to have so little to go on.

The image results also appeared to be a wash—there were a porn star and a motivational speaker of the same name (each calling herself "Dr.," no less), and the two of them dominated the first page of results.

The first image on the second page, however, caused Jennifer's mouth to drop.

It was a photograph, apparently taken at an institute event, of a woman in a pantsuit, standing with arms akimbo, regarding the camera with a daring, almost regal air. Her brown, spiky hair—dyed, Jennifer had always assumed, as the woman appeared to be in her mid-sixties—perfect posture, and overly large head balanced perfectly on her thin, elegant neck ensured that Jennifer would have known her anywhere. Dr. Diane Sexton was none other than the Shoe Lady.

As if Jennifer needed any further confirmation, she looked at the woman's shoes. Sure enough, one black, one red.

The Shoe Lady also lived on the nineteenth floor of 270 West Eleventh Street, though in a different wing of the building, and Jennifer had no idea which apartment was hers. She'd moved in several months ago, and the boys (especially Jack) had quickly become enamored of Lucy, her Great Dane. They were a bit put off, however, by her "weird" habit of always wearing one black shoe and one red one. Suddenly it hit her. *Ta-ta for now!* The Shoe Lady, or Dr. Sexton, as Jennifer supposed she should refer to her now, often said "ta-ta for now" when waving good-bye to the boys. A few weeks ago, Jack had informed her that "ta-ta for now" was Tigger's favorite way of saying good-bye, which had delighted her. It had been a hint, and a big one, and Jennifer had missed it completely.

Jennifer looked at the clock. It was 10:00 p.m. Should she run downstairs to the doorman, laptop in hand, and ask which apartment the crazy lady with the mismatched shoes lived in? Or should she simply hope to see Dr. Sexton in the elevator in the morning and say, *Excuse me, did you happen to put a time-travel app on my phone yesterday? And might I have it back?*

It was a moot point. She couldn't go running around the

building, knocking on doors, not to mention leave the boys
alone asleep in their beds. Best to wait till morning and, with a
clearer head (she was as tired as she could remember having
been in a very long time, which was saying something), decide
what to do. Plugging her phone into the charger for the night,
however, Jennifer felt a frisson of hope. Not only might the
app she so desperately needed be within her reach—it might be
right down the hall.

JENNIFER SLEPT, BUT THERE was a rub: rather than the
blank oblivion of peaceful sleep she'd longed for, she was
instead plunged into a sea of mind-wreckingly vivid dreams.
During them her brain snapped jarringly from one image to
the next, illuminating moments she had experienced that day
with the abrupt starkness of a strobe light. Owen touching her
shoulder. Julien plucking the guitar. Norman producing the
time log from his pocket. Bill Truitt impatiently glaring at the
staff meeting. And her hand gripping her phone as the
crushing heat of the tornado of light engulfed her.

In the midst of reliving another moment of transport,
however—the interior walls of the APT shredding into strips
and being replaced with the preening gleam of Wishful
Thinking's wand gallivanting about in 3-D—she felt a tapping
at the base of her spine, an irregular drumming, the pressure
light at first but starting to mount.

"*Mama!*" she heard a voice call.

Jack! *Wake up!* she thought, trying to scrape the heavy
sludge of images and sounds from her brain.

"Mama!" she heard again. And then: "*Wake up!*"

She did. And there was Jack, standing next to her bed,
clutching his blue blankie and smacking her back firmly with
his open palm.

She was soaked in sweat. It was 3:00 a.m. now. Wiping her brow, she sat up, pulling the covers back from the bed so Jack could climb in.

"You were talking," Jack said sleepily. "You were talking, but you were asleep."

"Shhhh," Jennifer said, lying down beside him. He snuggled up to her, and she began threading chunks of his soft curls between her fingers.

Jack threw an arm across her and let his small hand rest at the base of her scalp. He began running his fingers through her hair too. He got caught on a few sweaty tangles but managed to extricate his fingers from them with careful tenderness, even though he was only half awake. It felt wonderfully good. After a moment, however, Jennifer pulled away, placing his hand back on his side of the bed as he drifted off. Years ago she'd resolved not to let herself rely on her boys' physical affection too much, though it had been hard. In the months after the separation from Norman, especially, she had found herself powerfully drawn to falling asleep in one of their beds each night and staying there until morning, arms and legs intertwined. But she'd known she had to find other ways to fill her need for human touch. Not that she'd had much luck in that department. Hugs from girlfriends and pedicures went only so far.

With the sounds of Manhattan rumbling outside her windows, Jennifer closed her eyes. A few minutes later she opened them again. Pure exhaustion had knocked her out earlier, but now the Pandora's box of her mind, overflowing with all that had happened that day, had been opened again, and she knew from experience that very few things could close it. Turning onto her side and cuddling up with Jack (*Screw it,* she thought; she needed his touch right now), she took one of his hands in hers and ran her thumb across its dimpled back, fingering each tiny indentation where one day a grown man's knuckle would be.

And then she heard it.

A knock—soft but firm—at her door.

Jennifer sat up on one elbow. She looked at the boys' metal baseball bat, which she kept in the corner.

The knock came again, louder this time. Jennifer got out of bed, casting a quick look over her shoulder at Jack. He had not stirred. The cat sprang lightly up onto the bed and curled up next to Jack on the pillow, topping off his curls like a lady's hat.

On tiptoe she made her way to the door. As quietly as she could, she put one eye up to the peephole.

And there she stood. Wearing an off-the-shoulder gray sweatshirt from the *Flashdance* era, black leggings, and two unmatched slippers: one black, one red.

Taking a deep breath, Jennifer opened the door.

"Dr. Sexton?" she said.

"Yes," answered the woman, smiling. "I am."

seven | DR. DIANE
SEXTON

THE TWO WOMEN STOOD facing each other.

"You used the app," Dr. Sexton said.

Jennifer nodded.

"I am sorry," Dr. Sexton said. "That must have been quite traumatic."

Jennifer gave her head a little shake—*no worries*—as though Dr. Sexton had accidentally bumped into her on the street.

"It was unforgivably naive of me to expect that you would, as instructed, contact me first. I don't know what got into me. And now knocking on your door like this. At this hour. Not that I'm quite sure of the time."

Dr. Sexton tilted her head to one side, as though to examine Jennifer more closely.

There was a pause.

"There, now. You seem perfectly well. I am very sorry to have done something so careless. At this point, however," she said with a curt nod, "I hope we can consider the matter closed."

With that, Dr. Sexton turned to go.

"Wait!" Jennifer said. "You can't just leave me with . . . I need to talk to you. I have a million questions!" From the impassive expression on Dr. Sexton's face, Jennifer sensed that she might never have another chance at getting Wishful Thinking back if she let Dr. Sexton go now. "Like you said . . . what you put me through . . . it was the most traumatic thing that has ever happened to me in my life. 'I'm sorry' isn't enough. Do you think it's enough?"

Dr. Sexton seemed to consider this. She looked up and down the hallway, as though to be sure they had not been seen.

"I suppose you're right," she said. "A short interview. Now. Afterward, if we see each other again, I shall pretend we have never met. It's the only way."

Jennifer glanced back into her apartment, thinking of the boys. She couldn't just leave them there alone, but she didn't want to talk in her apartment, either. Then she remembered. When she had first moved into the apartment, and the ramifications of her decision to leave Norman had felt more and more like a noose around her neck, she had sometimes snuck upstairs for a glass of wine and some semifresh air on the roof of her building, where she could feel a little bit human again after wrestling the boys into bed. To do this, she'd MacGyvered a baby monitor of sorts by calling her landline from her cell phone, picking up the landline and putting it on speaker, then putting it in the boys' room. From the roof, with her cell phone tethered to the landline by the invisible string of a wireless phone connection, she could hear them cough.

"One minute," she told Dr. Sexton, leaving her door ajar as she went inside. First she picked Jack up and put him back in his bottom bunk. Then she dialed her landline, checked to see if the connection was clear, and set the receiver just inside the boys' door. Suddenly self-conscious of her cotton pajama bottoms and T-shirt, she opted for a pair of Uggs, sweats, and a hoodie, though when she caught a glance of herself in the hallway mirror, she realized all she'd done was upgrade her look from after-hours Liz Lemon to Britney Spears getting off an airplane circa 1999. Phone in hand, she opened the door. "Ready," she said.

The two women made their way wordlessly down the hall. At the elevator bank, Dr. Sexton turned left, heading into a section of the building that, though it was on Jennifer's floor, she had never had the occasion to enter. Dr. Sexton walked very briskly for a 3:00 a.m. jaunt, and Jennifer struggled to keep up with her. They came to the door at the end of the hall. On it were at least six locks, stacked one on top of the other, drug dealer–style.

Watching as Dr. Sexton's slender hands worked each one of the locks, Jennifer wondered if she lived alone. She had never seen her in the building with anyone but Lucy. At last the door opened, and Dr. Sexton flipped on the lights.

At the newly illuminated threshold, Jennifer stopped and stared. And for a New York minute, every thought of the app vanished in the wake of Jennifer's shock and awe at the size of Dr. Sexton's apartment.

"How is it that we live in the same building," she stammered, "and this your apartment, and my apartment is my apartment?" Taking a few steps inside, she turned her head from side to side, staring at the tall windows, the elegant drapes, the polished hardwood floors, the antiques, the walls of floor-to-ceiling bookshelves.

Dr. Sexton made her way into the room, obviously pleased by Jennifer's admiration. "It is something, isn't it?" she said. "I had to move in a hurry, but the movers I employed were extremely careful. There are collections here that require the utmost expertise in their handling." Jennifer attempted to focus her attention on the objects that Dr. Sexton gestured to proudly: several books and documents under glass, magnificently framed prints, and other instruments and artifacts. But she could not get over the sheer amount of space.

"You must have half the floor!" she said.

"A quarter," Dr. Sexton replied. "The previous owners consolidated several units." Dr. Sexton crossed into the open kitchen, gesturing somewhat disdainfully at the Poggenpohl fixtures. "Some of it isn't to my taste—I prefer a classic six to a loft, and all these fancy fixtures are a little nouveau—but it is more than satisfactory." Lucy, who was the size of a horse, approached languidly, and Dr. Sexton gave her head a pat. "Would you care for some tea? I bought some exquisite oolong during a recent . . ." Dr. Sexton paused, seeming to search for the right word. "*Journey.* To Paris."

At the word *journey*, Jennifer snapped out of her real estate–induced haze.

"Is that what you call it? A journey?" Jennifer said. "The wand . . . it was all so beautiful, like a game. That's why I didn't contact you first. I didn't think it was real. But then I made an appointment, and then . . ."

"You traveled in time," Dr. Sexton said, calmly proceeding with the making of tea, moving through a routine she evidently cherished. "By wormhole."

Jennifer sat down on a stool across the white marble kitchen island from Dr. Sexton.

"But that's impossible," Jennifer said.

"Is it?" Dr. Sexton replied wryly. "More than anything, Jennifer," she continued, "I want to assure you that it was perfectly safe. I know I behaved recklessly, but I never would have installed it on your phone had I harbored the slightest doubt in that regard."

"How?" Jennifer managed to ask dumbly.

"How what?" Dr. Sexton asked as the water began to boil. "How does it work, or how are you the only person with whom I have chosen to share it?"

Jennifer noted Dr. Sexton's use of the term *chosen*. Was there some hope in that? Something Dr. Sexton had seen in her, or in her phone, that had made her want to give the app to Jennifer and nobody else? If there was, maybe Jennifer could convince her to give it back again. But, she thought, first things first. "How does it work?" Jennifer asked. "I put my body through something today, and my mind too. I'd like to know."

Dr. Sexton took a seat opposite Jennifer, setting two cups of steaming tea to steep between them.

"Have you had any physics?" she asked.

"A little," Jennifer said, reddening a bit. "The high school kind."

Dr. Sexton sighed. "I never cared for teaching," she said. "I'm no good at that Neil deGrasse Tyson 'physics is for everybody!' kind of thing."

"I know what you mean," Jennifer lied, throwing her new physics crush under the bus in a feeble attempt to establish some physics street cred. "I'm a much bigger fan of the original *Cosmos*. Carl Sagan. You know."

Dr. Sexton raised an eyebrow, whether approving or disdainful of the Carl Sagan reference, Jennifer could not tell. Sighing, Dr. Sexton squared her shoulders and pinched the bridge of her nose, as though to hold it before embarking on the unpleasant task of giving a very dull person a lecture. "Are you familiar with the concept of a wormhole?" she began.

"I think so," Jennifer said.

"A wormhole, in essence, is a bridge between two points in space and time. As a concept stemming from the theory of relativity, wormholes are well established. Einstein himself, with a colleague named Nathan Rosen, mathematically proved their existence. They were originally called Einstein-Rosen bridges but later came to be known as wormholes." Dr. Sexton used air quotes when saying "wormholes" and rolled her eyes slightly. "It is typical of male physicists," she said, turning to open a drawer, "to give such an elegant concept such an irredeemably ugly name." She took out a yellow legal pad and a pen and placed them on the kitchen island. As she talked, she began to draw. "Basically, for reasons it would be too time-consuming to explain here, the theory was that through curvatures in space-time it was possible for one point in space and time"—she drew a funnel shape reminiscent, Jennifer thought, of what she had seen emerge from her phone that day —"to connect directly to another point not only in another place, but at another point in time." Dr. Sexton drew a second funnel shape, and then a tunnel connecting the two. "Einstein thought these bridges were stable structures, but they were later shown to be unstable—so unstable they would not exist long enough for even a particle of light to traverse them."

Dr. Sexton's eyes began to gleam. "Einstein was not the only one who had a misconception about wormholes," she went on. "The initial belief was that a black hole was necessary for their creation, which made wormholes, for many years, more science fiction than science. In graduate school my interest in them, and in their possible applications for time travel, was treated, to put it mildly, with disdain. The word *eccentric* came up a lot," Dr. Sexton said, smiling at Jennifer mischievously, "even in my younger years." Apparently Dr. Sexton suspected Jennifer had used a similar word to describe the Shoe Lady to her boys, and she wasn't far from wrong: the word had been *unique*. "While there was no question of the theoretical basis for wormholes," she said, "the difficulty— seemingly insurmountable—was the fact that an infinite, almost incomprehensible amount of energy would be required to keep a wormhole open long enough for even a photon to traverse it from one set of space-time coordinates to another, let alone a human being." Returning to her drawing, she took her pen and drew an arrow entering one end of the wormhole, drew a line through the connecting tunnel, and drew another arrow coming out the other side.

"That was until two extraordinary things occurred. The first was the discovery of the Casimir effect. The second was the construction of the Large Hadron Collider, neither of which, I am assuming, you are aware of." Jennifer admitted she wasn't. "In order to create a traversable wormhole, it was believed, two things were required: first, wormholes that could, in effect, be 'caught,' and second, matter possessed of a negative energy sufficient to provide the repulsive gravity required to keep the wormhole open. The name for the latter kind of matter is much lovelier than *wormhole*. It is known as *exotic energy*." At this locution Dr. Sexton practically shuddered with pleasure. "The Casimir effect postulated conditions in which negative energy density could be created from quantum foam, the theorized but undetected fundamental fabric of the universe. And I, when I was at last able to conduct experiments using the Large Hadron Collider—the largest particle collider on the planet—discovered a way to detect quantum foam."

Dr. Sexton paused, letting this evidently awesome achievement sink in, though Jennifer felt woefully unqualified to appreciate it. "From the quantum foam, I harvested wormholes. Using the negative energy of exotic matter, I enlarged and stabilized them, turning a wormhole from a theory into a method of transportation as reliable as the Holland Tunnel." Smiling, she took a sip of her tea. "And that, my dear, is how it works."

Jennifer wished she could say it all made sense now, but she felt more confused than ever.

"Sugar?" Dr. Sexton asked brightly, gesturing to her untouched tea. Jennifer nodded.

With a flourish, Dr. Sexton scooped a spoonful of sugar into Jennifer's cup. When Jennifer made no motion to stir it, Dr. Sexton did it for her.

At last Jennifer found her voice. "My phone is a wormhole."

"It creates one end of a wormhole. Your destination forms the other."

Jennifer looked down at her tea and began to stir for herself. "And why hasn't this been all over the news? Why am I here in the middle of the night, listening to an explanation I can't even understand? Why doesn't anybody else know? The people who *should* know?"

"The people who *should* know?" Dr. Sexton repeated, visibly amused. "Nobody else knows, my dear. Just you, and me."

"Why not? Why me?"

"Why doesn't anybody else know? Because I don't want them to. Imagine what would happen to a technology like this if it were to fall, though I'm loath to use such a melodramatic cliché, 'into the wrong hands'? It is inconceivably frightening. Can you imagine the violence, murder, and spying such a device would enable in the hands of the men who rule this country, or, God forbid, the men who wish to see it destroyed? Technology has made them far too capable of doing damage exponentially disproportionate to their judgment already. It is the last thing I would want to see come of my work. I had all but concluded, in fact, that I would never share my discovery with anyone—until I was inspired, in part, by the evening I spent with your phone. For a moment, anyway, I envisioned a future where the app was put to good use in the hands of women like you, struggling so mightily under the burdens of modern life." Jennifer considered this. If she got the app back, could she be trusted to use it wisely, and well? She wouldn't start any wars with it, to be sure, but there would certainly be other temptations. "Which leads me directly to your second question: Why you? The answer to that is both more complicated and more straightforward for me to explain.

"The simple explanation," Dr. Sexton went on, "is that it was fate. An extraordinary stroke of fate! I've come to believe in such things much more as I've grown older, though I must confess I've always had a mystical streak, like many another brilliant scientist. None other than Marie Curie believed that spirits could communicate from the dead. Science and magic have always been intertwined. As Arthur C. Clarke said, 'Any sufficiently advanced technology is indistinguishable from magic.' Part of the reason for the wand, you know." At the thought of the wand, Dr. Sexton permitted herself an unreserved look of pleasure—as close as a woman like her ever came to a silly grin, Jennifer thought, as she smiled too. "And then there is how it actually came about, which was in the most ordinary of ways.

"Last night, I was out walking Lucy very late—keeping these sorts of hours, as I often do," she said, waving at a grandfather clock in the corner of the living room, "and was just about to enter the lobby of our building, when a taxicab pulled up at the door." Jennifer immediately felt a stab of guilt, recalling her mental cursing of the cab driver that morning. "He wanted to know if I lived in the building. I told him I did, and he asked if I might give your phone to the doorman. Then he told me your name and your apartment number. How did he know that, by the way?"

"I have an entry in my address book, *If Found*, with an asterisk so it's the first thing."

"How clever," Dr. Sexton said. Suddenly, she clapped her hands together loudly and the sound of an aria came from the direction of her couch. Dr. Sexton walked over to it, picked up her phone, and silenced it. "I use the clapper!" she laughed. "For my senior moments." It was a bit difficult to reconcile the clapper with a woman who was evidently the peer of Einstein, though not so difficult if Jennifer thought of her as the Shoe Lady.

"What happened then?" Jennifer asked.

"By the time your phone came into my possession, it was dead. As soon as I charged it, however, and saw your home screen, I knew that Jennifer Sharpe was *you*. My neighbor." Dr. Sexton smiled. "I've become quite fond of you and your boys during the short time I've been here," she added. "It's been a lonely period for me. Your boys, with their energy and jostling and endless knock-knock jokes in the elevator, not to mention Jack's lovely way with Lucy, are an enlivening diversion I have very much come to look forward to." Dr. Sexton had likely observed her boys more often than she had realized, Jennifer thought, particularly at the park, where the boys played on the playground and Dr. Sexton often let Lucy off leash in the adjoining dog run. "And you, my dear," Dr. Sexton said, her voice pitching lower. "You are quite remarkable with them. I had a very distant mother. She was practically a stranger to me. Watching you—your naturalness, your humor, your patience as you teach them things—it has been a revelation to me." At this, much to Jennifer's surprise, she found herself on the receiving end of an expression of great sympathy and affection. Only her mother had ever looked at her that way. It was eerie, but, a motherless daughter now, she could not help feeling warmed by it.

"But then there was your phone! Speak of a revelation!" Dr. Sexton cried. "I hope you don't mind that I deduced your password," she confided sheepishly. "I can't help myself with that sort of thing. You might consider changing it from your apartment number combined with the inverse of your birthday, which is something even a common fool could work out with a bit of help from the Internet." Jennifer made a mental note never to leave her phone unattended in Dr. Sexton's presence again. "I didn't read any of your e-mails, rest assured. I just observed that there were thousands of them. I had no idea such a thing was possible. Thousands! And your calendar! The number of entries was staggering—to me, anyway, childless and free as I am of familial obligations or the traditional constraints of work, particularly of the barbaric American two-weeks-of-vacation variety—one after another after the next! It looked like a presidential candidate's agenda on her last day in Iowa, not a minute unaccounted for, morning to night. Even its cracked case," she said, glancing fondly at the battered phone resting on the table, "signaled a life overrun with both mundane tasks and urgent, unrelenting pressures at work and at home. I've read about this sort of thing, in the *Times*. Life of the modern woman, *Lean In* and all that. But to see it spelled out in the life of someone I've come to care about . . ." Dr. Sexton reached across the kitchen island and took Jennifer's hand. "And that's when I knew. I knew *you* were the one this app was for. That you, more than any teenage Cinderella, truly deserved to be granted a wish. And a feeling came over me. I wanted to be the one to grant it."

Jennifer's throat tightened. She looked away. It had been a terribly difficult three years—the hardest of her life. Could her phone really tell that story to a stranger? The invasion of her privacy, somehow, seemed secondary to the fact that Dr. Sexton, using only these digital clues and some chance encounters in their building, seemed to know her so well.

"As we know now, however," Dr. Sexton said, withdrawing her hand with a sigh, "it was a mistake. An arrogant and dangerous one. Thankfully, I took one true precaution, which was to ensure the app's disappearance should it be used without my knowledge."

"I noticed that," Jennifer said, sitting forward in her chair. "And I wanted to thank you," she went on, "for choosing me. Because you're right. My life *is* full of unrelenting pressures. Sometimes I feel like I can't possibly manage it all. Sometimes," she said, "making my life work seems more impossible than time travel!" She laughed. Dr. Sexton did not. "It scared me using the app today," Jennifer said, looking up at her and holding her gaze. "But I don't think you made a mistake."

Dr. Sexton said nothing. Her look of sympathy and affection had been replaced by a coolly skeptical expression.

"I need it back," Jennifer said, as levelly as she could.

At that, Dr. Sexton outright scowled. "Out of the question. As soon as you leave here tonight, in fact, I am going to destroy it."

"You're going to *what?*"

"Destroy it. And all evidence that it ever existed."

"What if I tell someone?"

"What, that you traveled in time through your cell phone? Who would believe that?"

"Nobody," Jennifer muttered, thinking back to her conversation with Vinita earlier that day.

"I'm sorry," Dr. Sexton said, "but my mind is made up."

"So no one will ever know that you did this? That you have achieved the most significant breakthrough in the history of science?"

"Aside from the discovery of nuclear fission? Yes. And we all know how that turned out."

"But couldn't you use it for something peaceful? To travel to other planets? Discover life in other parts of the universe?"

"I couldn't care less about life in other parts of the universe. Carl Sagan and all that alien mumbo jumbo. What nonsense." Jennifer winced slightly. "My concern is behaving with integrity and morality with regard to human life *right here on our planet*. First do no harm," she said. And then she repeated herself, closing her eyes tightly. *"First do no harm. When I was caught up in the sheer science of it, when I was in the deepest throes of my obsession, I chose not to think about its implications. But now that I have achieved it, I can think of nothing else. The accolades don't matter to me. I have never required more than my own intellectual satisfaction. And I have fulfilled it beyond my wildest dreams."

Jennifer put her head in her hands.

"Dr. Sexton," she said, looking up, trying to recapture the connection they had shared just moments ago. *"I* am a human being, right here on this planet. And you saw something in me —or in my phone—that meant something to you." Dr. Sexton narrowed her eyes. "My phone didn't tell you the half of it. My ex-husband, who basically abandoned us for two years after the divorce, has been spying on me, saying I work too much and using it against me to try to take away time with the children." Her voice broke. "The worst part is, he's right. I've been forced to take on 'private-sector hours,' which means sixty to eighty hours a week. If I choose my work, I will lose my children. If I choose my children, I will lose my job. And my work, while it may seem 'mundane' to you, is actually incredibly important to me, and to others, I hope." She looked Dr. Sexton in the eye. "So I'm asking you. Please. I really, really need to be in two places at once. Just for a little while."

Dr. Sexton shook her head sadly. "I wanted to grant you a wish. *One* wish. Not offer you a solution to a problem that technology cannot solve."

"Who says it can't? You were right. The app *could* help women like me, so much." She paused. "I need it."

Dr. Sexton shook her head again. "I'm sorry, Jennifer," she

said. "But your bourgeois plight does not pass muster as a humanitarian catastrophe."

Jennifer flinched, embarrassed. "I know," she said quietly.

"Is it money that you need?" Dr. Sexton asked, softening a little.

"No," Jennifer said. "It's time."

Recognizing defeat, and bone-splittingly tired, she rose and turned to go. "Thank you for the tea," she said. "It really was delicious." Dr. Sexton flashed a tiny smile. Assuming she would never enter the apartment again, Jennifer took one last look around before heading for the door. It seemed to take forever for her to get there, and it was not until her hand was on the knob that she realized Dr. Sexton was behind her. Feeling a cool hand upon her shoulder, she turned around. Dr. Sexton's eyes were shining again. In the half-light Jennifer could not tell: Were those tears? The two women looked at each other for a long moment.

"I don't want to destroy it," Dr. Sexton said at last, in a near whisper. "Though I feel that I should."

Jennifer, not daring to speak, simply nodded.

"You could tell no one," Dr. Sexton said. "We would approach it as an experiment. A trial."

Jennifer nodded again, doing her best to conceal her excitement, the sensation of her heart lifting.

"Perhaps some good *could* come of it," Dr. Sexton added cautiously, "if we proceeded with the utmost care."

At this, Jennifer allowed herself to smile a little. "If you could have seen the look on Julien's face today when I came to his recital," Jennifer said, "you'd know that even though it's in a small way, some good has come of it already."

"He's a wonderful child," Dr. Sexton said warmly. "I'd love to get to know him better."

"He is," Jennifer said. "And you will."

"All right, then," said Dr. Sexton. "Come around again tomorrow evening, and we'll talk."

Jennifer nodded. She was about to leave, when, feeling an overpowering rush of affection for this woman she hardly knew, she turned back to Dr. Sexton and kissed her on the cheek. "I always wanted a fairy godmother," she said.

"How lucky you are, my dear," Dr. Sexton replied, drawing back and smiling at her fondly, "that I am not a fairy but a *physicist.*"

eight | WEEK ONE: LIFE
IN THE FAST LANE

THE SATURDAY NIGHT BEFORE Jennifer was to begin her life as a time-traveling superwoman (whose feats would include things like cooking dinner for her children with non-frozen ingredients and working till ten o'clock on a school night) she found herself, as she almost always did on Saturday nights, alone. Saturday nights were still a struggle for Jennifer, though for the most part she had stopped using them as the one night a week she allowed herself to be self-pityingly depressed. She had not yet succeeded, however, in making them into the weekly funfest her married friends fantasized they would be. To begin with, it was practically impossible to make Saturday-night plans with married people with kids, which pretty much described everyone Jennifer knew. And while she had made several halfhearted attempts at online dating, agonizing over her profile and trying to crop her kids out of pictures (what adult

woman has photos of herself standing around solo, she'd
wondered, particularly the "full-body" shots the sites all
seemed to recommend?), the whole process still felt to her like
wearing a sandwich board in Penn Station, hoping one of the
thousands of men who walked by would either bother to grab
her ass or miraculously turn out to be "the one." Twenty-four
hours a week of being a thirty-nine-year-old single woman
with a cat, when the other 144 hours were spent as a working
mother of two active boys, did not seem a luxury. Instead, it
was just weird.

This Saturday night, however, Jennifer was feeling fine. In
a series of conversations since their rendezvous a week and a
half before, she and Dr. Sexton had settled on a one-year trial.
Dr. Sexton had suggested six months at first, but Jennifer—
having signed Bill's contract, which meant four quarters of
milestones to meet at work looming ahead of her—had argued
that it wouldn't be enough to test it thoroughly. She had
promised, however, to use the app only twice per week,
despite being immediately tempted to use it more. (That
Friday Melissa had officially asked to cut back to just two
afternoons a week, offering to help Jennifer find somebody to
fill in the other three afternoons. *No need*, she'd said, to
Melissa's astonishment. *I'll manage.*) In the meantime Jennifer
had gone for the testing Vinita had ordered—though without
telling Vinita—and both the EEG and the MRI had come out
fine. With confirmation of Jennifer's good health in hand, the
two women had agreed to start right away.

In a long meeting earlier that day, Dr. Sexton had outlined
Wishful Thinking's parameters and protocols in detail. Alone
now, seated at her kitchen table, Jennifer was about to book
her first appointments, for Tuesday and Thursday that week.
In preparation, she began to review the user's guide, of sorts,
that Dr. Sexton had prepared.

WISHFUL THINKING: A GUIDE

Part One: How to Use the App

1) Make an appointment in the Wishful Thinking calendar for the *second* place you want to be for a specified period of time. Enter the correct Google Maps coordinates and the length of the appointment. Confirm and book.

2) At the appointed time of travel, be sure to find a place where you will be unobserved, and be sure to have the phone in physical contact with your hand.

3) Any objects in physical contact with your person, from your clothing to your briefcase, will travel through the portal with you.

4) During the return trip to the original space-time coordinates, follow the instructions above: find a place where you can travel unobserved, and be sure to be in physical contact with your phone.

5) **Once a Wishful Thinking appointment has been scheduled, it cannot be altered in any way.** If, in the event of an emergency, such a need should arise, you will require my assistance in order to make any changes to an appointment.

Part Two: How You May *Not* Use the App

1) You may travel backward in time (departing the office at 6:00 p.m., for example, and arriving at the school at 3:00 p.m.), *but not forward*. In other words, you may not schedule an appointment to depart the office at 3:00 p.m. and arrive at school at 6:00 p.m. You may not use Wishful Thinking to *skip* hours of the day, nor to jet off to 2095. You may use it only to *add* hours to the day.

2) You may not use Wishful Thinking to travel more
    than six hours backward in time. (No hurtling back to
    the belle epoque for a quick cancan, either.) Six hours
    is the maximum length of an appointment, but shorter
    journeys, between one and three hours, are ideal.

3) While on a Wishful Thinking appointment,
    interacting with your "other self" or anyone who
    might be around her could result in a causality
    violation and is strictly forbidden. This applies to both
    physical interaction (observing the fixed boundary of
    the five-hundred-yard radius) and all other forms of
    communication. Causality violations occur when the
    relationship between cause and effect is disrupted by a
    time-travel paradox: if Jennifer were to run over
    Jennifer in a car, for example, or, far less catastrophic
    but no less disturbing to the universe and the people
    in it, if Jennifer were to e-mail a colleague about
    something that for Jennifer had already happened but
    for the colleague in question hadn't happened yet.
    Most physicists do not believe that such causality
    violations are permitted by the laws of physics (for
    further reading, see the Novikov self-consistency
    principle), but, as usual, the physicists in question
    concern themselves with grandiose ideas about
    shooting one's own grandfather, etc., and do not
    consider the implications of a woman in two places at
    once sending causality-violating text messages to her
    babysitter.

4) It is for this reason that the phone, while on a Wishful
    Thinking appointment, enters airplane mode. It is up
    to you to observe this moratorium in all other forms
    of communication and contact.

Part Three: Your Consciousness Is Not in Two Places at Once

This is less an instruction than a clarification, or perhaps a measure of reassurance. When using Wishful Thinking, the traveler, mind and body, is fully present in the location of her appointment. A Wishful Thinking user simply experiences hours *in addition* to the ones that those around her experience, and she experiences them sequentially: first, for example, experiencing the time period from 2:00 to 4:00 p.m. at the park, then experiencing the same time period, 2:00 to 4:00 p.m., at the office. She does not experience these two realities simultaneously.

THERE WAS ONLY ONE rule, after the two women had gone over all of them together, that Jennifer asked Dr. Sexton to change: having her phone automatically enter into airplane mode when she was in two places at once. "I can't function in either place without it," she'd argued. "How can I communicate with other moms about playdates, or stay in contact with the office if I go for a coffee at work, or do anything?" Her anxiety on this score wasn't solely practical. The idea of being phoneless in any space-time unnerved Jennifer greatly. When she'd lost her phone the year before, she'd felt as though she'd lost a limb, reaching for a phantom phone every time somebody else's rang or chimed. (She'd found a word for this affliction in the Urban Dictionary: *nomophobia.* She was without question a sufferer.) Dr. Sexton had conceded the point, though she had not liked it one bit. "Very well, though you will have to manage the separation of the two worlds manually," she'd said darkly, *manually* apparently meaning *relying upon your hopelessly flawed brain.* "And you will have to be extraordinarily careful."

She had also requested that Dr. Sexton remove the 3-D wand (a little too much flair), as well as the reminders before a journey and the notification of arrival after it (a little too much action from an app she didn't want anyone to know existed).

Jennifer had then raised one final concern. Even though Dr. Sexton had installed an ultraprecise version of Google Maps on her phone, capable of pinpointing her location with a margin of error no bigger than a roll of masking tape (apparently she had high-up Google friends who'd given her access to a prototype), didn't it still rely on a wireless signal, and didn't that mean she would be at the mercy of her wireless network? It was maddening enough when her phone suddenly displayed zero bars or, even worse, said it couldn't find the server when she was standing on a corner in TriBeCa right outside the AT&T building. Relying on wireless access when bad reception might translate into never putting your particles back together again seemed crazier than the idea of a traversable wormhole.

"I couldn't agree more!" Dr. Sexton had said, pleased as ever to demonstrate that she really had thought of everything. "Which is why, through some back channels, I procured an access code to GETS."

"Gets?" Jennifer asked.

"The Government Emergency Telecommunications Service," Dr. Sexton answered matter-of-factly. "A network created by the Department of Homeland Security to ensure that key personnel, from the president to disaster responders, would never encounter the so-called Mother's Day effect. Another very silly name, if you ask me, very likely coined by somebody on a morning television show, as though on Mother's Day the nation's cellular network would be crippled by millions of dutiful children calling their mothers at the same time. The phenomenon, however, is real. New York's

cellular network did become overwhelmed on September
eleventh, for example, as you might recall. GETS users are
given priority access to every wireless network in the country
and have an almost-flawless completion rate."

Almost? Jennifer had thought. Then she'd thought, if it was
good enough for Dr. Sexton, it was good enough for her too.

Upon rereading the guide alone on Saturday night,
Jennifer was grateful to have things spelled out so clearly and
printed on paper. Because while the tone of the guide
sometimes reminded her of a school principal's instructions to
parents about proper behavior on field trips, having it all laid
out for her like that was not just comforting; it was critical.
And this was because, as she discovered the moment she sat
down to book her first Wishful Thinking appointment,
keeping a clear head when it came to time travel was about as
easy as uncracking an egg.

First, Tuesday. Tuesday she planned to pick up both boys
—Jack first, at the New Day Preschool, then Julien. Jennifer
opened up the Wishful Thinking calendar. A few days ago, at
Dr. Sexton's suggestion, she had mapped the coordinates of the
inside of the cleaning-supplies closet at the Pecan Café, right
across from the preschool. It was where all the parents and
babysitters convened before pickup. She'd then saved the
coordinates as a Wishful Thinking "favorite." Jack's preschool
got out at 3:00 p.m., and so did Julien's elementary school.
They were only a few blocks apart, but still, how did Melissa
handle that? Maybe she could get Jack a little bit early? She
began to type: *Pick up Jack, Pecan Café, 138 West 10th Street,
Tuesday, October 6, 2:45 p.m. to . . . ?* How long should the
appointment be? And how was she going to create a seamless
transition from work to school to home and back to work, and
then back home again? Her brain began to hurt. First she
would "travel" from her office to the café. Then she would

spend the afternoon with the boys. What time should she leave home to go back to 2:45 p.m. at work? Eight p.m.? Yes. Less than six hours, which was the limit, and late enough that Bill and Alicia were likely to leave before she did, earning her major hard-worker brownie points. Once she had put in her hours at work, she would then *physically* travel, on foot or by train, back home, arriving by eight in order to relieve . . . herself.

The question was, without violating the five-hundred-yard radius, how would she get in her own front door?

Jennifer decided she would think about that on Tuesday.

Jennifer then booked a second appointment on Thursday, October 8, this time to arrive at Julien's school at 2:00 p.m. Julien wouldn't get out till three, but that Friday—while reading, perhaps for the first time, the school newsletter's "Get Involved!" section—she had read that the school's annual benefit committee's first meeting was to be held on Thursday from 2:00 to 3:00 p.m. *Annual benefit committee!* For three years, these three words had been as removed from Jennifer's reality as *Navy SEAL commando*. Volunteering for such a committee was sure to shut Norman up. And Jennifer actually liked that kind of thing. In college, in fact, she had been on so many committees that Vinita, who avoided all committees like the plague ("Committees make me want to vomit in my mouth" was a common refrain), had called her Committee Kathy. It was going to be hard to explain to Vinita her presence on this one, if she chose to join it. Was there a way to prevent her from finding out?

Jennifer decided she would think about that on Thursday. Since she'd already be at the school, she should be able to grab Julien right at three and hustle over to New Day to get Jack only a few minutes late.

Having successfully booked her two Wishful Thinking

appointments for the week, Jennifer sat back, surveyed her revamped schedule . . . and frowned. Two "extra" afternoons, which at first had seemed like a life-changing gift, really weren't much at all. What about Wednesdays? Could she convince Melissa to do three afternoons instead of two? Or take her up on her offer to find someone else to help out?

There was another option, of course. She could give the third afternoon to Norman. It irritated her to think he'd see this as a concession, however small, of his point. On the other hand, if she offered the afternoon preemptively, she'd look like the good guy, taking the high road and all that. A small concession might forestall his pushing her for larger ones.

Jennifer opened up her e-mail. She took a deep breath and began to type.

> *Dear Norman,*
>
> *I have arranged my schedule to be with the boys two afternoons a week. Would you like to pick them up on Wednesdays? Melissa will only be with them on Mondays and Fridays from now on.*
>
> *Best, Jennifer*

She waited a minute, her finger hovering over the ENTER key. And then she hit SEND. Some part of her knew it wasn't just the savvy thing to do; it was the right thing to do. She'd never admit it to him, but Norman's speech hadn't entirely missed its mark.

Her arrangements for the week complete, Jennifer put on her pajamas and climbed into bed. As soon as she did, a huge smile came over her face. Imagine the looks on the boys' faces when she was there to pick them up on Tuesday! (She planned to make it a surprise.) And on every Tuesday and Thursday after that, when she took them to the park to play, helped them with their homework, arranged playdates with the moms who didn't make playdates with babysitters but only with other moms, sang songs, gave treats. She knew it wouldn't all be Mary Poppins–ish bliss. She'd struggled with her sanity on enough long school "holidays" (*For whom?* she always wanted to ask), particularly in the dark winter months, to know that. But she had also been becoming increasingly aware of the fleetingness of these years in particular, when her children were still young enough to curl up in her lap and kiss her when she wasn't expecting it, but old enough to play chess; still young enough to build couch forts and be wowed by glitter glue, but old enough to clean up and put the caps back on things. She believed in the magic years, treasuring them even more than the boys' baby days, and she'd been frustrated and sad at missing so much of it. It had occurred to her, of course, that by doubling down on her hours two times every week, she would be exhausted. But wasn't sleep the thing that all working parents sacrificed? She'd just have to get as many hours as she could on the other five plain old twenty-four-hour days and live on coffee, which had gotten her through many a workday after a sleepless night when the boys were very young.

Was it cheating, using the app? Yes. Did she feel bad about it? No. Because if she was honest, she knew that the illicit, cheating part was one of the reasons that she—Jennifer Sharpe, type-A worker, straight-A student, and A-plus single mom—was so goddamn excited about it.

TUESDAY, OCTOBER 6, the day Jennifer was scheduled to make her first intentional Wishful Thinking journey, also happened to be Alicia Richardson's second day as the new cohead of the One Stop community-center project. Alicia,

apparently, had also been swayed by the bonus Bill had offered
—Jennifer could not imagine why else she would have
consented to be Jennifer's cohead when she'd been lured by the
promise of being Jennifer's boss. And it was with Alicia and
Bill, naturally, that Jennifer was sitting when, at 2:41 p.m., she
felt her stomach begin to churn. Her appointment was at two
forty-five. They were smack in the middle of a meeting with
the executive director of a nonprofit who had evidently been
as good as promised the contract to run all of One Stop's job-
placement programs. (The ED, naturally, was the wife of a
friend of Bill's.) The backslapping expediency of it all was
enough to make Jennifer queasy, but the prospect of rushing off
to the secret bathroom in two minutes, in order to give herself a
little cushion before closing her eyes, gritting her teeth, and
getting sucked into her smartphone again, made her feel
dangerously close to hurling more time travel–related vomit.

"Jennifer?" Bill was addressing Jennifer directly. The head
of the nonprofit, Work for Today, was looking at her
inquiringly. Obviously she had missed something.

"Yes?" she replied.

"Bill was asking you when you thought you could have a
budget drawn up for the job-placement program," Alicia said
impatiently.

"Right," Jennifer said. "And the idea is that Work for
Today would have a staff person on-site?"

"Yes, yes," Bill said. "So when can you complete a budget
proposal?"

"I'm sorry," Jennifer said, irritated enough to take her eyes
off the clock for a minute. "But have we considered taking
proposals from some of the nonprofit partners I suggested,
who have been working with the city for years? Aren't we
obligated to do that, in fact?"

Bill smiled. A big, broad smile. Then he shook his head, as

though Jennifer had said something funny. "You know, for someone with a business background, you sure know how to talk like a bureaucrat!" he said. Jennifer did her best not to roll her eyes at him. "Aren't we trying to change the way things are done around here?" Bill went on. "Aren't we trying to streamline and make things *happen*, rather than putting the same old players in the same old process?"

Jennifer was about to answer that if by "the same old players" Bill was referring to some of the most respected nonprofits in the city, then her answer was yes, when she looked at the time: 2:43. It was now or never. "I have to go the bathroom," she blurted, mortified.

"Now?" Bill asked incredulously.

"Yes, now!" Jennifer replied, smiling as cheerily as she could at the assembled scowls. Standing up briskly, she headed for the door before anyone could stop her. "I'll be back before you know it!" she added over her shoulder. "I promise."

Jennifer made her way into the hallway. *How is this little stunt going to play out when I get back?* she wondered. It hardly mattered now. It was 2:44, and by the time she'd grabbed the bag she'd stashed in her office, bulging with the bulk of a soccer ball for the boys and a pair of sneakers for her, she had to hit the stairs running. It was time to time travel, and she'd be damned if she was going to be late.

MOMENTS LATER, JENNIFER WAS in a broom closet. That had been the idea, but something this time around didn't feel right. The journey had been the same: the yawning, spiraling blue tunnel, the feeling of being compressed to the size of a paper clip and suddenly inflating like a bounce house, the pounding heart rate upon landing. But then a different feeling. A feeling of not quite having resumed her normal shape again;

a feeling of being folded up, as though she were squashed inside a box. As she came to and was restored to a sense of her body again, Jennifer realized, in fact, that she was in a crouch. The backs of her heels were digging into her butt, and something hard and flat was pressing against her back. It was pitch-black in the closet, and it took Jennifer a minute to maneuver around enough to produce her phone and switch it into flashlight mode. With her arm extended into the darkness, she swiveled her wrist, looked down, and stifled a scream. The floor was not beneath her feet. Instead it lay at least six feet below.

She was on top of something. When she tried to move, she realized she was squished between whatever that something was and the ceiling.

Hot with adrenaline, she turned her wrist toward herself to illuminate the object she was perched upon. It was a metal supply cabinet. *Goddamn cabinet!* she thought. That hadn't been there when she'd snuck into the Pecan Café broom closet to map the coordinates a week before.

"Frack!" she yelled to nobody in particular.

Thank God she hadn't ended up locked *inside* the supply cabinet, she thought. She made a mental note to add another item to the WT travel bag she'd packed that morning, which included an emergency battery-operated phone charger, a change of clothes, a first-aid kit, her passport (what if she ended up in Soho, London, instead of Soho, New York?), and a roll of quarters for APTs: lock-pick.

It took some doing, in tights, a business suit, and heels, but somehow she managed to hug the slick metal sides of the cabinet, unfold her legs, and, enduring a sharp jab to the stomach as she slid across the cabinet's corner, drop herself to the floor.

Earthbound again, Jennifer put her ear to the door.

Outside, she could hear the sound of women's voices, the rise and fall of prepickup chatter. It was just after 2:45 p.m. (*Amazing, incredible!* she thought, allowing herself a moment of awe)—time for her to join the fray. After opening the door just enough to see that the coast was clear, Jennifer smoothed down her skirt, reassembled her ponytail, and walked outside.

Facing the crowd of mothers and nannies, smiling and trying to appear as if she'd just come out of the bathroom, Jennifer almost felt more anxious than she had while awaiting her transport by wormhole. As a working mom, she always experienced the chatting trios and pairs of mothers at drop-off as a bit of a gauntlet—never quite feeling like she belonged, the mom who dropped off but never picked up, the mom who never chaperoned a class field trip or volunteered to run a booth at the annual book fair. Jennifer always felt as though the mothers who did everything viewed her as a freeloader . . . if they remembered her name at all.

But here they were, throngs of them in jeans and Uggs, talking of Suzuki and tae kwon do. (The nannies had their own cliques, usually organizing themselves by their countries of origin. The few dads who picked up tended to skip Pecan Café, apparently, and go straight to the school.) After making awkward eye contact with a few moms who seemed to recognize her but couldn't quite place her, Jennifer locked eyes with a mother she was sure she knew, and smiled. But what was her name? She racked her brain but found nothing there. The woman stood and embraced her with a warm "It's *so* good to see you" hug that would have made Jennifer feel terrible if she hadn't been so grateful for it. And then she had it, just in time. Caroline.

"Caroline!" Jennifer said warmly. "How are you? How's Charlie?" Charlie was an adorable redhead whom Jack often played with at the park after school. She knew this because

Melissa had often texted her pictures of them together.

"Where's Melissa?" Caroline asked. "We *love* Melissa!"

"She's just doing Mondays and Fridays now," Jennifer replied. "I'm going to start picking up on Tuesdays and Thursdays."

"That's great!" Caroline said, clapping her hands together. "Melissa is great, but Mommy's always better."

Mommy's always better? Jennifer's working-mom self chafed at this. But as she stood there, basking in Caroline's approval, part of her was eating it up. "Is Charlie free to play today?" Jennifer asked. "I could take him to the park with Jack and my older son, Julien."

"Oh, I know Julien. He and my daughter, Sasha, are in the same third-grade class, didn't you know?" Jennifer, embarrassed, apologized, making some comment about never knowing any of the girls. "Oh, please," Caroline said. "I can't remember what I had for breakfast. Charlie has fencing on Tuesdays," she went on. "But we would love a date on Thursday!"

And that was that. Jennifer, feeling punchy, experienced a surge of *love* for Caroline. (She'd tried to suppress her astonishment at the idea of a four-year-old taking fencing classes.) Armed with a freshly booked playdate and feeling like a very good mother indeed, she soon followed the pack of women across the street for pickup a little bit before 3:00 p.m. As she approached the school, anticipating Jack's blue eyes lighting up at the sight of her, her hunger for him became a craving, her palms practically itching at the thought of the soft, still-babyish skin of his upper arms warm against her hands.

Once inside, Jennifer wended her way through the hallways to Jack's classroom in back. Naively, she pressed straight on to the doorway, hoping to collect him early so she could get to Julien's school. Then she noticed the other mothers and caregivers, who had already lined up in an orderly row along the wall outside. Apparently each child had to be called from the rug, and each picker-upper had to wait her, or his, turn. As she waited, Jennifer craned her neck, trying to catch an illicit glimpse of Jack, whose movements were apparently as highly restricted as a maximum-security prisoner's, until finally she was at the head of the line. She heard his teacher whisper, "Jack, Mommy's here." Jack's head snapped up, his eyes widened as he met her eyes at the door, and then his whole face lit up like it was Christmas morning. Running right at her despite his teachers' protestations, he jumped into her arms, so thrilled and surprised to see her he was practically trembling. Touching each of her cheeks and looking into her eyes, he pronounced two sweet syllables with quiet satisfaction: "*Ma-ma*." She was smiling so hard her cheeks hurt.

They stayed like that for a moment, snuggling.

Then she put him down. "We have to hurry to get Julien!" she said. Jack nodded solemnly, though they both knew *hurry* was not in his vocabulary. The two of them wound their way through the crowd and headed for the door. Jack held her hand firmly. At last they were standing on the sidewalk together in the fresh air.

He looked up at her. "Did you bring me a snack?" he asked.

"Snack?" she asked blankly. "Don't you get a snack at school?" Jennifer seemed to remember two school snacks, in fact. She still could not believe how much snacking was always going on. On the weekends she often felt like a combination of a Sherpa and a vending machine, carrying backpacks, sporting equipment, and coats on one arm while dispensing an endless supply of Annie's Snack Mix and Honest Ade into the open mouths of her insatiable children with the other.

"Mewissa ahways brings snack!" Jack whined. The charm of her appearance, it seemed, was already a distant memory.

"Me*lissa*," Jennifer corrected. Jack ignored her. "Maybe we can get something at the park," she said. "Now, come on—it's after three o'clock!"

Jack began to walk again but, head downcast, refused to hurry.

Arriving at Julien's school at 3:10, Jennifer discovered they were criminally late. Apparently, Julien had to be picked up by 3:00 p.m. sharp every day or the family would be placed on probation. When she arrived, he barely acknowledged her, he was so distressed. (Melissa later explained the way to be at two pickups at once: skip Pecan Café and head straight to New Day School at 2:45 p.m. The teachers were happy to release Jack at ten or even fifteen minutes before three.) "Did you bring snack?" Julien asked as soon as they were out of the yard.

"Are you kidding me?" she fired back. "You're talking about Mommy here, who always remembers everything and is always on time!" Julien rolled his eyes at her, but she saw a hint of a smile. She held his gaze, and finally he laughed. She reached for him and gave him a big hug and kiss. He returned it and, relaxing in her arms, let himself be happy to see her.

"Why aren't you at work?" Julien asked. "I thought Melissa was picking us up."

Jennifer sat down on a bench and motioned for them to join her. "I actually have some big news for you guys," she said, putting her arms around both of them. "I made some changes at work, and from now on, I'm going to be picking you guys up *every* Tuesday and Thursday, and spending the whole afternoon with you!"

The boys clapped and cheered as if they'd won the lottery. Jennifer felt so happy to be telling them this, she was able to ignore the niggling guilt she felt for lying to them. But wasn't the fact that she was with them more important than why, or how?

"So," she said, hopping up off the bench, "let's go get a freaking snack, and *play!*"

Fifteen minutes later, armed with water bottles and "bars" (not the usual breakfast bars, but a chocolate-masquerading-as-health-food thing they both professed to love), the three of them walked onto the grass at the park. It felt wonderful to be outside. The day was so breezy and bright, Jennifer felt as though her heavy, office-bound body might lift and spin skyward like the autumn leaves. Her boys were invigorated by the early-autumn air, too, as frisky and playful as puppies and ready to run. Julien set about determining bounds and goals for their game, and Jack, a natural but more indifferent athlete, began dribbling the ball. Jennifer sat on a bench and put on the sneakers she'd transported through the wormhole in her bag, along with a soccer ball. As she laced up her shoes, she drew in a long, deep breath. She was at the park on a weekday afternoon, and for the next couple of hours there would be nothing between her and her boys, nothing between her and the sky, and nothing between her and the ball she couldn't wait to kick around. Best of all, this afternoon would be 100 percent free of stress, worry, or guilt, because during these same hours, she was at her office, getting all her work done too.

They played hard, and for the most part they had a blast. Jack had a meltdown when he thought Julien wasn't being fair, and Julien struggled to rein in his competitiveness, but as they finished their game of "World Cup" with a nail-biting penalty shoot-out, she against the boys, Jennifer couldn't remember having been happier in a very long time. (Jennifer had been a decent soccer player in high school, though not nearly as good as Norman, who'd played at Amherst.) Clouds began to gather overhead around four thirty, however, threatening rain, so the three of them headed home, red-cheeked and panting. The boys were happy, too, she knew. Both of them held her hands when they crossed the street without her having to ask them to, and when she asked about their days, they answered her with enthusiasm, and in multiple complete sentences.

They were home by five. Soon after they crowded into the small apartment, however, stuffy and cramped after all that glorious space and air, the wrangling began. The boys resisted her on every possible front, from baths to homework to dinner. They bargained and bickered, and Jennifer went from patiently requesting things to straight-up yelling at them. By six o'clock she was feeling less like bliss and more like making a run for it. Shouldn't she do *other* things, she thought, with this borrowed bonus time? Looking around her apartment, its surfaces covered in newspapers and school papers and work papers and unopened mail, its floor swept but in desperate need of mopping, the couch heaped with piles of clean but unfolded laundry, Jennifer was seized with an overpowering desire. In another life she had prided herself on her neat and orderly environment. Hadn't a new life kicked off today? So much for family dinner. While the boys ate, Jennifer cleaned. And cleaned. And cleaned.

She did not look up, in fact, until Jack tapped her on the shoulder, signaling for her to turn off the vacuum cleaner. "Can I have dessert?" he asked.

"Sure, darling," she said, standing up and stretching. "What time is it?"

"I don't know," Jack replied. Jennifer looked at the clock on the microwave and did a double take. *Seven fifteen? Wasn't it six o'clock five minutes ago?*

It was then that Jennifer remembered the difficulty she had decided, when booking her appointment, that she was going to figure out later: how to deal with the five-hundred-yard-radius problem she was presented with now. Her appointment ended at eight o'clock. If her stay-at-home-mommy self stayed in her apartment until eight, however, her work-till-eight self wouldn't be able to come near her building until at least ten minutes after she'd left in order not to violate the five-hundred-yard radius, meaning she'd need to leave her apartment in a little over half an hour to make it work. Not only that, but she'd have to find somewhere outside her apartment to travel from. How was she going to manage that?

Where was her phone? She'd buried it in her bag in order to focus on the boys and also to resist the temptation to use it. Now she dug it out and flipped on the sound. *Ping!* It was a text from Dr. Sexton, sent over an hour ago. *How r u?* it read. Jennifer was so panicked, she didn't even laugh at the incongruity of Dr. Sexton's using text-speak.

Help! Jennifer wrote back, the hair standing up on the back of her neck as she stared at the time. *How do I stay here with my kids until I get back from work to be with my kids? I will violate the five-hundred-yard radius, right?*

Good point, came the reply.

"'Good point'?" Jennifer cried.

Then came a second text: *I'll be right there.*

Of course, Jennifer thought. Dr. Sexton lived down the hall. Which meant that Dr. Sexton was about to show up at her front door.

"Boys!" Jennifer called. Julien was in his room, doing his homework. Jack, now holding a Popsicle he'd taken from the freezer in one hand, was shooting Playmobil knights off the counter with a Nerf gun with the other. "I have a friend stopping by!" At least she had cleaned her apartment.

Julien appeared, shirtless, in his flannel pajama bottoms. He was so lean he had a six-pack, though he would have had no idea what that was. *Oh, to be young again,* she thought, *with the metabolism of brushfire.* Jennifer's metabolism now burned at the rate of a damp kitchen match.

"Who?" he asked.

"A neighbor," she told him. "I forgot something at the office. I just have to run out for a few minutes."

There was a crisp knock at the door. "Mommy, *really?*" Julien wailed as he ran back to his room to get a shirt.

Jack put his Popsicle in a bowl on the counter and, gun in hand, marched to the door. "Who goes there?" he yelled.

"Dr. Diane Sexton!" came an equally booming response.

Jennifer, attempting to respect Jack's solemnity but suppressing a laugh, lowered Jack's gun and opened the door. There stood Dr. Sexton, in a belted black dress and knee-high boots (one red, one black), wearing nutty-professor glasses that dwarfed her face and bright red lipstick (dashingly applied), and holding a gigantic metal ball mounted on a wooden stand, with a smaller metal ball on a stick mounted next to it.

"I come bearing a Van de Graaff!" she pronounced, holding the machine out like an offering. Jack, for one, was impressed. He followed her at a trot.

Julien, however, took one look and grabbed Jennifer's shoulder, pulling her ear to his mouth hard. "Her?" he whispered. "The *Shoe* Lady?"

After some effort, Dr. Sexton managed to clear a space on the counter and plopped the Van de Graaff onto it. "Julien. Jack. My name is Dr. Sexton. I am your neighbor, as you know. And this," she said, eyes alight, "is a Van de Graaff generator. Would you like to see what it can do?"

Julien shrugged but inched closer. Jack climbed up onto a barstool.

Dr. Sexton flipped a switch. She then placed both of her hands atop the large metal ball. "*Watch,*" she commanded. A belt beneath the ball began to turn. The ball began to buzz. And Dr. Sexton's hair, to which she had apparently applied less product than usual that morning, as it was uncharacteristically limp, began to stand straight up on its ends.

"Is *that* how you make your hair do that?" Jack asked.

"I've seen one of these!" Julien cried, reaching for the ball. "Can I try it? Can I?"

Turning to Jennifer as the boys clamored for the Van de Graaff, Dr. Sexton, hair sticking out in every direction like a toilet brush, mouthed a single word.

Go.

Seeing her chance, Jennifer went.

Once outside, she headed south. She had to leave the perimeter set by the five-hundred-yard radius before her other self (her other self, or her, later? It boggled the mind) made her way home. There was only one place to go, Jennifer thought grimly, where she could be out of sight and ready for transport when the clock struck 8:00 p.m. It was time for a trip to the nearest automatic public toilet.

THE REST OF THE day at the office, thankfully, went remarkably smoothly. She reentered her meeting with Bill, Alicia, and Ms. Work for Today seamlessly, almost imme-diately abandoning her protests about the unconven-tional way Bill was running things. This pleased Bill greatly, who took it as evidence of what he believed to be his superior powers of persuasion. It was, of course, the five hours straight she'd just spent with her boys that had reduced the fight in her. After a full afternoon of meetings, Alicia left at six thirty, saying she had to be at home for dinner with her family. Jennifer smiled sunnily and waved good-bye when she left, enjoying Alicia's evident irk at being first to go. She was even more delighted when Bill exited his office and saw her sitting dutifully at her own. As master of the macho pissing contest of who stayed at work last, Bill could afford to give her an approving nod. Not only that, but she got a huge amount of work done, her productivity notably increased by the feeling of well-being that came from knowing she was with her children, too, and there was no need whatsoever to rush home.

She did not meet herself on her way back to her apartment. And Dr. Sexton, it turned out, was the world's best thirty-minute babysitter. The boys were still so busy with the Van de Graaff, in fact, that they hardly noticed when she walked through the door. It was very strange—from their perspective she'd been gone only a half hour, while from hers, she'd spent the last five hours at work.

On her way out, Dr. Sexton took her aside. "I've given it some thought," she said, "and it would probably be best if you did not use the app's default of traveling to a Wishful Thinking appointment and then traveling back to the place where you began. Better to work till the end of the day, then travel backward in time to get the boys at school. That way, you may continue your day in real time, without a return trip, and you will not encounter this difficulty."

Jennifer nodded. Good idea.

"I can amend any upcoming appointments," Dr. Sexton added. "Stop by tomorrow?" Jennifer nodded again. She was too tired to do much else.

"Ta-ta for now!" she called out to the boys, who enthusiastically waved their good-byes. The Shoe Lady, Julien later confided, had turned out to be pretty cool after all.

A little less than an hour later, it was all Jennifer could do not to pass out while reading Jack a story in his bed. Nine o'clock at night felt like five o'clock in the morning to her, and when she finally crawled into her bed, she fell asleep instantly. But her dreams were bizarre, flashing from memory to image to memory in a dizzying mash-up, just as they had after her first Wishful Thinking journey. Waking up the next morning was hard. Getting through the day at work was challenging. The following night, the night she had planned to catch up on sleep, the boys took turns disrupting it (they always seemed to have a sixth sense for when Jennifer most needed an uninterrupted night's sleep), first Jack with a bloody nose that took forty-five minutes to stanch and clean up, then Julien with a nightmare. Which meant that by the time Thursday rolled around, getting up was damn near impossible.

By Thursday morning, in fact, she thought she would have to snort the contents of her coffee grinder directly into her nose if she wanted to arise. At seven twenty, when she should have been showered, dressed, and pouring milk into waiting bowls of Cheerios, she remained immobile on the couch, and her sons had begun to poke her in the tummy with plastic swords.

Jennifer could not imagine how she was going to rouse herself. "Desist, good sirs!" she mumbled weakly, but the poking continued. Then, from somewhere in the murky depths of her consciousness, inspiration surfaced. "Remember when we went swimming in that freezing lake?" she said, partially unburying her face from the pillow. "And you guys counted to ten and I jumped in?" They nodded. "Okay. On ten, jump on me . . . and tickle."

Julien assumed a serious expression and spread his legs in a warrior stance. Jennifer steeled herself and began to count. "One, two . . . ten!"

With cries of "cowabunga!" and "charge!" they pinned Jennifer to the bed, two little balls of muscle, each sprouting what seemed like a thousand tiny fingers scribbling at her skin

—under her chin, in her armpits, on the bottoms of her feet. It was a frenzied, sloppy kid-tickle, and it did the trick.

Up and at 'em, Jennifer quickly got herself into shape, relying on her old dry-shampoo-and-ponytail trick. Then she fed the boys breakfast, aka buttered toast, made Jack's lunch, and got the three of them out the door only five minutes later than usual.

Work was murder, but she made it through with the help of roughly eight cups of coffee. Alicia left at six thirty for her family dinner. Bill left soon after, again giving her a chummy thumbs-up for working late. By seven Tim was gone, too, and Jennifer was alone. The silent office was like a tomb. She wanted to sleep in it.

But at 7:55 p.m. she trudged down the stairs to the secret bathroom to start her afternoon all over again, heading back to 2:00 p.m. for the appointment Dr. Sexton had revised for her.

Blue spinning tunnel of light. Contraction and expansion. Annual benefit committee meeting.

Superwoman, indeed.

HERE ARE WORSE PLACES to pass out cold than in a group of full-time moms. Mothers of young children may be the only audience, in fact, in front of whom you can go narcoleptic smack in the middle of a meeting—ending up facedown on a conference table, no less—and be immediately met with sympathy, ice packs, and arnica.

At some point during a rather heated debate about the "coolest" theme for that year's fundraiser (should it be an eighties night or Roaring Twenties?), Jennifer had begun to fade. Under the soporific buzz of the fluorescent lights in the school's conference room, with the soothing melodies of rest time floating in from the classroom next door and the aching absence of coffee in her system giving her a wicked headache (she just couldn't justify another cup), her eyes had begun to droop as heavily as they had in her business school statistics class, where she had been a notorious classroom sleeper. Her head had then begun to bob. She had wrenched herself wildly awake at least six times, snapping her neck backward every time her chin hit her chest à la Jack, who, when he was determined not to sleep, seemed to have a string attached directly to his eyelids that he could jerk violently upward whenever unconsciousness threatened. Ultimately, however, she'd lost the fight. She'd keeled right over onto the conference table, face-first, spilling somebody's Pellegrino Limonata in the process.

At least it wasn't coffee. She might have started licking it.

Upon impact with the wooden surface, Jennifer had awoken with a jolt and sat upright, though with a bit of drool still clinging to the corner of her mouth. The other five women at the table looked shocked and alarmed, but this quickly gave way to comfort and the aforementioned offers of ice packs and arnica.

"I am so sorry," Jennifer said, painfully embarrassed and in pain to boot. A knot was forming where her forehead had hit the table. *What a way to kick off my new career as a mom who does volunteer stuff!* she thought. They had all been so happy to see her there, though it had soon dawned on her that it was because these women, whom, she was ashamed to admit, she had looked down upon somewhat for the endless amounts of time they devoted to volunteering at the school, were desperate for help, and Jennifer was the first fresh face they'd seen at a meeting like this one in some time.

"When Charlie was a baby," said Caroline, who Jennifer had been glad to see was on the benefit committee, too, "I fell asleep once while I was standing up. While steaming vegetables. While he was strapped to me in the baby carrier." She laughed. "Luckily, I fell backward."

"Maybe this is a good note to end on," said Elizabeth, annual benefit committee chair, Harvard law school graduate turned professional supermom (for real), with plank-straight blond hair, ripped triceps, and no stories of falling asleep on the job. It was Elizabeth whom Vinita and Jennifer often had in mind when penning their "somewhere there's a woman" e-mails to each other, but this was partly because Elizabeth's very existence made them feel guilty—everyone knew that the woefully underfunded and overcrowded public school couldn't function without Elizabeth and women like her. "Let's all give some thought to what the different themes might take to execute, and come up with suggestions for venues, decor, et cetera. We'll make the final decision next week."

They all nodded, rising from their chairs, gathering bags and violin cases and tennis rackets, preparing for pickup and afternoons full of activities ahead. Jennifer attempted to rouse herself with the rest, but the temporary shot of adrenaline her face-plant had provided was already fading, and she was feeling wobbly. It seemed prudent to remain seated for another minute or two.

"Can I help you with anything?" Caroline asked. "Do you still want to do the playdate with Charlie and Jack today?" Jennifer grimaced. She had forgotten all about it. "I could pick Jack up," Caroline said. "Sasha is going to a friend's. You could come get him from my house later. We live right around the corner."

"Could you?" Jennifer said. She willed herself to stand up. She was already fantasizing about sneaking into Jack's bottom bunk for a nap when she and Julien got home—so much for helping Julien with his homework. Caroline assured her it was absolutely fine, though Jennifer worried it would be a black mark, or maybe just a question mark, against her.

At three o'clock sharp, Jennifer was in the schoolyard at PS 41, searching for Julien. In the afternoon scrum she did not even realize, until they were inches away from each other, that she was standing right next to Vinita.

"What are you doing here?" Vinita asked, as they each turned toward the other in the same instant. "And what happened to your head?" Vinita put a thumb to the tender spot and leaned in for a closer look. She lowered her voice to a whisper. "Did you pass out again?"

"You could say that," Jennifer said.

Vinita frowned. "Did you get those tests I ordered?" Jennifer couldn't muster much more than a weary nod. Turning to face her squarely, Vinita put a hand on each of Jennifer's shoulders and searched her eyes. "What's going on, Jay?" she said. "You don't look right."

"The app," Jennifer said, unable to stop herself. *"It's real."*

WITHIN MOMENTS OF JENNIFER'S proclamation, Vinita, never one to dither when immediate action was required, had arranged for her babysitter, Sandra to take Julien to her place with her three girls. (Sandra was at pickup, too, as a backup, because Vinita had been afraid she was going to be late.) Julien protested until Vinita told him he could play with her oldest daughter, Rani, on their 3-D Xbox—property of Vinita's man-child investment-banker husband, Sean—as soon as they finished their homework. Even then, however, he was reluctant. "I thought the point of you picking us up was for us to spend time with *you*," Julien said reproachfully. "Not for you to have coffee with Vinita."

"I know, sweetheart," she said, "but I really need to talk to her about something, okay?" She thought about giving him her stock "mommies are people too" speech, but she wasn't sure she could even remember it.

A few minutes later, over a cup of herbal tea at Le Pain Quotidien, Jennifer told Vinita the second half of her Wishful Thinking story.

When she was finished, Vinita sat back in her chair, crossed her arms over her chest, and pursed her lips. "So, you're at work right now too?" she asked, picking up her phone. "Why don't I just call you and find out?"

"Don't!" Jennifer cried, grabbing her wrist across the table.

"You can't do that. It would result in a . . . causality violation. Dr. Sexton told me. It would be very bad." Jennifer considered adding that Vinita couldn't call her at work because Vinita *hadn't* called her at work, but the implications of that were too much for her to wrap her head around at the moment.

"How convenient," Vinita said, putting her phone down and leaning toward Jennifer, "that the only way we could possibly prove the app is real is not permitted by the very person who has trapped you in the delusion that it is."

"It's not a delusion!" Jennifer said desperately. She had already shown Vinita the app, but Vinita's reaction had been similar to Jennifer's the first time she'd seen it. Yes, it looked like every overscheduled woman's fantasy, but that didn't mean it was real.

"I want to meet her," Vinita said, leaning back in her chair again and motioning for the check.

"She won't like that," Jennifer said, "and she'll probably deny everything."

"Do you know how you sound?" Vinita said, whispering. "You sound like someone who has joined a *cult!*"

"Fine," Jennifer said. She was too tired to argue, and the incident at the benefit committee meeting had scared her. "You want to meet her? Let's go."

Twenty minutes later, Jennifer and Vinita were standing outside Dr. Sexton's door. Part of Jennifer prayed Dr. Sexton wasn't home. Part of her prayed that she was. It had been crazy to think that she could do this for a year without telling Vinita, though she had thought she could manage it for more than two days.

Vinita eyed the plethora of locks. "Paranoid much?" she asked drily.

Jennifer rolled her eyes and knocked. "Dr. Sexton?" she called. "It's Jennifer." A few seconds later, Jennifer heard the click of heels on a hardwood floor. Then came the small sound of metal scraping against glass. Dr. Sexton, Jennifer knew, was peering out at them through the peephole.

"You're not alone," Dr. Sexton observed, her voice projecting easily through the metal door.

"She's my best friend," Jennifer said. "And she's a doctor." Dr. Sexton, apparently, did not find this compelling. "I passed out in a meeting today," Jennifer added, gesturing to the fairly dramatic bump that had sprouted on her forehead. "See? Vinita saw it at pickup. I had to tell her. But she doesn't believe me. She thinks I'm crazy. Could we come in? You can trust her. I promise. She's my best friend. And honestly, Dr. Sexton, I can't do this for a whole year alone. I should have realized that before."

There was a pause. "I'm sorry, Jennifer," Dr. Sexton replied, "but I can't let you in. You shouldn't have brought a stranger here. Come back alone, and we can talk."

"Dr. Sexton!" Vinita interjected forcefully. "I'm not leaving here until you answer some questions." There was no reply. Vinita was clenching and unclenching her jaw, as she always did when she was wrestling with her temper. "Please. Jennifer is my best friend, and she's, she's . . . This is very frightening. I'm deeply concerned." Jennifer looked at Vinita and shrugged. It was no use. But Vinita was not giving up. She placed a palm against the door. "If this is real," she said, choosing her words carefully, "and you are testing the app with the idea that others might use it someday, shouldn't a medical doctor be involved? What if Jennifer is being affected physically in ways you can't detect? Your taking her temperature and her pulse every week isn't sufficient or safe." Jennifer regretted having told Vinita that this was the extent of her and Dr. Sexton's plan to "monitor" her health. Vinita paused. "As a woman of science, I'm sure you would agree."

In the silence that followed, neither Jennifer nor Vinita

moved. "I can help," Vinita said. "And I'm not leaving." After what seemed like an eternity, the locks began to turn.

They turned so slowly that every click was a rebuke, but one by one they opened. Standing there, waiting to be let in, Jennifer felt terrible. What had she done? Why had she acted so impulsively when she'd seen Vinita in the yard? What had she been thinking, bringing her here without asking Dr. Sexton first?

At last the door opened, and the brilliant physicist Jennifer hoped would serve as irrefutable proof that Wishful Thinking was real was dressed not like a professor, but like a telenovela star about to go to a South American singles bar.

"What kind of doctor are you?" Vinita blurted bluntly, staring at Dr. Sexton's skintight black leather pants, pumps (one black, one red), cat-woman eyeliner, and low-cut shirt.

Dr. Sexton ignored this. She looked right at Jennifer. "I do not appreciate being ambushed," she said. "This clearly contradicts our agreement."

"I'm so sorry," Jennifer said, "but . . ." She trailed off, pointing to the bump on her head as though that explained everything. "Dr. Sexton, Dr. Kapoor. Dr. Kapoor, Dr. Sexton." The two women nodded at each other with the barest measure of civility. Dr. Sexton, stony-faced, stepped back and gestured for the two of them to enter her apartment.

"Excuse my appearance," she said with the slightest hint of embarrassment. "As you can see, I've just returned from an . . . appointment."

"Was he handsome?" Jennifer asked, hazarding a smile. The joke fell spectacularly flat.

As they entered the living room, Jennifer was struck by how dark the apartment was even on such a bright, sunny day. The curtains were drawn, and throughout the cavernous room were the objects, enclosed in glass cases and illuminated by very low light, that Jennifer had registered only as pieces from Dr. Sexton's "collection" on her previous visits. Vinita, however, who would not be one to gawk over the apartment's size, given that Sean's multimillion-dollar income paid for a West Village loft that rivaled—or surpassed—Dr. Sexton's in square footage, immediately walked over to one of the glass cases and peered over the top. When she saw what was inside, her eyes opened wide.

"Oh, wow," she breathed. Dr. Sexton smiled. This awestruck utterance apparently pleased her far more than Jennifer's stupefaction at the apartment's size had. Dr. Sexton joined Vinita at the case. Jennifer, curious, approached as well.

"You've seen them before?" Dr. Sexton asked Vinita.

"Florence Nightingale's rose diagrams," Vinita said reverentially. "An original?"

"Yes," Dr. Sexton said. "The coxcombs, as she more aptly called them, that she presented to Queen Victoria herself."

"I can't believe you have these," Vinita said. "She was my hero when I was a little girl. I read every book about her I could find, but I didn't hear about the rose diagrams until I was a medical student. Nobody talks about them. Or about her as a mathematician. They're so beautiful." Vinita turned to Jennifer. "Aren't they?"

Jennifer drew closer to the case. Inside was a worn book, its pages edged with age, opened to reveal the heading "Diagram of the Causes of Mortality in the Army of the East." Below this were two graphs that resembled pie charts, but pie charts with a twist, as the slices of the pie were of varying sizes in terms of not only width but length, with some pieces extending far outward on the page and others so small they barely reached beyond the center of the circle. Each wedge was divided into three colors: pale red, pale blue, and black.

"What does it mean?" Jennifer asked.

"Florence Nightingale was an accomplished mathe-matician," Dr. Sexton said. "And one of the first people to display statistics graphically to further the cause of social reform. Her hope was to convince the government of the United Kingdom that sanitation would save lives on the battlefield." Dr. Sexton pointed to the neat, handwritten text in the bottom-left-hand corner of the page. "The blue represents the number of deaths from infection in infirmary tents; the red represents deaths from actual war wounds." In the first diagram, the blue wedges were much larger than the red. "Here," Dr. Sexton said, pointing to a second diagram, "Nightingale showed what happened once she was able to improve hygiene in the field hospitals." The blue wedges diminished drastically with each passing month, like a pinwheel being trimmed successively shorter as you spun it around. "If Nightingale had merely illustrated her findings by handing over reams of documents and charts, it is very unlikely any of her reforms would have been implemented, much less made the law of the British Empire."

The three of them stood staring for a moment. Vinita, however, was the first to turn away.

"No great fan of women, Florence," she said, taking a seat on the couch after Dr. Sexton gestured to it. "I found that out when I read a less-than-admiring biography a few years ago."

"Would you have been a 'fan of women,' as you put it, if you had lived amongst the women of Victorian England?"

"I'm no great fan of Victorian England," Vinita answered, gesturing briefly to her brown North Indian complexion, "for obvious reasons." Following Vinita's lead, Jennifer sat down too. Dr. Sexton took a seat across from them. Leaning forward, she studied Jennifer's forehead.

"Are you all right, my dear?" Dr. Sexton asked. "That's quite a bump. You fainted after a journey?"

"I worked till eight o'clock," Jennifer said, "and then I went back, to go to a meeting at the school at two o'clock—a six-hour appointment, I know—and the whole time I could barely keep my eyes open, and then at the end, I couldn't do it anymore; my brain felt like it was going dry . . ."

Dr. Sexton took a pen and paper out of a side table and began to take notes. "Were there other symptoms?" she asked. "Dizziness? Sweating?" Jennifer nodded.

Glancing over at Vinita, however, Jennifer saw her regarding Dr. Sexton and her notebook with wry disdain. "You can put that notebook away," she said. Dr. Sexton ceased writing, but not before fixing Vinita with an icy glare. "Not that I believe any of this is real," Vinita said, leaning forward. "But if it were, her symptoms are easy to explain. She has jet lag."

"What?" Jennifer said.

"Think about it. If the app works the way you say it does, transporting you to another space-time and then having you go right back and add the additional hours to your day, it's jet lag."

Jennifer thought about it. Of course! The way she'd used the app that week was like flying from Moscow to New York two times in three days (with a poor night's sleep in between, thanks to the boys), putting in full workdays and full afternoons with her kids, and never taking a nap. She had jet lag. Unpleasant, to be sure, but nothing to be overly worried about.

"You see?" she cried, turning to Dr. Sexton. "We need her!"

"To tell us what?" Dr. Sexton asked tartly. "This is somewhat short of illuminating, though I ought to have anticipated it. But sleep holds so little appeal for me, lack of it hasn't been an issue in my use of Wishful Thinking." Jennifer tried to imagine sleep holding little appeal. Since she'd had children, sleep was more appealing to her than an all-expenses-paid vacation to a five-star hotel in the Bahamas—a vacation she would sleep through.

"I agree," Vinita continued, "which is why I would argue that you are actually feeling the aftereffects of some kind of drug this 'doctor' is administering through your phone. I can run some tests, Jay," she said, turning to Jennifer and away from Dr. Sexton. "Your phone could be emitting some kind of psychotropic drug. And if it is, we should report it to the police."

"That is quite enough," Dr. Sexton said sharply. Setting her notebook down on the coffee table, Dr. Sexton pinched the bridge of her nose and closed her eyes for a moment. When she opened them, she looked at Jennifer. "This must *never* happen again," she said. "If it happens again, I will do as I planned to do before we met: destroy the app and cut off all ties with you. Do you understand?"

Jennifer nodded. Dr. Sexton seemed to relax a bit. "I agree that having a medical doctor involved would probably be helpful," she said. "But we've got to be able to trust each other," she added. Jennifer nodded again. She was about to act on her impulse to hug Dr. Sexton, partly as an apology, partly as an expression of relief, when she felt Vinita's hand on her arm, pulling her back sharply and staying there across her body like a shield.

"Who *are* you?" she asked Dr. Sexton, seeming almost as unnerved by Jennifer and Dr. Sexton's intimacy as she was by the idea of the app. "And what have you done to my friend?"

Dr. Sexton was silent. She was clearly trying to decide what to do.

"Dr. Kapoor," she said, "would you like to try the app for yourself?" Dr. Sexton picked up her phone and held it out to Vinita.

Vinita stared at Dr. Sexton's phone. "It's a wormhole?" she asked. Dr. Sexton nodded. "And you travel through it from one set of space-time coordinates to another, and then back?" Dr. Sexton nodded again. Vinita shook her head. "A) I still don't believe you; b) even if I did, I like my technology government-approved. Unlike some people," Vinita added, shooting Jennifer a look.

"Interesting," Dr. Sexton replied, "as the government is the last institution I'd trust to do that." She stood up. "I am left with only one other way to show you," Dr. Sexton said. "Jennifer, please do not consider this license to violate the parameters I have given you." Dr. Sexton typed something quickly into her phone. "Please stand back," she commanded. Jennifer jumped up, grabbed Vinita's arm, and pulled her off the couch into the farthest corner of the room. She had a guess as to what was going to happen next.

Dr. Sexton, gripping the phone in one hand, closed her eyes. And then, right there in front of them, it happened. The wormhole—a fiery blue tunnel of light whipping outward from the phone as it took shape with a dull, muted whir, no louder than a noisy microwave—enveloped Dr. Sexton. The whole thing happened in an instant, faster than Jennifer, who had experienced the journey but never witnessed it, had realized. Dr. Sexton was gone. And Vinita, for the first time in the nearly twenty-two years Jennifer had known her, was speechless.

A second later, there was a knock at the door. Jennifer hung back and waited while Vinita approached the door cautiously, like the girl in a horror movie who can't help herself from letting in whatever is on the other side. Slowly, Vinita turned every single lock. Slowly, Vinita opened the door. Jennifer moved to stand next to her. And sure enough, just outside the door, stood Dr. Sexton.

"Cheap parlor trick," Vinita managed, though her voice was unsteady. "You're a magician. So what?"

"Not a magician," came a voice from behind them, inside the apartment. "A *physicist.*"

Vinita and Jennifer turned around to see, standing in the living room . . . Dr. Sexton. "Hello, Dr. Kapoor," that Dr. Sexton said quietly. When Vinita turned back to look at the Dr. Sexton in the hallway, she was met with a bright smile.

"Ever wanted to be in more than one place at the same time?" the hallway Dr. Sexton asked cheerily, though in an equally low voice, as though she did not wish to be heard by the other Dr. Sexton inside. "With Wishful Thinking, you can be!"

Shaking off her initial shock, Vinita sprang into action. First she ran into the apartment and grabbed the inside Dr. Sexton by the arm, examining her pulse, eyes, and reflexes with rough expedience, an examination Dr. Sexton patiently endured. Then she ran back into the hallway and did the same to the Dr. Sexton there. Then she stared at both of them, going from one to the other and back again.

At last, she spoke.

"Holy. Fucking. Shit."

Jennifer, also looking from one Dr. Sexton to the other, was enthralled. She couldn't believe her eyes. This was what *she* was doing. She was not simply "adding hours" to her day. She was commuting by wormhole.

Vinita returned to the Dr. Sexton in the living room, leaving Jennifer and the other Dr. Sexton alone in the hallway for a moment.

"Do you want to see yourself?" Jennifer whispered to the Dr. Sexton in the hall.

"Oh, no, I'd rather not," Dr. Sexton answered, whispering too. "And I'd rather not hear myself, either. I find it most disturbing. This is an extremely imprudent thing to do, my dear."

"I thought it was an impossible thing to do. The five-hundred-yard radius and all that."

"The five-hundred-yard radius is a rule I put in place to prevent all possible interactions between a Wishful Thinking user in one space-time and the same Wishful Thinking user in another space-time, in order to avoid paradoxes and other unforeseeable catastrophes. It is not, however, prevented by the laws of physics."

Abruptly, Vinita appeared in the doorway again, a little wild-eyed. Jennifer turned to her and put an affectionate hand on her arm. It was a lot, she knew, and this was a particularly jarring way to see it. But she was glad Vinita had.

The Dr. Sexton in the hallway produced her phone again. "I think I'll end this now," she said, "or begin it, depending on one's point of view."

"Home coordinates," she said, instructing her phone and tapping the screen. "Thursday, October eighth, four thirty-four p.m." Vinita looked at her watch. It was now 4:38. Dr. Sexton was about to go back in time and land in the living room—which, of course, had already happened four minutes ago.

"Since when can you use voice commands?" Jennifer asked. Dr. Sexton winked, obviously proud of this newest feature. Then, wearing a look of irrepressible triumph, the Dr. Sexton in the hallway vanished into the Wishful Thinking wormhole again, right before their eyes.

Still looking stunned, in Vinita's case, and grinning ear to ear, in Jennifer's, the two friends turned to face the only remaining Dr. Sexton, who was standing in the living room, arms crossed in front of her chest like a superhero.

"You invented time travel," Vinita said. Dr. Sexton simply smiled—almost, Jennifer thought, though only almost—modestly.

Jennifer turned to Vinita. "I know it's a lot to take in," she

said. "And I know you think I'm crazy to risk it. But Dr.
Sexton's been using it for months now, and really, it's perfectly
safe." Jennifer paused. "And I need it. You know that better
than anybody."

Vinita suddenly snapped out of the thrall in which the
app's dramatic demonstration had held her. She turned to
Jennifer, not angry now but instead looking deeply worried.
"One person has been traveling through space-time via
wormhole for a few months, and you think this is *safe*? Yes,
I'm impressed. I mean, *impressed* doesn't begin to cover it. But
just because this exists doesn't mean it's worth endangering
yourself to use it. Sweetie. Are things really this bad? Can't I
help? Sean could help you pay for a nanny who could work
nights, if you wanted, or—"

"I don't want a nanny!" Jennifer burst out. "I want to be
with my boys. I want to build this community center. I want
your *help*." Jennifer took a step toward her friend. "Will you
help?" she asked. She placed her hand on Vinita's arm.

"If I say no," Vinita replied quietly, "are you going to stop?"

Jennifer didn't answer. She wasn't sure she could do it
without Vinita. But she wasn't sure she could promise not to,
either.

"Because this isn't a solution," Vinita went on. "Setting the
physical risk aside for a minute, you could argue, in fact, that
doing this is an amplification of the problem. You're spread
too thin already, and now you're going to spread yourself even
thinner? You passed out at school today! The only thing
crazier than that is that you decided to use the time from the
app to volunteer for the school benefit committee!"

Dr. Sexton raised her eyebrows. "That is questionable, in
light of the reasons we discussed for your use of Wishful
Thinking," she said. "And who would serve on a committee if
she were not under extreme duress?" At this, Dr. Sexton and

Vinita exchanged their first sympathetic glance.

"I will totally resign from the benefit committee," Jennifer said. "But that isn't the point." She sighed, her exhaustion catching up with her again. "It's a simple question, Vee. Will you help me or not?"

"It is hardly a simple question," Vinita said, resignation in her voice. She looked at Jennifer, then at Dr. Sexton, then back at Jennifer again. "At the first sign of any physical distress—and I mean *any*—I am pulling the plug. I don't care if it's a migraine or a foot cramp. Everything will stop until we figure it out. Okay?"

"Okay," Jennifer said, nodding vigorously. "Whatever you say. I promise." Vinita grimaced, but Jennifer could also see a spark of excitement in her eyes. Vinita was a scientist, after all —she had graduated at the top of her medical school class—and while Jennifer knew Vinita was doing this for her, she also knew that the mind-bending significance of Dr. Sexton's discovery and the prospect of being part of their experiment was alluring to her too.

"We have your word you will tell no one?" Dr. Sexton said, stepping forward and extending her hand to Vinita.

"You have my word," Vinita replied, taking Dr. Sexton's hand and shaking it. Jennifer turned and hugged her tight.

"Thank you," she whispered.

"Don't make me regret it," Vinita whispered back.

And then there were three.

ten | DOUBLE VISION

TWO AND A HALF months later, Jennifer began what had become, since that fateful September day when she had first used the app, a typical Friday.

As in her life before the app, she awoke to the burble of Mr. Coffee, still perched like a loyal pet on the barstool next to her pullout bed. As in her life before the app, she rushed to get the boys ready for school, rushed to get them there on time, and rushed to the office to make it in by eight forty-five. Alicia was always there earlier than she; apparently her husband, Steven, whom Alicia had met when they were rookie teachers at a magnet school in the Bronx, dropped their two children off in the mornings. (*No fair!* Jennifer couldn't help thinking when she arrived to see Alicia's steaming cup of coffee and hour's worth of work done, managing to forget that she was using *time travel* to secure her advantage as the one who always stayed late.) By the time she arrived, however, Jennifer could dive in completely, with a level of focus that was exhilarating. The ambitious—she would have said crazy—milestones Bill had set in order to open the flagship One Stop community center in a year were beginning to be met, one by one, and with Wishful Thinking powering her efforts, she felt like an athlete with extra red blood cells pumping through her veins, doped and capable of anything. It helped, of course, that Bill had finally made official his directive to dispense with the usual protocol for vetting nonprofit partners, arguing as he had from the beginning that expediency, not bureaucracy, was in the best interest of the people the center would serve. Jennifer had made a last stand against this, opposing the involvement of yet another new nonprofit apparently founded by an FOB (Friend of Bill) solely for this project, but when she did, Bill bluntly informed her that unless she was prepared to take her concerns directly to the Office of the Inspector General, who would most certainly put their entire operation under review, she could either put her head down and cooperate or lose any chance of receiving her bonuses.

So she had let it go. It was not only the money that had swayed her. It was the progress they'd made. The community center, an unrealized dream for so many years, was becoming real: floor plans and artist's renderings taking shape in the form of concrete, wires, and steel. She and Alicia had donned their Lego-yellow hard hats several times now, touring the site with guys in Timberlands, seeing many of the NYCHA residents Bill's contractors had employed working overtime to complete the center's foundation before winter set in. The two of them had not come to love each other these past couple of months, it was true. But the wisdom of their pairing was apparent, to Jennifer anyway. Alicia had quickly been able to establish trust in the community they worked in. She was a natural leader, easygoing and warm, able to listen carefully while steering a conversation in the direction she wanted it to go. Her ease with residents made Jennifer jealous, and

Jennifer's private-sector pedigree made Alicia suspicious, but
they tolerated each other and the work got done.

It helped that they didn't often work directly together.
There just wasn't time. This Friday, however, they had agreed
to spend the afternoon meeting with a few key residents in
NYCHA housing in the Fort Greene section of Brooklyn,
gathering feedback in order to fine-tune the center's offerings.
With all the labor necessary to get the center off the ground,
neither of them had visited the residents in their apartments in
a long time—Alicia, in fact, had not paid a visit since her first
day.

It was a cold day in mid-December. By five o'clock, as
Alicia and Jennifer headed for their last appointment of the
afternoon, it was already dark, and a light snow had begun to
fall. When they walked into the lobby of the north tower of
the complex, however, it was light and warm. The walls were
festooned with little white lights, and a cheerful-looking fake
Christmas tree hung with plastic golden globes was tucked
into the corner. (A tiny menorah was placed next to it, looking
somewhat forlorn.) Alicia tensed up a little as they walked in,
but only in the way in which any girl who grew up in the city
and had some sense would. It helped that she carried herself
with the authority of a woman who could assess a situation
quickly; she had more than a bit of *just try it* about her. But her
forbidding air was disarmed again and again as she caught
sight of familiar faces and called out her hellos. (The school
where Alicia had been a principal for ten years, earning every
award the city had to give during her tenure there, was in the
same district.) "It's been a while," she would say as she stopped
for yet another chat.

They soon discovered the elevator was out. Alicia
immediately phoned the maintenance department at NYCHA
to report it, and the two of them huffed and puffed (or Jennifer

huffed and puffed; Alicia hardly broke a sweat) up seven flights of stairs.

Their last appointment was with a family Alicia knew well. Its matriarch was a seventy-three-year-old Dominican woman named Amalia Campusano, who greeted them at the door dressed to receive visitors, in a long black skirt and a white blouse tucked in around her ample waist, small gold earrings visible beneath the thinning, dyed-brown hair she'd pulled tightly into a bun. It was an unspoken truth that when a family stayed together in public housing, a matriarch was around, and these were the women whose support they needed most for the center to succeed. Three of Amalia's fifteen grandchildren had been favorites of Alicia's at the high school, and one of them, Noel, now twenty-eight, was in the kitchen now, scarfing down a late lunch of *sancocho*.

"These children," Amalia said in her heavily accented English, gesturing to Noel as she and Alicia drew apart from their embrace, "always eating, and always at the wrong time of day!"

Alicia walked in and smelled the meaty stew simmering on the stove. "You can't blame them!" she said. "Just smelling that makes *me* want to eat!"

Amalia laughed and squeezed Alicia's upper arm, beginning the ritual of offering food that Alicia graciously refused. Jennifer introduced herself and trotted out a few lame bits of Spanish, to which Amalia simply nodded absently and smiled. Alicia, meanwhile, pressed Noel for details about the classes he was taking at community college and, when he told her he'd recently gotten his forklift operator's license, encouraged him to check into the job opportunities available for people constructing the centers. Then she turned her attention to Amalia, switching to Spanish, which Alicia spoke fluently. Jennifer noticed that Amalia's response to one of

Alicia's questions seemed to upset Alicia a good deal. She couldn't understand what was said but made a mental note to ask Alicia about it later.

After a few more bites of *sancocho*, Noel took off and Amalia, Alicia, and Jennifer got down to business.

Alicia and Jennifer sat on the couch, which was covered with a white sheet to guard against the excesses of grandchildren great and small. Amalia sat in her easy chair with her feet propped up, waving wearily at her swollen ankles. Alicia then began to tell Amalia about the center and its offerings. Jennifer listened intently, trying to follow in Spanish. But after a few minutes, tired at the end of a long day and straining to translate, her mind began to wander.

It did not wander long.

It was only a few minutes, in fact, before Jennifer's brain was seized so jarringly, it was as if her head were riding in a roller-coaster car that had suddenly slammed right into a brick wall. One minute her brain was humming along just fine, processing the data streaming into the organic microprocessors of her eyes, ears, nose, and skin, planted firmly in the time and place her body occupied. And the next minute, *slam*—Jennifer's brain was in two places at once. Or at least in one and a half places at once. She was undoubtedly in Amalia's apartment. She could feel the scratchy-stiff sheet against the backs of her legs, hear the sound of Alicia's and Amalia's voices, see the wall of family photos, and inhale the smell of strong black coffee. But suddenly she also saw, heard, and felt another reality, too, as though it were projected on top of this one, sounds stuttering and snapping loudly through her ears as though she were listening to two radio stations jamming up the same frequency. And in that other reality she was seated in Vinita's familiar home office, and Vinita was hovering in front of her, peering with a small handheld light into the pupils of her eyes. Looking at Vinita's face as it hovered ghostlike over Amalia's, Jennifer tried not to react as she saw Vinita scowl and heard her say something in a worried tone. Jennifer didn't know what, because Vinita's voice merely skipped over the surface of Amalia and Alicia's chatter and was lost to it completely.

But it was real. So real that Jennifer could smell Vinita's perfume.

And then it was over, just as suddenly as it had begun. Vinita—her smell, her sound, her face—was gone, and Jennifer was in only one place again. Or so she hoped. Jennifer glanced at Alicia, who didn't seem to have noticed anything. She looked down at her hands and, as subtly as she could, pinched the skin on her right arm. Fear was coursing through her. *What was that?* In two and a half months of using the app, she had experienced nothing like it before, and Dr. Sexton's guide had assured her it never would happen. (Part Three: Your Consciousness Is Not in Two Places at Once.) But just now her consciousness *had* been in two places at once, hadn't it? Or, at the very least, one consciousness had bled into another. Remembering the concerned scowl on Vinita's face as she'd peered into Jennifer's eyes, she wondered: Had Vinita been able to tell that she wasn't all there, that she was in fact cheating by using the app to be at Vinita's with the boys and work late that Friday too?

She hoped not. Because Jennifer was not supposed to be using the app on Fridays, and if Vinita found out, there would be hell to pay.

When Vinita had agreed to take part in the experiment, she'd suggested that Jennifer stick to the twice-a-week usage she and Dr. Sexton had originally agreed to but use one of the two appointments to catch up on sleep, in order to combat the jet lag. Jennifer had quickly put the kibosh on that plan—only one day a week of being able to be at work and at home? What was the point? And so reluctantly Vinita had consented to Jennifer's proposal to add a third appointment to the schedule. But only reluctantly.

Jennifer had meant to stick to this twice-a-week-plus-one plan. She really had. But it had taken only a few weeks of using the app on a regular basis for her space-time commute to go from terrifying to humdrum, from sweaty, panicked ordeal to the *Star Trek* version of a subway ride. Which had made it seem such a small leap to use it, just once, on a Monday, to go on Jack's class trip to the Met. And just once, on a Friday, to go to Julien's guitar lesson and get a second look at the alluring Owen. And another time, on a Monday, when Melissa was scheduled to pick up the boys, to have one-on-one time with Jack while Melissa took Julien to a friend's house, and on another to go to the dentist, where she hadn't been in more than three years, and then on a Friday again for Julien's guitar lesson (and Owen), and one-on-one time with Julien afterward while Melissa was with Jack. And soon she was going to guitar with Julien every Friday and spending one-on-one time with Jack every Monday, helping him work on his speech. Nobody was monitoring her use. Their tiny band of experimenters was operating on the honor system. And Jennifer, quite dishonorably, now used the app every day of the week but Saturday, Sunday, and Wednesday, with an occasional extra nap appointment thrown in for some much-needed sleep, as one extra nap a week was not sufficient to sustain her. It had been so easy—and hadn't part of her always known, deep down, that it would come to this?—to fall right down the wormhole and into the two lives of which she'd always dreamed. Lately Jennifer was less awestruck by time travel than she was by the fact that with the app her life *worked*, on every level and in every way. Talk about a miracle.

That this life included deceiving her oldest friend, Vinita, and her newest one, Dr. Sexton, had not been lost on Jennifer. But as she'd begun to use the app more and more, she had assiduously armed herself with rationalizations. Central to these was that while she'd increased her use of the app considerably, as long as she'd kept up on her sleep, she'd felt no adverse effects.

Until now.

IT TOOK A MOMENT for Jennifer to realize that Alicia was calling her name.

"Jennifer?" Jennifer attempted to focus. "I've brought Amalia up to speed. Are you ready to start?"

"Oh, yes, of course. Forgive me."

Alicia smiled, but it was a fake one.

"First of all, thank you so much for taking the time today," Jennifer said to Amalia, who nodded amiably but a bit uncomprehendingly, as she'd done before. Jennifer wondered what she was doing wrong, because while Amalia was more comfortable in Spanish, she was perfectly fluent in English too.

"As I was saying a minute ago," Alicia said impatiently, "Amalia's hearing isn't what it used to be." Jennifer reddened. Of course. Amalia's hearing aid was plain to see. "One of the things she'd most like to see in the community centers, in fact," Alicia added, "are Medicaid clinics that offer basic services for elderly residents, like getting help with their hearing aids."

"That's great," Jennifer went on, projecting her voice forcefully now, "because we are planning to do that! So. My first question for you is about education. Do you currently take any of the free classes the city offers?"

Jennifer couldn't be sure of it, but she could have sworn

she heard Alicia, who turned away for a moment, emit an irritated sigh. Jennifer wondered what was bothering her; she'd gone from bubbly to snappish since they'd arrived at Amalia's apartment. As Amalia began to answer her question, Jennifer took notes. She was just about to ask her next question when suddenly she felt a sharp, painful poke inside her right ear. "What the fuck!" she cried, leaping up, her notebook falling to the floor. A hard, pointy object had been jabbed into the tender flesh of her ear canal. It hurt so much that all pretense of *frack* and *freak* had left her—which was unfortunate.

"Jennifer!" Alicia cried, horrified.

"There's something in my ear!" Jennifer said, sticking her finger in her ear, rooting around and grimacing.

Amalia knitted her eyebrows, looking at Jennifer with some combination of disapproval and concern as she winced and rubbed her ear.

"Not in here!" a voice suddenly said.

Jennifer turned to Alicia. "What do you mean, 'not in here'?" she asked, but Alicia simply stared at her angrily. And suddenly she knew. Alicia hadn't asked the question. It was Vinita talking. And Vinita must be checking her ears as part of her weekly exam—though more clumsily than she'd ever done before, that was for sure.

"*Lo siento,*" Alicia said quietly to Amalia, standing up and taking Jennifer, who was still squirming, by the arm. "*Perdone. Solamente un minuto.*"

By the time Jennifer and Alicia had stepped out into the hallway and shut the door, the pain in her ear had stopped. Alicia, however, did not share her relief.

"What the *fuck,*" Alicia said, "to use a colorful word you just threw out in front of a seventy-three-year-old woman, was *that?*"

Jennifer was just getting her bearings. Alicia, however, interpreted her dazed expression as apathy.

"Do you have no respect? For her time? For mine? For the years she has spent on this earth being treated with *no* respect by this city, dealing with the shit that goes down in these buildings, in these projects, in these hallways? Do you think you can come in here and make everything okay with your notebook and your bar graphs and your stupid senior-citizen yoga classes?"

Jennifer was fully present now. "Wait a minute," she began.

"No, *you* wait a minute," Alicia said. "Being here today . . . seeing this family again . . . When we come in here, asking these residents anything besides 'Is your faucet working?' and 'When was the last winter you had proper heat?' I question what we are doing. We're spending millions of dollars on this community center, and meanwhile these buildings are still falling down. Can't you see that? Amalia's granddaughter got bitten by a rat last week at Ingersoll. *Bit by a rat.*" Jennifer finally understood. It wasn't her ear dance, or her yoga question, that had so upset Alicia. It was the conversation Alicia had had with Amalia before their interview had begun. "Noel is living in a one-bedroom apartment with his girlfriend, three kids, one of whom is asthmatic, and two other adults who come and go, and the hot water doesn't work. How much of that federal stimulus money is going to infrastructure? To fixing the buildings that already exist?"

"I don't know," Jennifer answered honestly. "But I do know that the needs we are identifying here are real. And that our answers are real. I know it's only one piece of the puzzle. And most of that federal money *must* be going to infrastructure, right? But even when the elevator works, you need somewhere to go. Some way to improve your life and move on from here, not just make life here more livable. Right?"

Alicia was silent for a minute. She let herself lean against the wall, a rare sign of fatigue in a woman who almost never let her guard down. She looked around, at the decrepit hallway, the peeling paint, the sagging ceilings. There was graffiti on the elevator door.

"I hate being in these towers," she said flatly.

"I can't imagine," Jennifer said. "I admire you," she added, going out on a limb.

Alicia took a deep breath and stood up a little bit straighter. "Let's go back inside," Alicia said. "Amalia will be wondering what happened to us."

Jennifer nodded. "How do you say 'I'm sorry' in Spanish, again?" Jennifer asked. "*Lo siento?*"

"Wait a minute," Alicia said, stopping her. "What *was* that? Your ear. Are you okay?"

"Just this really sharp pain," Jennifer said, as nonchalantly as she could. "Out of nowhere! Weird."

"Weird is right," Alicia said. Then she laughed. "Maybe we're just cracking up under all this pressure," she went on. "Sometimes I feel like my mind is going too. I could have sworn I saw you on the street in the West Village with your kids Tuesday afternoon after I came out of a meeting with a funder, even though I knew you were on a site visit with Bill." Jennifer turned white. Alicia, shaking her head at the memory, didn't seem to notice. "Crazy. It's like all I'm thinking about is work, work, work. I can't get away from it. And you popping up like this little ghost, jumping out at me on the street when you aren't even there." She rubbed the back of her own neck. "Don't you miss your boys?" she asked. "I miss my kids, even though they're teenagers now and more interested in their friends these days. I never miss family dinner, but as soon as dinner is over, I go right back to work and Steven cleans up after everybody."

Jennifer, still reeling from what Alicia had just said about seeing her in the West Village, merely nodded.

"And you, missing sitting down to dinner with your boys at night, getting home after they're already in bed," Alicia went on. "How do you do it?"

It hit Jennifer then. By using the app to make Bill's "milestones" seem doable, instead of the impossible demands they really were, she was perhaps hurting Alicia, stuck trying to manage the workload in real time, the most.

"Alicia," Jennifer said hesitantly, knowing she should slow down but seized by an irresistible urge. "There's something . . . I'm thinking there's a way I could help. Help you, I mean."

Alicia was looking at her questioningly when a young girl, fourteen or fifteen years old, approached the door. "Ms. Richardson?" the girl asked.

"Luisa!" Alicia said, turning. "Oh my God, look at you! You're so grown! Come here." Alicia embraced the girl and immediately began peppering her with questions. Luisa opened the apartment door as she answered them, and before Jennifer knew it, all three of them were going inside. It was as though Jennifer's nonsensical, unfinished sentence had never begun, and when they walked in, Amalia was on her feet, hugging her granddaughter but worrying over Jennifer, too, offering her a cup of hot tea and inquiring about her ear.

Jennifer accepted the tea gratefully, apologizing for her outburst. And then she took the opportunity to collect herself. Had she really been about to tell Alicia about the app? Dr. Sexton would be furious if Jennifer brought anyone else into their tiny circle without her permission. And it wasn't only that. If she shared the app, she would lose the freedom to use Wishful Thinking however and whenever she liked. If she shared it with someone, that someone might experience an interspace-time brain meld like the one that she'd just had, and

tell Vinita and Dr. Sexton about it, in which case Vinita would
almost certainly pull the plug. But the incident hadn't been that
bad. Had it? It had been brief. It had never happened before.
Dr. Sexton had never mentioned having experienced anything
like that. None of the tests Vinita had run had shown anything
was physically amiss. And for now, nobody but Jennifer knew
about it. *If something comes up in my checkup today,* she thought,
I'll tell Vinita everything. If not, I won't.

Sipping her tea as she watched Alicia, Amalia, and Luisa
chat, she thought about how, in a few hours' time, she would
be with her boys again, drinking them in. And how, when she
was with them, she would be *totally* with them, knowing that
she had already put in a full and productive day at work.

Yes, what had happened this afternoon was a little bit bad.
But it wasn't bad enough to stop her.

eleven | FRIDAY CHECKUP,
FRIDAY TREAT

ACK AT THE OFFICE at 7:50 p.m., Jennifer was alone
at her desk, dictating notes into her phone's voice-
memo app in the semidarkness, as she now did at the
end of every "day."

"Incorporate fresh data from residents into the services
proposal. Finalize contract with Brooklyn Family Clinic.
Schedule lunch for Tim's birthday. Ask IT guy to look into
slow network connection . . ." Jennifer trailed off and sighed,
rubbing her temples. What else? Betty Friedan had once said
that housework expanded to fill the time available. Jennifer,
however, with more time now than ever, had discovered that
every kind of work—housework, child-care work, work-work
—expanded to fill the time available. Prior to that afternoon's
incident, in fact, her ballooning time commitments had been
the most worrisome thing about her Wishful Thinking life.
Yes, she had freedom she'd never thought possible to be both
superworker and supermom, and yes, when she was in the
thick of either role, it was mostly a good thing. She had noted,
however, that the more time she had at work, the more e-

mails she felt she should answer within minutes, or check late at night and on the weekends, and the more others expected it of her too. The same went for parenthood. The more time she spent with her kids, the more she obsessed over all the things she should be doing for them and with them, from taking them to every museum exhibit *TimeOut New York* recommended (enrichment the boys had made clear they could do without) to constructing wildly creative Halloween costumes from scratch, instead of buying them at Party City, as she'd always done. Modern life, it seemed, abhorred any kind of vacuum. Jennifer often thought wistfully of a day a year before when she had proclaimed it "family sick day" and the three of them had played hooky at home and made couch forts and taken a three-hour walk along the Hudson in the sun. You couldn't schedule that kind of time as a Wishful Thinking appointment—the kind of time you can find only by losing track of it. Moments like those had meaning only if they were spontaneous, snatched from the jaws of an over-scheduled existence. They had no place as another appointment on her smartphone's calendar.

Once she had finished recording her voice memos for the day, Jennifer checked the time: 7:55 p.m. She rose from her chair, stretching, and headed to the stairs. Time to go back in time, where she would meet Melissa and the boys, go to guitar with Julien, and then rendezvous with Melissa and Jack at Vinita's house for her weekly checkup and dinner. (Jennifer had told Vinita she'd managed to get Bill to let her out of work early on Fridays, given how late she stayed every other night. Another white lie.) She walked into the secret bathroom and shut the door behind her. Holding her phone in her right hand and waiting, she could not help but wonder, as she often did, *What if I dropped my phone in the toilet right now? What if I let the wormhole come and go?* And then she reminded herself that there could be no what-ifs. She had already done it. She had already been at Vinita's house, had already undergone her examination, including that painful poke to the ear. She couldn't *not* go. But how could it be that she didn't have a choice?

"'The only solutions to the laws of physics that can occur locally in the real universe,'" Dr. Sexton had intoned, quoting a paper by somebody named Novikov when Jennifer had posed just such a question, "'are those which are globally self-consistent.'" At the time Jennifer had only half listened to what Dr. Sexton had said. But when she'd returned to the office after the visit with Amalia (Alicia, very sensibly, had headed straight home from the towers), and after Tim and Bill had left for the day, Jennifer had tried to find a YouTube video explaining it. Unfortunately, searching for *Novikov self-consistency principle* had yielded nothing but two teenagers pretending to be physicists in the hallway of their high school, doing cartoonish Russian accents and referencing *Bill and Ted's Excellent Adventure*. As she contemplated the concept of free will from her seat on the counter of the bathroom sink, however, the clock struck eight, and there it was again: the yawning wormhole, the atomic squeezing, the coming to. Today her destination was the broom closet of the West End School for Music and Art, a sentimental favorite as her first Wishful Thinking destination ever. She had the coordinates down pat, though occasionally somebody stored a mop bucket in a new place and she ended up with her foot in it. This arrival, however, went smoothly, and, after making sure the coast was clear, Jennifer slipped through the door and into the hallway outside.

As always, she had to walk into the waiting area in the front of the school as though there was nothing unusual about her being in a building without ever having entered its front door. Nobody ever seemed to notice, but Jennifer still fretted

over it. Slipping her earbuds into her ears, she took a seat on a
pale green bench by the window and leaned her forehead
against the icy-cold glass. She pulled up the voice memo she
had recorded yesterday and pushed PLAY. "You promised Jack
you would take him for frozen yogurt. Pay Melissa back for the
pizza she bought Monday. Julien needs a long-sleeved black T-
shirt for a project at school. Caroline told you her best friend
from high school has skin cancer." Jennifer couldn't believe she
had to record things like the last one. But she'd learned from
her mistakes: with her mind so overloaded, she had completely
forgotten one mother's tearful confession that she and her
husband were taking a "break" (as a known Divorced Mom,
Jennifer was on the receiving end of a lot of those), and the
next day at drop-off, when Jennifer had received a mournful
shrug in response to her perfunctory "How are you?" she had
blithely asked, "Is something wrong?" causing the woman to
shoot her a look of wounded incredulity.

When the list ended, Jennifer pulled out the earbuds and
took a moment to sit in silence, soothed by the everyday kid
traffic around her. Outside, the air was gray and dense with
the heavy portent of snow—which would begin to fall, Jennifer
happened to know, in about an hour. She did her best to
ignore all happenings in the outside world until she was on her
second and last version of a particular day, but she could not
tune out the weather, and in truth she loved being able to
bundle up her children, or provide an umbrella, at just the
right moment. It felt like the all-knowing, mother-as-god kind
of thing she had never been able to pull off before.

She had a good view of the sidewalk and within minutes
spotted Melissa, Jack, and Julien as they turned the corner,
holding hands as they headed west on Warren Street. As she
rose from her seat, her boys in her sights, everything felt right
again, the worries of the day gone. Jack broke into a run,

despite Melissa's protests, and Julien couldn't help grinning at the sight of her standing in the window. As she waved and waited, she reveled in the unabashed expressions of adoration she knew her boys would outgrow before she ever tired of them. She opened the door for them and then knelt down to wrap her arms around Jack's puffy-jacketed body, pressing his pink, frosty fingers against her cheek. Julien hung back a little, guitar case in hand, but when Jennifer stood he went for her waist, sliding an arm around it and pressing his face against her belly.

"I feel like I haven't seen you guys *all day!*" Jennifer said.

"You saw us at breakfast!" Julien cried.

"I know," she said. It had been all day for her, of course. It was her private joke to herself.

"He-*llo*, Mama," Jack said carefully, emphasizing the *l* he had finally found after weeks of painstaking work with Jennifer and the speech therapist. Though she hated to admit it, it made a difference for her to do it with him, rather than Melissa (she did not like to think that before the app, she'd been failing him), especially because she'd been able to work with him one-on-one.

Jennifer greeted Melissa, giving her a quick squeeze. She had been easy to forgive once Jennifer had achieved super-woman status, and, she also reasoned, Norman had probably put Melissa on the spot anyway. After a few minutes chatting about the day's logistics (they were all to meet at Vinita's place at five), Melissa and Jack left to go to the library, and Jennifer and Julien headed for the practice rooms downstairs. Owen wasn't there yet, but he would be soon. At the thought of his arrival, a different kind of anticipation gave her heart a little jolt.

It had taken a few weeks after her promise, delivered so sincerely at Julien's recital, for her to come to a guitar lesson.

But when she'd walked into the practice room for the first time a little more than a month ago, so nervous that her eyes had darted between Owen, Julien, and the floor, she'd known immediately that the surge of electricity she'd felt when Owen touched her shoulder the day of Julien's recital had not been a fluke. It was obvious in an instant, that rare surge of warmth and recognition between two people who hardly know each other, the way they smiled an extra beat before looking away, the way their bodies practically shot out crackling zaps every time they came into each other's orbit. It was the kind of chemistry that doesn't grow over time but is (or isn't) there from the beginning. Jennifer couldn't help but wonder if it had ever been there with Norman. It was so hard to say. Her attraction to Norman was a memory now, buried under years of animosity, and even that negative passion had since faded into neutrality, spiked only occasionally by moments of sharp distaste.

As Jennifer and Julien waited in the practice room for Owen to arrive, Jennifer's thoughts went back again to that first day. The practice rooms at the West End School were cramped, and Owen, she remembered, had gone to a lot of trouble to find an extra folding chair so Jennifer could sit with them, rather than wait upstairs. When Jennifer had sat down, her chair had been so close to Owen's their knees had almost touched. And toward the end of the lesson, as Jennifer had watched Owen taking Julien through a new song, observing the respectful way he listened when Julien talked and his gentleness as he guided Julien's small, pale fingers on the frets with his own huge, callused ones, her knees had knocked against the music stand, sending the guitar book sliding onto the floor. They'd both gone to pick it up, and his wrist had grazed the back of her hand. It was the first time they'd touched since the recital, and even though the moment of contact was over almost before it had begun, the current that had leaped from his body to hers had been so strong that the rush of blood she'd felt, from her cheeks to her toes, had nearly taken her breath away.

Pulling away, she'd let Owen pick up the book. He'd tried to make eye contact with her as he did, but she'd looked away. Owen was Julien's guitar teacher, she'd admonished herself. For a few years, in fact, Owen had been one of the few stable men in Julien's life. Surely she possessed enough self-control not to mess up such a good thing! Since that first lesson, five weeks before, Jennifer had managed to avoid any further physical contact. Fridays with Owen, she had resolved, were a weekly treat and nothing more. But as her attraction—and his, she thought, she hoped?—grew, it was getting harder and harder to ignore.

TODAY OWEN WALKED IN a few minutes past their regular start time, with a little duck of his head to avoid hitting the door frame. "Hey," he said. "So sorry, the train." He was wearing a worn-out-looking baseball cap, which he removed as soon as he sat down. Jennifer loved that he was not wearing, nor had she ever seen him wear, one of those limp ski hats drooping off the back of his head just so, the kind that New York hipster dudes wore even in the summertime. Owen was a grown-up, not a little boy showing off for his friends, or so it seemed, anyway. These past few weeks her reserve had been such that she'd learned nothing personal about him except that he was from Austin (he'd worn an Austin City Limits shirt one day), an origin that explained some of the unhurried friendliness she found in his eyes. He took his guitar—dark red, solid-bodied, and glossy with good care—out of its worn black case.

"Has it started snowing yet?" Jennifer couldn't help asking.

"No," he laughed, "but you are definitely my best source on the weather. I can't believe you called that rainstorm last Friday! Out of nowhere!"

Jennifer smiled. The boys weren't the only ones she played her weather trick on.

"So, how are you?" Owen said. He looked right into her eyes when he asked, seeming to want to hold her there for a minute while Julien took out his guitar. There was something different about him today, she thought. A little nervousness. A little question. Was it a question for her?

"Good," she said cheerily, holding his gaze. "You?"

Julien plugged into the amp and hit an ear-splittingly loud G chord. "I wrote a song!" Julien said. "It's called 'T. Rexes Have Bad Breath.'"

"Let's hear it!" Owen laughed.

They got started. The lesson was going well, as always, when right in the middle, Julien, who had been squirming since he'd sat down, despite strenuously denying having to go to the bathroom, confessed his need. Owen, laughing, grabbed Julien's guitar. "Go, little man!" he said. "We'll be here when you get back."

As Julien walked out the door, Jennifer surreptitiously ran her hands through her hair. She had touched up her makeup, at least, before diving into the wormhole, and was wearing black leggings and a long gray sweater: not bad. Her legs looked good in tights. But *Owen's* legs. Oh my. Owen was so tall that when he sat on the piano bench, his knees were higher than his ass. And those white creases around the seams of his jeans, running along his thighs, his quad muscles filling up the denim till it was tight . . .

"Julien is doing so well," Owen said, smiling. "I showed a video of him to a friend the other day. I hope that's okay," he said quickly. "I wouldn't show it to a lot of people. But the way he concentrates! He's such a natural." Jennifer smiled back. It was almost sad how much she loved hearing this from another adult, how much she missed being able to talk with somebody else who appreciated her children, who gave her the slightest opportunity to say out loud how wonderful they were, to tell the little stories only parents have patience for. Her mother had been that person for her after Norman wasn't anymore, and now it was Melissa, but it wasn't the same.

"Do you think so?" she gushed. "He's really into it right now. He woke me up the other morning, playing." Better not to go on too much, she thought. "He used to cry when I sang to him when he was a baby," she added. "That's how I knew he was musical. I'm a totally terrible singer."

"Oh, I bet that isn't true," Owen said warmly. "Anyone can sing. You might not end up being the *best* singer or anything, but you could do it." He was looking at her again. Really looking at her. Her forearm erupted in goose bumps. "I sing with my band," he said. "Just harmonies, but I had to get over my fear of it. It can be really hard if you're shy."

Owen was shy. Jennifer was just thinking how cute this was when she registered the other part: Owen was in a band. Of course. A grown man in his forties, teaching music to third graders and singing in a band. Jennifer felt her heart sink. She couldn't help thinking of Norman. Actor, artist, lost boy, and now teacher. Was Owen Norman all over again? Everything told her no, but . . . guys in their mid-forties who were in bands and who had never been married? Major red flag.

"Have you ever been married?" Jennifer burst out, to her immediate regret. "I'm sorry. I don't know why I even asked you that," she said quickly. "I wonder where Julien could be." She looked at the door, trying to conceal the rip-roaring blush that had overtaken her face.

"It's okay," he said. "And yes, I have. But not anymore."

"Me too," Jennifer said. "I mean, me neither. I mean, I'm divorced too. You know what I mean."

"I do," Owen said. "Know what you mean, I mean." They laughed, then were silent. Owen was about to say something else, when Julien walked back inside. She didn't know whether to be grateful or relieved that he hadn't.

For the second half of the thirty-minute lesson, Owen put the book away, as he always did. It was time for Julien to work on his "fun" piece—Pink Floyd's "Wish You Were Here." After a few tries, Julien mastered the opening lines. He was just starting to work on a complicated chord when Owen looked at the time. It was almost four. "Maybe I can record my playing it?" he said. "So Julien can practice at home?" He took out his phone. He'd done this before: recorded an audio file and e-mailed it to her. But today Jennifer had a better idea.

"I'll do it," she said. "I can even take a video."

"Great!" Owen said. Jennifer took out her phone, swiped her thumb across the screen to bring up the video camera's view, and tapped the red button. She nodded to Owen when it began to flash.

He nodded back at her, then began. Jennifer turned her phone horizontally to get the whole guitar. Which just so happened to be balanced on top of Owen's thighs.

He'd been playing for almost a minute, occasionally talking Julien through what he was doing or naming a chord, when he began to sing. He sang in a whisper at first, as though to keep his place in the music, but his voice grew clearer as he went, and the sound of it, husky, deep, and steady, warmed her to her toes.

"So, so you think you can tell . . . " he began, half singing the familiar lines, almost as though to himself.

She tried not to look at anything but his hands. But looking at his hands and listening to him sing in that soft, deep voice was quite enough to make her wish that Julien had stayed gone just one minute more.

"How I wish, how I wish you were here," he sang. She moved the camera up, just briefly, to capture his face, then dutifully back down again to the guitar. And then it was over. Owen gently placed a flattened palm across his strings to silence them.

"It's a long song," he said, looking up and smiling at her. "I think you got enough."

She looked down and tapped the flashing red button with her thumb.

End of treat, she thought. *But enough?* Of that, she wasn't so sure.

A LITTLE BIT BEFORE five, it was dark (again) and the snow had begun to fall. Jennifer and Julien left the café where they often spent the hour between guitar and Vinita's house and walked to Vinita's, where they met up with Melissa and Jack outside. Remembering to hand Melissa cash for the pizza she'd picked up Monday, Jennifer saw her off, and she and the boys headed inside.

The doorman gave the boys high fives, and as they crossed the lobby on the way to the elevator, they passed a glassed-in Zen rock garden bounded by a shimmering wall of water, lit by floodlights dimmed to the frequency of candlelight recessed in the granite floor. The building was only a few years old, with an indoor pool and a spectacular roof deck Vinita and Sean sometimes used for barbecues or cocktail parties.

Sean and Vinita had met at a graduate school mixer at NYU, when she was in medical school and he was getting his MBA. Jennifer and Vinita had laughed, at the time, at the male business school students' obvious preference for women going

into specialties like pediatrics, rather than the more
demanding, macho field of cardiology or surgery. Sometimes,
however, Jennifer couldn't help feeling Sean had had the last
laugh. He traveled ten or fifteen days out of the month, never
remembered a birthday or picked up a sock, and had every one
of his domestic needs cared for by Vinita (with help from
Sandra and her housekeeper, to be sure). But with Vinita's
successful pediatrics practice, he got to enjoy the status of
having a doctor for a wife too.

Outside the door, Jennifer and the boys removed their
shoes and placed them in a pile beside the orderly rows of girl
shoes, ranging from patent leather flats to embroidered boots
Jennifer couldn't help sighing longingly over. (Her boys' daily
uniform of sneakers and sweats was hard to get excited about.)
The boys banged on the door, and when it opened, they all got
a surprise: Sean. A fair-skinned man with reddish-blond hair;
small, round, close-set blue eyes; fleshy red cheeks; and perfect,
orderly white teeth, Sean looked more like a cherub than like a
Wall Street shark. (One reason, perhaps, he was so good at it.)
He also didn't lack charisma, and Jennifer was always glad to
see him—though seeing him home at five o'clock on a Friday
was almost as startling as turning on *Dancing with the Stars* and
seeing Tom DeLay doing the cha-cha.

"Jennifer!" he said, welcoming her with a hug and a kiss.
"Boys!" he said, with even more enthusiasm. "What's
happenin'? Give me five!" He began the ritual of "down low,
too slow," to the boys' delight.

"You're home early," Jennifer observed teasingly.

"It's Friday," Sean said lightly, ushering them in. Jennifer
didn't press it. Vinita would explain.

The loft's floors were made of light, sanded pine, and track
lighting hovered from the high ceilings above the open living
room and kitchen. The couch was deep and welcoming,

covered in colorful throw pillows and cashmere blankets, and framed artwork hung on the walls. (Jennifer could not remember the last time she'd framed anything.) There was some evidence that three little girls lived there—a children's table next to the long, rustic farmers' table for adults, children's books and art supplies allocated to clean white shelves, an errant plaything here and there. But with housekeeping help twice a week and Sandra ensuring every day that things were tidy, Vinita's house always possessed an order Jennifer envied.

"Vee?" she called.

"In here!" Vinita replied, her voice coming from the bathroom. "The girls wanted to do baths before dinner."

Jennifer walked into the bathroom to see three little girls, ages three, five, and nine, standing on the bathroom rug in pink hooded towels, all monogrammed with their initials, dripping as they waited in an orderly row to have their hair combed. "Oh, Vinita, your daughters are so *beautiful*," Jennifer said fawningly.

"Shut up," Vinita replied, smiling. It was a joke between them: a common response from many (white) people upon seeing mixed-race children was "They are so *beautiful*," thinly disguised code for "Did you know they are half Indian and half white?" Vinita was crouched down on the bath mat, holding a comb in one hand and her youngest daughter, Preethi's, arm in the other to prevent her from squirming away. "I am always envious of your having girls," Jennifer said, "but I forget all about the hair."

Vinita grimaced. Her oldest, Rani, was trying to comb out her tangles herself. Outside, Sean and the boys were crashing around the apartment in a game of tickle monster.

"I want to go play with Daddy and the boys!" Preethi yelled, yanking her head away from the brush.

"Fine," Vinita said, rising. "But we have to finish before

dinner. The pizza is coming soon!" The girls took off. Vinita looked at Jennifer. "You ready for your exam?" she asked with a wink. They'd developed a routine in the past two and a half months, and Vinita's weekly checkups had become far less stressful than they had been in the beginning. Every Friday evening Vinita gave her a basic exam in her home office, and every month Jennifer went in for an EEG and an MRI.

They walked down the hallway and into the office Sean and Vinita shared. Jennifer sat down on the edge of the ottoman as Vinita opened her heavy black doctor bag—a gift from her grandfather, who had been a doctor too. Jennifer tried to relax, but it was hard. It was nearing the time when, in her previous experience of this same moment, her mind had been in two places at once. Simply having to wait for it, wondering if it would happen here, too, was unnerving. *Does it go both ways?* she wondered. Was this the moment Vinita would examine her eyes and look inquiringly at her face? Or would she take her blood pressure first?

A blood pressure gauge came out of the bag. *Okay. Not yet.*

"Sean's home early today," Jennifer observed.

Vinita strapped the black band to Jennifer's arm and began to pump. "Sean has been in Tokyo for a week and had the balls to book a ticket to Amsterdam tomorrow night to see Radiohead," she said. Radiohead was Sean's great passion. He traveled all over the world to see them, often for just one night, as only an investment banker with platinum status on six different airlines could. "I was so pissed I almost neutered him."

Jennifer laughed. "So he thought it wise to spend the afternoon at home?"

"He got here about an hour ago," she said, reading the gauge and making a note in Jennifer's file. "Whatever. I want to hear about *you*," she said, reaching into her bag again. This time she took out the ophthalmoscope. She was going to shine it in Jennifer's eyes. "How was guitar? How was Owen? *Oh-when Oh-when Oh-when?*" Jennifer tried to smile. Maybe if she freaked out, she thought, she could mask it as excitement over Owen. She clenched her fists under her thighs, preparing herself for whatever was next. Would she start to see and hear Alicia now? Feel Amalia's couch under her legs, the pen in her hand?

Squinting, Vinita shone the light into Jennifer's eyes. Then she leaned in closely and scowled, just as Jennifer had known she would. But that was all. The other side, the other self, the other brain . . . it didn't come through. Maybe it did happen only one way, Jennifer thought. Thank God.

"Your eyes didn't dilate," Vinita said. "That's weird." Jennifer wondered if her eyes had dilated at Amalia's, but not here, which would be really strange. Vinita shone the ophthalmoscope into Jennifer's eyes a second time, and this time she was satisfied. "Huh," she muttered, making a note.

Jennifer drew in a deep breath as Vinita's hands went back into the bag again. Now she was taking out the otoscope, fitting it with a sterilized cap, preparing to place it in Jennifer's ear. It was all Jennifer could do not to pull away as she approached. The anticipation of that sharp pain was almost worse than the pain itself. She couldn't imagine why Vinita would be so clumsy, but just as Vinita leaned down to peer through the scope, Jennifer got her answer. Jack burst into the room, squealing, and slammed into the back of Vinita's legs. On impact, the otoscope jammed into her ear canal.

"Damn!" Jennifer said, even though she'd been waiting for it. At least she'd managed not to say *fuck* in front of Jack.

"Mama!" Jack yelped. "Sean is going to get me!"

"Not in here!" Vinita said sharply, removing the otoscope from Jennifer's ear. "Sorry, sweetie."

Jack went running out. It was over.

"Everything look okay?" Jennifer asked as casually as possible, rubbing her ear.

"Yes," Vinita said, putting away her instruments. "You are the picture of health. Two and a half months now, and you haven't even had a cold."

"I know," Jennifer said. "It's good, right? Amazing!" She was filled with relief. No need to tell Vinita about the bleedthrough. She was fine.

Vinita sat down on the couch and took out her iPad. "It *is* amazing," she said. Then she patted the seat next to her, motioning for Jennifer to sit. "It is amazing. And hard to believe," she went on. "I still find it hard to believe. I find it hard to believe that we are the only two people on the planet, aside from Dr. Sexton, who are sitting around being amazed by it right now." Vinita was pulling up something on her screen. "I know you think Dr. Sexton hasn't told anyone about this because she's afraid of what would happen if she did. And that sort of makes sense. Sort of. But I keep wondering, what if there's another reason for all this secrecy?"

Jennifer watched as Vinita typed *Dr. Susan Terry* into her search engine.

"Who's Dr. Susan Terry?" Jennifer asked. The Internet soon supplied the answer. Dr. Susan Terry was a world-renowned physicist. As Jennifer looked on, Vinita pulled up a series of links. Dr. Susan Terry, recipient of the American Physical Society's Julius Edgar Lilienfeld Prize; Dr. Susan Terry, named one of *TIME* magazine's one hundred most influential people; Dr. Susan Terry, the third woman ever to be awarded the Nobel Prize in Physics. "Susan Terry is one of the most brilliant physicists on the planet," Vinita said. "After I met Dr. Sexton, I thought it might be wise to set up Google alerts for certain terms she was using. *Quantum foam* was one of them. I wanted to see who else was working on this stuff.

This morning, something came up about Susan Terry and quantum foam. I didn't see any connection between Dr. Terry and Dr. Sexton at first." Vinita clicked the images link to the left of the search results. "But then I started pulling up pictures. And that's when I saw it."

"Saw what?" Jennifer asked. And then she saw it too. In the photos from these events, Dr. Terry was almost always accompanied by none other than Dr. Sexton, wearing, unfailingly, one black shoe and one red one.

"They're friends?" Jennifer said. Vinita shook her head and pointed. "Look," she said. "Look." Jennifer looked. Dr. Terry was square-shouldered, with a confident, determined bearing; pale skin; thin, fair hair; and wide-set eyes that glittered with formidable intelligence. She was almost a foot taller than Dr. Sexton, and in almost every photograph of the two of them together, she stood with one hand placed on the small of Dr. Sexton's back. It was subtle, to be sure, but in the photos where Dr. Terry was with Dr. Sexton, as opposed to those of her alone, something softened in her. She looked happier. More relaxed. And in the photos where Dr. Sexton was looking up at Dr. Terry, something seemed to shine livelier than ever in her eyes.

It wasn't physics. It was chemistry.

"They're a couple," Jennifer said.

"Yes," Vinita said. "I mean, there's almost nothing online about Dr. Terry's private life. She deflects every question about it. But for as long as there are records of these things online, every time Dr. Terry is honored or given a prize, Dr. Sexton is there. And the way they look at each other—they were a couple, I'm sure of it."

"Were a couple?" Jennifer said.

Vinita pulled up more recent photos of Dr. Terry, dating back about a year, including some from a benefit at the

Institute for Strings, Cosmology, and Astroparticle Physics at
Columbia, and Dr. Terry appeared alone in every one of them.
Dr. Sexton, it seemed, had vanished. Jennifer thought about
what Dr. Sexton had said the night they met, about having had
to move into her new apartment quickly, and that it had been
a lonely time for her.

"Dr. Terry just won the Nobel Prize for her work on
quantum foam, Jay," Vinita said, "though if you read about her
work, or at least what the committee describes, it's all strictly
theoretical. My question is, what if Dr. Sexton stole Wishful
Thinking from Dr. Terry? Doesn't Dr. Terry seem more like
the kind of scientist who could invent it? Dr. Sexton has never
won anything, as far as I can tell. She's totally obscure. Dr.
Terry is the superstar."

Jennifer sat back on the couch. "So Dr. Sexton was Dr.
Terry's partner," she said. "That doesn't mean she couldn't
have invented Wishful Thinking herself."

"You have to admit it *is* suspicious," Vinita said, sitting
forward and putting a hand on Jennifer's leg. "What if Dr.
Sexton is operating totally out of her league? What if Dr.
Terry is the one who really understands all of this stuff, but
somehow Dr. Sexton has managed to make it work without
Dr. Terry's knowing, and you are entrusting your life to
somebody who is not only an inferior scientist but a thief?"

"Does she seem like that to you?" Jennifer asked.

Vinita sighed. "No. But I don't like how in the dark you
still are, and I still am, about all of this. You need to ask her
about it, Jay. You need to find out what happened with her and
Dr. Terry. You need to know the truth."

The buzzer rang. "The pizza," Vinita said, handing
Jennifer the iPad and standing up. "Promise me you'll ask her?"

Jennifer stared at the photograph of Dr. Terry and Dr.
Sexton, the happy couple, on the screen. "I promise," she said,

as Vinita headed for the door. "And, Vee, thank you. Thanks for looking out for me. Thanks for everything."

"Love you," Vinita answered.

"Love you too," Jennifer replied. Vinita was right. It was high time she got to know Dr. Diane Sexton a whole lot better.

twelve | HAPPY
HOLIDAYS

THE NEXT MORNING, Jennifer received an unusual
phone call. It was Norman, requesting that she drop
the boys with him at 5:00 p.m. that day, rather than
at 4:00.

"Okay," Jennifer said. She couldn't resist adding, "But I am
going to put that in the Bad Dad column of the time log I am
keeping for your lawyer."

"Very funny, Jennifer," Norman said. "You still owe my
attorney a response to the letter she sent you, you know."

"I know," she said. "I know."

Now that Norman was taking the boys on Wednesday
afternoons and for his weekly Saturday overnights, too,
Jennifer had hoped he would be appeased and drop his pursuit
of fifty-fifty custody altogether. She knew Norman was
intimidated by the new her, the practically stay-at-home mom
who, in every aspect of parenting, so obviously had him beat.
She'd hoped that if she left the ball in his court long enough, he
might not ever bring it up to the basket. But a month before,
Jennifer had received a letter from Norman's new lawyer

asking her to begin negotiations to officially amend their agreement. At first, Jennifer had simply ignored it. Hanging up the phone now, she thought of the list of divorce lawyers she'd compiled and resolved to make an appointment the following week. It had to be done. The 5-2-2-5 schedule Norman had proposed (supposedly a common custody arrangement that made 5-2-2-5 part of divorce parlance) would have the boys with her Monday and Tuesday, with Norman Wednesday and Thursday, and at her place every other weekend, meaning that some weeks she would have five nights in a row without them. It was completely untenable. She still didn't believe Norman would really take her to court to get it, but she'd be foolish to count on that.

She sighed. The change in plan meant an extra hour to kill on a dark, cold Saturday, and that she would have to wait an extra hour before her desperately needed Saturday-afternoon nap, which she always took after she dropped the boys off. It was too cold for the park—the beginning of those dark months when parents of young boys spend a lot of time in bowling alleys or at Chuck E. Cheese, trying to burn excess boy energy before it incinerated entire city blocks. Luckily, Julien had a birthday party to go to at a bounce-house place, and Jack was invited to bounce too. The party, however, didn't start until one, and it was only nine in the morning.

"I want to pway—I mean play—Mousetrap!" Jack announced after pancakes. "With *Mama!*" Mousetrap was Jack's new favorite game, and Jennifer had spent so much time circling the cheese wheel with her little yellow mouse (the forlorn color neither boy ever wanted), she had begun to wish the mice really were in a trap and would get picked off by a predator one by one, never to traverse the wheel again. "Julien," she said, as she sat down on a barstool with the newspaper, "will you play with him, please?"

"But we want *you* to play with us," Julien said. "And I don't want to play Mousetrap. I want to play Sorry."

"How about an hour of quiet time first," Jennifer suggested, "where everybody does their own thing, and then I will play with you guys?"

"Nooooo!" they both wailed. "No quiet time! We want to play with you now!"

Jennifer looked longingly at the paper. She had not always been successful at enforcing periods of "quiet time" on the weekends even before she'd begun using the app, but since she'd been around more, she had noted that the boys seemed less able, or perhaps simply less willing, to play on their own. "Did you know Grandma made me have quiet time every day after school?" she asked them. "And did you know that parents never used to play with their children? Like in *Little House*? Mary and Laura don't ask Ma and Pa to play with them. Can you imagine?"

"We know, Mom," said Julien. "But we don't live on a prairie. We live in an apartment building. We can't go around looking for animals and Indian beads. We can't even go alone into the elevator."

He had a point. But Jennifer did not want to play Sorry, or Mousetrap. She wanted to read the paper. "How about a movie?" she said, feeling like a lame, no-account mother the minute she said it. "Yes!" they cried. "With *Mama*," Jack said.

"No," Jennifer replied. "You are perfectly capable of watching a movie by yourselves. Especially if it's going to be *Swiss Family Robinson*. Again." Even as she said it, she felt pathetic. Observing them as they hungrily searched through the DVDs, fighting already about what to watch, she added, "Afterward, we'll do an art project."

They barely heard her, but she didn't care.

* * *

AFTER THE MOVIE (during which Jennifer attempted to read the paper but instead fell asleep in Jack's deliciously cozy, stuffed animal–filled bed), they did do a project, as planned. It was a simple project, one her mother had always done with her during the holidays to make gifts for her teachers. Naturally, Jennifer had never found the time to do it with her boys, and as she set the Styrofoam cones out on the table, with a big bowl of peppermints placed in the middle, and showed the boys how to pin the ends of peppermint wrappers in rows around the cones to make red and green and white peppermint trees, the way she and her mother used to do, she both missed and felt close to her mom in a way she hadn't for a long time. The boys, perhaps picking up on her good feeling, decided they loved making the trees so much that they made an extra one, for none other than Norman.

Jennifer couldn't wait for Norman to see it.

And so, after two hours of bouncing, pizza, and cake, and a spontaneous hour spent at a friend's house afterward to kill the rest of the afternoon, Jennifer brought the boys, the peppermint Christmas tree (placed carefully upright in a crisp white paper bag), and Jack's blankie to Norman's front door, ready to deliver them all. Or at least to what she thought was Norman's front door. She ought to know, as it used to be hers too. But now there was a wreath on it, and a cheery welcome mat with a snowman on it waving hello.

This was strange. So strange that she said aloud, "This is Daddy's, right?" The boys were too busy knocking to answer, and then the door opened and, sure enough, there was Norman, his thick black hair full of product, as usual. But then the scent of mulled wine and fresh-baked cookies wafted out around him and into the hallway, which was stranger still.

"Boys!" he said, lifting them up in the air with extra *I'm a great dad* enthusiasm, she thought, though there was nobody but her to perform for. "How are you guys?"

Jennifer tried to smile.

"Come in," he said. "Sorry about the five o'clock thing. We're just having some people over and we needed a little bit more time to get ready."

We? Jennifer thought. She looked around nervously, her heart beginning to pound. Peeking her head inside the apartment, she saw that it had been transformed. It wasn't just that it smelled like yummy holiday things, or that there was a five-foot tree in the corner (when was the last time Norman had gotten anything other than a tiny bush in a foil-covered pot to appease the boys, and decorated it with anything more than a single string of tinsel?), or that there were little white lights in the window. It was that it was neat, and clean, and homey, even, and there were new throw pillows on the couch. Some of the boys' recent artwork hung from clips on a wire strung on one of the walls. She had always meant to do that. There was no way Norman had.

With a sickening feeling, she realized she had not entered Norman's apartment in weeks, maybe even a month or more. She'd been sending the boys up and down from the lobby, which they loved because it was the only time she let them ride in the elevator alone. She'd come up this time only to show off her stupid peppermint tree, which she was beginning to want to crush beneath her snow boot.

There was somebody in the kitchen.

"Dina?" Norman said, holding Jack in his arms and tickling him. "Jennifer's here."

"Oh, sorry!" Jennifer heard a woman's voice cry. "I was just taking out the cookies!"

Jennifer felt like she was on an episode of *Punk'd*. Surely somewhere there was a hidden camera. Everything in her body was screaming at her to flee. She prayed that the smile she had managed to plaster on her face when she walked through the door would not fail her. And out of the kitchen she came: Dina, who looked like a pixie, barely five feet tall, with short, dark brown hair that curled in perfect little wisps on her forehead, and dark purple lipstick, adding a hint of downtown cool to her otherwise too-cute cookie-baking costume, complete with an apron and floured forearms. *Dina Lou Who,* Jennifer thought, *who could be no more than two.* Or at least born in the 1980s.

"Jennifer," she said warmly, and genuinely, Jennifer thought, which irritated her even more, "I'm so happy to meet you. I've heard so much about you, and I just love the boys."

They shook hands. And then it happened. The boys ran happily into Dina's arms too.

"Hi, monkey!" she said to Jack, kissing his head not once but *several* times, cooing and mooning over him without the slightest hint of reserve at Jennifer's being there. "I'm making cookies; want to help?"

Jennifer attempted to stand still, but she was beginning to shake. "Norman?" she said. "Can we talk for a minute, please?" Norman nodded. She could have sworn she saw the tiniest little smirk on his face. "Nice to meet you," she said to Dina.

"Nice to meet you too," she said. "Come on, peanuts; help me with the frosting?" *Peanuts? Monkey?* How many idiotic nicknames did this woman have for Jennifer's children? Dina led the boys, who followed her after a quick glance back at Jennifer, who nodded them on as encouragingly as she could, into the kitchen.

Norman and Jennifer went into the bedroom. The bedroom that used to be their bedroom. Three years ago, when Jennifer had realized that she could not live with Norman another day, that his combination of insecurity, self-righteousness, and emotional obliviousness was killing her, she'd known that she would have to be the one to find somewhere new to live. He would have made such a botched job of creating a new home that would be suitable for the boys, and she had already created this one. (Though of course until recently, they'd hardly spent any time there.) It wasn't much, anyway: small, like her place was. But still, it had been theirs together. And now there was another woman's underwear on the floor.

The bed was unmade. Apparently Dina did not do beds, just cookies.

"Who is that?" Jennifer asked.

"Dina," he said slowly, as though Jennifer had missed her name. "We've been seeing each other since school started. She teaches at St. John's too. Math," he added proudly.

"She's not a student?"

"She's twenty-nine, Jennifer. She'll be thirty in May." He said it as though she were about to reach retirement. Jennifer thought of all the fortysomething men, men Norman's age, who, in her brief forays on online dating sites, had specified they wanted to meet women between the ages of eighteen (*eighteen!*) and thirty-five, and then of the fifty- and even sixty-year-old men who "winked" at her there, viewing a thirty-nine-year-old as just their size. How things had changed since she and Norman had begun their courtship, when she, the hot young coed, had had all the power, and he had been the one, penniless but full of ambition, in hot pursuit.

"Do you know what that was like for me?" she asked him. "Walking in your door, getting ambushed like that?"

"What about Dina?" he said. "Do you think that was easy for *her*? She didn't expect to see you either, Jen. You never come up. You could have let me know." So it was her fault?

"Is it serious?" she asked.

"Yes," he said.

"How serious? I mean, it better be serious, if you are letting the boys get so close to her. And I assume she doesn't stay here when they're here."

Norman looked her right in the eye. "She does, actually," he said. "We just tell them it's a grown-up sleepover."

"Seriously?" she said, her face turning bright red. "A *grown-up sleepover*? You realize Julien is eight, right? You realize Jack is not a moron? And what about when they crawl into bed with you in the middle of the night? What is she . . . what does she . . ." Jennifer glanced at the underwear on the floor and grimaced. "How could you think it was okay for you to do this without telling me?"

"To do what?" he said. "To move on, Jennifer? To try to be happy?"

"Oh, come on," she said. "That's not what I'm saying, and you—"

He cut her off. "I finally found someone I can love," Norman said. "Someone who makes me believe I can have a family again." At the word *family*, Jennifer's chest felt like a real wooden chest—tiny, hard, and brown—that had suddenly snapped shut. She was fighting back tears. She could not let him see her cry. She could not let him think that she was crying because she still loved him, when she would have been crying because the day they split up she had lost her dream of a certain kind of family too.

"I'm sorry I didn't warn you before, but you've just been dropping them off, and we figured . . ."

"What?" she said, groping for her indignation again to steady her. "What did you figure? Can you imagine if I had been dating someone for months now and hadn't told you? And if that guy was sleeping in my bed while the boys were around, and you had no idea? What if they had asked me about Dina and I'd had no clue who they were talking about?" Jennifer wondered, briefly, why they hadn't. Jack probably hadn't thought of it, but Julien might have guessed she'd be upset. "Do you know how humiliating that would have been for me, and how confusing for them?" For the first time, Norman looked remorseful. She was getting somewhere. She kept it up. "Not only that, but have you thought about what it will be like for them if it doesn't work out with her? If they start to feel like they *are* part of a new family, and then that family breaks up too?"

Norman was silent for a moment. "You're right," he said. "I should have told you sooner. I'm sorry. But unless Dina leaves me, and I don't think she will, because we are talking about marriage now, just so you know, and she stays here most of the time—"

"Are you guys *living* together?" Jennifer demanded, feeling pathetic as her voice rose but past caring.

"Let me finish, Jen." She tried. She dug her fingernails into her palms. "No, we aren't living together. Not yet. But frankly, I'm not worried about her ever not being in their lives, or mine. Obviously I can't guarantee that it won't end. But I know that I don't want it to end. I feel sure about this. As sure as I've felt about anything since . . . You know."

He bit his lip. *Acting again*, she thought angrily. And then she thought, *No*.

She knew. Since her. Since the woman he'd loved and married and had two children with, who had left him. It was a betrayal he'd never been able to forgive, perhaps because it was a betrayal he'd never been able to understand. How can you explain to somebody that you once loved him but you don't anymore, when he still loves you? You can't. But Norman didn't love her, not anymore.

"That's wonderful," she said, as calmly as she could. "I'm happy for you."

"You know I'd be happy for you if you told me you were seeing someone," he said.

Jennifer laughed, more bitterly than she would have liked. "Please," she said. "I don't have time."

"You'd have time if you let me have the kids more often. They love Dina, and we've made the apartment a great place—"

"Norman," she said, cutting him off, "if you think that my getting a boyfriend or your getting a girlfriend is going to get you more custody of the boys—"

"I'm not talking about me or my time with the boys. I'm talking about you." *Oh God.* She could feel her emotions swelling again. She didn't want to feel this way—or any way, for that matter—in front of him. She wanted him to stop, but he kept going. "Don't you miss having a partner? Someone you can tell your daily story to? Someone who knows what's going on in your life, who takes care of you, who is your best friend?"

"I'm a mother, Norman," she said, mustering what was left of her authority. "I take care of our boys. And for a long time, I did it without any help from you. I'm sure I will meet someone someday. But I don't need someone else to make me feel whole."

"Not to feel *whole*," Norman said, his condescending earnestness making her hair stand on end. "To feel *happy*."

JENNIFER CAME HOME TO an apartment that was empty, dark, and quiet, and flipping on the lights didn't make it feel more cheery. The sink was full of breakfast dishes, including a bowl rimmed with pancake mix that had hardened into a patina of gummy glue (how had she forgotten to soak it?), and the detritus of peppermint-Styrofoam–Christmas tree making covered the kitchen table. Jennifer was still carrying the peppermint tree the boys had made for Norman in its white paper bag, having been too embarrassed to give it to him in front of Dina. She set it on the counter carefully, despite herself.

Jennifer took each cushion off the couch one by one and stacked them onto the floor, then wearily unfolded the sofa bed, retrieved the down comforter she stowed in a zippered cube in the corner, and laid it across the mattress pad and flannel sheets that just barely made it habitable. After taking off her boots, jeans, and sweater, she climbed into the bed in her T-shirt, did the gym-class bra-through-the-sleeve trick, and pulled the comforter up around her neck. She drew her knees into her chest and clutched a pillow in her arms. She tried not to think. She needed to sleep. But it was impossible to banish the sight of Norman, one arm around the tiny waist of his new "best friend"—she of the petite, perky butt and prebaby belly—guiding the boys as they carefully sprinkled red and green sugar onto gingerbread men, completing a picture in which Norman's last name would be not Bideau, but Rockwell. *A family*, Norman had said. Dina was likely to want to have babies of her own. And then they'd be perfect: husband, wife, baby, and two adorable boys (*her* adorable boys) too. The emptiness of her life without the boys frightened her. The romance propaganda Norman had fed her stuck with her, and stung. *A best friend. Someone to tell your daily story to. Someone who takes care of you.* She tried to laugh. A boyfriend would be just another boy to take care of, she told herself, not someone who would take care of her. But she knew—or hoped, at least—that that wasn't really true. Norman hadn't been that man. But Norman had moved on, and where was she? Living a double life that was doubly bereft of grown-up sleepovers or grown-up love.

Could it be that Norman was the one evolving, while she was frozen in time?

She needed to cry. She needed to talk to somebody. The healthy thing to do would be to call someone, get herself together, and go out. Instead she took out her phone and pulled up the video of Owen playing "Wish You Were Here." As soon as she pushed PLAY, however, she wished she'd shot it so that she could see his face. Staring at the frets of a shiny red electric guitar was not what the doctor had ordered. She stopped the video. But the song. She wanted to hear the song. Maybe if she heard the song, she could feel like Owen was keeping her company, just a little bit.

On YouTube she found a video of David Gilmour playing "Wish You Were Here" in an *MTV Unplugged* performance from 2009. At first, as she laid her head on her pillow and cradled her headphones to her ears, it was just right. The muscular strumming, the full chorus of two guitars, with Gilmour on lead and another guitarist playing rhythm, soothed her. Heartened, she cranked the volume up high and felt her balled-up fists relax. "A smile from a veil . . ." Gilmour's soulful voice filled the little living room, and the aching, enigmatic, Cambridge-boy lyrics were transporting. But then there was the guitar solo. The lyric suspended, Gilmour began to riff, softly, in a high, winsome scat, echoing each note of his guitar, his voice so full of sadness it was as though he had to remember to use it to make a sound. And in that pause, Jennifer's heart began to ache. When the whole band joined together for the chorus, her heart broke all over again.

How I wish, how I wish you were here.

She began to cry. Suddenly she was filled with a memory of her own little family two winters ago, in her tiny kitchen, cheery then, sprinkling colored sugar onto Christmas cookies, using the cookie cutters she and her mother had used when she was a little girl. Her, Julien, Jack, . . . and her mother, together.

Her mother. Her mother, her mother, her mother.

WHEN SHE WOKE UP, it was 4:00 a.m. An empty box of tissues sat next to her, and her eyes were still sore from sobbing. Waking up at this time on Saturday night, however—though it was technically Sunday morning—was not unusual. Even when her body was terribly sleep-deprived after a week of using the app, her circadian rhythms prevented her from simply banking the sleep she needed in one big twelve- or fourteen-hour chunk. Vinita had tried to help her, giving her suggestions about light and hydration, as well as bottles of melatonin and valerian root. She'd refused to prescribe a pharmaceutical sleeping aid, however, saying, with typical bluntness, "You are already walking around with your head up your app, and you want me to put you on Ambien so you can have sex and drive at the same time too?" (Vinita had been unmoved by Jennifer's objection that she was not having any sex.) Jennifer had finally had to make peace with her new sleep cycle, and had been encouraged by an article she'd found in the *New York Times* suggesting that the eight-hours-of-sleep standard was a relatively new invention, tied to the eight-hour workday. Apparently, the article said, it had once been commonplace for people to have a "first sleep," wake up for a few hours, and then settle back into their "second sleep," as Jennifer was now wont to do. Experiments had shown that subjects put into a sensory-deprivation chamber eventually settled into this pattern, too, suggesting it was the most natural one for human beings. Jennifer took comfort in this despite the fact that the reason for her first and second sleeps was about as far from natural as blue Gatorade.

This 4:00 a.m. awakening, however, came with a numb sense of sadness. Depression, her mother had once told her, could be like a warm blanket you pulled over yourself. It was hard to throw it off, because when you did, you were met not with a blast of happiness but with a blast of cold air. Jennifer had struggled with depression before, too, though nothing as crippling or long-lasting as the episodes that had plagued her mother, and she could feel it coming over her now. Her body felt immobilized, affixed to the bed like an insect with a pin through the thorax; her mind squirmed with anxious thoughts, painting the circumstances of her life progressively darker. She passed an hour this way, angry that she hadn't managed to extract at least one sleeping pill from Vinita, suffering and stuck and longing for the blackout of a truly restful sleep, the kind of sleep, frankly, that she hadn't known since Wishful Thinking had entered her life. These days her brain seized every sleeping minute to process and sort all that had happened during her double day, tossing through the jumble like a valiant but battered little brain ship trying not to capsize.

But there she lay. The world was asleep, and at least one of her children was very likely in bed right now with Dina, a stranger, who Jennifer prayed always wore a nightgown. (With sweatpants underneath.) The thought of this was enough to rouse her to a sitting position. She knew she should text Vinita. Throw up a flare. It was still dark, and she didn't bother with a light, instead squinting at her phone and typing like a drunk.

Norman has GF, she managed (autocorrect suggesting *God* for *GF*, causing her to snort), *29, sleeping in bed with the boys. Help!* She hit SEND. At least she had reached out to somebody from under her depression blanket. Vinita would see it first thing in the morning. That was enough for now.

To her surprise, however, Jennifer immediately heard a corresponding *ping*.

Norman has a 29 y.o. GF? came the reply. *How unoriginal!*

"How unoriginal?" That didn't sound like Vinita. Jennifer looked at the phone more closely. She had texted Dr. Sexton by mistake. Dr. Sexton was the last person she had texted that day, as they had been attempting to set up a check-in time to discuss the app. She laughed.

Sorry, Dr. S, she typed. *Meant to text V.*

The response was again immediate. *Would you like to come over for tea?*

Tea? At 4:00 a.m.? She wasn't likely to get another such invitation. She usually spent the hours between her first and second sleep reading. But given that she was currently reading a nonfiction book about a child trapped in the slums of Mumbai, where teenage girls routinely swallowed rat poison to escape the horrors of their impoverished lives, reading seemed unwise.

Yes please, she replied.

Excellent, Dr. Sexton wrote. *See you soon.*

Jennifer lay still for a moment. Did she really want to get up?

Then she heard it. Her mother's voice. *You may not want to get up,* the voice whispered, *but you have to.*

Shaking a little, Jennifer threw off the blanket and got dressed. Just as she was about to walk out the door, she glimpsed the white paper bag with the peppermint Christmas tree in it. She grabbed it by the handles, tucked it under one arm, and headed for apartment 19D.

J ENNIFER KNOCKED LIGHTLY ON Dr. Sexton's door.
After hearing her unmistakable, ringing voice call out,
"Come in, my dear!" Jennifer entered the apartment,
placing the white paper bag with the peppermint tree on the
table in the foyer. Upon entering the living room, she was
greeted by an astonishing sight: Dr. Sexton, curled up with
Lucy, in front of a crackling fire. It was a lovely picture, except
that Jennifer was quite certain Dr. Sexton didn't have a
fireplace. When a log suddenly lurched downward to join the
growing bed of ashes beneath the grate, however, and the
smell of wood-burning smoke drifted toward her, spurring her
to quickly close the door so as not to set off the smoke alarm in
the hallway, Jennifer could only stammer.

"You have a *fireplace?*" she said.

Dr. Sexton turned and smiled, patting a spot beside her on
the rug. "Isn't it lovely?"

Jennifer approached cautiously. The hearth was perfectly
positioned a few feet away from the couch, warming the
sitting area with its glow, and the chimney extended upward

directly to the center of the ceiling, an unlikely placement
indeed. Walking toward the fire, Jennifer told herself this had
to be one of Dr. Sexton's creations, despite feeling its growing
warmth as she approached. Entranced, she reached out her
hand to touch it.

"Jennifer!" Dr. Sexton cried, just as Jennifer yanked her
hand back in pain. "How do you think it could produce heat if I
hadn't made it hot? For goodness' sake. You ought to run cold
water over that." Jennifer, the tips of two of her fingers
turning pink from a very minor burn, walked briskly over to
the kitchen sink and turned on the tap.

"Is it real?" she asked.

"Of course not," Dr. Sexton answered. "How on earth
could I have a real fireplace smack in the middle of my
apartment, in this building? It took months of work, this
hologram," she said. "But it was worth it, with winter coming
on. I loathe winter. In the house I used to live in, we had a
magnificent fireplace. An indispensable comfort on nights like
these."

Jennifer noted the use of the word *we* (for the second time
that day, she thought), a term she'd never heard Dr. Sexton
utter before. Her thoughts turned to Dr. Terry as she entered
the kitchen at Dr. Sexton's suggestion that she pour herself a
cup of tea. Surely she and Dr. Terry were the *we* Dr. Sexton
was referring to.

Jennifer carried her tea into the living room. She sat down
on the floor next to Dr. Sexton, tucked her ankles beneath her,
and took a sip. "Is this from the tea shop you told me about?"
Jennifer asked. "Mariage Frères?" Mariage Frères was a
magnificent tea shop in Paris, apparently, a city to which
Jennifer had never been.

"No," Dr. Sexton said. "This one comes from none other
than Hanoi! I had a splendid time there. An unforgettable

landscape. Someday," she added, "when your children are older, we should do some traveling together. It would do you good." Dr. Sexton put an affectionate hand on Jennifer's knee. "So," she said, "tell me. What's this about Norman?"

"Oh, you know," she said, "he's got a girlfriend. They've been together four months, but apparently it's *very serious*. He didn't bother to tell me about it, of course, and when I brought the boys to his place, there she was, all perky in an apron, making holiday cookies, and there was a wreath on the door, the whole thing. She kissed the boys. A lot. In front of me. It was like I was being ambushed by a sitcom." Dr. Sexton patted her sympathetically. "Norman was quite impressed with himself that she'll be thirty any minute now." Jennifer sighed. "It isn't really her, or him, even," she admitted. "It's me. Suddenly I felt like I was on the outside of something, my nose up against the glass, out in the cold." Jennifer cupped her hands tightly around her teacup. "It's so strange and painful to have created this unit, this thing, that is supposed to keep you safe and last forever, and then to lose it without any idea of what to replace it with. You know?"

"Yes," Dr. Sexton said. "I do." They were quiet for a moment. Another log met its end.

"What happens when it burns out?" Jennifer asked. "Do you have to add virtual wood?"

"I let it," Dr. Sexton said. "That's part of the pleasure. A dying fire."

Another long moment passed. Dr. Sexton, it was clear, was not going to volunteer information about her personal life, even in response to Jennifer's sharing details of her own. Jennifer was just going to have to come out and ask her.

"So," she began, "where did you live before? And with who?"

"With *whom*," Dr. Sexton corrected, smiling. Sitting up a bit, she turned to Jennifer. "Surely you must have put this together by now," she said. "You or Vinita, as bright as you are." She turned back to the fire. "The Internet makes it relatively easy, of course, though I've done my best to avoid a presence there. But still there would be clues. About my partner, the great Susan Terry, and, for anyone motivated to look closely, about the nature of our relationship. The sapphic secret is no longer so secret that it can hide in plain sight. Am I right?"

Jennifer nodded, a bit sheepishly.

"I'm curious," Dr. Sexton said. "What did you make of it? Of her, Dr. Terry's, illustrious career? Of my place at her side, and of the fact that not once, in a single, solitary interview or acceptance speech, did she ever mention me by name?"

This took Jennifer completely off guard. Dr. Terry's failure to acknowledge Dr. Sexton as her partner had not been her or Vinita's focus. But now that Dr. Sexton pointed it out, it was glaring: nowhere in the articles or profiles of Dr. Terry was their relationship ever mentioned.

"We weren't really thinking about that," Jennifer said. "We, I mean Vinita, we were more thinking, it just seemed strange, you moving in here so suddenly, and then the app, relying on an area that Dr. Terry also works on, you know, quantum foam . . ."

"You are making no sense whatsoever," Dr. Sexton said sharply. "What are you trying to say?"

Jennifer took a deep breath. "Did *you* invent the app?" she asked. "Or did Dr. Terry?"

Dr. Sexton's eyes widened, and her head jerked back in naked disbelief. She remained frozen in this posture for a moment and then began to shake her head and laugh. "*Naturellement!*" she said. "How fitting. It is remarkable how rooted we become in our own view of things. I look at the public record of Susan's life and find *myself* missing. You look at the app and find *Susan* missing, or at least assume that I could not have done it without her." Jennifer began to apologize, but Dr. Sexton waved her off. "I don't come off too well in the record of all those journals and prizes, or in the annals of scientific achievement, I know. I never really went in for that sort of thing. It's a job in and of itself, my dear, seeking that kind of recognition. Very time-consuming. For most scientists, however, it's a necessary evil. It's impossible to do the work otherwise. One needs resources, institutional support, money. But I have money, and Susan gave me access to the rest. We were an open secret, in more ways than one— she the superstar, and a little lab space for me the price of acquiring her. They'd give her the professorship and bask in her glory, and in turn she always made sure I had access to what I needed to continue my research."

"But that changed?" Jennifer said.

"It's a long story," Dr. Sexton said, her slender fingers slowly scratching the soft skin behind Lucy's enormous ears. "I suppose I've never told it all the way through."

"Please?" Jennifer said. Smiling, she added, "I bet it's a good one, knowing you."

Dr. Sexton let out a little laugh and clasped Jennifer's hand warmly. "What a wondrous connection we've formed," she said. "And in so short a time."

Jennifer felt it too. For a moment she thought of her dishonesty, lying to Dr. Sexton about how much she was using the app. But somehow she knew: if Dr. Sexton ever found out, she would forgive her.

"So?" Jennifer said. "Will you tell me?"

Dr. Sexton nodded, and, after getting up briefly to pour herself a second cup of tea, settled in beside Jennifer again. With Lucy's heavy head resting in her lap, she began.

* * *

THE STORY BEGAN ON the Upper East Side of Manhattan, where Dr. Sexton and a younger brother, whom she evidently preferred not to discuss, were raised by aging parents, both members of old and established New York families, both on their third marriages, and, surprisingly, both previously childless. Dr. Sexton's father was fifty-six when she was born, her mother forty, and her household was a quiet, scholarly one, dominated by her father's gentlemanly but advanced pursuits of astronomy and linguistics, and her mother's love of entomology, which had resulted in a butterfly collection to rival Nabokov's. Neither parent was much interested in children, as it turned out, and it was not until Dr. Sexton reached the age of eight that her father began to take notice of her. She had an exceptional mind and was quick to grasp concepts her father assumed beyond her reach. By the age of ten, the acute loneliness of her early childhood behind her, the young Diane had become her father's prize student and intellectual confidant and was soon pulled from private school to pursue her studies with her father at home. Her mother had no objection, as she was often away for extended periods on collecting trips. Her brother, who was sent to boarding school not long afterward, was resentful.

Diane, for her part, wanted nothing more than to escape the dull goings-on at the all-girls school she'd been attending and threw herself into her new role with passion, quickly extending her studies well beyond her father's chosen fields. Colleagues of his became her informal tutors in a variety of subjects, but by the time she was seventeen, physics had become her great and all-consuming passion, and she had outgrown the ability of these men to teach her. She wanted to go to university. She wanted to jump into the quantum fray, where physicists had recently determined the existence of quarks, a discovery that thrilled her. It was, however, 1964.

Her world at home resembled an enlightened eighteenth-century household, headed by a gentleman scholar committed to the instruction of a brilliant daughter, while the world outside resembled, as Dr. Sexton put it, *Mad Men*. Undeterred, the young Diane applied to numerous physics programs and, with her money and connections, eventually found a place at the University of Chicago, home of Enrico Fermi and, most important, Maria Goeppert Mayer. Goeppert Mayer had been awarded the Nobel Prize in Physics in 1963—the only woman since Marie Curie. She was to be Diane's mentor.

Diane received this news in February. A month later, her father died suddenly of a heart attack.

"I was utterly lost," Dr. Sexton said, shushing Lucy, who was emitting a series of stifled yelps, her eyelids fluttering as she dreamed of squirrels. "I had no friends my own age, having immersed myself completely in my father's world. My mother, when my need was greatest—perhaps precisely for that reason —became more distant than ever. It was almost as though my brother and I had been orphaned, and soon we were. The summer before I was supposed to go to Chicago, we lost our mother too. She was killed in a climbing accident while giving chase to a Kaiser-i-Hind butterfly in the Himalayas." Dr. Sexton laughed darkly. "Can you imagine? My father had just died, and my mother dead not five months later, chasing a butterfly?" Jennifer couldn't. "My brother threw himself into his studies, determined to forget my careless parents and make his own fortune. We rarely speak now, but he ended up in your line of work, my dear. Politics, that sort of thing." Jennifer was about to ask Dr. Sexton more about her brother, but she went on, and Jennifer did not want to interrupt her.

"My memories of that time are scarce," Dr. Sexton said. "All I can tell you is that at the age of seventeen I came into a great deal of money, and there was nobody but an extremely indulgent trustee, an old friend of my father's who adored me, to tell me what to do with it. And so, with the impetuousness of youth, I told the University of Chicago 'no, thank you' and set off to see the world. Can you believe it?" Dr. Sexton said, shaking her head and laughing. "'No, thank you' to Maria Goeppert Mayer! I sent a telegram, like a coward, something I regret to this day." She paused, looking into the fire. "I flew to the Orient—an unfashionable way of saying it now, but quite exotic then. I was looking for my mother, I suppose. Driven by anger and grief." This time it was Jennifer who squeezed Dr. Sexton's hand. "Curiosity drove me, too, of course. Having spent my adolescent years masquerading as an eighteenth-century scholar, I wanted to channel my inner adventurer, to live the life of a fearless explorer." Dr. Sexton gestured to an illustration hanging on the wall. "Eighteenth-century women scientists, and the countless other women scientists I soon became obsessed with from centuries before and since, were better suited than anyone I knew to be my guides. In fact, the first piece I ever collected in the little museum I have here," she said, pointing as Jennifer rose to take a closer look, "was that plate, taken from *Metamorphosis insectorum Surinamensium* by the Dutch naturalist Maria Sibylla Merian, who, at fifty-two, after selling most of her belongings to fund the trip, traveled to Surinam with her daughter in 1699 to classify new species of insects." Jennifer studied the exquisite illustration. It depicted, in vivid ink that was both delicate and bold, painstaking and ravishing, the metamorphosis of a caterpillar into a butterfly. "As you can see," Dr. Sexton added quietly, "Merian's specialty was butterflies."

Just then, the last log in the virtual fire settled into the grate with a thud, its coals going from orange to red.

"But I digress!" Dr. Sexton said. "And the fire won't wait. Onward, to Susan. I traveled for several years. I will be forever grateful to my mother and these women," she added, glancing around her apartment at her treasures, "for inspiring me. During those years I learned to be alive, and to seduce men and women alike with a heady sense of conquest." At this she winked at Jennifer mischievously. "But it was not the life for me, mostly because I couldn't stay away from physics any longer. I had to come back to the United States to resume my work! The quantum universe was expanding so rapidly then, and I'd managed to keep track of things even when I was in parts of the world that were very remote. I could not apply to Maria again, however. And so, upon my return, I set out to find a place in another PhD program—to lie about my previous education if I had to.

"And so I did. Lie, which was much easier then, and enter a PhD program too. That was when I met Susan. At Caltech. They'd only just begun accepting women. There were only, in fact, we two. And the men—Murray Gell-Mann, Richard Feynman, William Fowler—an intimidating group, to say the least. But Susan had arrived a few years prior to me, and, rather than see me as a rival, she mentored me. Our first bond was intellectual, and it lasted many years before developing into something more. By that time, Susan had already established herself as one of the most gifted physicists in the country. I, however, had established myself as a mouthy crackpot, who could talk of only one thing when studying quantum mechanics, even after string theory emerged: *time travel.*" Jennifer smiled. "I was officially a kook. But Susan loved my passion, and she alone, perhaps, understood what I was capable of. You asked if Susan invented this app?" Dr. Sexton said, looking at Jennifer. Jennifer nodded, again feeling bad for doubting her. "I would answer that we did it together. Nothing exists in a vacuum, least of all invention. There are others I worked with over the years to whom I owe a debt, but none more than her. Which makes it all the more difficult that she has no idea that I've achieved it."

"That's what I don't understand," Jennifer said, interjecting at last. "How could that be? How could you have been so close to pulling this off without her knowing? And why did you leave Columbia?"

"So many questions, my dear!" Dr. Sexton said, as Lucy got up, stretched, and ambled over to her water bowl. "There is one simple answer, at least with regard to the suddenness of the breakthrough. The last piece of the puzzle, the harvesting of quantum foam, was made possible by a very recently completed tool: the Large Hadron Collider at CERN, a twenty-seven-kilometer loop and the largest hadron particle collider ever built. Susan knew that the LHC would change everything for me, but . . . she had lost some of her interest, shall we say, and perhaps some of her respect, for my off-the-beaten-path pursuits. Particularly in the last decade, when, with the Nobel, her coronation as the world's most brilliant female scientist was made official." Jennifer detected a rare note of bitterness in Dr. Sexton's voice. "It had been many years since we'd been truly intimate with each other. But we were still partners, and occasionally lovers too. There had been periods of estrangement before, of course. We'd always gotten through them. But in the last few years, things we'd ignored became impossible to ignore any longer, for me anyway. As her life became more public, her unwillingness to be public about our relationship was humiliating. And when everyone already knew! We fought about it constantly. And then there was . . . the incident."

"The incident?" Jennifer asked, shifting her weight. She was getting sleepy.

"The incident is something you won't find on the Internet," Dr. Sexton continued, allowing herself a wry smile.

"The university made sure of that." Dr. Sexton whistled softly to Lucy, who returned to her. "It has to do with this old girl, doesn't it, Lucy dear?" Lucy looked up at Dr. Sexton, and Jennifer was sure she saw the great beast raise an assenting eyebrow. "But first, a bit of background. Do you recall, about a year ago, when one of the most well-known men in the physics department at Columbia said that women would never be equal to men in physics, because physicists 'peak early,' at a time when women are most interested in family and babies and thereby unable to fully concentrate?"

"Seriously?" Jennifer said. "What a dick."

"What a *dick*," Dr. Sexton repeated, with some relish. "That's right! There was quite an uproar, as you might imagine, but not nearly enough uproar for me. I was getting close to completing the app, though I had not yet gained access to the LHC, as, with my lack of publications and slight reputation, I was a long way from being first in line. But laboring in obscurity, which had suited me so well for many years, suddenly chafed in a whole new way. I wanted to arm-wrestle this man, to show him what I was capable of. I wanted to see him fired and publicly flogged!" Dr. Sexton sighed. "However, as a lowly adjunct professor, without credibility or a platform, I could do little but rail privately to Susan. And do you know what Susan did? Susan, the most renowned woman physicist in the world, with a Nobel Prize in the cabinet and all the world waiting to see how she would respond?"

Jennifer shook her head. "Nothing," Dr. Sexton said. "She did not say a word." She was quiet for a moment. "I pressed her. I prodded her. I tried to shame her into it. And finally she came out and said it. 'I am childless,' she said. 'What could I possibly have to say?'

"It broke my heart," Dr. Sexton said. "To hear Susan, who had fought tooth and nail in some of the most sexist environments imaginable, essentially say that because she had not had children she was in no position to speak out about this man's attitudes toward women in science. She is a magnificent, brave, brilliant woman. And yet she denied who she was, and by doing so, I felt, issued a final, chilling denial of me. Of us. In that moment, in fact, I felt she denied our whole life together. And I was unbelievably angry at the man who, I felt, had had the power to make her feel she was not a 'real' woman but an aberrant exception to the rule."

"I'm so sorry," Jennifer said.

Dr. Sexton shook her head. "It doesn't matter now. It might have. But right after that conversation, I took Lucy for a walk. Didn't I, Lucy?" Lucy pricked up her ears at the sound of her name. "And it was very unfortunate that, at that moment, the professor in question happened to be out for a walk too. I tried to ignore him, but he saw me and, as arrogant as you please, approached just as Lucy was beginning to do her business, something that, as you can imagine for a dog of this size, is quite a production. I was stuck. He asked after Susan, who, while refusing to speak publicly on the matter, had not returned his calls, either. And then, just as I was bending down to pick up Lucy's steaming pile of stool, he said, 'I hope she knows that I have the utmost respect for her. Please tell her. I've always thought of her as *one of us.*' And then he had the audacity to stick out his hand to shake mine." Jennifer, who could see what was coming, began to giggle. "And yes, my dear, I filled that outstretched hand with a fistful of Great Dane poop." Jennifer burst out laughing. "It was glorious!" Dr. Sexton said, beginning to laugh herself. "The feeling of it, hot and squishy on the other side of the poop bag, which naturally I deployed to keep my own hand clean, oozing every which way as it enveloped his hand, the little hard bits of gravel and twigs poking into his palm through the muck, and the look on his face as he withdrew that insulting handshake and began to frantically wipe his hand on a nearby tree, with very little success at cleaning it."

"What did you do then?" Jennifer asked.

"I said, 'I hope I have conveyed how much respect I have for you as well,' gave him a little nod, and walked away."

"He was speechless," Jennifer said.

"Utterly," Dr. Sexton replied. "Susan, however, when she heard what had happened, was quite the opposite. She was beyond angry with me, telling me I had behaved like a spoiled child, that I had jeopardized her career, after all she had done for me, and demanding I apologize. Naturally, I refused. As for her esteemed colleague, he recovered his powers of speech very quickly, particularly when I was not in a position to defend myself. He called a private meeting of the faculty council of the institute and had me, for lack of a better term, banished. And what did Susan do?" Dr. Sexton asked, her voice flat and hard.

"Nothing," Jennifer guessed.

"The final blow," Dr. Sexton said, nodding. "A complete repudiation. I lost my access to the lab, I lost my academic standing, and I lost her. That is the loss I still regret the most. But I couldn't stay then. And she didn't want me to. She'd had enough, she said. She wanted to be left alone."

"And so you moved out and came here," Jennifer said. She couldn't suppress a yawn, though she was captivated. "And then you finally got into the LHC, and . . ."

"And my work was complete, but Susan never knew, and still doesn't," Dr. Sexton said, her voice growing quieter. There was a pause. "I think that's quite enough of me for one night!" Dr. Sexton said suddenly. "Or morning." Jennifer could see the gray hint of dawn illuminating a slit between the curtains. "My goodness," Dr. Sexton said, taking out her phone, "look at the time. I have to be ready to depart in less than an hour. It's nearly dinnertime in Tokyo, you know!"

The two of them got up. The fire was out—there were only embers now.

"May I ask you a question?" Jennifer said. "About the app?"

"Of course," Dr. Sexton answered, making the fireplace disappear with a wave of her hand.

"How often do you use it? Do *you* use it only twice a week?"

Dr. Sexton looked at Jennifer with curiosity, and then her eyes narrowed, as though she were trying to decide something. "I use it more frequently than that," she said after a moment. "But I restrict my appointments to two hours, as a rule, sometimes extending them to three, which is generally enough time to enjoy a dinner, or an exhibition, or a man." Now Jennifer was the one to raise her eyebrows.

"Yes," Dr. Sexton said, slipping an arm into the crook of Jennifer's elbow as she escorted her to the door, "a man! Men, after all these years, seem to be, for now, what I enjoy. Though perhaps it's because, by not taking up with another woman, I feel as though I'm remaining faithful to Susan somehow." Dr. Sexton paused, turning to face Jennifer. "I would advise you to listen to Norman, my dear, though I'll be the one to say it, if it helps you to feel you are acting on my advice, not his. Love, or another lifelong partner, may not be what you need, or what you are ready for. But adult companionship, physical pleasure —those are things one should never live without! Don't use the app to amplify your martyrdom, Jennifer. Use it to amplify your *life*."

They were standing together by the door, and Jennifer spotted the white paper bag, just where she had left it on the foyer table. Dr. Sexton followed her eyes and looked at it. "What's this?" she said. "For me?" She reached into the bag and produced the Styrofoam cone, covered in red and white peppermints. Turning it this way and that, she smiled. "How charming!" she said.

"See?" Jennifer said. "I *am* amplifying my life. With crafts! The boys made it," she added, feeling a little bit silly.

"Thank you," Dr. Sexton said, placing it back on the table. "I will take it into evidence, in hopes that, by year's end, you have considerably steamier, child-free adventures to regale me with."

"I'll try," Jennifer said, yawning again, hugging herself as she felt the cold in the absence of the virtual fire.

"Don't try," Dr. Sexton said sternly. *"Do."*

fourteen | NEW YEAR'S
EVE

TWO WEEKS LATER, when Jennifer found herself traversing cobblestone somewhere in deepest Brooklyn on the night of December 31, wearing nineties-era dark brown faux-leather pants that she'd had to wipe clean of dust, Jennifer blamed Dr. Sexton. If not for Dr. Sexton's prodding about "adult kinds of fun," she thought, she wouldn't have asked Owen, just a little bit flirtatiously, if he had plans over the holidays, in response to which he had handed her a flyer inviting her to see his band play on New Year's Eve. If not for Dr. Sexton, she thought, she probably would have tried a lot harder to ignore the tingling warmth she'd felt when, as he handed her the flyer, he'd leaned in to her ear and said, in a voice low enough that Julien couldn't hear, "I'd love it if you came." And if not for Dr. Sexton, she probably would have worked much harder to dismiss/repress the fact that she'd had three sex dreams about him in a row. (In the last one, they were trapped in the West End School broom closet and he was wearing nothing but a flannel shirt and black

ballet tights.) But Dr. Sexton's advice had awoken something
in her, or at least given her permission (or a mandate, more
like), to act on it. So two days after he'd given her the flyer,
she'd sent him a simple e-mail: *I'll be there.*

He'd sent an equally simple e-mail back: *You made my day.*

She'd now read that e-mail about fifty times, and it still
gave her a little spike of happiness. It had made granting
Norman and Dina's request to spend New Year's Eve with the
boys easy, though she hadn't told them that.

Now, however, as she stood outside the Brooklyn music
hall where Owen's band, the Dimes, was playing that night, in
a line that went all the way down Wythe Avenue, Jennifer felt
incredibly out of place. Scantily clad twentysomethings, who,
in the rearview mirror of Jennifer's life, were beginning to
appear even farther away than they were, were everywhere,
like skinny little mice, smoking and squeaking in the cold. She
knew that divorce made some people feel young again, as
though they were rejoining a party they'd never really wanted
to leave. But divorce made Jennifer feel old, or, worse, it made
her feel nowhere: caught between the countries of young
single life and middle-aged parenthood, without full residency
in either. Sometimes, as she did taking her place in line outside
the Brooklyn Bowl, she felt like an impostor, as awkward and
obvious in her attempt to "pass" for young as the old man in
Death in Venice, dyeing his hair and wearing rouge on the
beach. Like an idiot she'd shown up at ten thirty, only a half
hour before Owen's set, too nervous to arrive earlier alone.
But when she'd headed to the front of the line as though she
were someone important and actually uttered the words "I'm
with the band," she'd found there was a list, and she wasn't on
it. So much for being with the band. She was pretty sure she
heard someone snigger.

Afraid she would miss his set entirely, she texted Owen.

Hey, sorry, outside in long line, there's a list? Sure you are v busy, np to wait! Shivering, she shoved her phone back into her coat pocket. The faint smell of clove cigarettes and weed sweetened the dry, wintry air. Jennifer was just beginning to feel sorry for herself again, wishing she'd had a second glass of chardonnay while watching TV at home, when suddenly Owen materialized, almost out of thin air. Tall. So deliciously tall, with that little bit of light brown bang hanging over his eyes, his breath sending white puffs of steam into the black night air. In a heavy canvas jacket and work boots, he looked Brooklyn perfect (but not Brooklyn pretentious), and suddenly, despite the fact that a bulky black North Face coat completely covered her outfit, she felt foolishly glam in her makeup and strappy gold heels.

She looked up at him, and he smiled. She smiled back. It surprised her a little, just how happy she was to see him. It was the first time, she realized, she'd ever seen him outside the walls of the West End School. It was nice.

"Wow," he said, grinning.

"What?" she asked, pleased, starting to glow.

"*You.* Wow." Jennifer blushed. How good it felt to be looked at, *really* looked at, a good, long look that lingered, warming her to her nearly numb toes. Suddenly the leather against her thighs, faux or no, felt soft and sexy and exactly right, and, on an impulse, she opened her coat to reveal her outfit in full.

"Leather?" he cried. She was going to alert him to the fact that it wasn't real leather but was too pleased by his reaction to interrupt. "I have to concentrate, you know. I'm playing the Dobro tonight." She laughed. *What's a Dobro?* she wondered. Whatever it was, she wanted to hear him play it. "Come on inside," he said. "You were supposed to be on the list. I'm so sorry. Dummies."

Dummies was one of the words where she could hear his

Texas accent most clearly, the sound of his *u* softer than a New York's, coming from farther back in his mouth.

He grabbed her hand. Nervous, she squeezed it. He squeezed back. In an instant, Jennifer went from cursing Dr. Sexton to thanking her instead.

Owen was in a hurry, though he refused to listen to any of Jennifer's apologies for making him come to collect her. He whisked her inside, deposited her on a choice barstool with a view of the stage, and told the bartender to take care of her. Then, before she could register it, he had given her a quick kiss on the cheek and his hand had brushed against one of her thighs, all wrapped up in that buttery russet-brown leather. "I wish I could stay for a drink," he said. She shrugged—*no worries* —and wished him luck. Watching him as he dashed off to join his band for the show, however, she wished it were over already so she could have him back again. Suddenly she wanted to know everything about him, about his first marriage, about his parents, about where he'd grown up and where he'd gone to school. The idea of a long, adult conversation, especially when they'd never been able to exchange more than a few sentences out of Julien's earshot, was as alluring as his blue jeans. But she would have to wait.

The last band was wrapping up its set, the singer skinny and bald and tattooed, with a kinetic delivery that made Jennifer think of a less corporate version of Adam Levine, though you could already see visions of sponsorship sugar-plums dancing over his head. Looking around the room as she waited for her drink, she immediately felt antsy, with an overpowering urge to reach for her phone, to consult it and fiddle with it and scroll through it and find something to *do*, someone to talk to. But she willed herself to leave it in her pocket, instead taking an extrabig gulp of the wine the bartender placed before her. The music was deafeningly loud.

Jennifer's heart sank slightly. How had she thought she could possibly get to know Owen better in a place like this? she wondered, doubt seizing her. Not only that, but Owen probably handed those flyers to every single person he knew, which meant there were probably throngs of his friends out on the dance floor, showing up just like her to listen to him play and count down to midnight, people without nine-to-fives or kids, ready to hang till the wee hours when the set was done. What had she been thinking, getting all gussied up like this was a date? *Who cares?* she told herself. Even if she was going to go home alone once the clock struck midnight—her stint as Cinderella concluding as soon as she returned to her apartment and resumed her life as a mother–scullery maid—Owen liked her. She was sure of it, and for that alone, showing up (and even dressing up) had already been worth it.

Finally the jittery punk band wound down and it was time for Owen's band to take the stage. She spotted him in the semidarkness, nimbly hopping over and around foot pedals, amps, and cords, accompanied by another guy of a similar age, who darted around beside him with an acoustic guitar slung around his neck and bushy black eyebrows that lent an intense seriousness to him as he plugged and unplugged and began to tune. They were yin and yang, she thought, Owen's lightness in marked contrast with his bandmate's slash of dark. Jennifer was beginning to suspect they were the whole band, when two other musicians took the stage. One of them was a stout, balding, ex-hippie type with a jovial *hey, man* vibe, and the other was a woman (Jennifer would have said *girl*, though she knew she shouldn't) who couldn't have been more than twenty-two. She had thick, black, flowing hair that seemed the very reason for the word *tresses.* Loose strands of it fell provocatively upon her pale white cleavage, which was bound up and boosted by a satiny red top with a deep V-neck. She was wearing cat-eye liner painted on so thick Jennifer could see it from the bar.

"They play with Sarah Fair?" the bartender asked her. From the tone of his voice, Jennifer could tell he was impressed. *Who the hell is Sarah Fair?* "She's the lead singer for the Dixons," he said, seeing she was clueless. "She's awesome." Jennifer didn't really want to hear how awesome Sarah Fair was. She turned toward the stage. Sarah Fair, about to take her seat behind the drums, raised her arms in a little half salute and was met with whoops and hollers from the crowd. "Be my Lady Fair!" somebody yelled. Owen's bandmate, the lead singer, grinned, then gave Sarah a nod. Stepping up to center stage, he gave Owen a nod too. And in that loud, cavernous space, the small, dark guy at the mic tuned his guitar one last time and, just like that, began to play.

What came from that guy, and that guitar, was an utter surprise. He looked like a brooder, but he sounded like a troubadour, his voice clear and without irony, singing sweet, simple notes that rose and fell unhurriedly, quiet and calm. It was lyrical, lilting, easy. And as the lead singer began the lyric, his voice quieted the crowd just as his guitar had quieted her. "It felt like winter / everywhere except for Summer Street. / There the flames were all anybody anywhere could see. / And from the top of Beacon Hill / we watched the fire spill / over Water Street." Just then, Owen and the other two leaned in to their mics with a dipping, arcing "ah ah" that filled the room with a rich, four-part harmony that ran over Jennifer like honey. It was just measures in, and Jennifer was hooked. This was music that was the opposite of a sneer: an airy, folky sound, a sound of soulful joy. Even Sarah Fair, a world away from music-video theatrics, treated her drums lightly, smiling and keeping time, using brushes on the snare.

It was the first time she'd heard their music, despite the

fact that the Dimes were on iTunes. Jennifer loved music so much she'd been afraid that if she downloaded the Dimes album before the show, she might be downloading a cold shower, so she'd held off. But this was good. Really good. A flush rose in her cheeks and stayed there. For the first time in months, Jennifer didn't think about her phone, her kids, her calendar, her job, or her to-do list. Listening to that music, Jennifer didn't even think about Owen. She just floated in the sound, happy.

All spells, however, must come to an end. Owen's applause-inducing riff on the slide guitar brought the song to a close, and Jennifer cheered. *I'm with the band!*

"Hey," the lead singer said. "Thanks. Good to see you guys tonight. We're so happy to be here. That was 'Damrell's Fire,' from our Boston album, *The King Can Drink the Harbor Dry.* And we're the Dimes." Then, with disarming charm, Mr. Dark broke out into a grin. "And goddamn it, it's New Year's Eve! Anybody wanna dance?" The next song was rollicking good fun, exuberant and punchy on the drums, with a beat that sent Owen and the hippie bass player bouncing on their tiptoes. It was called "Celia's Garden," and Jennifer couldn't help thinking of Simon and Garfunkel's "Cecilia" as Sarah Fair let it rip. She loved that she didn't have to figure out how to feel about it, that it so effortlessly carried her away. Perhaps most of all, she loved that it didn't sound like it was made by a bunch of guys who were still in high school.

They played three more. It wasn't until the final song that Owen played the Dobro. The Dobro, it turned out, was a guitar that the musician laid across his lap and played with a pick and a slide. As Owen set up, Sarah Fair strode to the front of the stage. "Owen and I wrote this one together," she said. "Hope y'all don't mind if we end on a quiet note, even on a night like tonight." The crowd cheered, then hushed. Jennifer, less thrilled by this news, clenched her jaw. "She's going to sing," she could hear a guy next to her say excitedly. Everybody loved this girl. *Y'all?* Jennifer thought. Was she from Texas too? She tried not to think about Owen and Sarah Fair writing songs together. She tried to let her mind float away as the song began, to ignore the beauty of their combined voices, the minor key, the effortlessly entwined harmonies. She tried to concentrate on him, on those long, strong legs, on the shiny metal glare that occasionally flashed off the Dobro on his lap, on his fingers, working the pick and slide. She tried to tell herself Owen was not one of those guys who looked for girls eighteen to thirty-five on Match.com. But at the end, Sarah Fair kissed Owen's cheek, and he grinned and pulled away from her, fixing her with a look of such affection it was like she had just baked him his favorite chocolate cake. Or like she *was* his favorite chocolate cake.

With that kiss and that grin, Jennifer's confidence, already riven with hairline fractures after listening to the two of them sing together, cracked completely.

"Good set," the bartender said loudly. "Not what I expected!"

"Me neither," Jennifer said. "One more for the road?" she asked, tapping her glass. For a moment she thought about leaving, but Owen had told her to stay put, and stay put she did. It seemed like an eternity, however, and as she waited and sipped her wine, her brain began to fuzz around the edges, her head suddenly aching in a way that made even the inside of her skull feel dry. "Water?" she said to the bartender, realizing it was high time to hydrate. The next band was covered in facial hair, and every one of them was wearing duck boots and sunglasses, carrying a can of Pabst. If there was anything Jennifer loathed, it was ironic beer drinking. These guys had already launched into their set, straining every indie-music cliché in the book (including trotting out a cellist and a girl with a banjo), when Owen, all smiles, appeared at last, heading toward her. Which would have been great if Sarah Fair, also smiling, had not had her arm tucked in his.

The bartender brightened up immediately. Jennifer wanted to slug him.

"Hey," Owen said as he approached. "Sorry it took so long to get over here. We had to get all the gear packed up and into the van."

"It's, like, impossible trying to fit everything in there!" Sarah laughed, extending her hand. "Sarah," she said.

"Jennifer," Jennifer replied, wondering how she must look to this girl, an old, divorced mom with a crush on her son's guitar teacher, alone on New Year's Eve, wearing 1990s pleather.

Sarah ordered a shot of Maker's Mark.

"You guys were so great," Jennifer said, turning to Owen. "I loved it. Julien will love it too."

"Thank you," Owen said sincerely. "Thank you so much." It was so nice, she thought, that he didn't glower, or avert his eyes and pretend not to care, the way Norman always used to do after a play. His reaction was as unaffected and genuine as his music. But then there was this creamy-breasted siren with the whiskey.

"She liked it!" Owen said, turning to Sarah.

"Of course she liked it, you dork!" *Dork?* Even as Sarah said this, her eyes had begun to scan the room distractedly.

"Who are you looking for?" Owen said, a little sharply.

"None of your business," Sarah said. Then, with a quick good-bye to Jennifer and one more kiss on the cheek for Owen, she excused herself and walked away.

Well, Jennifer thought. *If he likes being condescended to by a girl born during the Clinton administration . . .*

"I have to go," she said, standing abruptly, stumbling a little on her heels.

"Really?" Owen said. He did look disappointed. But then he said, "Okay."

Okay? she thought. All these months of looks, and hinting, and "I'd love it if you came" and "Leather!" and just . . . *Okay?*

The bartender brought the check. Suddenly Jennifer didn't want Owen to pay it. She stood up and, with a little slap, palmed the black vinyl holder. Owen stood, too, and covered her hand with his.

"Let me get it, please," he said. "Not that I'm being such a gentleman," he added, smiling at her. "I think we get free drinks."

Jennifer looked down at his hand, covering hers. She couldn't bring herself to look up. But she couldn't bring herself to just walk out of there, either.

"Is this a date?" she blurted, still looking at his hand.

"What?" Owen asked.

"Because I thought maybe . . . but I didn't realize . . . I mean, you and Sarah . . ." She trailed off, having succeeded at completely embarrassing herself one incomplete sentence at a time.

What a disaster, she thought. *I am going to have to find Julien a new guitar teacher.*

When she finally did manage to look up, though, she saw that Owen was smiling. Very sweetly. At her. "Sarah?" he repeated.

"Yes," she said, smiling back. "You know! Drummer, singer, the one who kissed you on the cheek? Sarah!"

Owen sat back down on the barstool and motioned for her to sit next to him. She did, but her stool was a few feet away from his. He reached out and pulled her and the stool to him, a hand on either side of her butt, the stool's legs skittering and stuttering across the uneven concrete floor, until they were so close their knees were touching.

"Sarah," he said, leaning in still farther, and not taking his hands off her stool, "who is twenty years younger than I am, and a much more successful musician than I am, and who is my *little sister?*"

"Your sister?" Jennifer exclaimed. "Well, how was I supposed to know *that?*"

"We don't look much alike, I know," Owen said. "My dad had her with wife number two, and she definitely got better genes in the looks department."

"I wouldn't say that," Jennifer said quietly. The wine was making her loose and bold. She put a hand on one of his thighs. Pressing her palm against the fine-ribbed grain of the denim on his knee, she fit the ball of his kneecap into her palm and gave it a gentle squeeze. Not daring to look up, she just stared at her fingers, wrapped around his leg. Owen was quiet too. Then he said something she couldn't hear.

"What?" she said, looking up at him and meeting his eyes.

He leaned in, his cheek against hers, his stubble prickling her skin. "I think you *should* go, actually," he said, his mouth just grazing the rim of her ear.

"Really?" she said.

"With me," he said.

Leaning back, Owen then took her hand for the second time that night. And with the sure-footed confidence of a man a head taller than just about everybody else in the room, he escorted her to her feet, maneuvered them away from the bar, across the dance floor, past the bowling alley (were all those hipsters bowling ironically too?), and through the people, the crowd, the noise, the bouncers, and the line . . . until they were on the sidewalk again, safely across the street, alone at last. Outside, a fine-grained snow, cloudy white under the pale green streetlights, had begun to fall.

Owen squinted, snowflakes on his eyelashes. They

looked at each other for a minute. He took both of her hands.

"To answer your question," he said, "this definitely isn't a date." Jennifer waited. "I wasn't sure if you would go on a date with me," he went on. "It's been a little hard to tell. I didn't know if it was because I'm Julien's teacher, but sometimes it seemed like you were sort of, I don't know, avoiding me."

Jennifer was about to explain, to pour forth with confessions and excuses, but, thinking better of it, she bit her lip and smiled.

"So would you? Go on a date with me?"

She nodded slowly.

"Right now?"

She nodded again, grinning from ear to ear.

"Yes!" he said. "That's good." He looked at her again. She loved the way he looked at her. "And now we have to get out of here for real," he added, laughing, "because I would never ask someone for a first date to see me play a show with my baby sister on New Year's Eve. That would be the worst!"

But on New Year's Eve, at this hour, Jennifer thought, where would they go and have any chance of finding a quiet place to talk? "I wish I could ask you to my place . . . ," she began, thinking of her cat and her pullout couch.

"How about mine?" he said. "I live in Manhattan, too, not far from you, I don't think." At that, Jennifer had to laugh. She'd been so sure he lived in Brooklyn. "And I have wine. Or hot chocolate. Whatever you want. I can make you something to eat. I bet you didn't eat yet tonight." Jennifer nodded again, realizing he was right. She was starving. "We can watch a movie. Play cards. Pretend it's only eight"—he checked his watch—"on any old Thursday."

"I would love that," she said. Tipsy and turned on, she brought his hands to her lips and kissed his knuckles, one by one, while looking up at him. "There's one good thing about it being New Year's Eve just before midnight," she added, smiling.

"What's that?" he asked her, shuddering a little as she placed each light, barely there kiss, letting her tongue lightly flick the V's between his fingers.

"Because there is no better time," she said, pulling away playfully, "to get a cab!"

With that, she dropped his hands and turned toward Wythe Avenue, breaking out her best city-girl cab whistle—perfected after numerous sessions with Julien when he was five and just beginning to learn. Owen whooped, impressed. And as though she had summoned a chariot, a yellow cab arrived just then, depositing a carload of stumbling revelers yelling at one another to hurry up so they wouldn't miss the countdown, their sloppy bodies the first sign of the least appealing part of New Year's Eve, when men began to piss on the street and their dates began to puke on it.

Jennifer and Owen slipped inside.

"Suckers," Jennifer said, throwing a leg over Owen's lap.

"Big time," Owen replied, tucking a hand behind the small of her back.

As the cab began to pull away, he leaned over, leaned in, took her face in his hands, and finally, slowly, *finally*—how many times had she imagined it?—kissed her. For a good, long, back-of-a-cab-in–New York time, as the taxi moved through the dark, deserted, snow-softened streets on its way over the bridge and into the sparkling city. And as Jennifer's hands found their way under and up and beneath Owen's shirt, causing his stomach muscles to tighten and contract with a shiver from the cold still clinging to her fingertips, and as Owen threaded his fingers through the hair at the base of her skull, pulling her head back to bare her neck and kissing her there, somewhere a crowd cheered, and a ball fell, and Jennifer could feel herself falling too.

fifteen | DAMN THE
TORPEDOES

S HOULD IT REALLY HAVE come as any great surprise
that by March, three months into the year and three
months after her love affair with Owen had begun,
Jennifer, with the help of Wishful Thinking, was living not
two lives but three?

In her defense—or at least in the defense she had carefully
constructed in the event Dr. Sexton or Vinita ever found out—
it didn't happen right away. At first, in fact, it had been easy to
keep her time with Owen to Saturday nights. The Saturday
sleepovers that began soon after New Year's Eve were such an
astronomical upgrade from her chaste Friday-guitar-lesson
treats that in the beginning, they satisfied. This was not least
because, like a virgin touched for the very first time, it was
with Owen, and at the age of thirty-nine, no less, that Jennifer
felt she had finally discovered what the sex fuss was really all
about. Sex with Norman had been short and to the point, and,
having met him in college, she'd had little to compare it to. Sex

with Owen, however, awoke in her an appetite for the carnal she'd never known she possessed. She relished every minute of it, from the breathless, fluttery bits at the beginning to the wanton "tell me what you want and I'll do it" splayed-limb abandon at the end. From the start, however, it was not just the sex that drew her to him. It was his friendship. He was such a good friend, emotionally present, intuitive, funny. He loved to talk, about her boys or her divorce or her job, or his band or his divorce or his job—teaching not just at the West End School, it turned out, but at a public junior high school in Washington Heights too. He was kind, always remembering to stock up on chai tea for her and, one night, sewing a button on her shirt. He loved movies and was giving her an education about the French New Wave on his plump, worn-out couch, nicknamed the Velveteen Sofa because it had been loved threadbare and he couldn't bear to part with it. Snuggled up there, watching Netflix under a blanket Sarah had knitted for his birthday (so sweet, Jennifer thought, those Brooklyn girls with their rock bands and their knitting), Jennifer felt like she was home.

Not that Owen—or his place—was perfect. That had been amply evident from the first night Jennifer had set foot in his apartment. It was cluttered at best, and showed little evidence of having once been inhabited by a married couple or, for that matter, anyone more than two years out of a dorm. (Jennifer soon found out that it was not the apartment Owen and his ex-wife had shared, which did not surprise her a bit.) There was grime on the bathroom sink and gunk around the shower drain. Owen, lacking the cash for a cleaning lady or the inclination to do much housekeeping, hardly seemed to notice, while Jennifer could not understand how anyone could fail to see the contradiction in showering while standing barefoot in mildew. But things were so good between them, Jennifer would have relieved herself in an outhouse if she'd had to, and she soon settled for wiping down the bathroom with Clorox every time she came over.

Soon, seeing each other once every seven days—not including Julien's guitar lesson—was not enough. A few weeks after they began dating, Owen asked her to come to a poetry reading that one of his friends, a fellow teacher, was having on a Tuesday. She couldn't, she said; she had to work late. (She did not mention that not only would she be working late, but she would also be picking her boys up from school and taking Julien to one of the multiple after-school activities she had enrolled him in in her Wishful Thinking–fueled mother-of-the-year frenzy that fall.) Then he asked her to come to one of his gigs on a Thursday, a benefit for the West End School. She couldn't, she said; she had to work late again. (She did not mention that she would also be picking her boys up from school that day, or that the boys now believed she was *always* home for homework, dinner, and bath, and became apoplectic at the mere suggestion that she wouldn't be.) Then he asked her to come to a dinner party that Johnny, the lead singer for the Dimes, was having, because he wanted her to get to know his friends. It was on a Wednesday, and Jennifer could have asked Norman to keep the boys for the night. But he and Dina had been getting so horribly smug, and Dina had been courting the boys' affections so aggressively, bringing homemade granola to soccer games and coming to Jack's preschool class to bake cookies, that Jennifer just couldn't bear to give them (or was it her?) the satisfaction.

So she'd thought, *I could be in three places at once, just once.* Why not?

When it came to Wishful Thinking, of course, it was easy for the exception to become the rule.

And so before she knew it, two Jennifers became three.

Owen thought she had a flexible work schedule and a babysitter who could stay late a few nights a week, and they saw each other at least that often. Norman thought she had accepted a pay cut to do flextime and morphed into the mother of the year. Her boys thought she had gone from harried, I-promise-I'll-make-it-up-to-you mom to let's-build-another-skyscraper-out-of-Popsicle-sticks mom practically overnight. And Bill Truitt thought his notion of running a government agency like an investment bank was the best thing since sliced bread, with Jennifer as the evidence that productivity could be increased tenfold and nobody (least of all he) would suffer. For her part, Jennifer felt, at last, that life was the way it should be. Or at least the way everyone she knew advertised his or her life on Facebook.

In all of this, Alicia remained the person Jennifer felt the most guilty about deceiving. They'd gotten closer after Jennifer's "episode" at Amalia's, having finally let themselves be a little bit vulnerable in front of each other. They'd become closer still at year's end, when Jennifer had volunteered to help Alicia meet her milestones in order to get her first bonus check. (It seemed the least Jennifer could do.) But every time Bill, like the stern headmistress of a boarding school, reviewed the reports of the Employee Time Clock and commented on Alicia's leaving at six thirty on days where there were deadlines (days Jennifer stayed past eight, sometimes), or taking an afternoon off to take her daughter to a doctor's appointment, or leaving the office for an hour for a parent-teacher conference, he humiliated Alicia by noting that she, unlike Jennifer, was struggling to meet her milestones. Jennifer felt like a traitor.

She also felt, however, like there was no other way. Not only that, but that *this* way was pretty great. True, she was tired a lot, and the solution of using the app to pack in extra hours of sleep each day didn't really solve the difficulty of her body's circadian rhythms being profoundly out of whack. It was also true that she often forgot things and had become more dependent than ever on her phone to remember them, not just recording voice memos but taking photos and videos of things she didn't want to lose in the increasingly cluttered files of her mind. And yes, it was sometimes hard to transition from one Jennifer to another, from girlfriend to career woman to stay-at-home mom. But, she reasoned, she had been tired and forgetful and somewhat schizophrenic before Wishful Thinking had changed her life. That she was now more tired and forgetful, while able to do three times what she had been able to do when she was somewhat less tired and forgetful but also stressed, guilty, grouchy, and overwhelmed, seemed a small price to pay.

And so it was that when Jennifer woke up on a cold, rainy Saturday at the end of March, which also happened to be her fortieth birthday (she was hoping for a blessedly unremarkable one), she felt, more than she had for many a birthday past, that she had everything she could possibly want, and more.

WAKING UP THAT MORNING took some doing, as usual. The day before, she'd worked until seven, picked the boys up from school at three, gone to guitar with Julien (whom she and Owen had thus far managed to keep in the dark about their relationship), and had dinner at Vinita's, chatting and getting her checkup. Then she'd thrown another couple hours of Wishful Thinking time on top of that to accompany Owen to a dinner party. All of which meant that at 7:00 a.m., when the boys roused her with cries of "Happy birthday!" it was all she could do to hug and kiss them before telling them to put on a movie ("Mama needs *sleep* for her birthday"), stumbling down the hallway, and collapsing into the warm stuffed-animal burrow that was Jack's lower bunk. She needed sleep in the worst way, and for a blissful couple of hours, she got it. But then, wafting into her senses even as she was still in a coma-like slumber, came the smell of something unexpected: pancakes.

She willed herself to open her eyes and saw what was simultaneously the cutest and most terrifying thing she'd ever seen in her life: her boys, bringing her freshly cooked pancakes.

"Happy birthday, Mama!" Jack said. "We made you breakfast!"

"You guys are amazing!" she replied. "And you turned on the stove!"

"We turned it *off*, Mom," Julien said, rolling his eyes but beaming with pride as they presented her with the tray. "Jack got out all the ingredients, and I made the batter, and then I put some butter in the skillet and I poured the batter in. And then," he continued, pausing for dramatic effect, "I *flipped* it!"

"We even spilled some pancake mix," Jack said, "but *I* cleaned it up!"

Jennifer tried not to think about what might have happened if something had caught fire. She also tried not to think about what her kitchen probably looked like right now. Instead, she concentrated on sitting up without hitting her head on the upper bunk, and then on thanking them. "I am the luckiest mommy on the planet," she told them, mugging her insane delight as she took the first bite of slightly chewy pancake. "Thank you so much for making me breakfast. And don't ever turn on the stove alone again." Julien had just begun to protest this in his best "Come on, Mom" pretween way when the doorbell rang.

"Dr. Sexton!" he cried, lighting out of the room like a shot.

"*Mama*," Jack said, promptly taking advantage of Julien's absence to take the best mama spot available, snuggling up under her non-pancake-eating arm.

In the radical transformation of Saturdays that had begun with her evenings with Owen, Jennifer had added Saturday brunches with Dr. Sexton to her list—a ritual the boys enjoyed just as much as she did. They never met at Dr. Sexton's, however, as, after the demise of an antique vase, it had been quickly established that it was best for the foursome to convene at Jennifer's, land of the valueless and unbreakable, as opposed to Dr. Sexton's, land of the irreplaceable and exquisite. But Dr. Sexton often arrived carrying instruments of physics or plans for experiments to conduct, just as she'd done the first evening she'd visited. Dr. Sexton and Julien had taken a particular shine to each other, but Jack was an exuberant participant in the activities, too, particularly when propulsion was involved.

Jennifer assumed Dr. Sexton and Julien would immediately set to work on something, so she continued eating her pancake, Jack tucked solidly under her arm. A moment later, however, and much to her surprise, Dr. Sexton appeared, arms akimbo, in Julien and Jack's doorway. Even stranger, Dr. Sexton was as disheveled as Jennifer had ever seen her, her hair damp with spiky bits stuck to her forehead, her cheeks shiny with rain. In a glossy black slicker and galoshes (one red, one black), she looked a bit loony, and the pronouncement that followed did little to dispel the impression.

"There has been," she declared in a booming voice, her eyes bright with an uncharacteristically girlish look of excitement, "a delivery."

"What is it?" Julien cried, tugging at Dr. Sexton's coat. "*Where* is it?"

"Come to my apartment in twenty minutes," she answered, smiling at him, her eyebrows lifted high, "and you will find out!"

With that, she disappeared.

"Do you think it's a spaceship?" Jack asked, his eyes wide.

"No, Jack," Julien said impatiently. "A spaceship would be way too big to fit in Dr. Sexton's apartment."

"Don't be so sure, Julien," Jennifer said, picking up the tray to carry it back into the kitchen, dreaming of coffee. "Knowing Dr. Sexton, I wouldn't rule it out."

THE BOYS COULD NOT have been more pleased with the "delivery" if it had been a spaceship after all. For when they arrived and Dr. Sexton ushered them inside, hair blown dry and looking a bit more put together (though still wearing a look of manic joy), she stood back and revealed nothing less than a torpedo, smack in the center of her living room.

Army green, twenty feet in length and nearly two feet in diameter, with a yellow nose at one end and a rudder and propeller at the other, the massive object was displayed on a stand. Even more startling, on its metal body was painted, in vibrant colors and fine, nearly photographic detail, a voluptuous, smoky-eyed woman. Richly adorned and reclining in the manner of an odalisque, she had dark eyes and thick, shiny black hair, gold jewelry hanging from every finger and toe, and thin, arched eyebrows that presided over an air of commanding seduction. Together, the woman and the torpedo were a knockout.

"Well? What do you think of her?" Dr. Sexton asked.

"Wow," Julien breathed. Jennifer could not help but smile to herself, knowing that Julien was still at an age when the "wow" was a reaction to the torpedo, rather than to the pinup.

"Wow indeed," Jennifer said, moving toward the alluring object.

"Wait!" Dr. Sexton said. "Not yet! I need to show you the

coolest part!" Jennifer, who had never heard Dr. Sexton utter any variation of the word *cool*, stopped in her tracks.

"Jack," Dr. Sexton said, "will you assist me?"

"*I* want to assist!" Julien cried.

"You may assist too," Dr. Sexton said. "Jack, hold this transmitter for me, just like that." She handed him what looked like a simple remote control. "Julien, go over to the torpedo with your mother and open the door, just under Hedy's—I mean, *the woman's*—leg." Jennifer and Jack did as they were told, locating a panel placed provocatively under a thigh and opening the torpedo's small compartment. Inside, they saw a mechanism that included perforated tape on a scroll with rods underneath it, each positioned over a panel of tiny switches.

"All right, Jack," Dr. Sexton said. "Would you like to steer?" Jack nodded enthusiastically. "Julien," she said, "you watch what happens inside the receiver when we launch, and afterward I'll explain it to you."

"Launch?" Jennifer cried.

"Don't worry, my dear," Dr. Sexton said. "I haven't gone completely bonkers." Then, with a flourish and a cry of "For Hedy!" Dr. Sexton pushed a button on the remote control in Jack's hands. Immediately, the propeller started spinning, the perforated tape in the receiver began scrolling, and the switches beneath it commenced switching, one at a time, in an apparently random pattern.

"All right—now, send a signal!" Dr. Sexton cried, as the receiver clicked and buzzed. "Tell the torpedo to turn left!" Jack, an experienced Xbox player, immediately moved the joystick on the remote control to the left, and the rudder of the torpedo swayed dutifully to the left too. "You've got it!" Dr. Sexton said. "Keep going!" She then joined Jennifer and Julien. Julien was watching the mechanism like a hawk, though clearly without a clue as to what he was looking at. Dr. Sexton joined him, peering into the receiver. She pointed.

"Do you see how the perforated tape has a very specific pattern imprinted on it?" she asked him. He nodded. "An identical pattern is printed on a perforated tape inside the transmitter that Jack is holding. The pattern tells the receiver and the transmitter which radio frequency, or channel, to use to send the signal. If the transmitter is on channel A, the receiver is on channel A, but a second later the transmitter has hopped to channel B, and the receiver has too."

"Why?" Julien asked.

"During World War Two, the German army would try to stop torpedoes from communicating with their home ships by detecting the frequency that the ship was using to communicate with the torpedo and jam it. The idea behind this torpedo was that by randomly switching between frequencies all the time, the Americans could keep the Germans from jamming the signal, because the Germans would never be able to break the code. Its inventors called it *spread spectrum*. Sadly, the US government failed to recognize the brilliance of the innovation in time to implement it during the war. But now cell phones and bar-code readers and a whole lot of other things use it too."

"Did this torpedo ever sink a ship?" Julien asked.

"No," Dr. Sexton said. "This torpedo was never in a battle. It was made only a few weeks ago. It is a gift to me from a friend who knows how much I admire the woman who invented the idea of frequency hopping. A way of imagining what her torpedo *would* have been like had it ever been built."

"Let me guess," Jennifer said, smiling. "Hedy?"

"The same," Dr. Sexton replied. "None other than the nineteen-forties movie star Hedy Lamarr. A brilliant woman, who was barely acknowledged, and never rewarded, for inventing, with the composer George Antheil, one of the most widely used technologies of the century." Julien stared at the woman on the torpedo with new admiration, and Jennifer did too.

A few minutes later, the torpedo had been shut down and the boys were playing with Dr. Sexton's gyroscope collection by a window on the other end of the living room, out of earshot. "So?" Jennifer said, sitting down at the island to a plate of vegetable quiche and a green salad. (Dr. Sexton always had something delicious and elegant in her refrigerator: a quiche, a torte, a goose liver pâté. The only things Jennifer always had in her refrigerator were ketchup and string cheese.) "Who gave you this magnificent—and extremely sensual, might I add —weapon?"

Dr. Sexton took a seat across from Jennifer. "Susan," she said triumphantly, her eyes lighting up with pleasure.

"Susan?" Jennifer asked. "Really? I didn't know you two were speaking to each other, much less exchanging torpedoes."

"It's been several months, actually," Dr. Sexton said, pouring the tea. "I didn't want to say anything, but it was around the new year—a propitious time for romance, as you know." Jennifer smiled at the reference to Owen, a development that had very much pleased Dr. Sexton. "Susan telephoned. She wanted to talk. I was reluctant at first. But I have missed her. Very deeply." Dr. Sexton cut into her quiche and smiled. "It was wonderful to know that she had missed me too. Enough to swallow her pride, which for Susan is no small feat."

"And?" Jennifer said.

"We met for coffee, but it was impossible to say all that needed to be said. I wanted to take it slowly. I needed to know, if we were going to attempt to reconcile, how things would change. If she would publicly acknowledge our relationship. Susan asked for some time to consider."

Jennifer gestured toward the torpedo. "And then she sent that?"

"Two weeks ago I was in Marrakesh on a 'journey.'" (*Someday,*
Jennifer thought, *I have got to get out of the five boroughs.*) "Susan
and I had spent a very romantic weekend in Marrakesh many
years ago and had discovered a particular tea shop we loved—
the same shop where I purchased the leaves for this extraordinary brew." Jennifer took a deep breath of the tea Dr.
Sexton had made for them, inhaling the fragrant vapor. "I was
drawn to it, of course," Dr. Sexton went on. "And when I
arrived, Susan was there—in Marrakesh—for a conference on
quantum mechanics! Can you believe it?" Dr. Sexton asked,
beaming. "It was fate. One thing led to another. It was very
passionate. We were together again."

"So are you?" Jennifer asked. "Together again?"

"Once I was back in New York, my doubts returned.
During our night in Marrakesh, we avoided, so to speak,
difficult subjects. However . . ." Dr. Sexton picked up an
envelope and took out a handwritten note. She read: "'Display
it anywhere you like (on the quad, maybe?), and tell anyone
who asks it was a gift from the woman who loves you, and
always will: Dr. Susan Terry.'" Setting the note down, Dr.
Sexton smiled. "It is an extravagant gesture," she said, turning
to the torpedo, "which is just the sort of gesture I like."

Jennifer laughed.

"And you?" Dr. Sexton said, regarding her playfully. "Don't
think I've forgotten that it's your birthday, my dear. What do
you and your handsome guitar player have in store? Not that I
can testify to his handsomeness, as you refuse to let me meet him."

"I don't 'refuse,'" Jennifer said. "I just like to keep things
separate, that's all. Everything in its place."

"But you are not divided into parts. You're a whole person.
A mother, a career woman, and my friend." Dr. Sexton said.
"Surely Owen appreciates all those things about you. Surely
you wish to share all those things with him."

"Does Susan know about the app?" Jennifer asked challengingly.

Dr. Sexton paused and took a long draft of tea. "Touché," she said quietly. "I suppose I'm in no position to judge on the subject of transparency."

Jennifer had clearly struck a nerve, and she looked down, feeling bad. Telling Susan or Owen or anyone else about the app was not the same as introducing Owen to Dr. Sexton, or her friends, or otherwise integrating the rapidly diverging parts of her life. It was something Owen had lately been pushing her about too.

"It's all right, dear," Dr. Sexton said, affectionately patting Jennifer's hand. "There is no need to rush. That is what the app is for, after all. To slow down and let yourself be fully present in the world at each moment, without constantly feeling as though you ought to be somewhere else."

"Is it?" Jennifer said, thinking of the lists, videos, voice memos, and calendar reminders that had increased threefold since she'd begun to use the app to live life in triplicate. "Sometimes," she added, "I just feel like I should be in more places than ever."

sixteen | SURPRISE!

THE BOYS PLAYED INDOOR soccer at Chelsea Piers (Norman had gotten Jack a spot after all), a massive sports complex on Manhattan's West Side. Weekends at Chelsea Piers were a madhouse, teeming with the comings and goings of thousands of New York families desperate for open space for their children in the wintertime. That afternoon they arrived late, as usual (Jennifer often wished she could pop the boys through the portal of Wishful Thinking when they needed to get somewhere on time), and as soon as they got there, Jennifer hastily outfitted them in their shin guards before sending them onto the Astroturf fields. She then took her place in the parent pen, as the grown-ups not so affectionately referred to it—an area at one end of the fields with benches where parents were allowed to sit. It was Jack's first year, but Julien had been playing soccer there since he was four, and there were families they had been seeing every winter Saturday for years. This included Tara and Josh, whose son, Frank, was Julien's age. As soon as Jennifer sat down, Tara ambled over to her, holding a coffee.

"At least he didn't show up with Dingbat today," she said, gesturing to Norman, who had just arrived and was giving the boys some last-minute soccer tips. He was showing off a trick he'd perfected when they were in college, where he flipped the ball neatly over his head with one foot—a trick Jennifer had always thought was kind of cool. Smiling at Tara, Jennifer rolled her eyes and shrugged. "I'm sure she'll be here soon," she said. Tara had provided Jennifer with some much-needed comic relief when it came to dealing with the Norman-and-Dina situation. She was a loyal friend, but she was also a bit of a curmudgeon and clearly enjoyed having something to make cracks about on otherwise-uneventful soccer Saturdays.

"Hello, ladies," Norman said, approaching them jauntily. "Any good gossip this morning?"

Jennifer didn't reply. She knew that Tara really liked Norman—she had worked in the entertainment business, too, as a casting director, and she was soon offering him a few choice bits. But while Norman usually ate up Tara's industry chatter, today he seemed distracted as he listened. He kept looking over at Jennifer, trying to catch her eye. *Oh God*, she thought. *He wants to talk to me about something.* For months she'd been successfully managing to avoid him, relying on the glacial pace of their lawyers' communications (she'd finally gotten one) to stall any further discussion on the subject of custody.

"I gotta go to the bathroom," she said, making her escape. When she emerged, however, Norman was there, standing next to the vending machines.

"Jen," he said, "do you have a minute?" He gestured to a bench in the hall, covered in sweatpants and coats, and cleared a space for the two of them.

"You got that last e-mail from my lawyer, right?" she said, reluctantly taking a seat beside him.

"Yes," he said. "This isn't about that." Then his face broke into a grin, the sight of which made her toes curl. "There's something we're going to tell the boys tonight, but I wanted you to be the first to know. So that you don't feel, you know, ambushed."

"Okay," she said.

"We're getting married," he said.

"Good for you," Jennifer said quickly. "Congratulations." She stood up, a little shakily. "Can I go now?"

"There's something else," he said, touching her on the arm, motioning for her to sit back down. He did it gently. He was being gentle with her. And then she knew.

"She's pregnant," she said flatly, sitting down next to him in a little heap.

"How did you know?" he asked, genuinely surprised.

Because I know you, she wanted to say. Instead she asked, "How far along?"

"It's just six weeks," he said. "I know it might not take, but—"

"You're not going to tell the boys *that*," she said. "Not until she's further along."

"No," he said. "We'll wait."

They were silent for a minute. Looking over at the parent pen, Jennifer searched for Tara, wanting to meet her eyes, looking for a lifeline, something, anything, to pull her out of that moment. Why did she care? she wondered. She didn't love him anymore. And Dina loved her boys. Vinita was always reminding her—gently, and sometimes not so gently—how much worse it could be. What if Norman had chosen a woman Jennifer thought was cruel, or thoughtless? Someone she didn't trust? What if it was a different woman every weekend, sleeping in Norman's bed? Dina was good with the boys, and Norman was better with them when she was around. But something was hurting her. Something was making her feel really, really sad.

A baby.

"It's my birthday today," she said, almost to nobody.

"Oh my God!" Norman said. "Happy birthday!" He turned toward her, giving her an awkward but affectionate little hug. Pulling away, he added, "That's so weird. I don't think I've ever forgotten your birthday before. Not for twenty years."

"Twenty years," Jennifer said. "That's scary."

"You're finally forty," he said. "Welcome to the club. You look great, you know."

It cost him nothing to say it, she could tell. And that was the moment she knew that Norman, finally and for good, was over her.

JENNIFER LEFT SOCCER EARLY, before Dina got there. The boys weren't happy about it, but she wasn't ready to offer her congratulations—not yet. Not in front of all of the other moms, who were likely to notice a new diamond ring in their midst, and ooh and aah over it while rubbernecking to see the look on Jennifer's face.

When she got home, she permitted herself a good cry. Then she stopped. Then she went running. She hadn't gone for a run in years, it seemed—she hadn't used Wishful Thinking for that—and cruising through the wintry air on the path along the Hudson, even though she got winded faster than she'd wished, cleared her head a little.

A few hours later, when Owen arrived to pick her up, she was no longer puffy-eyed, but she wasn't dressed for dinner, either. In fact, Owen found her curled up on the sofa, showered but still in her bathrobe.

"Hey there, sweetheart," he said, walking over to join her. He sat down, lifted her chin, put a hand on each of her cheeks, and pressed his forehead firmly into hers. She really hated it when he did that. It made her feel like she was in an affection vise. She pulled away. "Birthday blues?"

"Norman's marrying Dingbat," she said. "And she's pregnant."

"With a baby dingbat?" Owen asked, smiling. "Awww," he said, pulling her into him and doing the forehead thing again.

"Stop it," she said, "please?" And then, "Sorry."

"No, I'm sorry," he said. "That must be really hard. I can't imagine what it's like for you to have to see him all the time." Relaxing a little, she snuggled up next to him. "For all I know Rachel is married by now, back in North Carolina, living a whole new life." Neither of them said it out loud, but it went without saying that Rachel almost certainly wasn't pregnant. She'd never been able to conceive, even after years of treatments that a music teacher and a restaurant sommelier could hardly afford. Owen had been open to adoption, too, but Rachel had refused to consider it. It was one of the main reasons their marriage had ended.

It was not a direction in which Jennifer wanted their conversation to go. Owen still wanted a baby, she knew, and he could have one—tests had confirmed that Owen was fertile. But a baby was something she could not begin to imagine right now. Hoping to preempt the possibility the conversation would head in that direction, she kissed him.

They kissed for a while. It was just what she needed. She could feel the life coming back into her body, his arms around her sending a feeling of well-being flowing through her, until her body hummed with warmth and she was present and alive again. Now *this* was a birthday, she thought, as she slipped one of his hands inside her bathrobe. Home alone, no kids, with her hunky man rising to the occasion on the couch. She put her hand on his inner thigh and began to walk her fingers upward, caressing him as she went.

"Wait a minute," Owen said. "I'm taking you out tonight! For your birthday! Remember?" She looked at him petulantly.

"Do we have to?" she said. "Wouldn't it be so much nicer to stay here and do the things we do? Like this? And then, like, nothing?"

"We never do hang out at your place," he said, pulling away and looking at her a little reproachfully.

"Not because I don't want you here—you know that. You have a bed. I have a pullout couch."

"Sometimes I feel like my place has become a little hideout from the world," he said. "I mean, I think it's great that Norman has moved on. Good for him, right? Don't you think it's time we talked to the boys? Maybe introduced them to the idea of my being around?"

She cut him off. "No," she said. "I don't." He held her gaze for a minute. He seemed to be deciding something. Thankfully, he decided, apparently, that it was not the time for that conversation. She couldn't have agreed more. He stood up. "All right, missy," he said. "It's time for you to get your ass up off of that sofa bed and put something sexy on. Tonight I am taking the hottest piece of tail north of the Rio Grande out on the town, and I cannot have her in her bathrobe."

Grateful to be let off the hook so easily, Jennifer jumped off the sofa and started hunting for something fabulous. She wasn't going to let Norman's announcement ruin her birthday, she told herself. She was going go out and have a good old time with her man.

AN HOUR LATER, wearing her pleather pants for nostalgia's sake, Jennifer was walking with Owen somewhere in Chelsea, following him to a restaurant the name of which he refused to disclose. He was checking his phone more than usual as they walked, receiving a barrage of texts.

"Who *is* that?" Jennifer asked, trying not to sound annoyed but instinctively reaching for her phone, too.

"It's just Johnny," he said. "Somebody wants to use one of our songs on a soundtrack, and he's wigging out about it." Glancing up as he put his phone away, he saw Jennifer fiddling with hers. Suddenly he reached over and grabbed her phone from her hand. She stared up at him indignantly and then lunged at him to get it back. He didn't let her have it.

"Hey!" she said. "Give it back to me!"

"No," he said, using his considerable height to keep the phone just out of her reach. He was laughing, but she wasn't. A feeling of panic had shot through her the minute he'd torn the phone from her grasp, and she was angry, disturbingly angry, at his having taken it, even as a joke.

"I said give it back," she said, stopping on the sidewalk.

Stopping too, he looked at her, knitting his brow a little. "You actually look pissed off," he said.

"Just give me my phone back," she said.

"Don't you want to unplug for tonight?" he said. "You sleep with this thing under your pillow, you know. It isn't healthy."

"It's in case something happens to my kids," she said sharply. "I've told you. I need it." Slowly, Owen lowered the phone. As soon as it was within reach, she grabbed it.

"Touchy," he said. "Someday," he added, taking her in a conciliatory bear hug, lifting her off her feet, "I'm going to whisk you away to a tropical island, and you and I will both throw those things in the Caribbean."

"How romantic," she said, pulling away and stroking her phone surreptitiously as she returned it to her pocket. "Now, where are we going, Mr. Romance? I'm hungry! I want to stuff myself on a huge dessert and test the limits of these pants!"

Owen checked his phone again, studying the GPS. "Here,"

he said, looking up at a nondescript building on Ninth Avenue. It looked like the kind of place that would house an off-off-Broadway performance space, or a bunch of artists' lofts. It was hard to see how it could contain a fortieth birthday–worthy restaurant.

"Trust me," he said, noting her skeptical expression and winking. She loved it when he winked. So few men could wink without looking like idiots. Someday she was going to convince him to wink at her from under the brim of a cowboy hat, though she'd had no luck so far. ("Cowboy hats are for kickers," he'd said, though he had neglected to explain just what that meant.) Softening, and eager to see where they were headed, she followed him inside, smiling and holding his hand as they boarded a gigantic freight elevator. He pushed 10.

"This better not be anything weird," she said. "Like some kind of spanking club or something. Don't get the wrong idea just because I'm wearing pleather." Giving her a playful swat on the rear, he grinned. A moment later, the elevator doors opened onto a darkened room. And then she heard it. The unmistakable sound of several dozen adults waiting with bated breath. And then the lights flipped on and she saw it: Vinita, Tara, Alicia, Tim, Caroline, and a whole bunch of other people she knew, some of whom she hadn't seen in years, gathered together under a big HAPPY 40TH BIRTHDAY, JENNIFER! sign.

"Oh my God," she whispered.

"SURPRISE!" they answered.

"Happy birthday, baby," Owen said.

It was all she could do not to kill him right then and there.

seventeen | BUSTED

I T WAS JENNIFER'S WORST Wishful Thinking nightmare: everybody she knew together in one room. The
room, however, was a dream sprung straight from
Vinita's head. Vinita had always fantasized about opening a
restaurant specializing in the North Indian food she'd grown
up with, and Jennifer knew this was what it would look like,
awash in richly colored fabrics, draped from the ceiling to the
floor and sweeping across the windows of the loft, with music
from one of her favorite Bollywood movies playing in the
background. Dozens of mango-colored paper lanterns hung so
low that Owen was in danger of hitting his head on them. To
Jennifer's left was a long table laden with platter after platter of
the food she'd stuffed herself with so many evenings at Vinita's
house: yellow dal, curried chicken, *saag paneer*, and more,
accented by hundreds of golden tea lights housed in rosewood
carved with a paisley pattern.

It was beautiful.

Vinita stepped forward immediately to greet her. She was
dressed for her part as hostess, her hair up in her signature

shiny black French twist, her body wrapped in a dark crimson sari accented by dangling earrings of ruby and gold.

"Happy birthday, Jay!" she said, leaning in to hug her. "Please don't kill me," she added, as soon as her mouth was near enough to Jennifer's ear to whisper. "I didn't know how else I was ever going to meet this guy." Pulling away, she beamed at Owen, apparently her new best friend, and added, "And besides, I've always wanted to throw you a big Bollywood birthday party!" Gesturing to the room behind her, Vinita smiled radiantly, and Jennifer gave her an extrabig kiss, a smile spreading across her face, too, in spite of herself. She was touched.

"You outdid yourself, Vinita," Owen said, greeting her with a kiss. "This place smells amazing." Jennifer tried not to react to the strange sight of Vinita and Owen on seemingly intimate terms, given the fact that she had never been in the same room with them together.

Sean then appeared at Vinita's side, wearing his impish man-child grin. "What's up, rock-star girlfriend?" he said teasingly, sizing up Jennifer's outfit and making her blush. (What was it about the frat-boy investment-banker types that made them so uniquely capable of doing that? It was infuriating.) Turning to Vinita, he said, "Where are your hot pants?" Vinita rolled her eyes. At this, Owen, the rock star in question, put a hand out, introducing himself to Sean, who promptly whisked him off to get a drink. Jennifer could see Owen's little sister, Sarah, cat-eye eyeliner in full effect, standing by a massive window and taking in the view with Johnny. She waved hello.

Taking Jennifer's arm, Vinita led her to the bar. "You are the belle of the ball, of course," she said, "which I know you hate as much as you hate surprise parties." Vinita gestured to the bartender. "So, to help you through it, how about an

Indian martini?" Jennifer raised her eyebrows skeptically as Vinita handed her a glass rimmed in rose-colored sugar, displaying it with a little Vanna White flourish. "Saffron vodka," she added, and sipped her own. "Indian enough for me, Indian enough for you."

Jennifer laughed and took a sip of her martini too. Now that the initial "surprise" blast had dissipated, little groups had formed all around the room, each composed of the friends and colleagues she'd so carefully kept apart during the last six months of her Wishful Thinking life. Vinita seemed to read her mind.

"Don't worry, Jay," she said. "The work people and the moms aren't going to talk to each other, much less compare notes on your schedule."

Jennifer nodded weakly. Watching all the people from every part of her life mill about, however, politely waiting for her to settle in before coming over to say hello, Jennifer thought, *This could be very bad.* Glancing at Vinita, the one person there who would not assume, if her memory of Jennifer's schedule on a given day didn't match up with somebody else's, that she was simply remembering things wrong, she thought, *Very, very bad.*

In one corner stood Alicia with her husband, Steven, a scholarly, genial-looking man with thinning gray hair, who was chatting with Tim and, to Jennifer's dismay, Bill Truitt, too. Admiring the food table were Caroline, Elizabeth, and Jane from the elementary-school benefit committee. Jennifer had opted out of the committee after the face-plant-on-the-conference-table episode, but she had lately taken to spending Monday afternoons with the three of them (who all had younger children at New Day, as it turned out, just as she and Caroline did) when she and Jack had their one-on-one afternoons together. Jennifer had even gotten to like, or at least appreciate, Elizabeth, but of course Vinita didn't know that.

"So, Owen did the guest list?" Jennifer asked Vinita under her breath, attempting to appear welcoming as Alicia, Tim, and Bill made their approach.

"Yes," Vinita said. "And, honey, I know you hate surprises, but he worked so hard. He wanted to be sure not to miss anyone. Though I don't know where he got Elizabeth Stick-up-her-ass over there." Apparently Owen hadn't turned up Dr. Sexton, which was the only thing about the evening that wasn't surprising at all.

"I can't believe he invited my *boss*," Jennifer managed to whisper, just before breaking into a warm greeting as the work group joined them. "Team One Stop!" she said. "How sweet of you to come celebrate my getting old!"

"Oh, please," Alicia said. "I'm ten years older than you!" As ever, it was hard to believe. Alicia, in the Saturday-night version of her trademark ivory suit, was sporting gold pumps and a waistline that any woman would envy, looking better at fifty than Jennifer had at twenty-nine. Jennifer gave her a kiss hello as Alicia's husband looked on, smiling and eyeing her proudly over his spectacles. "That's my girl," he said. "Like the day I met her, but better with every day that's gone by."

"Well, it's a party now!" Bill Truitt boomed, pushing his way forward to kiss Jennifer and interrupting Tim just as he was about to say hello. "How are you doing tonight, Ms. Sharpe? How does it feel to be a forty-year-old superwoman?"

"Superwoman? Please!" Jennifer laughed, a little forcedly.

Alicia met her eyes, and Jennifer detected a note of challenge in them. "We were just discussing your status at the top of the I-don't-know-how-she-does-it list. My husband wanted to come tonight just to lay eyes on you and make sure you were real."

"Alicia doesn't often feel anybody can outwork her,"

Steven confirmed. "I'd say there are some days—only some days, of course—when it gets to her just a little bit when you do." Alicia elbowed her husband in the ribs, then formally introduced him to Jennifer.

"Superwoman," Alicia said, "meet my superman." Alicia had often said that without Steven, she could never have made it through the last six months. He did not view picking the kids up from school as doing Alicia a favor, and he was an expert at laundry, though he drew the line at housekeeping, which apparently was Alicia's job no matter how many hours she worked. For a moment, as Jennifer caught Owen's eyes across the room, she wondered what her life would be like with a true partner in it. Owen wasn't too handy at housekeeping either, but he was the kind of man who ironed his own shirts and, more important, always offered to iron Jennifer's too. He was always asking, "How can I help?" But deepening their bond beyond dating, she reminded herself—as long as she was using Wishful Thinking—was wishful thinking indeed.

"I am not the superwoman here," Jennifer said. "I mean, what about my friend Vinita? Can you believe what she did with this space? *And* she has three little girls, *and* she's a doctor." Vinita, still at Jennifer's side, laughed gamely.

"Does *she* work till eight o'clock every night of the week?" Alicia asked, nodding toward Vinita. Vinita looked puzzled.

"Jennifer doesn't work until eight o'clock every night," Vinita said. "What about Fridays?" Now it was Alicia's turn to look puzzled.

"What about Fridays?" Alicia asked. "She stays till eight on Fridays, too." At this, Vinita turned to Jennifer with a look that, at its most benign, would have been described as curious.

Jennifer was about to do something drastic, like launch into a polka, when Bill Truitt's complete lack of tact saved the day.

"That's our Jennifer Sharpe," Bill said, thunking her on the back so hard her martini almost hit the floor, "putting the work ethic back into the sinkhole of city government, one twelve-hour day at a time!" At that, Jennifer threw back what was left of her drink and began hunting for the next one. One more word from Alicia, she thought, and Vinita would know that Jennifer used the app not just on Tuesdays and Thursdays, but on Mondays, Wednesdays, and Fridays, too, if she hadn't figured out the Friday part already. One word from Caroline, Elizabeth, or Jane, who were making their way over, and Alicia would know that Jennifer picked her boys up from school every day but Wednesday. One word from Owen, and her fellow moms would know she went out to bars to see bands play on school nights. One word from just about anybody in this room, in fact, regarding the last time and place they'd seen her, and all hell was going to break loose.

She had to think. She had to figure out what to do. She needed, just for a minute, to be alone.

It was time to go to the bathroom. Where else? She cleared her throat, preparing to make her excuse. Bill, of course, just kept on talking. "I'm sorry I can't stay," he was saying, "but the wife is waiting for me at a charity function. Not that I wouldn't dress up for Superwoman's soiree on any night of the week." Leaning down and in, he gave her a cheek-to-cheek air kiss like the practiced member of the benefit circuit that he was. "Enjoy yourselves," he said, departing. "And I'll see you all bright and early on Monday!"

There was a pause. "Sorry, guys," Jennifer said, jumping in to fill it, "but I really need to go to the bathroom."

"I'll come with you," Vinita said. From her tone, Jennifer knew that Vinita knew something was rotten in Denmark.

"Oh no, Vee," Jennifer said, "you stay here! That food looks so amazing! Doesn't it need you?" Pushing Vinita away firmly, she deposited quick kisses hello on Caroline, Elizabeth, and Jane as she passed them by. "Back in a sec!" she chirped merrily. "Bathroom break!"

Vinita, Jennifer knew, had let her go only for the moment. Glancing over her shoulder as she hurried off, Jennifer was relieved to see that everyone else, however, had gone back to admiring the decor, sipping their sugar-rimmed saffron martinis and chatting with their friends.

Just as she was about to open the bathroom door, Jennifer heard Vinita's voice cut through the crowd. "Don't be long!" she called. "Owen has a surprise for you!"

Another surprise? Jennifer thought as she hauled open the heavy metal door of the loft's bathroom, which Vinita had had the good sense to fill with cardamom-scented candles. "I'll be right back!" she called, just as the door swung shut. She locked it behind her.

I'll be right back, she thought, finally safe inside yet another bathroom, the latest stop on the underground railroad of bathrooms she relied on as a time-traveling fugitive in New York, *just as long as I don't decide to jump out a window first.*

Jennifer looked at herself in the mirror. "Deep breaths," she told herself. "Deep breaths."

She reached into her clutch, took out her phone, and stared at it. She opened her calendar. Saturday, March 26. Surely her phone contained the answer to this problem. Didn't it always? But how could Wishful Thinking help her now? The app couldn't get her out of this predicament, not unless she really wanted to send everybody to the funny farm (including herself) by making three appointments to be at the party, so that each version of her—one in leather pants, one in Uggs and mom jeans, and one in a business suit—could attend, dressed for her part. *Superwoman,* she thought, with some irritation at Alicia's having put her on the spot like that. They had no idea.

Forget the phone, she thought, putting it back in her bag. She could get herself out of this without it, couldn't she? She could just leave. Pretend she had just thrown up. Blame it on a bad oyster. Too bad she hadn't had any oysters that day. She hadn't eaten anything more menacing than a low-fat yogurt—not that anyone would know that. Maybe she could fake a nervous breakdown and blame it on a sudden hormonal change caused by the onset of her fifth decade.

And then she heard it: Johnny, counting in. "A one-two-three-four . . ." A simple melody on the piano—a tinny, old-timey upright, with just a little backroom-bar sound to it. A sweet melody, so Dimes-y, tripping up and down on the piano lightly, and then the chords on the guitar joining in.

Owen.

She knew this song. It was one of her favorites: "Abigail, Don't Be Long." (These guys had actually written a song about Abigail Adams for their Boston album. There was a Susan B. Anthony song and a Clara Barton song too.) For a minute, she let the music transport her, as it always did. For a minute, she let herself just listen and breathe. Then she smiled. They were repeating the opening hook over and over. Owen was waiting for her to come out before they started to sing.

Her heart filled with a surge of love and tenderness, and her throat tightened even as her foot began to tap. Meeting her own shining eyes in the mirror, she gave her head a little shake. *Stop with your fretting, you lucky girl*, she thought. Owen was out there with all the people she had not yet allowed him to meet, trying to be a part of her life, asking her to let him in. She had met a man who had given her hope for a future bigger than herself and her boys, who had given her hope in love again, and he was singing to her on her birthday.

She had to go out and kiss him. She had to stay.

* * *

BEING SERENADED WAS WONDERFUL. After finishing
"Abigail," Owen and Johnny played "Save Me, Clara," with
Sarah joining in to harmonize and keep time on the
tambourine. Looking over at Sean, who never listened to
anything but Radiohead, Jennifer could see that he was getting
through it by paying more attention to Sarah's cleavage than to
her vocals. This was not lost on Vinita, either, with whom she
exchanged a *what are you gonna do?* smile that reassured
Jennifer, though only a little bit. After a third song, the show
was over. It was time to eat.

Which meant it was also time for people to start talking to
one another again. Which meant that after a few heavenly
moments of being that girl in the audience the band really *is*
playing for, Jennifer was beset anew by panic. Watching
nervously as the guests began to choose their seats at the
round tables throughout the room, however, Jennifer was
relieved to see that a common human social phenomenon was
working beautifully in her favor. The guests were self-sorting,
gravitating to tables populated by people they already knew.
Her work friends sat with her work friends; her college friends
sat with her college friends; her mommy friends sat with her
mommy friends. Even Owen, who she knew was eager to meet
all the people in her life he'd never met, was too much of a
gentleman to go around shaking hands with everybody and
had settled down at a table with Johnny and the Dimes.

Jennifer joined him there. For at least half an hour, as
everyone concentrated on the delicious food, sighing with pleasure as they ate, everything was fine. Then Vinita appeared next
to Jennifer's chair and placed a hand lightly on the back of it.

"I hate to steal her, Owen," Vinita said, "but she can't stay
here all night. She's got to mingle!" Owen nodded and stood,

pushing his chair back. "Want me to come with you?" he asked Jennifer. His face was so sweet, so open. She wanted him to meet everyone in her life, she really did. Someday.

"Maybe later, sweetie?" Jennifer said, standing on her tiptoes to kiss him. Owen pulled away, looking, she couldn't deny it, a little hurt.

"Okay," he said, "but don't be long." Jennifer nodded, smiling as warmly as she could even as Vinita began to steer her firmly across the room.

"Where are you taking me?" Jennifer asked her.

"To the table where *I've* been sitting," Vinita said, approaching the mommy table, where Caroline, Elizabeth, Jane, and a few other mothers from school sat.

"It wasn't easy, ladies," Vinita announced, smiling, "but I managed to pry the birthday girl away from that gorgeous guitar player!"

Everyone laughed. Vinita pulled up an extra chair, and, uneasy, Jennifer sat in it. She was clutching her clutch, which contained her phone. As soon as she set it down on the table, Vinita eyed it meaningfully.

"So!" Jennifer said, determined to match Vinita's bright tone. "What are you hot mamas talking about?"

"Oh, you know," Vinita said. "The usual. Scheduling. After-school activities. *Pickup.*"

"I was telling Vinita she needs to join us for one of our mommy Mondays!" Elizabeth said enthusiastically. "We could do an Indian night. Vinita could teach us to cook Indian food, and we could have Indian martinis! These are so delish." Elizabeth took another swig. Jennifer would have enjoyed watching Elizabeth swerve outside her carefully scripted self outline with the help of the vodka if Vinita hadn't been looking at Jennifer like she was a mean girl Vinita was gearing up to destroy in the final scene of a movie.

"Mondays," Vinita said. "*Every* Monday. Pickup, playdate, early dinner for the kids, cocktails. Sounds heavenly." Jennifer smiled weakly. "But I told these guys," Vinita said, "that I can't make it on Mondays. Because on Mondays, I work."

"Jennifer works only on Wednesday afternoons now," Melissa, who was seated at this table, too, piped in. Melissa was thriving at night school. She had brought her new boyfriend with her and looked as fresh and confident as Jennifer had seen her in years. Jennifer was happy for her. But at the moment, she just wanted Melissa to shut up. "I pick up Julien on Mondays so she can spend time with Jack, and Jack on Fridays so she can spend time with Julien."

"But her coworker Alicia calls her a workaholic," Vinita said darkly. "Strange, isn't it?"

Jennifer looked at Vinita pleadingly. *Not now*, she wanted to say. *Please?*

Vinita, however, had waited quite long enough. "Will you guys excuse us for a second?" Vinita said. She motioned to Jennifer. Jennifer got up, but not before grabbing her clutch. "Oh, right," Vinita said, practically growling, "God forbid you should be separated from *that*!" Jennifer smiled at the moms, who looked confused.

"My phone," she explained. A collective "ah" rose over the table.

"I once grabbed mine from a toilet I'd already peed in," Elizabeth said as they walked away—another gem Jennifer was too stressed to appreciate.

The moment they were out of view, in a secluded hallway near the bathroom door, Vinita whirled around and, in a movement the force and vehemence of which stunned Jennifer, grabbed her by the arm, hard. Jennifer wrenched free, wincing.

"Ow!" she said.

"You've been lying to me!" Vinita hissed. "For weeks! Months? How long?"

"No!" Jennifer said. It was startling how easily she said it, the firmness with which she stated the biggest lie of all. "I've only used it a few extra times! I don't see those guys *every* Monday. And Alicia's going overboard. I don't work late every night. You know that. On Friday afternoons, I'm with you!"

"If that's true," Vinita said, "then you won't mind letting me see your phone. If there are only two Wishful Thinking appointments per week on your calendar, plus one more for sleeping, which was our agreement from the beginning, I'll drop this." She held out her hand. "That's okay, right, Jay?" she said, the sarcasm in her voice setting Jennifer's teeth on edge. "If you've got nothing to hide?"

Jennifer's grip on her purse tightened, her fingernails digging into the cheap, shiny fabric. "No," she said.

"*No?*" Vinita said. "No? You are using the app *way* more than we agreed. Way more! It's the only explanation for your after-school mommy hangouts and your workdays that go till eight every night and your Friday afternoons with me and Melissa working only two afternoons a week. Which means that you have been lying to me for *six months*. I feel so betrayed I don't even know what to say to you right now. And scared, Jennifer. This really scares me."

Jennifer didn't respond. She was thinking. Would it be better to tell Vinita everything? To be honest about how much she'd been using the app, and also to tell her about the bleed-through she'd experienced in December, which still worried her even though it hadn't happened again? But then she would have to stop using the app so often. She'd have to go back to their agreement, and there was no going back now.

"How many times a week?" Vinita repeated in a low, hard voice. Jennifer shrugged, feeling like a bullied and busted teenager. "And don't stand there slouching like you're a thirteen-year-old in trouble with her mom." (Vinita, as ever, knew her too well.) "Look at me," she said more tenderly, reaching out for her. "Jay. I love you, and I am crazy worried about this. I was crazy worried already, when I thought you were putting your body through a wormhole only *two* afternoons a week, with an app invented by a physicist who puts dog shit in the hands of university professors and has a torpedo in her living room."

"I never should have told you about the torpedo," Jennifer said, as though that were the point. (She hadn't been able to resist texting Vinita a picture that morning.) Taking her cue from Vinita's I'm-your-friend approach, she softened. "Vee," she began. "Have you forgotten the position I was in when this started? Norman putting together a time log so he could sue for custody of the boys? And at work finally getting a chance to build One Stop, but having to do it the Bill Truitt way—"

"This isn't about your *reasoning*," Vinita said, cutting her off. "I know why you did it. But now I need to know how often you are using the app. Honestly. Every day? To be with the boys and at work? And what about Owen?" Jennifer could not stop the guilty expression that overtook her face at the mention of Owen's name. "Oh my God—how stupid am I? Owen mentioned to me last week that he was having dinner with you, and it was a Tuesday. . . . Are you using it to see him too? Are you in *three* places at once, not just two?"

"You're not asking for my reasoning?" Jennifer said, her voice growing high-pitched as a wave of indignation overtook her. "You don't care *why* I'm doing this? Or about what was happening in my life with work, or my kids? Or that maybe, just maybe, I wanted to have a little bit of something for *me*, to spend time with the man I'm falling in love with?" At this, tears sprang to her eyes. She liked the sound of *the man I'm falling in love with.* She'd never said it out loud before. Who could be indifferent to that?

Vinita, apparently.

"Do you think you are the only person who struggles with this?" Vinita asked, her eyes even brighter with anger now. "Do you have any fucking idea what I had to do to make this party happen for you tonight? I didn't use time travel. I ran to Patel Brothers in between seeing patients. I cooked every night this week. I stayed up late after the girls went to bed to put together fifty paper lanterns. I—"

"Had the nanny stay late?"

"What?"

"Did you have the nanny stay late? Or did you have your night sitter come and take the dry cleaning and have the housekeeper buy the groceries so you could put together paper lanterns late into the night in your impeccably clean, three-thousand-square-foot loft?"

In all their years of friendship, neither Jennifer nor Vinita had ever mentioned this—the wildly different fortunes that had befallen them since Vinita's marriage to Sean, and the inevitable ways in which Vinita's resources and Jennifer's constraints divided them. For a moment, Jennifer thought Vinita might slap her.

But instead, after an initial angry stiffening, her oldest friend's whole body collapsed into a sigh, her expression going from tight fury to a worn, crumpled look of hurt. Jennifer felt terrible. But for the first time in their conversation, she felt she had regained a little bit of the high ground too.

"I'm not the enemy, Jay," Vinita said, breaking the silence. "You know that, right? I'm your best friend. I'm not trying to get you to stop using this thing because I don't want you to have a full and happy life. It's because I want you to *have* a life. Have you considered the medical implications of this?"

"You've been checking me out," Jennifer said, "and I'm fine. I would have stopped if I weren't. I would stop."

"I've been giving you basic checkups on Friday afternoons, yes. But you are due for an MRI, and now that I know what's happening, or at least now that I've guessed what's happening, since you're still lying to me like an addict"—Jennifer rolled her eyes, but Vinita went on—"there are a lot of other tests we need to run too. For one thing, you think you're forty today, right?" Jennifer was unable to stop herself from emitting a impatient sigh. Of course she was forty! It was her birthday! She was beginning to worry about how long they'd been arguing. Pretty soon, people were going to suspect something.

"*Wrong,*" Vinita said. "If you have been using this thing the way I think you've been using it, you turned forty weeks ago. Nobody else may know that you are living three days for every one that passes for the rest of us. But your body knows. Keep this up, and you'll be fifty before I turn forty-three, and you'll get Alzheimer's when the boys are in their twenties!"

Jennifer knitted her brow. *In their twenties? Really?*

"You can't cheat the body, Jay," Vinita went on. "You may be able to be in three places on the same day, but you are not in three places *at once*, remember? You are in one place for six hours, and another place for six hours, and another place for six hours, and all those hours add up. Think of how tired you've been. Have you had memory loss? Exhaustion? Cognitive issues? Is your menstrual cycle going haywire?"

Jennifer had been about to interrupt, to argue that memory loss and exhaustion were hardly anything new, but Vinita's mention of her menstrual cycle stopped her cold. Jennifer's period had never come very regularly, but for a while now it had been coming often—weirdly often. At first it had been every three weeks, but lately, sometimes, it was every two. The periods were light, as hers had always been, and she'd just figured her body was stressed. But now it hit her: Her ovaries still counted time by minutes elapsed, not by daily rotations of the earth. By adding hours to her day almost every day, she had made her body as out of sync with the calendar everyone else kept as she was.

"All of us get a certain amount of time in our bodies," Vinita went on, gesturing to her own. "And that time *cannot* be extended. Dr. Sexton hasn't solved that problem yet. Keep this up, and you will age faster than everyone around you. Do you understand that? Is that what you want?"

Jennifer remained silent. Vinita had succeeded in scaring her. So she had chosen to concentrate on something she did well: math in her head. "Eight hundred hours, give or take," she pronounced. "Thirty-three days."

"What?" Vinita asked, flummoxed.

"It isn't three days for every one, Vee," she said. "It's an extra five hours a day, four days a week, with some more hours added for sleep." Vinita fixed her with a withering stare. "And yes, *fine*, with some more hours for Owen. But I'm pretty sure it hasn't added up to more than thirty-three days over the last twenty-five weeks. I could go back and look to make sure, but—"

"And?" Vinita said, her voice rising. "Your point is?"

"Let's call it five days per month. Just to make it easier. So what would be better? Four days? Three? I could cut back on the Owen weekday time. Let's say I did that only once a week." Jennifer squinted, continuing to calculate in her head, while Vinita's eyebrows shot up.

"Are you kidding me?" Vinita asked. "Did you hear anything I just said?"

"I could get it down to three days per month, I'm sure. Which is only thirty-six days a year! That's not so bad, right? And when the boys are in high school, I won't need it anymore."

"'When the boys are in high school'?" Vinita repeated incredulously.

"Or junior high, maybe?" Jennifer said.

"Give me that phone," Vinita replied.

"No," Jennifer said.

"Give it to me!" Vinita said, reaching over, yelling now. With Jennifer parrying and dodging as Vinita attempted to seize her phone, they soon moved into full view of the seated guests, and everybody was staring. Undaunted, Vinita took another swipe, and Jennifer whirled around, holding her bag to her chest with both hands wrapped tightly around it, going totally Gollum. "Get away from me, Vinita!" she said. "Stop it!"

The next thing she knew, Owen's arms were around her. But she fought him, too, lashing out until she freed herself from his embrace.

"Easy," he said, backing away. "Is this some kind of birthday tradition I don't know about? 'Cause you guys are scaring the customers."

"This is what happens," Jennifer said, opening her bag, locating her phone, and taking it out to stare at it, reassuring herself that it was still there, "when you *attack* someone with a surprise party. With the help of someone who knows I *hate* surprise parties."

"You hate surprise parties?" Owen said. He looked at Vinita. Then he looked at Jennifer. He was moving quickly from worried to pissed off, she could tell.

"Surprise!" Vinita said, throwing up sarcastic jazz hands. "She's full of them."

"Vee . . . ," Jennifer began.

"I'm leaving," Vinita said.

"But you're our host!" Owen said, backing up. "Why don't I give you guys a minute?" Then he turned to Jennifer. "You okay?" he asked, looking down and meeting her eyes. She nodded. As he headed back to his table, he threw some easygoing bullshit out to the assembled party, which seemed to reassure everyone.

Taking advantage of the interruption, Jennifer furtively stuffed her phone back into her bag. Then she took a deep breath and reached out for Vee.

"Stay?" she asked softly. "We can talk afterward, I promise. Or first thing tomorrow, if you want. No lies."

Vinita simply looked at Jennifer's bag. Pursing her lips, and looking so sad it made Jennifer's heart ache, she shook her head. "I don't believe you," she said. "Not anymore."

Without another word, Vinita grabbed her coat, grabbed Sean—who'd apparently had enough Indian martinis not to think too much of their premature exit—and left. And Jennifer could not deny a feeling of relief as she watched her best friend of twenty-two years walk right out the door.

eighteen | TROUBLE

THREE WEEKS LATER, Jennifer and Vinita still weren't speaking to each other. Or, to put it more accurately, Jennifer had made many attempts to speak to Vinita, but Vinita was not responding to any of them. The day after the party, Vinita had e-mailed and said that she wouldn't talk to Jennifer again until she agreed to stop using the app immediately and underwent a full battery of physical and cognitive tests administered by specialists qualified to do things like assess organ function and measure telomeres, whatever those were. Jennifer had pleaded with her by text, voice mail, and e-mail, and had even made the grand old-school gesture of showing up at Vinita's door. *Somewhere there is a woman,* Jennifer had written in a recent e-mail, *who misses her best friend.* Even in the face of that entreaty, however, Vinita remained resolute.

Jennifer was resolute too. There was no way her life could work anymore without the app. (At this point, she wasn't sure how it had ever worked without it in the first place.) It was awkward and painful for them both, saying curt hellos but otherwise avoiding each other at school. But they were at an impasse. *I just have to get to the end of the school year,* Jennifer thought, *and* then *I will stop using the app and take every test Vinita asks me to.* But then she thought about summer looming ahead, and juggling the boys' cobbled-together summer-camp schedules during those long months when working parents are burdened with filling the inevitable gaps, on top of the pressure of completing her fourth-quarter milestones at work, and she revised. *I just have to get to the* fall, she told herself, *when the One Stop center is done and school starts again, and then I will stop using the app and take every test Vinita asks me to.* It was not lost on Jennifer that, even with the app, she was still chasing the moment when she could finally be in the moment, and it was a moment that never seemed to arrive.

To add to her isolation, things with Owen were strained too, namely because after her birthday dinner, and after the fight with Vinita—which she'd managed to avoid explaining to him but had not quite put him at ease about—Owen had finally, definitively, outed the elephant in their room.

"I want to have a baby," he'd said.

It was the morning after her party. They were wrapped up together in bed like strands of a warm cinnamon roll, and Jennifer was only half awake. All she wanted to do was have morning sex and fall back asleep. So she was silent, hoping he'd let it drop. But he didn't. "If you aren't open to it," he went on quietly, but without a hint of hesitation in his voice, "I need to know. Soon. Or . . . now."

Now?

"Are you saying that if I don't want to have another baby, you'll break up with me?" She was lying with her back to him, in the spoon position, and turned to look up at him with a playful expression of mock surprise.

"I want to have a child of my own," he said earnestly, tucking a strand of hair behind her ear. "You know that."

And then Jennifer did a very bad thing. Turning away from him, she laughed.

"Wow," Owen said. "Seriously?"

"I'm sorry," she replied, attempting to diffuse her gaffe by pulling his arms more tightly around her, though trying to keep them above her belly, which hung from her ribs in a loose little heap of flab on the bed. (Jack had once written a poem called "Mommy's Squishy Belly," with lines like *Mommy's belly is like a piece of mashed potato you can sleep on.* She shuddered to think of what it would take to recover what was left of her figure if, at forty, she blew up her baby-belly balloon again.) "I just know so many women my age who are dying to have children, and they have this conversation with a guy on the first date. You know, 'If you aren't interested in having children, I need to know so I can go find somebody else.' I never thought a guy would be saying that to *me*. Guys aren't supposed to have biological clocks!" Owen laughed, too, snuggling into her neck and making an ominous ticking-clock sound in her ear, followed by the theme from *Jaws*. She loved him for laughing in that moment. He had such a good sense of humor about himself, and a gift for knowing when to nudge her and when to back off.

She loved him. She did. But how could she be sure it would last? She had loved Norman so much she'd wanted to marry him, and at the time her love had been as true a thing as she'd ever known. Ten years later, she'd had to leave him to survive. It seemed impossible that both of those things could be true, and yet they were. Which made it hard, now that she was disabused of the romanticism of her youth, to imagine having a baby with someone else. What if the love she felt for Owen left her? What if Owen's feelings changed? She could not bear the thought of being separated from another child, of fighting over "access" to her baby with another adult who claimed her or him. And what would it do to her boys to take Owen into their hearts, only to see him go? They were already exposed to that risk with Dina. If Norman's new choice of partner turned out to be unreliable, fine. Norman was unreliable anyway. If hers did, she feared it would shake the boys loose from the foundation she had worked so hard to construct.

She believed it was possible to love for life. It was getting harder and harder to imagine a world with Owen in it where she would not want to be by his side. But she also knew there were no guarantees in matters of the heart. Which meant that unless Owen could produce a crystal ball and prove to her without a doubt that they would never, ever part, her fear of their relationship ending very nearly exceeded her need for it.

Not to mention the fact that it was unlikely to be wise to be pregnant in a wormhole, with a uterus working on Wishful Thinking time.

She hadn't said any of this to Owen that morning, of course. She'd just started kissing him, turning her naked body toward his and hoping, afterward, that he would let it go.

But he hadn't. "We need to talk about this," he'd said a few days later. She wasn't ready to talk about it, so she'd been avoiding him instead. In the three weeks since her party, she'd seen him only three times, pleading that she was too busy with work deadlines and her kids. Which she was—especially if she didn't use the app to make time for their time together.

Strangest of all, however, was another estrangement, or, in this case, an absence. In the three weeks since her party, Jennifer had not seen or heard from Dr. Sexton. Three Saturdays now, she and the boys had trooped to Dr. Sexton's door and knocked on it, despite Jennifer's suggestion that if Dr. Sexton were around, she would have knocked on their door instead. The last Saturday Julien had insisted on bringing a bulky insect-collecting kit Jennifer had ordered for him online in anticipation of spring. Long after it was obvious that Dr. Sexton was not going to open her door, Julien stood stubbornly at her threshold, clinging to it and knocking.

"Come on, darling," she'd said gently. "I'll work on it with you, okay?"

"But I want to do it with Dr. Sexton," Julien had said.

Jennifer had raised her eyebrows and smiled. "What am I, chopped liver?"

Julien had turned to her and rolled his eyes. "Whatever, Mom."

"Really?" she'd said. "'Whatever'?" He shrugged his shoulders and began to walk down the hallway. "That's not respectful," she called after him. "And you know it."

He mumbled an apology. But as she trailed behind him on their way back to her apartment, Jennifer felt, as she had felt often lately, that for an eight-year-old he was acting an awful lot like a teenager. She couldn't remember ever having talked to her mother that way when she was his age. On the other hand, she thought, at Julien's age Jennifer had hardly ever been home. Every day after school she'd gone straight out to play with the kids in her neighborhood, riding bikes all over the subdivision if the weather was good, sometimes even playing on the railroad tracks near her house, leaving pennies for the trains to flatten and building forts out of the junk they found nearby. It was a world her mother had known nothing about, and that kind of freewheeling, unsupervised kid universe was unimaginable now—not just because they lived in New York. Modern parenting, it seemed, required witnessing, monitoring, and supervising every move your child made, and while part of Julien expected this of her, part of him was driven crazy by it. Little wonder he sometimes exhibited a teenager's need to differentiate himself from his mom, even at eight. Little wonder she sometimes felt that being able to be with her children all the time was better in theory than it was in practice.

Dr. Sexton's sudden and unexplained absence wasn't just worrisome to Julien, of course. Jennifer was worried too. She had tried to track her down by text, e-mail, and phone, and when she had asked the doorman if he knew anything, he said she'd asked him to hold all her mail and packages for an indefinite period of time. One day Jennifer saw Lucy out with someone she didn't know and approached him hoping to find out what was going on. But the young man turned out to be a dog walker who said Dr. Sexton had simply told him she had personal business to attend to. What that business was, or when she would be back again, was a mystery.

Vinita had noticed Dr. Sexton's absence too. In their only communication since the party—if you didn't count Vinita's e-mailed ultimatum about the app—Vinita had texted Jennifer to ask if she had heard from her.

Trying to tell on me? Jennifer had texted back.

Aren't you worried, Vinita had replied, ignoring Jennifer's jab, *that the woman who invented the thing you are hurling your body through multiple times a day has disappeared?*

It did, a bit. But what was she supposed to do about it? Dr. Sexton was not a child, and she had clearly planned for her journey, making all the necessary arrangements, so there was no reason to send out a search party. Jennifer assumed that when she returned, she would explain everything.

She just hoped it would be soon.

* * *

JENNIFER HAD CHOSEN TO cope with the sudden absence of the three most important people in her life by doing something she'd always excelled at: throwing herself into her work. It helped that it was an important, even fun, time to do this. The first phase of construction of the One Stop community center was complete, and to mark the occasion there was to be a ribbon cutting and an open house, showing off the building's large, enclosed interior courtyard (the rest of the center was still under construction), where agencies, nonprofits, and other service providers would have their outposts all in one place. After the ribbon cutting, the mayor, with Bill Truitt at his side, would update the press on their progress, which was impressive indeed, so impressive Jennifer couldn't wait to show it off. Alongside Alicia and Tim, she'd been working harder than ever over the past few weeks to prepare. She'd been working so hard, in fact, that even with the app she was having trouble keeping up.

Alicia, however, app-less and living in real time, arrived most mornings looking like she'd been run over by a truck. Her husband had recently taken on a new job as principal at an elementary school in Brooklyn, and the strain of two superhuman work schedules on one household was weighing heavily on her family. The morning of the event, however, Alicia arrived at the office rested and fresh, wearing one of her perfectly tailored ivory suits. She'd left early the day before when Jennifer had volunteered to take over the last items on her to-do list.

"Thank you so much for helping me out last night," she said when she walked in, putting her bag on the table in the conference room where they'd agreed to meet and handing Jennifer a tall iced coffee. "I felt like I hadn't seen my kids in weeks, never mind gotten any sleep."

"Of course," Jennifer said, feeling guilty for taking credit.

Tim approached, carrying two cardboard boxes in his hands. "One Stop tote bags for all the residents who attend," he said. He made a face as he produced a sample. "Lemon yellow. Bill's idea. Do you think they'll be a hit?"

Alicia took the tote bag. "I don't know," she said, pretending to hunt inside the bag. "Is there a voucher in here for kitchen repairs?"

"Come on, Alicia," Jennifer said, rising and attempting to rally herself and the troops. "Today we can finally show the residents that a promise from this agency, for once, has nearly become a reality!"

"*Nearly* become a reality," Alicia repeated, sighing as she handed the tote bag back to Tim and hoisted her own heavy bag onto her shoulder. "It's a little early for a press conference, if you ask me," she said, as they headed for the door. "Given the history of this agency, *nearly* isn't nearly good enough."

Even Alicia's spirits, however, couldn't help but lift when they got to the site. Many residents had brought their families, several local schools had brought classrooms of children to attend, and the place was bustling. Around the perimeter of the site, food trucks from all over Brooklyn had gathered seeking some positive press and were handing out everything from doughnuts to tacos. Multicolored flags flew brightly in the chilly April wind, and various local street performers whom Tim had recruited, from bongo players to human statues, were scattered throughout too. A local first-grade class was on the stage behind the podium, preparing to sing for the mayor when he arrived, their thirty energetic little bodies mostly under the control of their determined teachers. This was Tim's moment to shine, and Alicia and Jennifer both gave him a congratulatory squeeze for conjuring a lively happening out of a nonexistent budget, expertly using Twitter to rally parts of the city Alicia and Jennifer would never have known existed. Print reporters and satellite trucks had begun to gather around the dais. It wasn't big news, but it was news, and luckily for them not much else was happening in the city that day.

Because they were in Brooklyn, Alicia was in high demand, and soon began greeting old friends, chatting warmly with residents, and saying her hellos to the local press. With another twenty minutes to go before the press conference was scheduled to begin, Jennifer quietly excused herself. The community center she'd dreamed of for years was right in front of her, its vaulted glass skylights glittering in the sun. She wanted to stand inside it.

It was still a shell, of course. The floor of the hexagonal interior courtyard was unfinished concrete, and the offices where various agencies and nonprofits would have their outposts (like a philanthropic food court, Tim had said) were nothing more than skeletal structures, without walls or the large glass windows that would eventually encase them. But the space was airy and peaceful, and to Jennifer, who had spent countless hours poring over blueprints and flowcharts, it soared with a sense of purpose too. She could see it as it would look when it was finished, filled with social workers and government employees and nonprofit agencies, residents filing in to do business, pay their rent, or take a class, and seeing her vision so close to becoming a reality filled her with pride.

She took out her phone and was about to snap a picture to send to Owen, when she heard the doors to the center open behind her. She turned to see Bill Truitt walk in, wearing a lemon-yellow tie.

"Fancy meeting you here," he said. "Admiring your handiwork?"

"Your handiwork," she said. "The building looks fabulous."

He walked over and stood next to her. "I like walking around when a project is at this stage," he said. "I like seeing it in a way few other people ever will. Like a secret between me and the building, and, of course, the team who takes part in it." He turned to her with a conspiratorial smile. "You probably won't appreciate this metaphor," he added, "but it's like seeing a woman in her underwear."

Jennifer did her best to smile back. "Not how I would put it," she said, "but I do see what you mean." Jennifer had never been part of building something from the ground up, and while the underwear analogy made her cringe, she could see what Bill meant about the intimacy. It had been moving and satisfying, in a way she hadn't experienced before, to witness the physical space taking shape.

"I'll leave you to it," Bill said after a minute, heading for the door. "You should be very proud."

"Thank you," Jennifer said. "I am."

A FEW MINUTES LATER Jennifer was outside again, checking in with the mayor's assistant by text. Tim brought her a taco.

"Who's Alicia talking to now?" Tim asked, taking a gigantic bite out of an organic corn dog. On the opposite side of the building site, Alicia was engaged in an intense conversation with a young man whose back was turned to them.

"I don't know," she answered, "but it looks serious." Jennifer strained to see. The man handed Alicia something, and she studied it intently. When she looked up, Jennifer saw an expression of concern—even alarm—on her face. She was looking for Jennifer, and when their eyes met, Jennifer gave her a little wave, raising her eyebrows inquiringly. Alicia waved her over. Jennifer handed Tim the uneaten portion of her taco.

"Hold down the fort for a second," Jennifer told him.

"But the mayor is going to be here any minute now!" Tim cried.

"So go over to the dais and make sure the news crews have what they need," she replied. "Hold Bill's hand. Or, better yet, bring him a corn dog."

As she drew closer, Jennifer recognized the young man Alicia was talking to. It was Noel, Amalia's grandson, the one Alicia had encouraged to find work at the building site back in December.

"You remember Noel?" Alicia said as Jennifer joined them. She spoke in a markedly low tone. Taking Alicia's cue, Jennifer nodded and said a quiet hello. Noel looked nervous and avoided Jennifer's gaze.

"Well, I was just asking him how it was going," Alicia said, "working on the site, about benefits, conditions, et cetera. It all sounded fabulous," she went on, "until he told me what he was getting paid." She handed Jennifer a pay stub. *Noel Campusano, Forklift Operator.* Alicia pointed to the hourly wage. Fourteen dollars per hour.

Jennifer did a double take. Fourteen dollars an hour? Noel had a forklift operator's license. He should have been earning nineteen.

"This can't be right," she said, staring.

"I know," Alicia said. "That's what I was telling Noel." Noel's check was issued not by the city but by the contractor for the residents' job program—which just so happened to be Bill's private foundation, BTE for Good. The accounting was done by a junior employee named Greg Schloss—a really nice guy, Jennifer thought. Every pay period, Greg submitted BTE for Good's certified payroll reports to Jennifer, and, upon receipt, Jennifer wrote a check to BTE for Good from the city. According to those payroll reports, Noel and all the other forklift operators had been paid nineteen dollars an hour. Where had the other five dollars an hour gone?

Her stomach was churning.

Alicia spoke to Noel quickly in Spanish, and he rejoined his friends. Jennifer and Alicia moved away from the crowd until they found a quiet spot.

"Can he bring us more of these?" Jennifer asked. "He has friends working on the site, too, right? I need to see all of his pay stubs, and we should look at others if we can. But we need to do it quietly. We can't let anybody else know, not until I have a chance to figure out what's going on. And we can't tell Noel or the others why we want the stubs. Okay?"

Grim-faced, Alicia nodded. In the near distance, the sound of sirens approached. It was the mayor's motorcade. From the dais, Tim was motioning frantically for them to hurry up as a band began dishing up the requisite fanfare. It was disconcerting, the hoopla, in light of what they'd just found.

"After the press conference," Alicia said, "I'll get Noel to help me collect as many as I can so we can at least round up a larger sample." Jennifer nodded. The two of them hurried toward the dais as the mayor exited his limousine, greeted by Bill Truitt, in his tailored dark navy suit and lemon-yellow tie, grinning widely as he shook the mayor's hand. "I'm sure it's just a clerical error," Alicia said. "I know he's not the easiest person to work for," she added, turning to Jennifer, "but Bill is a good man."

Jennifer said nothing. But as she watched Bill take the stage next to the mayor, preening for the cameras and looking every bit the politician himself, she couldn't help wondering if there was a far bigger secret between Bill Truitt and his building than what it looked like in its underwear.

BILL LEFT THE OFFICE at five that day, first to go home and pack (or to pick up the suitcase Mrs. Bill had packed for him), then to head to the airport to catch the red-eye to London for

an international conference on poverty. He was buzzed and
upbeat after the press conference, which had already resulted
in some positive hits in the media that afternoon, and had
even hinted at taking everyone out for a celebratory lunch
when he got back. Jennifer's, Alicia's, and Tim's moods,
however—Jennifer had told Tim about the pay-stub discrep-
ancy on their way back to the office that morning—were less
than ebullient. As soon as Bill left the building, the three of
them gathered solemnly in the conference room.

Tim brought a stack of file boxes, Jennifer brought her
laptop, and Alicia brought a small cache of pay stubs in a plain
manila folder, having collected as many as she could from Noel
and other men he knew who worked at the site. At Jennifer's
suggestion, Alicia had simply told them that the city needed to
double-check the deduction amounts for Social Security and
Medicare—no big deal. Trusting Alicia more than they would
have any other agency employee, the men had readily agreed.

As Jennifer and Tim sat down at the long conference table,
Alicia closed the door behind her. She then pulled a chair over
to block the entrance to the room. Jennifer and Tim
exchanged a look. Outside, the fickle spring clouds were
quickly turning from streaks of yellow to banks of gray.

From the manila folder Alicia produced the pay stubs.
She also took out a thick packet with a cover sheet that read:
New York City Housing Authority, Office of the Inspector General.
She pushed it in front of Jennifer. Something about the way
she did it, and the look on her face as she did, put Jennifer on
her guard. They'd all had the long afternoon hours to think
about this, without being able to breathe a word to one
another. What had been going through Alicia's mind?

"'Contractors and Vendors Anti-Corruption Guide,'"
Jennifer read.

"You're familiar?" Alicia asked pointedly.

Jennifer nodded, avoiding her gaze. She knew this was a document she should have memorized front to back, but her review of it when she had joined the agency years ago had been cursory at best, and since Bill had arrived, she had to admit, she'd been reluctant to review it. She knew their practices hadn't been what they should be, particularly in fast-tracking contracts with nonprofits and vendors owned and operated by people Bill knew. But he'd insisted—and threatened the loss of the bonuses if she didn't go along. And so she had. Not just for the money, but for the results. But now this.

Jennifer opened the packet briskly. "Most of it is about proper bidding practices, and bribery," she said as she flipped through. When she came to the page she was looking for, she stopped. "Here's the passage that might be relevant," she added, relieved that she was able to find it so quickly.

Jennifer showed the document to Tim, who read aloud. "'Pay prevailing wages, where legally required. Prevailing wage violations and the submissions to NYCHA of falsified payrolls are against the law and prosecuted to the fullest extent of the law.'" He looked up. "So if the payroll says Noel is being paid nineteen dollars an hour and he's getting fourteen, it's being falsified. And somebody is pocketing the difference."

Jennifer opened Excel on her laptop. "It's not a new scheme," she said matter-of-factly. "If what we think is going on is going on, that is."

"I don't think we know what's going on," Alicia said. "Not yet." Jennifer kept her eyes on her laptop screen and nodded. Tim pulled the certified payrolls out of their files.

"The first thing," Jennifer said, "is to see whether or not Noel's paycheck was an isolated mistake."

In the half hour that followed, the three of them set up a sort of assembly line, checking and double-checking payroll records and bank balances, attempting to reconcile the pay stubs with the funds that had been paid. The more they looked, the more Jennifer's head began to ache; the more they found, the more her chest felt like it was being squeezed into a barrel of concrete. To begin with, Noel's stub wasn't an isolated error. That was obvious right away, as none of the other residents' paychecks were right either. What she couldn't understand was that no two of them were wrong in the same way.

"It's all over the place," Tim said. Jennifer nodded in agreement. Some workers, like Noel, were being paid fourteen dollars an hour. But a friend of Noel's was making seventeen, while another forklift operator was earning twelve. It was a small sample size, but the discrepancies were glaring.

"Noel had a friend who just got hired at twelve," Alicia said. "That's why he showed me what he was earning. To ask why."

"Wait a minute," Tim said. Studying the stubs, he began to reorganize them. "What if what these guys get paid is tied to when they were hired?" Alicia and Jennifer leaned in. "Noel was hired in December, meaning he was part of the second round of residents hired through the program. All of those guys are getting fourteen. But the guy who's earning seventeen came on at the very start."

"And the new hire is at twelve," Jennifer said, nodding, "but all the while the certified payroll stays the same: nineteen dollars an hour."

"Which means that whoever is taking the difference between what the city is paying and what the residents are getting has been getting greedier," Tim said. "With every new hire, they push the wage down more."

"So?" Alicia said.

"So," Jennifer said, "somebody at BTE for Good, whether it's Bill or one of his administrators, is getting rich." She did some mental math. "How many residents have we employed at the building site?" Jennifer asked Tim.

"Close to a hundred by now," he replied.

"Which means, if this is widespread—say somebody is shaving off between two and seven dollars per hour, on a fifty-hour workweek; call it four-fifty an hour per employee, just to get a general idea—that's as much as forty-five thousand dollars per pay period. Maybe more. Which could mean as much as half a million dollars so far."

"Oh my God," Tim said.

For a moment, there was silence.

"It seems to me we should identify *all* the points where the money could be disappearing," Alicia said, looking directly at Jennifer. "Not just at BTE. I know Greg Schloss, the accountant. He has an impeccable reputation." She paused, seeming to bite her tongue. "And Bill. I know he likes to cut corners sometimes, but he does it in order to get things done. And what he's done for the community with the foundation—you have no idea." She paused again. "Not to mention the fact that he's got more money than the mayor does. It just doesn't make sense." Jennifer had to agree with Alicia there. "We need answers from *anyone* who is in a position to reroute funds," Alicia continued. "On our side or his. And we need to take this to Bill and tell him everything we know. Right away."

Jennifer felt Alicia's and Tim's eyes on her. For a minute, she couldn't understand why. And then she realized. *Anyone in a position to reroute funds. On our side or on his.* Alicia was talking about her.

Suspecting me is ridiculous! she wanted to shout. Always, in these cases, the most likely culprit was the entity that acted as the go-between, in this case BTE for Good. It was much too difficult to cook the books on the city's end. Not only was suspecting Jennifer ridiculous, but they couldn't take this to Bill, not yet. What if he was the guilty one?

She opened her mouth to speak. But just as she did, there

was an explosion in her head—a white-hot burst that rocked the inside of her skull like a sonic boom. She felt like she was having her ears boxed and raised her hands to cover them, emitting a little cry. And suddenly she heard the sound of city traffic passing her by, as though she were outside. Sirens. Honking horns. The usual New York clatter. Jennifer looked up at Tim and Alicia, who were talking as though nothing had changed. *Didn't they hear it too?* she thought. And then she knew. It was happening again. The bleed-through.

Her senses were now feeding her two sets of data, just as they had when she and Alicia were at Amalia's apartment. In one data set, her eyes were scanning a darkening city sidewalk, a solid gray mass of cloud cover above. Her ears fed her chatter from another woman walking alongside her—it was Tara, Julien's soccer pal Frank's mom. And her bare arms, feeling the chill of a damp breeze, telegraphed to her brain that she ought to put her rain jacket on. In the other, her eyes registered the baffled looks Tim and Alicia were giving her, her ears strained to hear their inquiries, and her body felt stuffy and hot inside the windowless conference room. The two inputs rattled and snapped and made nonsense of each other, and Jennifer was caught in the crossfire. Squeezing her hand around her phone, which she held in her lap beneath the conference table, Jennifer looked down, desperate for an anchor. What day was it? Wednesday, she told herself. The day she picked the boys up from Norman at five thirty. What time was it now? She willed herself to focus on the numbers on the screen: 5:35. She would have just picked them up at the park. So where were the boys? She had heard only Tara's voice.

"Give me a minute?" Jennifer heard herself to say to Alicia and Tim. "I just need to think." Alicia accepted this, though clearly only for a minute. She and Tim returned to the paperwork, casting glances her way as they chatted quietly.

Grateful, Jennifer turned to face a blank wall in the room and closed her eyes, letting the city block fully occupy her vision. She saw that it was West Eleventh, her street. They must be walking back to her place from the park, she thought. But where were Julien and Jack? She tried to look in front of her, but she had to wait until the Jennifer walking down that block looked. She could see only what her other eyes were seeing, apparently, not choose where to point them. Finally her self on the sidewalk looked away from Tara, who was serving up some delicious gossip about a teacher and the psychologist at the elementary school, and peered up the block, her eyes searching and finding the boys, a habit as ingrained in her as breathing. They were at least half a block away, running around on the sidewalk with Tara's son, Frank. Who was watching them? Then she saw Norman and Tara's husband, Josh, ambling nonchalantly a few paces behind. The boys were tossing a football. How many times had she told Norman never to let them do that on the street? She heard herself say something to that effect to Tara, who rolled her eyes, muttered something about how useless Josh was, and kept on telling her story. Norman and Josh were on boy duty, evidently, while she and Tara were bringing up the rear.

"Jennifer?" Alicia's voice was like an insistent tapping on her buckling brain. *"Jennifer!"* Alicia repeated, upgrading from tapping to pounding. "Are you done 'thinking' now?"

Jennifer nodded, willing herself to open her eyes. She turned to Alicia, made eye contact, and smiled, albeit weakly, as Tara's face and voice continued to sputter and snap over Alicia's visage. She had to make this stop, she thought. She had to be at work now. This was far too important. As she struggled to respond, however, she saw the boys again. And then she saw the football, sailing into the air as Julien pursued it dangerously close to the curb. He caught it like a wide receiver, on his toes, just barely keeping to the curb's edge. Why wasn't Norman saying anything?

"*Stop it!*" she yelled, loudly enough for them to hear her over the city din.

Unfortunately, however, the voice she found was not the one the boys could hear. Instead she had yelled at the top of her lungs right there in the conference room.

"Stop what?" Alicia said. "Asking you tough questions? And why are you *yelling?*"

Gingerly, Tim put a hand on her arm. It felt incredibly strange, as, just in that moment, it had also begun to rain, and her forearm felt chilly and wet even underneath his warm, dry touch. She had to leave the room, she thought. She would tell them she had to go to the bathroom. She had just begun to rise when another boom pushed her back down into her seat again. And then, just like that, it was gone. The boys, the drizzling rain, the sidewalk, Norman and Josh walking ahead—all of it switched off like a light, disappearing from view.

She was in the conference room again, all of her.

Alicia repeated her question. "What do you want us to stop, Jennifer?" Still reeling, Jennifer could do nothing but give her a blank look. "I thought about this all afternoon," Alicia continued levelly. "Nobody has had more time with those books than you. Especially at night, after the rest of us are gone. I have never been able to understand the hours you keep here, or why you spend so much time in the office alone. Something isn't right, and Bill is too easy for you to blame."

Jennifer tried to concentrate. The last thing she needed right now was to seem evasive. But why, *why* hadn't she asked Dr. Sexton about the bleed-through when she'd had the chance? Especially now that Dr. Sexton was nowhere to be found? Was it over now? Was it going to start again?

She couldn't think about it. She had to focus on the reality at hand.

Squaring her shoulders, Jennifer met Alicia's gaze. "Of course something isn't right," she said, finding her ground. "But the foundation is in the middle, not me. The checks aren't cut to me. They're cut to BTE for Good. I know it's the last thing any of us wants to believe, but it happens. In New Orleans after Katrina, a nonprofit took government money to rebuild houses and pocketed it. The San Francisco school district was defrauded by an education charity in 2010. It's always the same. A charity takes city money, and a bad apple siphons chunks of it off before it gets where it's supposed to go."

"I understand that," Alicia said, barely masking her impatience. "But I hope you agree that we should examine the entire process, from bottom to top. *And* that we should take this to Bill. Now."

"No," Jennifer said. "We should take it to the Office of the Inspector General. Not to Bill. The payroll company we are using was forced down our throats by Bill, too—don't you remember that? Even though BTE for Good had been using a different one for years?"

"You've already convicted him," Alicia said, emotion in her voice. "Which would be an excellent way to detract attention from yourself."

Jennifer was just about to protest when she felt her head slammed sideways again. This time the force of the signal was overwhelming, the invading images and sounds even stronger than before. There was nothing she could do but give in to them.

They had crossed Washington Street and were headed toward Greenwich. The football continued to be tossed around close enough that she could see it, but not close enough for her to interfere. And the story Tara was telling was juicy enough to keep her hanging back and letting it slide.

Suddenly Tim's voice was in her ear. She was so immersed in her other reality, she almost jumped out of her chair.

"Are you okay?" he was asking. "Do you want me to get you some water or something?" His question came as if over a great distance. She felt him rub her arm, saw him peer into her face, but she couldn't shake the other inputs enough to answer him. Her arms were pricked with goose bumps from the wind. She could feel the rain in her hair.

Alicia looked concerned now, too, though she was clearly struggling to balance her concern over Jennifer's odd behavior with her suspicion regarding its timing.

"Jennifer?" Alicia said. "You look pale."

Pushing back her chair, Jennifer got to her feet.

"I'm sorry," she managed. "But you have to excuse me."

"Now?" Alicia said, standing too.

"Yes," Jennifer said. "I'm sorry. But I have to . . . go to the bathroom. I'll be back."

She lurched for the door and willed herself into the hallway. And then it happened. Standing on the carpeted floor, staring down the featureless office hallway that seemed to extend into eternity, she saw it. The ball, lofting into the air just as the boys approached the driveway of a busy parking garage. The image, reflected in the fun-house mirror meant to serve as a warning to pedestrians, of a massive black SUV, lurching over the steep incline out of the garage and accelerating toward the street. And Jack, desperate to get the ball away from Frank and Julien, seizing the opportunity to run after it when, for a reason he obviously hadn't registered, the two older boys suddenly stopped short at the entrance to the garage. And Norman, leaping into action, only a few feet away from Jack but not there yet, not to where little Jack, her baby boy who was hardly the size of a fire hydrant—distracted, off-balance, and seeing only the ball—would be. Then she heard the terrible sound of brakes, screeching.

She screamed, or thought she did. The hallway was strangely still. Her scream had been like the scream in a dream, the one you labor to extract from yourself but can barely manage to whisper. The stifled scream that wakes you up from a nightmare.

Then, suddenly, like a nightmare, it was gone. Norman, Jack, the SUV, all of it. "No!" she cried out, reaching for the vision, clawing at the air, trying to bring it back. *Jack!* What happened next? What was happening now? Had the driver seen him? Had Norman gotten to him in time? Was Jack all right, or . . . ?

Or?

Right there in the hallway, she began to run.

"Jennifer!" she heard Alicia call after her. "That is not the way to the bathroom!"

My boy ran in front of an SUV after a ball! she wanted to yell. She was calling herself to come. That was why the signal was so strong. That was why the bleed-through had happened. Something terrible had happened. She had to go. She had to go.

She had to go.

"Jennifer!" Alicia repeated, in full high-school principal mode. "You come back here right now!"

But Jennifer didn't answer her. She just ran faster.

MOMENTS LATER, JENNIFER WAS safely inside her secret bathroom. The problem was, she had no idea what to do there.

One thing was clear: she had to get herself to West Eleventh Street. She had to warn Norman or throw herself in front of the oncoming SUV. Could she change something that had already happened? What *had* happened? She didn't know, but she couldn't wait to find out.

Hands shaking, she opened up her calendar. As always on Wednesdays, she had scheduled a Wishful Thinking appointment to leave work at 8:00 p.m. and arrive at her apartment at five fifteen, which gave her time to walk to the park (where Norman and the boys always went when the weather was nice) and pick up the boys at five thirty. Was it as simple as changing the appointment to leave now, rather than at eight, and going back with the knowledge of what was about to happen? But the guide Dr. Sexton had given her had been very specific: Wishful Thinking appointments, once made, could never be altered. This was made plain when she opened the entry and searched in vain for an EDIT button.

That appointment was set. Of course it was. She had already kept it.

There was only one person who could help her now.

Jennifer dialed. The phone rang five times, as usual, and then Dr. Sexton's voice mail picked up, just as it had for weeks. Jennifer let out a wail and slapped the counter with her fist. "Dr. Sexton!" she said after the beep. "Where are you? Jack's in danger and I have to go back, or go there, now, to where he is. But I'm already there. I was already there, and I didn't do anything." A sob caught in her throat. "I *have* to go to him. Please call me right away. Please." The image of the black SUV hurtling out of the garage, and of Jack racing toward the ball in its path, kept running through her head. Her breath was coming faster now. Panic whipped through her nervous system, needling her blood. She knew she had time—she could manipulate time, for Pete's sake; there wasn't *actually* a rush— but she couldn't bear another second of not knowing what had happened to her little boy. What if, at that very moment, he was being rushed into an ambulance? Better to summon the wormhole than to wait. But better *not* to land in her bathroom in her apartment, so close to her arrival at the same location at five fifteen. So where? As always, she accessed her mental map of bathrooms in New York.

There was an APT across the street from the park, she remembered, a five-minute walk from where she needed to be by 5:35, outside the parking-garage entrance on West Eleventh Street between Washington and Greenwich. She had used the APT once to travel to an appointment with Owen while Melissa played at the park with the boys. If she arrived there fifteen minutes ahead of time, she should have plenty of time to get to the parking garage before the boys did. She searched her saved locations in Google Maps and pulled up the coordinates.

Fingers trembling, she began to type. *Neighborhood Park APT, Wednesday, April 6, 5:20 p.m. to 6:00 p.m.* Once she'd either intervened to rescue Jack or seen that he was okay (she didn't want to consider any other alternative), she'd travel back to the bathroom at the time she'd left it, and Alicia and Tim would never know she'd been gone.

The seconds ticked by. Jennifer wished she had a watch with a second hand. It would be much less startling when her appointments began if she did. "Jack," she whispered to herself, just as she had whispered Julien's name the first time she used the app. "Jack, Jack, Jack."

Then she felt it. Her body heating up, almost seeming to liquefy. The roaring in her ears, like her blood had turned into jet fuel. Her fingers adhering to the screen and the wormhole opening, its swirling, crackling tunnel of blue light enveloping her.

And then she was gone.

THE APT, THANK GOD, was empty. Because the instant Jennifer materialized there, her phone began to screech. *EEEK! EEEK! EEEK!* It was the warning that had gone off the only other time she had wandered within five hundred yards of herself, and it was blaring now at an ear-splitting pitch. *STOP! STOP! STOP!* the phone's screen flashed in red.

WHEN USING WISHFUL THINKING, YOU MUST MAINTAIN A DISTANCE OF FIVE HUNDRED YARDS FROM THE ORIGIN OF YOUR WISHFUL THINKING APPOINTMENT. REPEAT: YOU CANNOT GO WITHIN FIVE HUNDRED YARDS OF NEIGHBORHOOD APT, OR A CAUSALITY VIOLATION MAY OCCUR.

"I know," Jennifer shouted at her phone, "but this is an emergency!" Her ears were smarting from the unbearable, stabbingly shrill sound. How could she have been so dumb? She had arrived early, fifteen minutes before the incident occurred on the street. But that had also placed her squarely within the five-hundred-yard radius that her other self, walking to the park at that very minute, was bound to occupy. When she walked out of the APT, she would be making such a commotion it would be impossible not to attract attention. What if Norman saw her? The boys? How was she going to get anywhere near Jack without ditching her phone?

Pulling her jacket over her face like a white-collar criminal avoiding the paparazzi, Jennifer squeezed out of the APT as soon as its door had opened wide enough to permit it and began to run—out of the park and in the opposite direction from her apartment—as fast as her legs could take her.

She crossed Greenwich. She crossed Washington, pedestrians and traffic cops cursing her. She was about to cross the West Side Highway, wondering if she would eventually have to dive into the Hudson River to make it stop, when her phone fell silent at last.

There was a bench at the corner. Jennifer sat on it. She could barely catch her breath.

Why hadn't she thought of this before? There was no way for her to get to Jack—with her other self only half a block behind—with her phone in hand. There was only one thing she could do: hide her phone somewhere and come back for it later. The idea of being separated from it terrified her—she had not let it out of her sight for more than a few minutes in the last six months. But it had to be done.

Jennifer was looking for a planter she could stash it in, when the phone rang. "Dr. Sexton!" Jennifer cried, picking up. It was 5:25 now. She had only ten minutes left. "Thank you so

much for calling. Something has happened, or I think
something has happened—"

"Jennifer," Dr. Sexton replied, cutting her short. "First of
all, I am sorry I have not been returning your calls of late.
Please forgive me." There was a pause. There was something
about the tone of Dr. Sexton's voice—both weary and resigned
—that frightened her.

"Are you all right?" Jennifer asked.

"No," Dr. Sexton said, her voice dropping to an uncharacteristically low register. "Susan has cancer. We found out just
after your birthday."

"Oh no," Jennifer breathed. "I'm so sorry."

"It's very serious," Dr. Sexton said. "She went into
treatment immediately, and she has needed all my care."

"What kind?" Jennifer asked. "What stage is it?" The
questions she had been asked again and again when her
mother had been ill.

"I will tell you everything when we see each other, and I
promise it will be soon," Dr. Sexton said. "I gathered from your
message, however, that time is short, so perhaps we should
focus our attention on the crisis at hand. Where are you now?"

Jennifer explained as quickly as she could. The bleed-
through, the everything-at-once horror of what she had seen,
and how, just as Jack had leaped into harm's way, the
transmission had suddenly stopped. "So you see," she said. "I
had to come."

"No," Dr. Sexton replied brusquely, "I do not see. I did not
write the Wishful Thinking guidelines for your entertainment. I wrote them for your safety, and for the safety of
everyone around you. You must schedule a return appointment to your office now, to leave immediately. Once you are
back, you must then do everything exactly as you had
planned."

"How can I?" Jennifer asked. "What if the bleed-through happened because something was about to happen to Jack and I was trying to tell myself to come, to rescue him?"

"Nonsense! What you have experienced is nothing more than a coincidence. Your actions in response to this coincidence, however, have the potential to be catastrophic. What has happened has happened. If you interfere, it is possible you will make things much worse. What if you distract Norman, who otherwise would have rescued Jack? What if Julien sees you and is so shocked—knowing you are also walking behind him—that he attempts to run to you and he is hurt? What if you are the one who is hit? The scenarios are endless, but they share one commonality: they disrupt the relationship between cause and effect."

"But what if I don't go, and Jack is . . . is . . ." Jennifer fell silent. She couldn't say the words. She let out a little cry, and her eyes filled with tears.

"Jennifer," Dr. Sexton said gently. "Search your heart, my dear. Do *you* believe that Jack is gone?"

Dr. Sexton had said what Jennifer could not, and it was almost unbearable to hear it said out loud. The cars on the West Side Highway whizzed past, their indifferent drone sickening her. Soon a drizzle would begin to fall. How many times had she had a scare with one of her boys like the one she'd witnessed? In New York, walking down the sidewalks and crossing busy streets, it happened more than she liked to admit. But this time she had seen it start to happen, and then she had screamed, and then—nothing. *Nothing.* In that moment, the moment the vision had left her, she did not recall a feeling of relief. But she did not recall a feeling of her heart breaking, of being ripped into pieces that would never mend, of dying a little death of her own.

"Are you saying I would know?" she asked. She stood.

Time was running short. She needed to hang up. She needed to go.

"Susan's brain tumor was discovered," Dr. Sexton said, "because one evening while she was running water for a bath in our upstairs bedroom, she fell. Fainted dead away. She did not hit her head, or fall into the water unconscious, or otherwise injure herself too badly. But it was a terrible scare."

"And you were there?"

"I was in the house, yes, but downstairs. I heard nothing. The running water muffled the sound. It was not until I observed that the bathwater had been running for a strangely long period of time that I went upstairs and discovered what had happened. I, too, however, had had an experience like the one you have described. Earlier in *my* day, while on a Wishful Thinking appointment at the same hour in Paris, I had experienced bleed-through, as you call it—though the proper term, I believe, is *entanglement*."

"You saw her fall?"

"I could not have seen that, as I wasn't there. I saw myself discover her on the bathroom floor. I was in the middle of a performance at the Palais Garnier, when suddenly I was also climbing the stairs of the house and then finding Susan unconscious. But before I was able to see whether she was all right or not, the signal stopped."

"But don't you see?" Jennifer cried. "This means it *isn't* just a coincidence. It *is* you, in one time, trying to signal to yourself, in another, that something bad has happened!"

"Not a conscious signal," Dr. Sexton said, "though the traumatic event may explain why the entanglement was so pronounced. It has happened to me, however, at other times, when there was no significant event to trigger it."

"It happened to me once before too," Jennifer said. "Why didn't you tell me?"

"I didn't think it would happen to you," Dr. Sexton replied, "since you are using the app so infrequently." Jennifer winced. Caught in her lie, again. How reckless she'd been! "When we have more time, I will share my theory regarding what causes it. All you need to know now is that I am absolutely convinced of two things. One, I would have known if Susan's fall had been bad enough to kill her. I would have *known* that she was dead. There is no science behind that, but I believe it all the same." Jennifer looked at the clock on her phone: 5:28. Very soon, she would have to decide what to do, or she would not have any choice left. "Two," Dr. Sexton continued, "whatever action you take, it cannot change the outcome."

"How can that be? What if I took the football before they even left the park?" Standing up, convinced by her own argument, Jennifer began hunting again for a hiding place for her phone.

"The only solutions to the laws of physics that can occur locally in the real universe are those that are globally self-consistent!" Dr. Sexton barked, exasperated. "This principle allows one to build a local solution to the equations of physics *only* if that local solution can be extended to be part of a global solution, which is well defined throughout the nonsingular regions of space-time!"

Jennifer sat back down again.

"I don't know about all that," she said. "But *you* are being inconsistent. On the one hand, you are telling me that if I go to Jack, I could put everyone in more danger. On the other, you are telling me that if I go back, I can't change anything."

There was another pause. "I didn't want to say this," Dr. Sexton said cautiously, "when you are in such a fragile state. But I suppose I must." Jennifer waited. "You are correct in the contradiction you just described. The Novikov self-consistency principle is, at best, untested theory, and, at worst, scientific gobbledygook. I truly do not know which. We have ventured into territory that goes beyond my knowledge—beyond, I believe, the meager cognitive capabilities of any human being. When I saw Susan fall, everything in me wanted to rush back in time to her side, to arrive before she fainted or at least to catch her in my arms. But somehow I knew—or at least I believed—that if I did, the consequences could be far worse than anything I could imagine. I am asking you to accept something very difficult here, Jennifer," Dr. Sexton continued. "I am asking you accept the limits of knowledge, of our ability to control events. I'm asking you to let go of your belief that you have a choice. Because you don't. You must let things unfold as they have, and recognize that you are part of a design far beyond your, or my, understanding."

Jennifer tried to imagine doing what Dr. Sexton was asking her to do. Return to her office. Wait there until eight o'clock and keep her Wishful Thinking appointment to go home at five fifteen. Change clothes and go meet Norman and the boys at the park. Listen to Tara's story while keeping one eye on the boys. Lamely express her frustration at Norman's less-than-rigorous approach. And then watch, from a distance, as the football shot into the air, Jack ran to get it, and the SUV lurched forward with her child directly in its path, all while doing nothing but screaming his name, because to do more—to run to him, to take the football away, to interfere with events as she had already seen them—would be to put Jack and everyone around him in a kind of danger she couldn't begin to comprehend.

"I don't know if I can," Jennifer said in a whisper. Tears filled her eyes.

"You must," Dr. Sexton said.

I would know, she told herself, trying to believe it. *I would know.*

"Go back to your office, my dear," Dr. Sexton continued. "And tomorrow, we will talk about it over tea."

"All right," Jennifer said weakly. She wiped her eyes with a tissue, just as the light rain began to fall. "Though something pretty bad is happening at work too," she added, remembering for the first time what she was walking back into.

"All the more reason," Dr. Sexton said, "for you to go back to where you are supposed to be."

twenty | REAL TIME

AT 5:42 P.M., with the usual fireworks, Jennifer arrived back at the secret bathroom.

Standing in the doorway, openmouthed, was Alicia.

Alicia had found her secret bathroom. And Alicia evidently had just witnessed what she did there.

Her dark skin was as pale as Jennifer had ever seen it. "What on earth," Alicia said quietly, breaking the silence at last, "was that?"

Jennifer tried to remember what it looked like—what had Alicia seen? She'd seen Dr. Sexton do it only once, months ago, when she had demonstrated the app for Vinita. A tunnel of blue light? A human body being sucked into it and spit back out again? Was there an excuse she could make? A way to convince Alicia she was seeing things? Staring back at Alicia, Jennifer thought not. Alicia was not the type of person to doubt her own senses.

"Alicia," Jennifer began cautiously, "I can explain."

"Do," Alicia said, trembling slightly but steely too.

"It's an app," Jennifer said. "A time-travel application that a physicist invented. It lets me, or anybody who uses it, be in more than one place at the same time."

"A time-travel application?" Alicia repeated. "Like, from the app store? That nobody else on the planet has ever heard of? Just how dumb," she asked, venom in her voice now, "do you think I am?"

"I know it sounds crazy," Jennifer said, taking a step toward her. Alicia put out a hand, motioning for her to stay right where she was. "I didn't believe it either, not at first. But it's real. As for my having it and your never having heard of it —it's a long story, but I can explain that too. And if you don't believe me, I could show you; I could demonstrate it. . . ." Jennifer held up her phone.

"No!" Alicia said, taking a step backward. "I don't want to be anywhere near that, ever again."

"I understand," Jennifer said, putting the phone down on the bathroom counter. "But it's safe, I promise. It's called Wishful Thinking. I'm telling you the truth, Alicia. Just think about it. How do you think I've been doing what I've been doing the last six months? The whole superwoman thing? Working every night till eight, without seeing my boys before they go to bed, paying for all those hours of child care, which even with our bonuses I'd be struggling to cover?" Alicia raised her eyebrows. Clearly she had been wondering that for some time. "Being at every single work meeting, never leaving the office, available at any time, day or night? The answer is: I haven't. I've been using this"—she held up the phone again, and again Alicia made a gesture for her to stay back, as though it were a weapon—"to be in two places at once. Sometimes three. How else would I be able to have a boyfriend on top of it all?" Alicia seemed to consider this.

"But what *is* it?" she asked. "That blue tunnel—how does it work?"

"It's a wormhole," Jennifer said. "By traveling through it, you can go to one set of coordinates in space and time and then travel back, or forward, to another one."

"And I've never heard of this because . . .?"

"There's a physicist—her name is Dr. Diane Sexton. She lives in my building. That's how we met. She'd been keeping her discovery to herself because she was afraid of how it might be used. But we agreed to see if I could use it safely." Alicia had balled one hand into a fist, looking very much like she'd like to punch Jennifer in the gut. Desperate, Jennifer decided to share something she'd been thinking about lately, something she thought Alicia might warm to. "And, Alicia, I've also been thinking—can you imagine what this could do for women in the community?" Alicia was silent. Jennifer went on. "With Wishful Thinking, a single mother could attend GED classes *and* be with her children at the same time. Or get job training *and* go to a doctor's appointment. Can you imagine? Think of what it could do!"

"Enough!" Alicia roared, causing Jennifer to shrink back and cringe. "First of all," Alicia began, placing one hand on the bathroom counter and leaning in, "none of this makes one bit of sense. I don't even know where to start, it sounds so crazy. You got a wormhole on your phone from a physicist who lives in your building? Like, *Here's a time-travel app and a cup of milk?*" Jennifer began to respond, but Alicia kept going. "Second of all, if this *is* true, you haven't been sacrificing time with your kids, or sacrificing anything, for that matter, to be Little Miss Office Superstar for the past six months. Is that right? Have you also been picking your boys up from school every day, playing supermom on top of it all?" Jennifer nodded weakly. "And meanwhile, for the last six months *I* have had to compete with *you*, and be judged next to you, to sacrifice time with my husband and my children, never mind my health and my sanity, while you have been running around with your new boyfriend too? And then—this I truly can't believe—you have the gall to suggest that this would be a good thing for the women in 'the community'?" Jennifer dug her nails into her palm. What had she been thinking, suggesting to Alicia, of all people, that a time-travel app was the solution to the problems of women in poverty? "Are you talking about *my* community? You didn't even think highly enough of me to let me in on your little scheme, and now you think it will be God's gift to throw a bunch of poor women through a wormhole every day so they can take care of their children and collect their welfare checks at the same time? That's your solution? *Time travel* is easier than passing affordable child care?"

Jennifer said nothing. Alicia, of course, was right. Years ago she had chosen to name the center It Takes a Village because, from the beginning, she had hated the every-person-for-herself attitude that isolated and blamed so many of the residents the agency worked with. Yet she had just suggested that the answer to the multiplying burdens faced by single mothers, in particular, was not for the village to gather around them, but for these women to multiply themselves instead.

The same answer, she thought, that she had applied to herself when her own burdens had seemed too much to bear.

"I have never trusted you," Alicia said, stepping toward Jennifer now, the last traces of fear long gone. "I have always known something was not right about you. My husband thought I was playing into Bill's hand, letting him set up a competition between us when we'd be better off as a team. So I tried to let it go. And I did. Or at least I started to." Alicia shook her head, looking sadder now than she did angry. "I started to believe you. That you were the real thing. That maybe I had found a colleague who could truly be a partner."

"I *am* the real thing, Alicia," Jennifer said. "And I *have* been a partner. I know I've broken your trust. But I have to believe your gut would still tell you that."

"My *gut?*" Alicia shot back derisively. "When Tim told me you had a secret bathroom, I thought maybe there was something in here you were trying to hide. I guess I was right, but I thought it had to do with the payroll. I would never have guessed it was some wacko Harry Potter type of shit like this."

"I have nothing to do with the embezzlement, Alicia," Jennifer said. "The only secret I've been keeping is the one you just found out about."

Alicia put two fingers to her temples and massaged them. She had been suffering from migraines lately. The stress she was under was enormous, Jennifer knew, and Jennifer felt awful about the role she'd played in it. As ill-timed as this revelation was, Jennifer was glad it was over. She'd been deceiving Alicia long enough. What she didn't know was what to do now that her secret was out.

"I'm going to go now," Alicia said at last. "I'm going to get those pay stubs and payroll reports from Tim, and tomorrow morning I'm going to fax them to Bill's hotel in London."

"You can't trust him, Alicia," Jennifer said firmly. They stood only inches from each other as Alicia placed her hand on the bathroom door.

"Maybe not," Alicia said. "But Bill is the devil I know. And in that phone, and in what I just saw it do . . . well, that's a devil I don't know at all."

twenty one | DOING IT ALL
OVER AGAIN

WHEN JENNIFER GOT BACK to the conference room, she found Tim with his cheeks so splotchy he looked like Prince William after a polo match in Bermuda. She could not imagine why. Had he seen her use the app too? Her brain was so scrambled by the events of the afternoon, she would not have been surprised.

"I'm sorry I told Alicia about your bathroom!" he burst out.

"Oh, please," Jennifer said, sitting and letting her body slide down into a deep slouch in her chair. "Don't worry about it." Tim looked at her dubiously. He'd seen a lot of strange behavior from her today.

"Alicia took all the paperwork," he said uneasily. "She's going to fax it to Bill at his hotel."

"I know," Jennifer replied.

It was six o'clock. Two hours from now, she would have to travel back to 5:15 p.m., first to her apartment, and then to meet Norman and the boys at the park. Two hours from now, she would have to do what she had already done all over again, exactly as she had already done it. A shudder went through her.

"Alicia has taken everything we could be looking at," she said to Tim, managing a smile. "Bill is gone, and the event this morning was a huge success, thanks to you. It's six o'clock. Why don't you go home early? Or not exactly early. More like at a humane time."

"I won't say no," Tim said, rising. "But are you sure there isn't something else we can do?" Jennifer shook her head. She was already thinking about how she was going to put several conference-room chairs together to make a nap bench. The only way she could imagine getting through the next couple of hours was by being unconscious, if she could manage it.

Tim slung his messenger bag over his shoulder. When he got to the door, however, he hesitated, patches of pink creeping back into his cheeks.

"Do you think Bill has something to do with this?" he asked.

Jennifer shut her laptop and began to gather what remained of the paperwork on the table. "I don't know," she said honestly. "But Alicia seems to think that once she talks to him, this will all be cleared up and we can get on with our lives."

"And if she's wrong?" Tim said quietly.

"For now," Jennifer said, "I'm going to hope that she isn't."

AT 7:45 P.M., Jennifer's alarm went off. To describe the fitful, sweaty, anxious hours she'd spent tossing and turning on her makeshift bed as a nap was beyond an overstatement, but at least now the waiting was over. At 7:55 p.m., she was in the secret bathroom again, preparing to travel, and at five fifteen Jennifer landed in her own bathroom, at home, and changed into her park clothes. As she did, she couldn't help thinking:

What if I wear a different pair of pants? Would that be the beat of the butterfly's wings? But she changed nothing, doing it all exactly as she'd planned—and as she had promised Dr. Sexton she would.

When Jennifer entered the playground at five thirty, however, she had already started to sweat. She did her best to act normal as she walked up to Norman, Tara, and Josh and said her hellos. Jack, Julien, and Frank were playing together on the jungle gym. The football was under a park bench—in a prime position to be left behind. The temptation to pick it up and throw it in a garbage can was enormous, but she forced herself to let it be. Her heart did stop for a moment when the seven of them began to head toward the park's exit and the football remained under the bench. Could Dr. Sexton have been wrong? Then Julien, ever vigilant, called out, "The football!" and ran back to retrieve it. "Go long!" he said to Frank, who was already beginning to run. They headed out onto the sidewalk.

"*Guys!*" Jack cried after them, always the little one trailing behind. "Throw it to me!" Jennifer was just about to say something to the boys, or to Norman, about tossing the football on the street—she knew she would have said that, in any time or place—when Tara, grabbing her by the arm, pulled her back and away from the rest of the group.

"You are not going to believe," she said, "the story Elizabeth just told me about the gym teacher and Dr. Kate."

So that was how it happened.

Doing her best to concentrate on Tara's story as they walked, Jennifer felt her body tensing as they approached the intersection of West Eleventh and Greenwich. This, she knew, was where she would begin to remember, and as her foot hit the sidewalk on the east side of the street, she did. Crossing over from a single, integrated reality into a realm where her memory of the moment began, she entered a discomfiting double reality—a waking nightmare of déjà vu. The sky was darkening, just as she knew it would. The chilly, damp breeze pricked her forearms as the drizzle began to fall. In a kind of daze, she put her rain jacket on, just as she had before. And at exactly the same moment in Tara's story, she complained briefly to her about Norman's lax attitude as the boys ran around playing catch. Tara, on cue, rolled her eyes, disparaged Josh, and continued to talk. It was coming, and then they were upon it—the entrance to the parking garage. Seeing it, however, Jennifer did something she couldn't have done before but couldn't stop herself from doing now. She clenched her hand into a fist, digging her fingernails into her palm so hard she thought she might draw blood.

"Julien!" Frank yelled, cranking his arm back.

"I got it!" Julien said, running down the sidewalk as Jack chased after him. Frank launched the football in a high, arcing spiral. Watching as it flew through the air, Jennifer froze. Julien and Frank stopped obediently at the threshold of the parking garage, letting the ball go. But Jack, his four-year-old legs scrambling beneath him as he surged ahead, desperate to get the ball away from the bigger boys, pursued it directly into the driveway. In the convex mirror hanging at the entrance of the garage, Jennifer saw the reflection of the gleaming black ton of steel hurtling out of the cavernous garage, briefly airborne from its forward thrust, heading straight for her child. But just as she thought she could not stop herself from running to him, cosmic consequences be damned, a feeling overtook her—a feeling she never could have believed she'd have in this moment, not in a million years. It was a feeling of calm. Profound, peaceful calm. Her balled-up fist relaxed. The adrenaline racing through her bloodstream receded, dissipating. And, standing there on the sidewalk as the ball hung in the air, she almost smiled. Jack was going to be all right. She knew it. If she hadn't known, she thought, she would have interfered with events even if she'd thought it would cause the moon to crash into the Empire State Building.

First there was Norman calling, "Jack!" just as she had, impotently, in the hallway of her office that afternoon. Then there was Norman acting fast—so fast, in fact, it was as though he had seen it all before too. He lunged forward and reached Jack in an instant, pulling him into his body and lifting him up and back and out of harm's way, rebuking him as he cradled him in his arms. He even got the SUV to come to a full stop just short of where Jack had been, delivering a few choice words to the driver before rescuing the football from the middle of the street too.

It was a moment, and then it was a memory. It was over.

"Jesus," Tara said, still wide-eyed. "What an asshole!" She was referring to the driver of the SUV. "I swear, sometimes I want to lock Frank up in a box and keep him under my bed until he's twenty-five. Thank God Norman was watching." Jennifer nodded. "Josh never seems like he's watching, but he usually is, in his way."

Turning to Tara, Jennifer smiled. "Finish your story?"

As Tara began to talk, Jennifer looked ahead at Norman, thinking he would look back at her, proud of himself. But he didn't. Instead the men and the boys kept walking, Norman waving them off when they clamored for the ball back, Josh admonishing the big boys for ignoring Jack when he'd called for the ball before.

They reached the corner. Tara, Frank, and Josh peeled off, saying their good-byes. As Jennifer, Norman, Julien, and Jack waited in their little group for the light to change, Jennifer felt Norman's hand on her shoulder. "You didn't think I was watching," he said. "Did you?"

"I knew you were!" she said, and she meant it. But Norman didn't believe her.

"Oh, ye of little faith," he said teasingly. *"Oh, ye of little faith."*

Moments later, feeling light and spontaneous for the first time that day—maybe for the first time since her fight with Vinita three weeks ago—Jennifer found herself asking Norman if he wanted to join her and the boys for dinner. Surprised but pleased, she thought, he said yes (after a quick text exchange with Dina, who was apparently out with friends), and the four of them ducked into a diner.

"This is so cool," Julien said as they scooted into a booth together, Julien and Norman on one side, she and Jack on the other. "We never have dinner together like this, with Mommy *and* Daddy."

"I know!" Jack said, snuggling up against Jennifer. "It's the whole family."

Jennifer and Norman exchanged an awkward glance and, just as quickly, looked away. It was true that they were very infrequently in each other's company like this with the boys, but, Jennifer realized, she had convinced herself that it was the boys (not she) who preferred it that way. In the past that might have been true, when the boys preferred having her to themselves and griped about having to be with Norman when he was in town. But something had undoubtedly changed between Norman, Julien, and Jack. Seated in the booth with them, watching him interact with the boys in a way she didn't often have the occasion to observe, it was impossible to deny. First Julien pulled some math homework out of his backpack and began to discuss it with Norman—evidently it was an assignment they had worked on together over the phone earlier in the week. (Had Julien called Norman on his own?) Then Jack, after being informed of his choices on the menu, mentioned that Dina always made fried chicken on Saturdays, and that fried chicken was his favorite food in the universe. (Since when?) Then Norman asked Julien about a girl in his class, and if there was any update on the "carrot incident."

The carrot incident?

Jennifer pulled Jack even closer. He responded exactly as she needed him to, burrowing into her like a baby bunny and saying, as he always did, "Mama."

Their food arrived. She and Norman chatted over their garlicky, mayonnaisey Caesar salads about the boys and other things, as much as they were able. She asked about his teaching. He asked about her work. Then, out of nowhere, Norman asked her when she had seen Vinita last. Jennifer made up an excuse, then asked, "Why?" as casually as she could.

"I saw her at pickup today," he replied. "She asked me to keep an eye on you."

"That's weird," she said, stabbing a crouton with her fork and shattering it.

He shrugged. "She said you've been working too hard. Which is even weirder considering what a flexible schedule you have now."

Jennifer took a big bite of crouton. She didn't know if she should feel touched or annoyed. She was leaning toward the latter.

The boys made quick work of their dinners, and after some talk about what was happening at school, Julien asked if he could play on Norman's phone. Norman, to her surprise, said yes. Jennifer raised an eyebrow, smiling. "I thought you didn't believe in Angry Birds," she said teasingly.

"It's Candy Crush," he replied curtly. "Helps with spatial reasoning."

Norman could always be counted on, Jennifer thought, to say something stupid like that just when she was beginning to warm up to him.

In an instant, the boys were totally absorbed, enclosed in a video-game bubble, Julien holding the phone and Jack craning over the table to see. The boys' bickering over who got to play and when was so irritating, however, that Jennifer asked them to slide into the next booth, which was empty.

This had the unfortunate effect of leaving her alone with Norman.

"We have a custody hearing coming up," he said quietly the moment the boys were settled.

It was true. Jennifer hadn't been able to put it off any longer. The wheels of the judiciary had been set in motion, and while Jennifer's lawyer had assured her that once a custody schedule had been set, as it had been in their mediated agreement, it was enormously difficult to change, the fact that she was likely to win had seemed less and less like the point. Instead she'd felt, over the past few months, that while a judge probably would not force her to give Norman more time with the boys, her conscience might.

"Did Melissa help you with that time log of yours?" she suddenly found herself asking. "The one you gave me last fall?" All this time, and she had never asked. But the suspected betrayal had clouded her relationship with Melissa enough to sadden her, and she wanted to know.

Norman put down his fork, took a sip of his Diet Coke, and looked at her. "No," he said. "Julien did."

Jennifer gulped. She hadn't expected that.

"He didn't know he was helping me," Norman added quickly. "I would just ask him things. He's like a little tape recorder, you know. He doesn't forget a thing." Jennifer nodded, trying not to let her expression betray her—the idea of

Norman's quizzing Julien like that made her furious. But Norman, as usual, misinterpreted the look on her face. "Oh, man," Norman said. "I could see how you would have thought Melissa did it. That must have been hard, thinking she and I were in cahoots together."

"It's okay," Jennifer said. "I should have just asked you in the first place."

"There's something I probably should have told you in the first place, too, Jen," he said. *What now?* she thought. "The time log wasn't my idea," he said. "It was your mom's."

"My *mom's?*" she repeated incredulously.

"Well, no, wait," Norman said, backpedaling. "Not the time log specifically. It was more . . . your mom pushed me to ask for more time, to take on partial custody of the boys. When she was so sick. She worried that you wouldn't let me help you after she was gone. She worried that it was too much for you, trying to do it all by yourself. And, frankly, she gave me quite a talking-to. About how I had been as a dad."

This revelation was more than either of them could bear in front of the other. Norman immediately took advantage of a minor squabble between the boys to turn away and scold them.

Watching him referee as the boys' verbal disagreement quickly devolved into punches and thrown elbows, Jennifer remembered the afternoon when Norman had come to visit her mother in hospice. "You've got to try to forgive him, sweetheart," her mother had said after he'd left. "For your sake, and for the boys'." Jennifer had nodded noncommittally, hearing but not hearing, overcome with her grief. Her mother had then clasped her hand, hard. "You can try to be everything to them," she'd said, "but you can never be their dad."

How had she forgotten?

Leaning over into the booth where Norman was grappling with the boys, Jennifer forced the words out before she could think twice. "Do you guys want to stay with Daddy tonight?"

Norman looked at her, eyes wide.

"I mean, if that's okay," she said.

"No, no," he said, smiling. "I'd love it. And I'm sure Dina would too."

"Yeah!" Jack said.

"Okay," Julien said, more doubtfully.

Once they were outside, Julien motioned to her to come over to the edge of the sidewalk, where he was standing. She leaned down to listen. "Mommy," he said, "why don't you come to Daddy's too? You never come to Daddy's. I want to go to Daddy's, but I want to be with you too." Before Jennifer could answer, Julien called out to Norman. "Daddy, can Mommy come too?"

"Julien," Norman said, shifting uncomfortably, "you know that isn't how it works. Dina will be home later, and—"

"I don't *want* Dina!" Julien cried with a fierceness that nearly knocked Jennifer off her feet. "I want *Mommy!*"

Now Julien was the one with tears in his eyes. Her stoic boy, who kept it in so tightly, who so rarely melted down. Pulling her toward him, he whispered, "Why does Daddy have to marry Dina? Why can't Daddy marry *you*, so we can all live together like before?"

Julien still remembers those days, Jennifer thought. Jack, she knew, did not.

Julien's tears were coming fast now, dropping off his cheeks and landing on the sidewalk. His expression was both so hopeful and so heart-wrenching, she almost lost her composure completely. *Oh, to protect him from everything!* she thought. *To guard him against all pain!* To give him what he wanted—his mommy and daddy, living together, with him, and for it to be a good thing, and not something miserable, as she knew it would be for all of them.

"I'm sorry," she said. She paused for a moment, wanting him to hear it. "I know it's hard for you. But when Daddy and I live together—"

"You can't be friends," he said quietly, wiping his tears away as he delivered the second half of a line she and Norman had cribbed from a therapy book somewhere and relied on heavily ever since.

"That's right, darling," she said softly. "But I'm still sorry that it's hard for you sometimes."

Just then Jack, joining them, elbowed his way into Jennifer and Julien's embrace.

"I don't want you to marry Daddy," he said defiantly. "I want you to marry me!"

Julien, taking a deep breath, laughed out loud. "You can't marry Mommy, dummy!" he said. "She's your *mom*!"

"Don't call your brother a dummy," Jennifer said to Julien, but she was smiling at him. She stood up. Norman looked at her inquiringly. *Is this really okay?* She nodded. She wanted them to go now, before she thought about it too much longer. The boys didn't know that Dina was pregnant yet, and she wasn't sure how they would feel once they found out. Better to let them get used to spending more time at Norman's now, when he could still focus on them completely.

Norman turned to the boys. "Who here," he said, clapping his hands together, "would like to stay out a little bit later and go get ice-cream sundaes?"

Ice-cream sundaes? Jennifer thought. *When Julien hasn't even done his homework yet?* It was nearly seven o'clock! Jennifer opened her mouth to say as much, when she stopped. "Oh, ye of little faith," Norman had said earlier. She needed to let him be their dad, his way. It was time.

* * *

IT WAS THE RIGHT thing to do, she knew. But that didn't make it any easier to watch as the three of them walked away from her, a merry band of boys, Jack perched up on Norman's shoulders, turning to wave to her every few seconds, Julien blowing her kisses like a silent-movie star, until, after a block or two, they rounded a corner and left her sight. Jennifer stood there for a few minutes, looking into the empty space where they had left her.

Space. Taking out her phone and smiling to herself, she texted Owen.

Hi love, she wrote.

The response came immediately. *Thinking of you. What are you going to wear tomorrow?*

Tomorrow? And since when did he care what she was going to wear? Jennifer opened her calendar. It was hard to sort through the legions of colored blocks representing her appointments for the day stacked two and three deep on the barely visible white background of her calendar. There were meetings and conference calls and reminders accounting for every minute at work, a midnight-blue Wishful Thinking appointment on top of them sending her back in time to pick up the boys and take them to swimming lessons at the Y, and then, sure enough, yet another Wishful Thinking appointment to go to a costume party with Owen at 7:00 p.m.

It was nuts.

No idea, she wrote. *Call later?*

K, he replied. *Don't forget.*

Xoxo, she texted back. She sighed. Just thinking about all she had planned the next day made her head ache. If she did it all, she would live thirty-five hours tomorrow, not twenty-four. She would be the perfect worker, the perfect mother, and the perfect girlfriend, and she would lie to her coworkers, her children, and her boyfriend to do it—never talking about her kids at work, or about her boyfriend to her kids, or about her job when she was with her boyfriend. The worst lie of all, she thought, was leading all of them to believe that, wherever she was, she had made a choice to be there and nowhere else.

When you can do anything all the time, she thought, *what does anything you do mean anymore?*

Leaning against a lamppost, Jennifer looked heavenward, gazing into the milky reflection of the city's lights in the dense cloud cover above. Somewhere beyond the clouds, she thought, lay a kind of order, a rhythm of days and nights and hours and atoms that her body and mind had, over the course of millennia, been built for. Right here on Earth was another kind of order, a set of choices and sacrifices everyone she knew wrestled with and made every single day as they balanced work, family, and love. An order Jennifer was longing to be part of again. It was time to rejoin the world she knew, she thought, as flawed and difficult as it could sometimes be: to jump back onto the merry-go-round and hang on just like everybody else. What did she have if she didn't have that? Suddenly she realized: in these past months using the app, she had felt like a superhero, but, like every superhero, she had also felt terribly alone.

The wind was strong that night, pushing the clouds swiftly across the purplish sky. After a moment they cleared, revealing a single star—something of a rarity in New York. But Jennifer was done wishing.

She looked down at her phone. Her calendar app was still open. With a tap of her thumb, she closed it. With another tap she pulled up her Favorites. First was Melissa. Then came Vinita Kapoor. She pressed her friend's name, and a throwback Thursday photo of the two of them from college—

Jennifer with bangs hair-sprayed to ghastly proportions, Vinita looking as beautiful as ever—appeared. She was about to call when she realized that Vinita wouldn't pick up. She'd said she wouldn't until Jennifer promised to stop using the app. So she texted instead.

You were right, she wrote. *I'm not going to do it anymore.*

twenty two

B R E A K F A S T
M E E T I N G

J ENNIFER WOKE UP THE next morning with a skull-
crushing hangover—perhaps because Vinita, ecstatic that
Jennifer had finally come to her senses, had decided to
celebrate by coming over and whipping up some of the
deliciously deadly Indian martinis she had concocted for the
surprise party. The timing of Jennifer's call had been perfect, as
Sean was back in town after having been away for two weeks
and owed Vinita big-time. Vinita had left him with the girls
and come over immediately. After some apologizing and
hugging it out (more than was generally comfortable for
Vinita), Jennifer had caught Vinita up on all that had
happened since her birthday.

Vinita had been dismayed, but not surprised, by the
apparent embezzlement from One Stop. She also harbored no
doubt that Bill was to blame. "That guy called me 'honey' at
your surprise party and told me to get him a drink like he
owned the place," she'd said. "Guys like that take whatever they
want because they think everything belongs to them
already." (Being married to a guy who worked in the upper

echelons of finance, Vinita had some authority in this regard.) She was most saddened to hear the reason for Dr. Sexton's disappearance. "What kind of cancer is it?" Vinita had asked. Jennifer realized she didn't know. They considered calling Dr. Sexton and asking her to join them, but Jennifer had already texted her to tell her Jack was all right and hadn't heard back from her. So they decided to wait, figuring she was probably with Susan.

At around midnight, way past the bedtime of two early-to-rise moms who had just downed three martinis each, the two friends had decided they might as well have a sleepover too. ("I can't wait to see what Sean does about packing lunch," Vinita had said gleefully.) In the end, however, this had entailed little more than passing out at roughly the same time on Jennifer's pullout couch, right in the middle of a rerun of *Top Chef*. And now it was morning, and Vinita was already dressed, looking snappy and fresh, pouring coffee. "Oh my God," Jennifer groaned. "You're so peppy!"

Vinita laughed. "One of the tests I should run on you," she said, "is to see how alcohol affects the time-traveled brain." Vinita handed Jennifer a cup.

"I'll take that test," Jennifer said, sitting up, "as long as I never have to drink another Indian martini." It took a moment or two for the coffee to begin to clear her head. She looked at the time. "Nine o'clock?" she said, shocked. "You let me sleep until nine o'clock on a workday?"

"You needed it, Jay," Vinita said. "You haven't slept properly in months."

Jennifer whirled around, nearly spilling her coffee on her comforter. "Where's my phone?" she said.

"Remember?" Vinita said, frowning a little. "You decided to sleep without it under your pillow for the first time in six months?"

"But did I charge it?" Jennifer said, getting up quickly. "Is it dead?"

Vinita picked up Jennifer's phone from its place on the kitchen table, displaying it to her. "I pronounce this phone dead," she said. "And good riddance!"

"Fine," Jennifer said, walking over to grab it. "But this morning—Alicia was going to fax Bill in London. Remember? What if she's been trying to call me?"

"You have a landline, don't you?" Vinita replied.

"She doesn't know that number! I don't even know it. I never thought I would sleep this late."

Frantic now, Jennifer searched for her charger. She found it, plugged it in, and quickly snapped the charger's pins into their counterparts at the base of her phone. After what seemed like a long moment, the empty battery symbol with its thin red line appeared on the black screen, signaling her phone's return to life. Jennifer sighed deeply, feeling as relieved as if she'd had to pee for fifteen blocks and had finally made it to a bathroom. Cradling her phone, she stared at it, waiting for it to fully awaken.

"We're going to have to work on your attachment issues," Vinita said, walking by and giving her arm a gentle squeeze.

There was a knock at the door. "Who could that be?" Jennifer wondered aloud, checking to make sure her flannel pajama top was fully buttoned.

Vinita opened the door. It was Dr. Sexton, holding a steaming pot of tea.

"I called, but I got no answer," Dr. Sexton said, "so I thought I'd try the old-fashioned way. Though I did assume you'd be at the office by now." Jennifer smiled, happy to see her.

"May I come in?" Dr. Sexton asked, an amused expression crossing her face at the sight of Jennifer's unkempt appearance.

She was impeccably dressed as ever, in a black suit accented by a silk lavender shirt, wearing her trademark shoes—pumps today—one black, one red. She quickly deposited the tea on the counter and, turning, opened her arms to Jennifer.

"You see," she said, "Jack *was* all right. You knew he would be."

"Yes," Jennifer said as she pulled away, "I suppose I did."

Dr. Sexton smiled and turned to Vinita. "My dear Vinita," she said, "I owe you an apology. I am very sorry not to have returned your calls these past weeks."

"Diane," Vinita said, leaning in and giving Dr. Sexton a warm embrace. It always took Jennifer aback to hear Vinita call Dr. Sexton "Diane" so easily, as she still said "Dr. Sexton" after all this time. "Jennifer told me about Susan. I'm so sorry."

The two doctors discussed Susan's diagnosis and treatment, Vinita inquiring about the hospital and the clinical trial Susan was soon to begin. It was brain cancer, and the prognosis, Jennifer gathered, wasn't good. Beneath Dr. Sexton's customary panache, Jennifer could see a drawn, tight tiredness on her face, a weary sadness that saddened her too. And then she had a terrible thought: *Thank God it's Susan and not Dr. Sexton.* It was inexcusably selfish, but she felt it all the same.

"I'm going to get myself together," Jennifer said, glancing at the clock. "I'll be right back." Just then, however, her phone sprang back to life. And as it did, a barrage of *ping*s poured forth. She walked over to the phone. "Alicia," she said. "Shit."

"What does she want?" Vinita said, without attempting to disguise her disdain. "Has she called the cops on you yet?" Vinita was indignant that Alicia had suspected Jennifer of doing anything wrong.

Jennifer ignored Vinita and read the first text aloud. "'Spoke with Bill. Please call immediately.'" Then the next: "'BT

flying back first thing after speech this afternoon. Please call.'"
After that: "'Are you coming in? Here with Tim. Call ASAP.'"
And then the last: "'Worried. Please call. Sorry I suspected you.
It's Bill.'

"Oh my God," Jennifer said.

Vinita slapped the counter with her hands. "I knew it!"

"What's going on?" Dr. Sexton asked, furrowing her brow.

"Somebody has been skimming off of the residents'
paychecks," Jennifer said, "the ones we hired through my boss's
foundation to work on constructing the centers. It could be a
half a million dollars or more." She was scrolling through her
e-mail as she talked, looking to see if there was any more
information to review from Alicia before she returned her call.
"And it sounds like my boss, Bill Truitt, is the one behind it.
Which, on the one hand, doesn't surprise me at all, because
he's kind of a sleazeball, but on the other makes no sense
because he's, like, a billionaire sleazeball."

"It isn't about money for those guys," Vinita said. "It's
always about something else."

"That could be devastating for the center," Dr. Sexton said,
distraught. "Will the whole program suffer as a result?"

"Suffer?" Jennifer said as she listened to Alicia's cell phone
ring, confused by the fact that she didn't immediately pick up.
"It will die." She was about to leave a voice mail, when the
intercom next to her front door buzzed. The doorman's voice
came through.

"An Alicia here to see you?" he said.

"Send her up," Jennifer said, hanging up her cell phone.

"Let her in?" Jennifer asked Vinita and Dr. Sexton. "I won't
be a minute; I promise."

"Of course," Dr. Sexton said. Jennifer was scurrying down
the hallway when she heard Dr. Sexton call after her. "Should I
cancel your Wishful Thinking appointments for today?"

Jennifer hadn't thought of that. "Yes!" she cried. "All of them."

"Not just for today," she heard Vinita say to Dr. Sexton. "For good."

AFTER A LIGHTNING-FAST SHOWER, despite the usual limp water pressure—no small feat—Jennifer was dressed and reasonably presentable when she returned to her kitchen/ living room. She arrived to find Alicia chatting, if a bit awkwardly, with Vinita. Dr. Sexton was busying herself at the sink, humming as she wiped clean a martini glass. As soon as she saw Jennifer, Alicia fixed her with an anxious but slightly accusatory look. "Where have you been?" she said.

"I'm sorry," she said. "I had a long day yesterday. I thought Jack was in danger. That's why I ran out of our meeting to use the app. But he's all right."

"She knows about the app?" Dr. Sexton said sharply, whirling around.

"Who are you?" Alicia said, turning to face her.

"Dr. Diane Sexton," Dr. Sexton replied. "And the app is my invention."

"Of course it is," Alicia said, looking Dr. Sexton up and down, her gaze lingering meaningfully on her shoes.

"I didn't realize we'd brought somebody else into our circle of confidence," Dr. Sexton said to Jennifer stiffly.

"She saw me," Jennifer said. "At work. In my secret bathroom."

"How careless," Dr. Sexton replied.

"You could say that," Alicia said. "But, believe it or not, there is something I'm more worried about right now than trying to understand how—or why—anybody would want to get sucked inside her phone to beam herself all over town and, to top it off, lie to everybody about it." Dr. Sexton was about to object when Alicia turned to Jennifer and put a hand on her arm. "Bill is getting on a plane now," she said urgently. "He lands at five o'clock New York time. Tim is at the office, waiting for us to tell him what we want to do."

"How do you know Bill is the one who has been embezzling from the residents' paychecks?" Dr. Sexton asked.

It was Alicia's turn to question Jennifer angrily. "She knows about this?"

"Apparently there are overlapping circles of confidence in this room," Dr. Sexton said pointedly. Vinita sighed and took a sip of her coffee. "Ladies," she said, "aren't we all on the same side here?"

"How *do* you know, Alicia?" Jennifer asked. She was hurriedly packing her briefcase.

Alicia pursed her lips and directed a warning look at Dr. Sexton, then lowered her voice. "This morning," she said, "after I sent the documents to Bill's hotel, he called me. And the first thing he asked me was, 'Have you taken this to the OIG?'"

"Office of the Inspector General," Jennifer explained to Dr. Sexton, who, she observed, was listening rather intently, much to Alicia's irritation.

"Then he told me he would take care of everything," Alicia continued, "and make sure the residents were paid. Said it must be an accounting error with his payroll company. When I said it seemed like a pattern, not just a mistake, he just said, again, that he'd take care of it."

"Not exactly an admission of guilt," Jennifer said.

"No," Alicia said. "But then I said I thought we should take it to the OIG. To see what he would say."

"And?"

"He mentioned our bonuses."

"What about them?"

"We've been getting those directly from BTE for Good, remember? Apparently they've been off the books too," Alicia said. "He said unless we want to explain those 'illegal' disbursements to the OIG, too, we should back off and let him take care of it."

"Great," Jennifer said, sitting down heavily at the kitchen table. "I knew those bonuses were too good to be true. He wanted it to look like we had our hands in the pot, too, in case he ever got caught. Which means he was planning this from the beginning. Or at least from when he accelerated the timetable on building the center." Alicia nodded. "Now what?"

Alicia's phone rang. "It's Tim," she said, picking up. She listened for a moment, then turned to Jennifer, holding her hand over the receiver. "Bill just cut off all Tim's access to Bill's e-mail, calendars, everything," she said. "He had someone from the department lock up his office too." Turning her attention back to the phone, she listened. "Wait," she said to Tim. "Jennifer should hear this." She placed her phone on the table, put it on speaker, and sat down. Vinita excused herself, walked over to the sofa bed, and began folding it up. Dr. Sexton, however, took a seat at the table too. Alicia glared at her. Dr. Sexton smiled serenely.

"Tell Jennifer what you just told me," Alicia said into the phone.

"Well, I don't know if it's anything," Tim began, "but you know how Bill has been having me help him with a lot of . . . personal errands? And Mrs. Bill too?" They did—the week before, Mrs. Bill had had poor Tim stuffing confetti-filled party invitations for her sixteen-year-old daughter's birthday cruise on the Hudson. "Well, I've spent a lot of time at their apartment, in the high-rise, you know. And I noticed that Bill has a locked file cabinet in his office, under his desk. He never lets me near it and never lets his wife near it, either. He's always filing stuff in there."

"And?" Jennifer said.

"Last week, I saw Greg Schloss drop off the payroll report. He handed it to Bill personally. And Bill told him he would review it, as always."

"But I've been getting them electronically," Jennifer said. "Directly from Greg."

"From Greg's e-mail account, yes," Tim said. "But how do you know Bill isn't the one writing up the false reports and then e-mailing you from Greg's account? Why would he tell Greg to deliver him a copy by hand?"

"Where did he put the report Greg gave him?" Alicia said.

"In the file cabinet. And I know where he keeps the key."

"You naughty boy," Jennifer said, smiling.

"He can't get to it until he gets back from London," Tim went on, his not-quite-broken-in-voice quavering. But then he paused. "Not that it matters. You can't get into that apartment building without being checked out by five different doormen, and Bill and his wife have never let me have a key. Plus you need a key for the elevator. Plus you can be sure he's told them not to let anybody in today. So even if there is something in there, we'll never get our hands on it. Which is why I didn't say anything in the first place."

"Is Mrs. Bill usually home during the day?" Jennifer asked.

"Sometimes," he said. "But she left this morning to see her sister in DC."

Jennifer and Dr. Sexton exchanged a look. Vinita, who had evidently been listening in from her seat on the sofa, walked back over to the table, frowning.

"They're redoing the bathroom, though," Tim added. "There's a whole crew of construction guys there all day today."

"What time do they usually leave?" Jennifer asked.

"Five o'clock on the dot," Tim said. "Those guys never stay a minute more."

Jennifer looked at Alicia. Alicia was staring at Jennifer's phone, which was sitting next to Alicia's on the table.

"Let us call you right back, okay?" Jennifer said. Tim agreed. Alicia hung up.

"Are you thinking what I think you're thinking?" Vinita said, her hands on her hips. "You *promised* me, Jay," she said. "You promised me just last night!"

"It's true," Jennifer said, looking at Dr. Sexton resignedly. "I've been using the app way too much. More than we agreed to. More than you know."

"More than you'd believe," Vinita said sharply. She turned to Dr. Sexton. "I'm going to run some tests on her tomorrow," she added. "And I should run them on you, too, Diane."

"Perhaps," Dr. Sexton said briskly, squaring her shoulders. "I've recently decided to stop using the app, too, at least for the time being."

"Why?" Jennifer asked.

"Because of Susan," Dr. Sexton said simply. "Her illness. It just doesn't seem right, somehow."

For a moment, everyone was silent. Then Alicia slowly rose to her feet. "I know I'm new to this," she said, "and God knows I think it's crazy. But if using that app is the only way to bring Bill Truitt Jr. to justice for stealing money from public-housing residents, some of whom are my friends, and all of whom have worked every bit as hard as we have to build One Stop, I say use it."

Jennifer looked up at Alicia, astonished.

"What's that look for?" Alicia asked. "After all you've put me through with your bullshit superwoman routine? How about now that we need the real thing?"

"But Superwoman *isn't* real," Jennifer said. "She can't just bust into Bill's apartment and go through everything in that file box for an hour all by herself. What if there isn't enough time? What if the payroll reports aren't in there and we have to look for something else?" Alicia began to shake her head, but Jennifer kept on going. "It takes a village, right?" Jennifer said. "I'll use the app to break into Bill's apartment. But you have to come too."

twenty three | SHOWTIME

THIRTY MINUTES LATER, after quizzing Vinita thoroughly regarding her medical opinion of the app's safety (this after Alicia's first response to Jennifer's proposition, which was an emphatic "hell, no"), and after Vinita had left for the office, and after Dr. Sexton had then spent several minutes explaining the physics behind how the app worked, Alicia was still not convinced. Though she did admit that the chances of succeeding in finding something incriminating in Bill's file cabinet between the time the workmen left the apartment and his arrival back from the airport were far greater if two of them went, rather than Jennifer alone.

"But why do *I* have to use the app?" Alicia asked. "Can't you just transport yourself and then let me in the front door the old-fashioned way, on foot and all in one piece?" Alicia was tapping the table nervously with her fingers, as antsy and anxious as Jennifer had ever seen her.

"You heard Tim about the security in that building,"

Jennifer said. "How will you get up to Bill's floor? The elevator requires a key, too, remember?"

Dr. Sexton laid a hand on Alicia's arm, stilling, for the moment, the tapping. "Alicia," she said, "I know it seems frightening. But I assure you, a single use of the app will be absolutely safe. It has been tested again and again, and it is completely stable."

Alicia took a deep breath. She looked from Dr. Sexton to Jennifer and back several times. "How many times have you all used it?" she asked.

"Hundreds," Jennifer said.

"Thousands," Dr. Sexton said at the same time, causing Jennifer to shoot her a look of amused surprise.

"And you've never gotten smashed up, or scrambled, or stuck?"

"Do I look smashed up or scrambled?" Jennifer asked.

"And no one has ever been stuck," Dr. Sexton said.

"'No one' meaning the two of you, the only two human beings on the planet who have ever used this thing?" Alicia asked.

There wasn't much Jennifer or Dr. Sexton could say to that.

As was her custom when she was trying to make up her mind about something, Alicia closed her eyes, put two fingers to each of her temples, and rubbed them, as though attempting to summon the spirit guide who would know what to do when the only way to catch one's corrupt boss was by jumping into a wormhole invented by a woman wearing two different-colored shoes. Dr. Sexton, for her part, had requisitioned Jennifer's laptop and was clicking away on the keyboard, determining the coordinates for Bill Truitt's fifty-fifth-story apartment in midtown.

After several minutes, Alicia opened her eyes. Jennifer knew. She was in. She smiled, but Alicia did not smile back. "If

I come out missing any of my parts," she said grimly, "I and my parts are going to haunt both of you for the rest of your lives."

"You won't," Jennifer said. "I promise."

"So we may proceed," Dr. Sexton said, turning Jennifer's laptop to face them. "As you can see, I have located the proper coordinates."

Alicia's phone chimed. She glanced at it. "Tim wants to know the plan."

"We can't tell Tim," Jennifer said.

"But Tim is the one who knows where Bill keeps the key to the file cabinet," Alicia answered. "And where the file cabinet is."

"But how will we explain to him that we can get in?" Jennifer asked. "Wait!" she said, turning to Dr. Sexton. "I know. Can you make one of those flashy thingies like in *Men in Black*, so we can explain the plan to him and then wipe his memory clean?" She was half kidding, but only half. Dr. Sexton, however, was not amused.

Dr. Sexton closed Jennifer's laptop and took a long sip of her ever-present tea. "It is very tiresome," she said at last, "to hear one's work described in the language of adolescent Hollywood movies." Jennifer was going to apologize, but Dr. Sexton went on. "Clearly, Tim needs to be included," she said, "in order to locate the file cabinet and key. Not only that," she said, "but I suspect Tim could be very useful as—to borrow from a Hollywood genre I much prefer to science fiction, the western—a lookout. Tim arranged the car to collect Bill at the airport, correct?" Alicia nodded. "So he will have some knowledge of when the pickup is made. Tim will be able to warn you when Bill is on his way home."

"We don't need to tell him anything about how we're going to get in," Alicia said. "We can just tell him we've found a way and it's better that he doesn't know about it."

"Plausible deniability," Dr. Sexton quipped. "How Nixonian."

"We should also tell him to go home for the day," Jennifer said. "We may need to take whatever we find to the office this afternoon, and he'll never understand it if we bring the files there before five."

As Alicia texted Tim back, Dr. Sexton picked up Jennifer's phone. "I deleted your Wishful Thinking appointments for today, my dear," she said, "as you requested." Apparently there *was* an EDIT button somewhere Jennifer didn't know about. "But now to make a new one." Dr. Sexton pulled up Wishful Thinking and tapped the button that had started it all so many months ago: CREATE AN EVENT. Alicia circled the table and stood behind Dr. Sexton to peer over her shoulder.

"You ought to see the wand," Dr. Sexton said, turning to Alicia, unable to resist the opportunity to show off her creation in front of a new audience. "It emerges from two dimensions to three and hovers over the screen! Jennifer found it distracting, but it's really quite wonderful. I can pull it up quickly if you'd like—"

"Later!" Jennifer said, taking her phone back. She read the entry, which was not in the form she was accustomed to: *Depart home, Thursday, April 7, 10:30 a.m. Arrive 157 West 57th Street, Thursday, April 7, 5:15 p.m. Return home, Thursday, April 7, 6:15 p.m.* She looked up at Dr. Sexton. "We aren't going to wait until five fifteen? I thought you couldn't travel into the future," she said. "Didn't the guide say that?"

"The laws of physics don't prevent it," Dr. Sexton said. "But I thought it wise to dissuade you, or anyone, from using the app in that manner, which would distract from its purpose: to provide individuals overwhelmed by modern life with a means to cope with it."

"Cope, or cheat?" Alicia asked.

"As you can see," Dr. Sexton said, ignoring her, "you will

depart at ten thirty, which is fifteen minutes from now. That way you will have time to review whatever you find—and formulate a plan of action—well before Bill's return."

Jennifer looked at the appointment again. The return: 6:15 p.m. It was reasonable to assume it would take Bill that long to get back, given that he had to go through customs (though she was sure he had some sort of mogul fast pass) and deal with rush-hour traffic. But still. "What if Bill comes back before six fifteen?" Jennifer asked. "What do we do? Hide?"

"I thought of that," Dr. Sexton said, smiling. She took Jennifer's phone and tapped on the Wishful Thinking appointment. Then she pointed to a button in the bottom-right-hand corner that had never appeared there before: EDIT. Jennifer smiled. Dr. Sexton had handed her the keys to the car at last, at least temporarily, and she felt much better traveling with them in hand.

"Are you sure this will work? For me to go with her?" Alicia asked.

"Just as long as she is touching both you and the phone, you will both be transported," Dr. Sexton replied. "I know this because I once traveled with Lucy—my dog—quite by mistake, which was very unpleasant."

Jennifer pictured Dr. Sexton departing for an evening of tango lessons in Buenos Aires only to find herself trapped in a chic nightclub bathroom with a very disoriented Great Dane.

"I will be here when you return," Dr. Sexton said. "Which, of course, will be almost instantly after you depart."

Jennifer stood, stretching. "I'm going to use the bathroom. Always wise before a long trip."

"You make it sound like we're driving to the Rockaways," Alicia said, standing too.

"It's almost as mundane by now, isn't it, my dear?" Dr. Sexton said, winking at Jennifer playfully. "But not quite."

* * *

HAVING INSTRUCTED TIM TO go home immediately and
to notify them as soon as the car picked Bill up at the airport,
and having secured Vinita's help in picking up the boys that
day (they'd have to skip their swimming lesson), Jennifer and
Alicia regrouped by the kitchen table.

"Are you ready?" Jennifer asked Alicia. Alicia, who was
tapping the table again with her bright, glossy nails, nodded.

"What's it like?" she asked, almost in a whisper. "How does
it feel?"

"Like a hot flash on steroids," Jennifer said. "And then it's
over."

"And how would you know what a hot flash feels like?"
Dr. Sexton asked, laughing. Alicia did her best to smile. "You
should both put your hands on the phone now," Dr. Sexton
said, glancing at the clock. "And don't forget, Alicia—be sure to
put one hand on Jennifer too."

Alicia lifted her hand from the table, ceasing her
drumming. Her hand was shaking. Jennifer remembered the
first time she'd used the app (the first time she'd used it
knowing it was real, anyway), and her heart went out to Alicia.
She clasped Alicia's hand in her own and placed them together
on top of her phone. "Think of Amalia," she said. "Think of
Noel."

"I think," Alicia said, placing her other hand on Jennifer's
forearm as they watched the clock, now at 10:29, "I will think
of Jesus."

"Whatever works," Jennifer said. "Because here . . . we . . .
go."

* * *

JENNIFER AND ALICIA LANDED in the middle of Bill
Truitt's vast living room, surrounded by floor-to-ceiling
windows with views of Manhattan only the fifty-fifth floor of
a midtown high-rise could provide. "Wow," Alicia breathed,
looking out over the city, Central Park, still mostly bare from
the winter months, laid out beneath them. "I've never seen the
park like that before."

Jennifer took a quick look, then turned her attention to
the layout of the apartment.

"Tim said the office was off the living room," she said,
scanning their surroundings. She pulled up the e-mail they'd
asked him to send with his instructions. "He said to look for
dark wood double doors." To the right of the foyer and to the
left of a hallway that appeared to lead to the kitchen, Jennifer
immediately spotted the doors. The wood was so dark it was
almost black, in keeping with the apartment's austere, modern
look. Together, the women walked toward them. Alicia
reached for the handle, but Jennifer stopped her. She fished in
her bag, took out a scarf, and wrapped it around her hand.

"It's silly," she said, "but we probably shouldn't leave
fingerprints. Right?"

"Seriously?" Alicia said. Jennifer, chagrined, put the scarf
back in her bag. Alicia turned the knob.

The doors opened. Unlike the bright white, modern living
room, Bill's office was luxurious, old-school, covered in deep
mahogany, every inch of it shining as glossily as Alicia's
fingernails. Cabinets and shelves, some encased in glass, were
everywhere, lit by perfectly placed recessed lights that pulsed
subtly to life when Jennifer pressed the switch by the door.
Lining the shelves were what Jennifer recognized from her
corporate days as "deal trophies": Lucite tombstones commem-
orating the dates and details of deals Bill Truitt Enterprises had
done over the years, mini-monuments to massive amounts of

money changing hands, awarded to the men who'd made the biggest financial kills.

"Where did Tim say the key was?" Alicia asked, stepping into the room cautiously.

"Under a vase," Jennifer said, surveying the contents of the cabinetry. "To the left of a photo of Bill and Tiger Woods." Sure enough, just as Tim had described, there was, to the left of a framed photo of Bill and a much younger Tiger Woods, an ornately decorated antique-looking vase, the value of which she did not even want to contemplate. "Imagine what Tiger would have done with that app of yours," Alicia said drily. Jennifer tipped the vase upward as gently as she could and, reaching underneath it with her other hand, probed with her fingers until she found what they sought: a tiny, round-topped key. She smiled. She'd half thought it wouldn't be there.

"Thank God," Alicia said. Key in hand, Jennifer walked over to Bill's desk, which was twice the size of her kitchen table. After wheeling his office chair aside, she got down on her hands and knees and peered underneath it. It was so dark in the room, not to mention under the desk, that it was difficult to make anything out at first. But as her eyes adjusted to the low light, she saw it: a heavy black file cabinet that looked like it was designed to survive a plane crash. It was just as Tim had described.

"I can't believe we're doing this," Alicia said, as Jennifer, on all fours, pulled the heavy cabinet out from under the desk. Just as she did, her phone emitted a loud *ping*, causing Jennifer to start and bang her head against the underside of the desk.

Rubbing the back of her head and standing, she looked at her phone. It was a text from Tim. *Flight just landed*, it read.

Pray for traffic, she replied.

Alicia knelt down next to her. Having given up on her stealth scarf, Jennifer placed the key into the lock and opened it. Expecting to see an orderly set of hanging file folders inside, however, Jennifer groaned when she saw what greeted them instead. The cabinet was stuffed to the gills, and there was nothing orderly about it. It looked, in fact, like a miniature storage locker from an episode of *Hoarders*.

"Oh my God," Alicia said. "It's the world's tiniest man cave."

The cabinet did look as though it were the only place in the world a man kept under tight control by his fastidious wife had left to shove things. There were scores of handwritten notes, Post-its, receipts, newspaper clippings, and other miscellany that neither Jennifer nor Alicia could make heads or tails of, and none of which seemed to relate to BTE for Good. There was no sign of Greg Schloss's payroll report, though Alicia did find a folder marked *Memoirs*, inside which was a handful of legal paper covered with Bill's neat, tiny print. "'Women I've Loved,'" Alicia read, sticking it back into the folder in disgust. Before they knew it, twenty minutes had gone by, and, despite being surrounded by papers and the occasional file, they seemed not to have begun to scratch the surface, let alone find what they'd come there for.

"What time is it?" Alicia asked.

"Five forty," Jennifer replied, looking at her phone. "Bill is in the car. Tim was tracking the driver with GPS, but he seems to have lost the signal. We might have another thirty-five minutes," Jennifer said. "Or we might have ten."

"There's got to be *something* in here," Alicia said. She reached into the bottom of the file cabinet, pulled another folder out from under the pile, and looked at it. Cocking her head, she read, "'BTE Investment Securities, LLC.'"

"Bill runs an investment firm?" Jennifer asked. She began to thumb through other files to see if any was similarly labeled.

"I don't think it's really an investment firm," Alicia said. "I think it's just something he's done for the last few years for his friends. He mentioned it to me when we got together to discuss the job. I know a couple of the investors." She peered at some of the statements and whistled. "I recognize a lot of these names, actually," she added. "It reads like a who's who of black people with money."

Jennifer found another folder related to BTE Investment Securities, marked *Correspondence*. She opened it.

"He started doing it right after the recession, I think," Alicia said. "He had a lot of big real estate deals go bad. But obviously," she said, gesturing to the room they were in, "he recovered."

"Alicia!" Jennifer said, her eyes widening as she paged through the contents of the correspondence folder faster and faster, her pulse quickening. "Look at this." She handed Alicia one of the letters from the file.

Alicia took the letter and began to read. "'Dear Bill,'" she began. "'This is the fifth letter I have written asking you to repay the two hundred and sixty-four thousand dollars I placed with you for investment in April of 2012. As you know, I have urged other of your investors—and, might I add, not just "investors" but mutual colleagues and friends—to do the same, as I have come to believe that the returns you have promised are not sustainable and were, perhaps, fiction to begin with. Out of respect for your late father, I'm willing to let the matter drop if you are able to fully disburse my original investment in the next thirty days, but otherwise I will be forced to take this matter to the SEC. . . .'"

Alicia read silently through to the end. "I know this man," Alicia said quietly. "He was a major donor to the mayor's education charity when I was superintendent."

Jennifer produced another letter. And another. Some of them were typed and written in formal language, like the first, but some were handwritten, striking more desperate, pathetic tones. *Dear Bill,* one began, *we have been friends for twenty-two years now, and you won't answer my calls? I have been trying to explain to my wife why we have not gotten our money back. As you know, she has been talking to Richard Stuart, and he has got her very worried about all this....*

Alicia and Jennifer set the folders down and looked at each other.

"Maybe he *didn't* recover from those bad real estate deals," Jennifer said. "Maybe he sustained huge losses in the crash and decided to offset them by running a Ponzi scheme." It was all beginning to make sense. "His investors are calling him on it. Which would explain why a billionaire would bother to steal from the government."

"He could have sold the house in Aspen," Alicia said, sighing. "Or the yacht." She set the folder down next to the only photo on Bill Truitt's desk—a picture of Bill Sr., who had passed away more than a decade ago, with his arms wrapped proudly around his son on his graduation day from Yale. "His daddy must be turning over in his grave," she added. "Junior is none other than the black Bernie Madoff."

ONCE THEY KNEW WHAT they were looking for, it didn't take long to find the proof to support Jennifer's theory. Greg Schloss's payroll reports weren't there—shredded, Jennifer guessed—but, in an unmarked folder buried at the very bottom of the file cabinet, Jennifer and Alicia found bank statements showing transfers from BTE for Good directly to BTE Investment Securities. The rate of the transfers had increased markedly in the last few months, as Bill had grown more and more desperate to appease his investors with cash, and correlated with the bigger amounts he'd been taking out of the residents' paychecks. Jennifer's calculations had been correct—the total transfers added up to more than half a million dollars. Bill, having tapped a cash cow, had only just gotten started milking it.

"We should start packing up," Jennifer said, indicating the time to Alicia on her phone. "He probably won't get here for another twenty minutes, but when he does, I want to be long gone."

Alicia nodded and began to replace papers carefully into their files and place the files back into the file cabinet. "I'll edit our return," Jennifer said, opening Wishful Thinking. Just as she did, however, there was a *ping*. It was a text from Tim.

HE'S IN THE LOBBY. It was 6:00 p.m.

R u sure? Jennifer texted back.

Doorman, Tim replied. *I will call, try to stall him. Get ready!!!!*

"We've gotta go!" Jennifer yelled. Alicia rose quickly from Bill's chair, closed the file cabinet, locked it, shoved it under the desk, and replaced the key while Jennifer used the EDIT button, which had come in as handy as she'd suspected it might, to change their Wishful Thinking return time.

Pulling up the entry, she changed the appointment's end time to 6:01 p.m.

"Oh my God," Alicia said. "He could walk in here any minute!" She shut the office door and joined Jennifer behind Bill's desk. Editing complete, Jennifer set the phone on the desk between them.

"We'll be gone in less than sixty seconds," she said. "Don't worry."

Alicia put one hand on the phone and one hand on Jennifer's upper arm. "I can't believe I'm actually looking forward to being turned into atomic soup," she said with a nervous laugh.

Jennifer smiled. "You got everything?" she asked.

"Yes," Alicia said, patting the folder tucked under her arm.

Looking at the clock on the wall, Jennifer and Alicia watched as the second hand swung past the six, beginning to count down the last thirty seconds they would have to wait. Steadily it glided past the seven, the eight, and then the nine. There were just five seconds to go when Jennifer, her eyes darting down to her phone, saw something that made her heart stop. Against Wishful Thinking's familiar dark blue background was an unfamiliar screen, unlike anything she had ever seen before. *A notification from Wishful Thinking.* Jennifer tapped it.

Unable to connect to the Internet to secure location coordinates, the notification said. *Please wait while Wishful Thinking searches for a wireless network. As soon as a connection is established, your appointment will begin.*

"Fuck," Jennifer said quietly.

"Why are we still here?" Alicia asked, turning to her. Jennifer motioned dumbly to her phone.

Alicia stared at the screen. "She invented a time-travel app that uses *3G?*"

"No," Jennifer replied, trying to think, her brain spinning just like the little wheel. "It uses GETS. Some network for government emergency responders. It's fail-safe—Dr. Sexton got the code! This never happens; it's impossible!" She motioned to Alicia to take out her own phone. "Call Dr. Sexton," she said, and dictated the number, which she had memorized months ago in case of an emergency, "but don't let go of me while you do."

Alicia dialed. "The reception is terrible in here," she said anxiously. "It's not even ringing."

Ping. Another text from Tim. Somehow *his* texts were coming through. Maybe he had Verizon.

COMING UP NOW, it read.

"*Whisper*," Jennifer hissed to Alicia.

Please, Dr. Sexton, Jennifer thought. *Please pick up.*

"It's ringing!" Alicia cried, her hand over her phone.

"Voice mail!" Alicia said. There was a beep. Alicia began to whisper-babble. "Dr. Sexton it's Alicia we're trying to get out of Bill's apartment but somehow we aren't getting a signal." She paused. "Please call us back." Alicia hung up. Jennifer's eyes were glued to her phone. At the top of it that wheel, that goddamn endlessly spinning little wheel, with its flashing and fading tiny little cheery spokes flashing and fading again and again, all of it adding up to nothing, to zero, to zilch, jammed up and pointless and impotent at precisely the moment she most needed it to work—if that little wheel didn't stop spinning soon, she thought, she was probably going to go to jail.

But the little wheel spun on.

She wanted to scream, but screaming, she knew, would be a very bad idea. Because by now Bill must surely have come off the elevator and onto the fifty-fifth floor. And then they heard it. Footsteps approaching the door.

"Put your phone away," Jennifer whispered, concentrating on keeping every muscle still.

Alicia gripped Jennifer's hand so tightly, Jennifer had to bite her lip to keep from crying out in pain. "Our father," Alicia murmured, "who art in heaven, hallowed be thy name . . ."

The door opened, and Bill Truitt was there, standing inside it. And for a split second—a moment so fleeting Jennifer knew that later Bill Truitt would doubt whether it had ever occurred, if only to preserve his sanity—Jennifer and big Bill Truitt locked eyes. And just as they did, just as that tiny wheel finally stopped spinning and just as the wormhole, her old, faithful friend, yawned out of her phone, the blue tunnel of light lashing outward and upward in all its swirling, tremendous glory, enveloping Jennifer and Alicia inside, Jennifer managed to say the three words she most wanted to say right to that arrogant asshole's stunned, disbelieving face.

"We got you."

And then they were gone.

twenty four | NOW WHAT?

BREATHLESS AND SHELL-SHOCKED but triumphant, Jennifer and Alicia appeared—the evidence inside the folder tucked under Alicia's arm—in the exact spot where they had begun their journey in Jennifer's apartment an hour before. For Dr. Sexton, of course, it had been only a minute, and when she saw the folder Alicia held, she sat up in her chair, eyes glittering with excitement. "You found what you needed?" she asked.

Sitting down, still shaking a little, Alicia placed the folder on the table. "It turns out that Bill Truitt was in big financial trouble," Alicia said. "So he set up a dummy investment business and took money—millions, we think—from his wealthy friends, promising them huge returns. But in the last year or so," she said, pulling out some of the correspondence, "some of his investors got suspicious and started to demand their money back. He was embezzling from One Stop to get the cash to hold them off."

"And this is the proof?" Dr. Sexton said, skimming the

documents. Jennifer, who'd taken a seat next to Alicia, nodded.

Dr. Sexton clapped her hands together. "Bravo!" she said. But Jennifer and Alicia were silent. The thrill of their find, and of their narrow escape, had already worn off. Jennifer sighed.

"I know," Alicia said, sighing too.

"Why so glum?" Dr. Sexton asked. "You got what you needed, didn't you?"

"Yes," Jennifer said. "The problem is, what do we do now?"

"Why, you take it to the inspector general you mentioned, and you have this greedy thief put in jail!"

"But what happens to One Stop?" Alicia said. "We're so close. Just six months away from opening our doors. This will blow up the whole project completely. There will be an investigation, which could take months, even years, and the breach of trust with the community will be nearly irreparable. There will be protests, demonstrations . . . We caught it, yes, but the damage will be crippling."

"Not only that," Jennifer added, "but the new mayor is a maniac about corruption. He campaigned as Mr. Clean, and Bill is connected to him personally. Which means it's a scandal that will taint *him*, and he'll want to stay as far away from it—and us—as he possibly can."

"We got Bill," Alicia said, "but in the end, he may have gotten us instead."

Alicia didn't have to say it. They should have been more vigilant. They should have known better.

It took a moment for them to register that Dr. Sexton was smiling. Grinning, in fact, from ear to ear.

"What's got you so cheery?" Alicia said, jerking her head back.

"I believe," Dr. Sexton said, "I may be able to be of some assistance."

"What?" Alicia said. "Do you have an app that saves public-housing projects from being sunk by corrupt, ego-maniacal businessmen?"

"No," Dr. Sexton replied. "I am not an app maker, or whatever such people are called. I am a physicist who happens to have made the greatest discovery in the history of science." That shut Alicia up. "In this case, however," Dr. Sexton continued, softening her tone, "I believe I can offer a more traditional sort of help, of the nepotistic variety. Do you remember, my dear," she said, turning to Jennifer, "when I mentioned my younger brother to you? And that he had gone into your line of work? Government or, more accurately put, politics." Jennifer nodded—she did remember, vaguely. "My brother's name is . . . Aldon!" When Jennifer and Alicia met this declaration with blank looks, Dr. Sexton added, slightly exasperated, "Fitch. *Aldon Fitch.*"

"Oh my God," Jennifer said. "Your younger brother is the mayor?"

Alicia's eyes were wide. "Seriously? Why isn't your last name Fitch?" she asked.

Dr. Sexton's eyes widened with horror. "Diane Fitch?" She shuddered. "I took my mother's name when I entered the physics program at Caltech. Infinitely more elegant, wouldn't you agree? Not to mention I had long been an admirer of the great poet Anne."

"So you're saying," Jennifer said, still trying to process this news and what it might mean for One Stop, "that if we have evidence that Bill has been embezzling and take it directly to the mayor, your brother, with you as our . . . liaison, or something, he would . . . what?"

Dr. Sexton was about to answer, when Alicia leaned in. For the first time since yesterday's press conference, she was all smiles, her eyes practically dancing. "Oh, I think our mayor would much prefer a quiet cover-up to a public airing of the city's dirty laundry," she said, "particularly when it involves one of his biggest campaign donors—not to mention the most prominent black businessman in the city—stealing from public-housing residents on his watch."

"But could the program survive?" Jennifer asked.

"If the mayor is behind it, as he very publicly declared himself to be yesterday morning, and wants us to keep this to ourselves, then yes, it could," Alicia said. "Bill goes away, and we move on."

"You mean Bill *gets* away," Jennifer said.

"Lesser of two evils," Alicia said. "Better to get rid of him and save the center if we can."

"So it's settled, then," Dr. Sexton said, obviously pleased. "I will call Aldon."

"We'll need to see him today if we can," Jennifer said. "Before Bill gets back."

"Consider it done," Dr. Sexton said, rising. "Though perhaps I'd better make this call in private. Aldon and I haven't spoken in a while." Jennifer walked Dr. Sexton to the door.

"Dr. Sexton," she said in a low voice, "I think you should know. There was a complication involving the network. We tried to call you—"

Dr. Sexton swiftly raised her hand, signaling Jennifer to stop. "Not another word," she said.

"But—"

"Not another word!" Dr. Sexton repeated emphatically. "Please. I'd hope you would have learned this lesson quite clearly after the events of yesterday. Whatever happens at six o'clock today is what must happen, and what *has* happened, and I cannot interfere. Susan will be finishing her chemo-therapy then. I will be with her at the hospital, and I will not have my phone turned on." Jennifer nodded. It wasn't urgent, she supposed, if Dr. Sexton wasn't using the app anymore either. But she'd have to let her know eventually.

Dr. Sexton opened the door, then turned to Jennifer, flashing her an amused smile. "I must say I find it amazing," she said. "Who would ever have thought Aldon would turn out to be a person from whom one would require a favor!"

HOURS LATER, JENNIFER AND Alicia were cooling their heels in Alicia's office on the twentieth floor, with no word from Dr. Sexton. It was nearly two o'clock, and they'd been trying to stay busy while also trying to keep Tim calm. He was waiting around at home, as instructed, but texting incessantly to express his growing anxiety about Jennifer and Alicia's need-to-know plan to break into Bill's apartment—an event that, as far as he knew, hadn't happened yet.

Jennifer was becoming increasingly nervous too. If they didn't get an audience with the mayor before Bill returned, their chances of settling things quietly would diminish fast. What would Bill do when he came home and discovered his files were missing? Leave the country? Come clean? Alicia and Jennifer had spun out a variety of outcomes, but none of them was favorable to One Stop.

Alicia, drumming her fingernails on her desk, pulled the mayor's schedule up on her computer for the fifth time that afternoon. "Department of Ed meeting finally wrapped up," she said. "Dr. Sexton probably couldn't have reached him until noon at the earliest." She looked over the top of her screen at Jennifer. "Don't stress," she said. But Alicia, apparently having difficulty following her own advice, resumed her incessant fingernail tapping.

Moments later, to their great surprise, Dr. Sexton appeared, out of breath, in the doorway to Alicia's office.

"Thank God!" she said exasperatedly. "I've been in the building half an hour now. Do you know how hard it is to navigate the corridors in this place? Everything so monotonously taupe! It's like being trapped in a Soviet Holiday Inn."

Jennifer and Alicia looked at her expectantly.

"Well, hello to you too," Dr. Sexton said, taking a seat next to Jennifer and opposite Alicia.

"*Well?*" Jennifer asked.

"He's not answering my calls," Dr. Sexton said. "It's strange. It isn't like him. I so rarely call. I thought he'd be pleased."

"Could he be unhappy with you about something?" Alicia asked.

"What could Aldon possibly be unhappy with me about?" Dr. Sexton replied indignantly. Placing both palms emphatically on Alicia's desk, she looked Alicia, then Jennifer, in the eye. "We just have to go in and see him," she said. "That's all there is to it." She stood, then stepped into the doorway again, poking her head out into the hallway. "I just hope you two know which way to go."

ON THEIR WAY FROM NYCHA to city hall, Alicia called the mayor's assistant, who reported that the mayor was due any minute at his office, where he had set aside some time to debrief with his chief of staff. "Perfect!" Dr. Sexton said. "He'll have a moment, then." Jennifer and Alicia thought that was unlikely, but time was running short, so they followed Dr. Sexton through one security checkpoint after the next. Entering the mayor's chambers, however, they were stopped by a security guard, who asked if they had an appointment. "I am the mayor's *sister*," Dr. Sexton replied haughtily. "I hardly think I need an appointment." Unsurprisingly, the security guard disagreed. Reluctantly, he consented to call the mayor's office and inquire whether a Dr. Diane Sexton should be allowed in to see him. This time, apparently, the mayor took the call.

"All right," the guard said, waving them through.

"Honestly," Dr. Sexton muttered as they gathered their bags from the conveyor belt after passing through the final checkpoint. "You'd think he was—"

"The mayor of New York City?" Alicia shot back. It was clear to Jennifer that Alicia was beginning to wish she had not thrown in her lot with Dr. Sexton—and perhaps not with Jennifer, either, for that matter. For her part, Jennifer was hoping Dr. Sexton's younger brother liked her a lot more than his response to Dr. Sexton thus far suggested.

Jennifer was not reassured when the mayor stepped out into his reception area and Dr. Sexton stood up to greet him. Upon seeing her, Mayor Fitch exhibited all the filial warmth of a tuna fish. "Diane," he said icily, "what's so important? You do know I'm running the country's largest city? Are you here about GETS? You couldn't possibly expect me to reinstate your access, having so utterly abused it."

"What do you mean?" Dr. Sexton said.

"GETS," the mayor practically snarled, though his face remained so expressionless that the malice in his voice seemed to come from another body. "Remember? You asked for the code? Have you been using it as your *wireless* provider? Do you know how restricted access to that network? When I gave you the code, I told you it was strictly for emergencies, like tsunamis or terrorist attacks. Not to be used multiple times on a daily basis because you are too impatient to suffer through commercial service like the rest of us." Dr. Sexton quickly took a step closer to the mayor and placed a hand on his arm.

"Aldon," she said in a low voice, "let's discuss this privately." The mayor, who had not so much as glanced at Jennifer and Alicia, nodded curtly and showed Diane into his office.

"Oh my God," Alicia said as soon as he'd shut the door.

"*That's* why we were hanging by a thread on AT&T or whatever-the-frack," Jennifer said. "He must have cut off her GETS access today!"

"I am battling the urge to run right out of this office," Alicia said.

"Keep battling," Jennifer said. "We've come too far to quit now."

At least fifteen minutes passed before Dr. Sexton opened the office door, during which time Alicia practically drilled a fingernail hole in the armrest of her chair. Stepping out into the reception area, Dr. Sexton seemed relieved to see that they were still sitting there. "Thank you for waiting," she said, motioning for them to come in. Dr. Sexton gave each of their arms a quick squeeze as they passed. "My apologies," she whispered. "It should be all right now."

The mayor was seated behind a large but not ostentatious desk, somewhere between the kind of gilded corporate veneer Bill had imported to his government digs and the more modest, conservative tones that had characterized it before. An aide was standing beside him.

"I met you both yesterday," the mayor said, regarding them matter-of-factly, "at the press conference for One Stop. Alicia Richardson, formerly superintendent for district—don't tell me —thirteen?" Alicia nodded, impressed. The mayor was clearly impressed with himself too. Dr. Sexton was looking at him, however, like he was a third grader showing off his knowledge of state capitals. "And you are Jennifer Sharpe, author of the One Stop community-center model, formerly a management consultant at—don't tell me—Bain?"

"McKinsey," Jennifer said. "And you have an incredible memory."

"I always have," the mayor responded, gesturing for them to take a seat. "Indispensable in this line of work." Jennifer and Alicia sat down. Jennifer glanced over at the folder of documents in Alicia's lap. The mayor, not one to miss a trick, eyed it too.

"Terrific project, One Stop," the mayor added, with a hint of a smile. "We got some great press yesterday. But my sister tells me there's a problem? Something that couldn't go through the usual channels?"

Diving in, Jennifer and Alicia made their case as quickly and concisely as they could. When they had finished, the mayor asked for the documents supporting their claims. He opened the folder and reviewed them silently, thin lips pursed, face frozen in an expression so blank it was impossible to interpret. After what seemed like an eternity, he whispered something to his aide, who whispered something back. Then the mayor whispered back to him. Then the aide whispered back to the mayor.

"Oh, for God's sake!" Dr. Sexton burst out. Jennifer nearly kicked her in the shin.

"First of all," the mayor said, after shooting his sister a withering look, "I want to thank you for bringing this to my attention, and for being so discreet. It's a terrible thing for those residents, and I'm incredibly disappointed in Bill. Frankly, I can't imagine why he'd do this." He paused, seeming to consider something. "Is it your belief that Bill, confronted with the evidence, will pay the money back? So that the project can move forward without a scandal? Without Bill as its head any longer, of course."

Jennifer and Alicia looked at each other. They had never said that. They didn't know how deep Bill's financial troubles went, but it seemed unlikely he was in any position to pay back the funds. But how could they tell that to the mayor? It had already been difficult to explain how they'd attained the records they'd brought, which they had confined strictly to the payroll discrepancies and the transfers, in matching amounts, between BTE for Good and BTE Investment Securities. They could not say they had read Bill's personal correspondence about his investment fund, or that he had embezzled from the city because his Ponzi scheme had caught up with him.

"*Is* that what you are suggesting?" the mayor asked impatiently.

Suddenly Dr. Sexton spoke. "Suppose I were to make up the difference," she said, leaning forward, "as an anonymous donor?"

"What?" Jennifer and Alicia gasped simultaneously.

The mayor sat back in his chair, knitting his brow and studying his sister. "Jennifer Sharpe is your neighbor. That's how two know each other?" He shook his head. "Even for you, Diane, this is extremely eccentric."

"She is my neighbor. And my friend. We've come to know each other very well, in fact," Dr. Sexton added, "and having been witness to her passion for the community center for many months now, I've become very passionate about it too. It seems to me that it would be very reckless, and endanger this important work further, to involve a criminal in financing it, even if he were repaying what he stole."

"It's almost half a million dollars, Dr. Sexton," Jennifer said softly, as though she were addressing a pitiable old lady who was beginning to go dotty. "You can't do that."

"Oh, she can do that," the mayor said with a wave of his hand and the faintest eye roll. "She can do that easily."

Alicia and Jennifer exchanged a look. *Really?*

"It is a public-private partnership, is it not, Aldon?" Dr.

Sexton went on, determinedly making her case. "Isn't that part of the innovation Ms. Sharpe has brought to the project, combining government funding with private donations? And I have the foundation Daddy set up for me. As you know, I've spent many years looking for a worthy cause."

Jennifer almost laughed at hearing Dr. Sexton utter the word *Daddy*, but she was too riveted by the exchange to breathe.

"It is about time you took your duties seriously with regard to philanthropy," the mayor said, though still a bit uneasily. The aide leaned in and whispered something else into his ear. The mayor seemed to brighten a bit. "And it would certainly be good publicity for the city, and the project, a gift of that size," he continued. "A major vote of confidence from the private sector, a half-million-dollar gift."

"A major vote!" Dr. Sexton cried, sensing victory. "To compensate for all the times I've failed to vote for you in the past!" Mayor Fitch scowled, and for a minute Jennifer could see the face of a little boy eternally made to feel like an also-ran by his brilliant older sister. "Don't be cross, Aldon," Dr. Sexton said, evidently making the same observation. "You know perfectly well that I never vote for anybody. After all, Daddy was a communist." At this the aide's eyebrows shot up, and the mayor abruptly stood.

"All right, then!" the mayor said, standing to shake Alicia's and Jennifer's hands. "I will inform Bill when he returns from London and ask him to write his letter of resignation. He shouldn't get away with this, of course," he added, "but you've convinced me. Tarring and feathering him would punish more people than it would help." The mayor turned to Jennifer. "I trust you can process the grant from my sister's foundation?" he asked. She nodded.

Jennifer and Alicia were gathering their things quickly,

wanting to leave before the mayor changed his mind, when the mayor appeared in front of them, having come around from behind his desk to stand between them and the door. "I trust we can all keep what's been said in this room confidential?" he said sternly. "Including," he added, letting out a little cough, "that bit about Daddy's, um, political affiliations?"

"Oh, really, Aldon," Dr. Sexton said with a hearty laugh. "This is New York. Everybody's daddy was a communist at one point or another, if he were at all interesting, that is. It was quite the rage amongst the intellectual class." The mayor reddened. Dr. Sexton leaned in. "Thank you," she said sincerely, giving him a kiss. She drew back. "You've done me a great favor, Aldon. If you ever want to play the 'my sister is a lesbian and I couldn't be prouder' card, I stand ready to oblige."

And with that, Dr. Diane Sexton, newly minted benefactor of the One Stop community center, made her exit.

twenty five | SAFE AND
SOUND

IT WAS FOUR O'CLOCK by the time they walked out of
city hall and into City Hall Park. "This is where I will
leave you," Dr. Sexton said. "It's time for me to meet
Susan at the treatment center. But perhaps we can reconvene
at my apartment tonight to celebrate?"

"I'd love to," Alicia replied, with a warmth that surprised
Jennifer. "Thank you," she added. "For what you've done. And
for what you are going to do."

Dr. Sexton smiled at them both. "I'm terribly sorry about
the GETS network, by the way," she said. "I assume that is the
difficulty you wanted to alert me to this morning?" Jennifer
nodded. "It must have been quite harrowing, standing in Bill's
study, evidence in hand, waiting for reception to kick in!"
Then Dr. Sexton laughed, and, despite themselves, Jennifer
and Alicia laughed too.

Dr. Sexton headed for the subway, and Alicia and Jennifer
headed back to the office. Both of them would have liked
nothing better than to leave after the day they'd had, but the

day wasn't over yet. There was one more thing they had to do —something Jennifer had to admit she was quite looking forward to.

When the moment arrived at 6:01 p.m., Jennifer and Alicia were ready, seated at their respective desks. Jennifer's phone was the first to ring.

She picked up, smiling brightly. "This is Jennifer," she said.

For a moment there was silence.

"You're in the office right now?" Bill asked, his voice cracking slightly.

"Is that you, Bill?" Jennifer asked innocently. "Of course I'm in the office. Where else would I be?" There was another pause, and Jennifer thought she could hear the sound of Bill's head exploding.

"Transfer me to Alicia," he barked. *"Now."*

Holding her hand over the receiver, Jennifer waved to Alicia in her office, who nodded and picked up the instant the call was transferred.

"Hello, Bill," Jennifer could hear her say, as calm as you please. "How was your flight?"

Bill hung up.

TOGETHER THEY CALLED TIM.

"Did you find anything?" he asked as soon as Jennifer put him on speakerphone. Alicia and Jennifer were sitting in Jennifer's office now, Alicia's ankle elevated on Jennifer's desk.

"We got proof," Alicia said.

"You did? I knew there was something in that file cabinet! I *knew* it! And I stalled him for a minute on the phone; did you notice that?" Jennifer and Alicia gave Tim a moment to savor his triumph.

"Bill agreed to step down," Alicia said, rehearsing the story she and Jennifer had agreed upon. "As long as we agreed not to tell anybody why."

"*What?*" Tim said. "And you said yes?"

"It's better for One Stop this way," Jennifer said. "And for the community."

"How? Better how? Letting a criminal rip off the residents and get away with it? Letting him walk around being a big fat hypocrite, talking about giving back and how he understands what people in poverty are going through, and after all that he gets some kind of honorable discharge?"

"Jennifer found a foundation today that will make it right with the residents," Alicia said. "They will be fairly paid."

"But how about making it *right* right? Like, right in the world?"

Jennifer and Alicia exchanged a look. Alicia muted the phone for a moment. "He's right," she said. "It's like the mayor said. He shouldn't get away with it."

"I agree," Jennifer said. "But what can we do?"

Alicia raised her eyebrows ever so slightly and smiled. She unmuted the phone. "Tim," she said. "If we told you that Bill was the black Bernie Madoff, would you believe it?"

"Hell, yeah," Tim said. "Are you kidding me?" There was a pause. "*Are* you kidding me?"

"Bill was embezzling from One Stop because he needed cash to cover a Ponzi scheme he was running—a big one, Madoff-style," Alicia said. Jennifer reached into her desk drawer and took out the folder marked *BTE Investment Securities: Correspondence* and handed it to Alicia. "If he burns for the embezzlement, we might as well burn down the community center, too . . . ," Alicia began.

"But if he burns for the Ponzi scheme . . . ," Jennifer added, trailing off.

"He burns," Tim said, "just like he should."

"If I gave you a list of names," Alicia said to Tim, "could you make it happen fast? Because my guess is that the minute he figured out those bank statements were gone, along with the letters from the investors he cheated, Bill Truitt headed for the airport."

"I can make it happen," Tim said. "Just give me the names." His voice seemed to have dropped an octave, and Alicia and Jennifer tried not to giggle at his sudden James Bond seriousness. "After all," he added, with even more swagger, "I'm not the One Stop social media coordinator for nothing."

NOT AN HOUR AND a half later, Tim not only had Bill busted; he had Bill busted on CNN. As Alicia had predicted, Bill had apparently decided shortly after discovering the two of them in his office—or at least thinking he saw the two of them standing in his office, until they disappeared into a snaking blue tunnel of light—that it was time to go on the lam. Having been tipped off by Tim, however, the powerful men he'd cheated acted faster than Bill could. It was a last-minute phone call from the mayor's office, in fact (many of Bill's victims being close chums of Aldon's, too), that resulted in his apprehension at JFK airport, holding a suitcase full of cash, attempting to board a plane headed for Ecuador.

"Ecuador!" Dr. Sexton snorted. "Who does he think he is, Julian Assange?" Dr. Sexton, Alicia, and Jennifer had just finished watching the clip Tim had sent them on Jennifer's laptop, having gathered together at last at Dr. Sexton's apartment at the end of a very long day. As it turned out, however, watching Bill with his hands in front of his face as men in black suits escorted him away from the international terminal was a bit of a buzzkill.

"There won't be a movie, that's for sure," Alicia said, sighing. "It's all too pathetic."

Jennifer closed the laptop, feeling weirdly sad too. Just yesterday morning, she and Bill had stood side by side in the One Stop atrium, admiring what they'd built together. One Stop had been a dashed dream before Bill became NYCHA's chair, and he had resurrected it because he believed in it—Jennifer still believed that. In the end, however, he hadn't cared about anything as much as he'd cared about saving his own skin. Jack, at four, had a stronger moral compass. At least he cleaned up his own spilled milk.

Dr. Sexton handed Alicia and Jennifer each a generous glass of red wine. "That man got exactly what he deserved," she said decidedly. She poured herself a glass, too, then raised it. "A toast! To your fearless daring as you stared into the face of time travel under the threat of spotty wireless service!"

"To your generosity," Alicia said, raising her glass, too, "which has truly saved the day."

"To Tim," Jennifer said, smiling. "May he never have to pick up anybody's dry cleaning but his own again!"

They clinked glasses and drank. The wine was superb, and Jennifer let out a grateful moan.

"Shall we boot up the fire?" Dr. Sexton asked, moving into the living room.

"Definitely," Jennifer said, looking at her watch. "Vinita will be here with the boys soon. Last time I checked, they were just finishing up watching a movie at her place." The boys, apparently, had been more than happy to skip swimming lessons. She guessed they weren't going to mind taking things down a notch now that she no longer had the app—though resuming a schedule where she never picked them up from school at all wasn't going to go over well. Though perhaps with Bill gone, she thought, that would change? It was hard to imagine what would happen now.

Alicia and Jennifer had just sat down on the couch when the fire began to blaze. "Wow," Alicia said, staring. "I want one!"

They settled in. Alicia and Jennifer took turns doing imitations of the look on Bill's face when he saw them standing in his office, file folders in hand. Dr. Sexton recounted her brother's outrage at having been threatened with an audit by the FCC and the lengths she'd had to go to placate him—including doing her best imitation of a "woman of a certain age," dim-witted and helpless in the face of technology. ("It's shocking how quickly, if I simply tilt my head a certain way and bat my eyes, my brother forgets I have a doctorate in theoretical physics.") Alicia wondered what Mrs. Bill's reaction to her husband's fall from grace was going to be. Jennifer asked how Susan's chemo had gone. Before they knew it, half an hour had gone by, and there was a knock at the door.

Dr. Sexton opened it, and the sights, sounds, and decidedly unrelaxing energy of five children under the age of ten rushed into the room, instantly transforming their cozy campfire into an unruly zoo. The children were all being corralled, if somewhat unsuccessfully, by a harried-looking Vinita.

"Sorry to bring my girls over too," Vinita said to Jennifer apologetically, "but Sandra had to leave." Lowering her voice so the children couldn't hear, she added, "And I'm dying to hear what happened with Bill!" Vinita knew that the break-in had been successful, but Jennifer hadn't updated her since.

"I'm delighted to meet your girls!" Dr. Sexton said, introducing herself to each of them. Jennifer gave Vinita a hug. She had done her a huge favor by picking the boys up that afternoon. Or, more likely, Sandra had, but Jennifer had not been about to look a pickup gift horse in the mouth.

Jennifer then turned to embrace Julien, who headed

straight for her open arms. Or so she thought until he ran straight into Dr. Sexton's.

"Where have you been?" Julien asked her plaintively. "We've been knocking and knocking on Saturdays! I wanted to show you my insect-collecting kit!"

"I'm sorry, Julien," Dr. Sexton said, bending down to his eye level, as she always did. "I'm back now."

"Should I take the kids to your place?" Vinita asked Jennifer as Preethi, Vinita's youngest, began zipping around like a pinball, coming dangerously close to smacking into one of Dr. Sexton's exhibits at top speed. "Put on a movie? Though they just watched a movie. And it's a school night."

"Not necessary," Dr. Sexton pronounced. "Children!" she said, clapping her hands. "Do you like virtual reality?"

"We do, we do!" cried Julien and Jack. Julien turned to Rani. "It's supercool. It's a game she made where you pretend you're in the Wild West, and you're cowboys, and you shoot—"

"You better not say Indians," Vinita said warningly.

"*Aliens,*" Dr. Sexton said. "You shoot aliens. I may be a child of the nineteen fifties, but I'm not as bad as all that."

"I thought you didn't like those 'adolescent Hollywood movies,'" Jennifer teased. Dr. Sexton ignored this.

"And it's safe, as well as PC?" Vinita asked, directing a meaningful look Jennifer's way.

"Absolutely safe," Dr. Sexton said. "Nothing more than bits and bytes, assembled together to create perfectly harmless, perfectly delightful illusions."

"Fine," Vinita said, picking up the open bottle on the counter and glancing at the label. "And for me, if you don't mind, a delightful, if not entirely harmless, glass of this gorgeous red wine."

* * *

TWENTY MINUTES LATER, all was remarkably quiet again. Rani and Julien were playing Cowboys and Aliens in Dr. Sexton's computer room, and Neela, Preethi, and Jack were huddled up in a squirmy kid ball on Dr. Sexton's four-poster bed, watching *Toy Story* on her big-screen TV. Alicia, Jennifer, and Vinita, who had been fully brought up to speed, were seated comfortably in front of the fire at last. Dr. Sexton was in her office, uninstalling Wishful Thinking on Jennifer's phone. It was almost seven months to the day, Jennifer calculated, since she'd gotten it.

"What do you think is taking so long?" Jennifer asked, attempting to tuck her legs under her in the elegant way Vinita did so effortlessly. (Another thing Jennifer had never managed to do, even with the superpowers of Wishful Thinking: yoga.)

"One would hope it's a relatively complex technology," Vinita said drily.

Jennifer tried not to let Vinita see the regret, tinged with panic, she could feel overtaking her as she waited for Dr. Sexton to return. But it was hard. After seven months of being able to do, be, and accomplish everything she wanted, never having to sacrifice one part of her life for another, she was about to return to the sacrifice and scarcity inevitable to a life in real time. Maybe she should move to Sweden, she thought, land of government-mandated five weeks' paid vacation and universal child care. Too bad she didn't like meatballs—and her life was in America, land of two weeks' paid vacation . . . if your employer felt like giving it to you.

At last Dr. Sexton emerged from her office. She approached Jennifer, holding her phone out in her upturned palms. "I must confess it pained me to carry it out, if only a little bit. But there is no going back now. The deed is done." She placed the phone into Jennifer's hands. "Ms. Sharpe," she said ceremoniously, "I present to you your phone, restored to its status as a merely 'smart' phone—yet another insufferably silly name."

Jennifer pressed the slim, rectangular button on top and watched as her phone blinked uneventfully back to life. A photo of Julien and Jack the morning of her birthday, when they made her pancakes, appeared. When her home screen was loaded, Jennifer swiped to the right with her thumb. She pressed on her calendar to open it. The familiar bars of color, stacked like Jenga blocks atop each day, were still there: orange for work, green for personal, red for the family calendar she shared with Norman, baby blue for the boys' schools. But one calendar was no longer there: the calendar graced by that beautiful midnight blue.

Looking up at Dr. Sexton, Jennifer did her best to smile.

"I suppose I'm a little sad too," she said.

"But it is the right thing to do," Dr. Sexton replied firmly. "Our experiment was just that. An experiment. And I believe we both learned a great deal."

"What about you, Diane?" Vinita asked, standing and going back into the kitchen to refill Dr. Sexton's glass of wine. "Did you uninstall it on your phone too?"

"I did," Dr. Sexton said, settling into a Victorian armchair. "Though my resolve was aided by the fact that I have not excluded the possibility of putting it back again. After Susan has recovered, of course."

"Jennifer told me your partner has cancer," Alicia said. "I'm so sorry."

"As am I," Dr. Sexton said, sighing as Vinita handed her the glass.

Vinita sat back down on the rug, across from Dr. Sexton. She looked up at her. "I hope it's all right," she said quietly, "but I just *have* to ask." Dr. Sexton nodded, seeming to know what was coming. "Did you ever think of it? Of going back? Of telling her earlier about the tumor?"

"You can only go back six hours," Jennifer said. "The app won't let you go back any further than that."

Dr. Sexton cleared her throat slightly.

"What?" Jennifer said. "Is that not true either, like the future thing?"

"It is another 'guideline' I put in for your own safety, my dear," Dr. Sexton said.

"How far can you go back? As far as you want?" Jennifer asked, her heart rising in her throat.

"You cannot go back to a time before the app existed," Dr. Sexton said gently, seeming to intuit the meaning behind Jennifer's question. Her mother. Could Jennifer have used the app to see her mother again? "And that was only a little more than a year ago." Jennifer's shoulders dropped, and she leaned her head back against the couch. Her mother had been gone for a year and a half now. Part of her was relieved. Going back in time to see her mother, who was gone now, would have been wrong, the way using the app to rescue Jack would have been wrong. But if she'd thought she could have, the temptation would have been nearly impossible to resist.

"A year would have been plenty of time to detect Susan's cancer much earlier than it was discovered," Vinita said.

"Yes," Dr. Sexton replied simply.

"So why didn't you," Jennifer asked, "if you could have saved her? I mean, not that she needs saving—I know she'll pull through this—but . . ." Jennifer did not finish her sentence.

"I thought about it a great deal," Dr. Sexton said quietly. "And, at one point, I made the trip. I was standing on the sidewalk, ready to walk through the front door of our brownstone and tell her everything. But just as I was about to enter, I caught sight of Susan through the window." Dr.

Sexton paused, remembering. "None of you has truly aged yet," she said, looking at the three women around her. "You may think you have, Alicia, but you'll see." Alicia smiled ruefully. "It is a very surreal experience. When you reach a certain age, your body, even the contours of your face, can suddenly take you by surprise in the mirror, as though you have been replaced by someone not yourself, someone you don't remember, or someone you have never even met." Jennifer thought ashamedly of how rashly she had dismissed the idea that she would age faster than everybody around her: a Faustian bargain indeed. "That was what it was like when I saw Susan through the window. I saw her as I hadn't seen her in many years, without the memory of our youth disguising the realities of our aging. She looked old! Her hair, which used to be so blond, is white and thinning now. The soft places on the undersides of her arms, where gravity has pulled her skin earthward, bear little resemblance to the arms that, when we played tennis together on Martha's Vineyard during our courtship, were so tan and taut and fine. And while I'd like to think I'm aging well"—all three women cut in in the affirmative, but Dr. Sexton waved them off, laughing—"I am getting old too. Susan and I have grown old together. And it is in time that Susan and I are most profoundly bound. My body is not what it once was, but it is Susan who remembers me as I was before. And it is Susan to whom I owe courage, and even acceptance, in the face of time's ultimate fate—the linear inevitability of our bodies. Death."

The tips of the virtual logs were turning ashy in the fire. "Susan and I have been *in time* together," she continued after a moment or two, in a voice so low the three women strained to hear it, "for so long now." She paused. "And it seemed to me that if I used this technology to disrupt our shared experience of time, to alter the course of her life and mine irrevocably, I would not only break with her but also with some part of myself. With some fundamental part of my humanity. And that act would separate me from her and everyone I've ever loved in a way more profound, perhaps, than dying will."

Jennifer looked up at her. Looking down, Dr. Sexton met her eyes. "Do you understand?" she asked. Jennifer nodded.

Suddenly Dr. Sexton sat forward in her chair, her voice clear and animated again. "Do you know what the chances are of our being together, on this planet, alive, at this exact moment in time?" Dr. Sexton asked, looking from Jennifer to Vinita to Alicia and back again. "The odds against it are on a scale that is almost incomprehensible. *Is* incomprehensible, I should say. And yet it could not be otherwise. We are bound together by the incomprehensible, impossible coincidence that we are here, at this precise space-time coordinate in an infinite universe, alive in the same nanosecond of time in this galaxy, on this planet, in the same country, in the same city, and, at this moment, in the very same room." The four women looked at each other. Vinita grabbed Jennifer's hand. Jennifer grabbed Alicia's. "Take that away," Dr. Sexton said, "break with that . . . and you are lost."

The fire crackled, and a log broke into pieces as its charred body collapsed farther into the virtual grate. "Forgive my speechifying," Dr. Sexton said. "A bad habit, learned at my father's knee." She stood. "The fire is dying," she observed. "I could restart it, but I'm expected at Susan's home tonight. Soon to be my home again too."

"What?" Jennifer asked, putting a hand to her heart. "You're moving back in?"

"That's wonderful!" Vinita said, standing, too, and hugging Dr. Sexton.

"Why do you have to live there?" Jennifer said. "Couldn't

Susan move in here? After all the work you've done on this place? What about the virtual fire?"

"When I could have a real one?" Dr. Sexton said lightly, laughing. Jennifer wanted to laugh too, but her disappointment was too great. She felt like Julien, trudging down the hallway forlornly with his insect-collecting kit in his hands.

Alicia left a few minutes later, promising Dr. Sexton she would be in touch. Vinita walked into the hallway with the children and began to collect coats and shoes. Jennifer hung back.

"I'll miss you so much," she said to Dr. Sexton.

"I don't plan on missing you," Dr. Sexton said. "You will come visit me, and I you. Often. You must come, with Julien and Jack."

At that moment, Jennifer's phone went *ping*.

Where r u? the text message read. *Waiting at costume party!*

"Oh my God," Jennifer said. "Owen!" In the mad dash that had been the last twenty-four hours, between thinking Jack was going to be run over by an SUV, discovering her boss was embezzling and using time travel to bust him for it, and drinking too much red wine, not to mention the Indian martinis of the night before, Jennifer had completely forgotten about her sweet, thoughtful, impossibly wonderful boyfriend.

"Owen!" Dr. Sexton said cheerfully. "Bring him over to visit Susan and me too!" Ducking her head into the hallway, she called to the boys, who were already beginning to make their way back to Jennifer's apartment. "Ta-ta for now, you two!"

"Ta-ta for now!" Jack cried.

"Maybe Saturday I can show you my insect-collecting kit," Julien said. "Will you be here?" Dr. Sexton nodded. *Not for long*, Jennifer thought ruefully. But there was no need to tell Julien that now.

A few minutes later, back in her apartment, Julien and Jack went to their room to put on their pajamas, and Jennifer took out her phone again. She reread Owen's text. She couldn't go to the party. But she wanted to see him. She wanted to see him, right now, more than she wanted anything.

Can't make costume party, she typed. *Boys are with me.* Then, her heart rate accelerating, she added, *Come here? We have ice cream.* She hit SEND. They'd been together long enough. It was time.

Ditching costume party now, came the reply, *for officially the best invite ever.*

Jennifer stared at her phone. It was no longer capable of producing wormholes. But she had used it to make a wish come true.

T WAS AN UNUSUALLY warm night in early May, and Jennifer was opening windows. This was not something she could ever have done in her tiny apartment in the West Village—partly because the windows opened only a crack before window guards stopped them, partly because of the noise from Bleecker Street, which hadn't been bad by Manhattan standards but had been bad enough that it was unpleasant to sleep through. But now she was in Brooklyn, in a house with windows that had screens. The pace of life was slower here—streets were residential for blocks and blocks and lined with leafy green trees. You could play football on the street and rarely have to yell, "Car!" Aside from garbage day, in fact, the world around her had gotten remarkably quiet for still being part of the breakneck city of New York.

What a difference, Jennifer thought as she moved quietly through the hallways of the half brownstone she, Owen, Julien, and Jack now shared, turning off lights and readying the apartment for bed, *a year makes.*

She poked her head into Julien's room. The cat was curled up at the foot of his bed. Even the cat, Jennifer thought—if a marked decrease in cat vomit was any indication—seemed happier in the more relaxed environs of Brooklyn. "Do you want your window open?" she asked him.

"Sure," he said. He hopped out of bed and opened it himself. As he climbed back into bed and resumed reading, Jennifer looked happily around his softly lit room, and particularly proudly at the desk—Julien's first—Owen had somehow managed to wedge into the corner. It was tiny, to be sure, but big enough to display his prized possessions: two soccer trophies, a guitar pick that had once belonged to Chuck Berry, and a framed photo of Norman, Dina, Julien, Jack, and their new baby half brother, Sam. Jennifer wished she could look at the picture without rolling her eyes a little, but she hadn't gotten that far yet—Norman and Dina were so unfailingly pleased with themselves, with their organic steamed vegetables, cosleeping, and cloth diapers. Jennifer had taken secret delight in the fact that, according to Norman, Sam was more colicky than Jack had been, something she would not have believed possible—some consolation for the fact that Dina's thirty-year-old body had almost instantly resumed its previous shape, perky butt and all.

She was still getting used to being without the boys half the time, from Sunday to Wednesday every week. (She might never get used to it completely, she knew.) But the nights without her boys were spent with Owen now, which made the separation from her children far easier to bear. And now the nights with her boys were nights with Owen, too, a transition they'd made relatively smoothly, albeit with some bumps along the way. Owen was out tonight, playing a show in Hoboken. But he'd slip into bed with her when he got home, and when he did, she'd marvel, as she did every night, at her great good luck in finding him.

"What chapter are you on?" she asked Julien.

Julien was rereading all the Harry Potter books. They'd

been like comfort food for him as he'd struggled with transitioning to his new school in Brooklyn. It helped that he'd ended up in a school where Alicia's husband, Steven, knew the principal—particularly since Steven and Alicia lived upstairs. The brownstone belonged to them, purchased with a modest amount of money by the two schoolteachers twenty-five years before, when Park Slope had been a very different place to live. The previous tenants had moved out in August, and Jennifer, Owen, and the boys had jumped at the chance to move in and have a go at making a little village of their own.

"Twenty-one," Julien said, barely looking up from his book. "Where Hermione tells Harry about the Time-Turner."

At the mention of the Time-Turner, Jennifer suppressed a smile and quietly closed Julien's door.

Jennifer had to turn only a half step to the left to be standing in the doorway of Jack's room. She could hear him humming to himself, and, as her eyes adjusted to the low glow of his Winnie-the-Pooh lamp and crescent-moon night-light, she saw him sitting on his knees on his bed, carefully arranging his enormous collection of stuffed animals in an order that never varied by a paw or a whisker. (The orderly stuffed animals were his comfort, she thought, in the absence of his big brother, with whom he had always shared a room.) She was just about to enter and open his window, too, when he began to sing in his off-key, absentminded, little-boy voice. It was the song he'd sung that day at his kindergarten's Spring Sing: "Puff the Magic Dragon."

A dragon lives forever, but not so little boys . . .

Her boys were not little anymore. They were growing, and that was what she wanted, of course! But she couldn't help wondering: Would it be so bad to slow time down, just a little bit? Wishful thinking, she knew. The app had added hours to her day. But what she really wanted, she thought, was to hold on a little bit longer to her boys as they were now, to freeze the frame a few more hours, a few more minutes, a few more days.

I'm happy, she thought. And it was her happiness, too, that she wanted to bottle and, most of all, to last. There was the urgently romantic love she still felt for Owen, which she knew would mellow and change, hopefully in ways that would sustain them over time. There was the balance she'd found in her new job, continuing her work with One Stop but now as cohead of Dr. Sexton's foundation. Alicia was her counterpart there, just she had been when they'd worked for Bill, but the two women were now free to set workplace policies and goals and did not require themselves or their employees to put work above all else, or reward participation in the who-stays-latest-at-the-office-for-no-reason contest. (Tim, whom they'd brought along with them, appreciated this too.) They worked hard, of course, but made time for family too—Alicia having noted that her last child at home, a teenage daughter, needed more from her than her teenage sons ever had.

Things weren't perfect, of course. The One Stop community center, which Dr. Sexton's foundation was now largely responsible for funding, wasn't improving residents' lives as much as they'd hoped—infighting and territorial disputes among the participating government agencies had made Jennifer's vision of putting all of them under one roof impossible to achieve. They'd also faced an array of unanticipated challenges in getting residents to use the center in the first place. They were still forging ahead with the plan to build a second One Stop, in the Bronx, however, and the prospect of expansion was thrilling. At home Owen was still messy and sometimes idiotically optimistic about everything, and Julien had dealt with some of his anxiety at his new school by getting into fights. But all in all, life was better for Jennifer than it had been in a very long time.

Somewhere there is a woman, she'd written to Vinita recently, *who is done trying to do everything all of the time.*

I like her, Vinita had written back. *Let's not talk about that other woman anymore.*

It was time for bed. "Jack?" she said softly, reluctant to interrupt his reverie.

"Mama!" he said, patting his bed and beckoning her to join him.

She sat down and helped him get settled as he nestled under his covers. At the foot of the bed, he had carefully folded his blue baby blanket, its edges now frayed and filled with holes. She picked it up and began to wrap it around his shoulders.

"No," he said decisively, sitting up a bit. "I'm not a baby. That blanket is for Pooh. Pooh-baby."

"Oh," Jennifer said, "excuse me." She placed the blanket gingerly over Pooh.

"Maybe the new baby could have that blanket when she's born," he said tentatively.

"You think so?" Jennifer said. Smiling, she ran a hand over her taut, six-months-pregnant belly.

"Maybe she could just borrow it for a little while," Jack said, settling down on his pillow again. "Pooh might want it back someday."

That was the other thing. Jennifer was pregnant. When she'd said yes to Owen, she'd said yes to that, too. If she was going to make a leap of faith, she'd decided, she had to make it with both feet, leaving nothing behind her. Part of her still couldn't believe she'd done it, but a swift kick to the ribs was an effective reminder, as was the simple silver band she'd been wearing for the last four months on the ring finger of her left hand.

Jack turned onto his side. "Cuddle?" he asked.

"It's getting harder!" she answered, lying down on her side next to him in his narrow twin bed, her bulging belly barely fitting up against his tiny tummy.

"Tell me the story again?" he asked.

"About the two tiny particles of light?"

"Yes," Jack said, taking one of her hands and placing it on his head, a mutually understood request that she run her fingers through his hair and pretend to cut it, something her mother had done to her hair when she was a little girl.

"Okay," Jennifer said. Every night for weeks now, Jennifer had told Jack this story—the story that Dr. Sexton had written for the boys, but really for herself, not long after Susan died, five months before. It was a story based—though quite loosely —on the quantum theory of entanglement.

"Once upon a time," Jennifer began, "there were two tiny particles of light, so tiny no human being could ever see them. The two particles were happy, living in the universe and going everywhere they pleased, shooting around outer space in ways that nobody, not even they, could predict. One moment they might be spinning up and down as they hurtled through space; another moment they might spin around and around. But they were so tiny and fast that nobody knew for sure. These particles of light were called photons. Aside from that they had no other name, and both of them were very lonely in the vast, infinite emptiness of space.

"One day, however, something amazing happened. The two photons, who had never collided with each other or even been in the same room together for longer than it takes a fly to beat its wing, found themselves trapped inside the same beautiful diamond.

"Well, neither of these photons had ever been inside a diamond before! It was full of strange crystals, and shapes like towers, only they were towers turned upside down, and sideways, and hanging from the ceiling at every angle you can imagine. For a while, the two tiny photons bounced all around inside the diamond, feeling alone, as usual. But suddenly something that had never happened to either of them before happened to both of them at exactly the same time.

"They crashed into each other!" Jack cried.

"That's right," Jennifer said. "And just as they began to get up to say 'excuse me,' and 'my apologies,' and 'oh my, are you all right?' they realized something. When one of the particles tried to go on her way, spinning and careening as usual, the other particle was pulled along with her. 'Oh no!' the first particle said. 'What are we going to do?' the second particle asked. They didn't know. But where before they had been all alone in the universe, suddenly they were coupled. Where there had been only one particle, there were now two. And whether they liked it or not, from that point forward, everything they did, they did together."

"So they needed names," Jack said. "So they could tell who was who." Jennifer nodded. "And one was named Diane," Jack said, "and one was named Susan, like Susan who died."

It was so simple and direct, the way Jack said it. *Susan who died.* Jennifer wondered how Dr. Sexton was getting along just now, packing up the brownstone she and Susan had shared for more than thirty years, and where they had been married in a quiet ceremony in the garden just a few months before Susan passed away. Dr. Sexton had decided to donate most of her scientific treasures to the American Museum of Natural History, as part of a *Women in Science* exhibition she was helping to curate in Susan's memory. The collection was too big for the small apartment she'd chosen to live in, just blocks from where she'd grown up on the Upper East Side.

Jack yawned loudly. "Tell the next part, Mama," he said.

"From that day onward, Susan and Diane traveled all over

the universe together. Everywhere one of them went, the other went too. At first it was hard. Neither one was used to traveling with somebody else. But after a while they learned how, and soon they were good at it. If one of them spun around and around, the other one spun up and down, so they were always in balance. The best part was that even though it was hard at first, traveling together turned out to be much better than traveling alone.

"Then, one day, after many years had gone by, something terrible happened. The photons were separated. Neither one of them understood how it had happened. One minute they were traveling along as usual, and the next minute they were torn apart, sent in two entirely different directions, hurtling away from each other at the speed of light. What had disjoined them? How would Diane know which way to spin if Susan wasn't there? And how would Susan know which way to spin without Diane to guide her? Light speed is the fastest speed there is, and the black and empty space between them grew infinitely vast in one irrevocable instant.

"But then another very strange thing happened. A spooky thing. Even though they were so far apart they could not see or hear or reach each other, when Diane spun up and down, Susan spun around and around. And when Susan spun around and around, Diane spun up and down. Stranger still, if one of them tried to do it differently, she couldn't. It didn't matter how far away they were. It didn't even matter if Diane was on Earth and Susan was on some other planet, a planet Diane could not begin to imagine. The two tiny particles of light were connected forever. They were entangled, and once they had been entangled—which is a way of being enchanted—not even the vastest distances in space could part them ever again.

"The end."

"That's a true story, right, Mama?" Jack said sleepily.

"It's based on a true story," Jennifer said. "Someday I'll explain what it means." Propping herself up on one elbow, she prepared for the enormous effort that had become sitting up. She hated being pregnant. She had never been one of those women who loved it. But when she stood up she felt the baby move, and she stood still for a moment, watching in wonder as an elbow, or a knee, swept across her belly. She placed a hand on her stomach. "Good night, Elizabeth," she whispered. Owen had agreed to let her do the naming. Her baby—her *daughter*—would be named Elizabeth, after her mother. Her middle name would be Susan.

Turning out the light, Jennifer thought of something Dr. Sexton had told her when she had explained entanglement—the quantum theory that two particles, once entangled, will be affected by what is done to the other, no matter how great the distance that separates them (a theory Einstein himself called "spooky" but accepted as fact). "It's a bit wacky, and unlikely, perhaps, but it is possible that when we used the app, the particles in our bodies, bound together by a particle yet unknown to us, may have remained connected somehow, entangled despite being separated by two different points in space-time." She had then eyed Jennifer's growing belly, which to Jennifer's dismay had already blown up to the size of that of a full-term mother of triplets. "And if that is true, my dear," she'd added, "imagine the connection between the particles in a mother's body and her baby's!"

Jennifer didn't know about all that. What she did know was that while she had managed to strike a remarkable equilibrium in her life at that moment, it was about to end, for a little while, at least. Nothing blew up balance, she kept trying to tell the hopelessly naive Owen, like a newborn.

Having kissed a sleeping Jack good night, she hurled herself out of his bed and stood. She was so tired already. How was she going to do it? The breast-feeding, the working, the pumping, the sleeplessness, the exhaustion, the poopy diapers, the endless neediness and crying—not to mention dealing with the demands of the children she already had and attending to Owen's needs too? And then a thought popped into her head before she could stop it.

Maybe, she thought, *there's an app for that.*

acknowledgments

There are so many people to whom I am grateful for supporting me, in ways great and small, in the writing of this book. First, the teachers, editors, and friends who contributed most directly to its creation: Alexandra Shelley and the members of the Jane Street Writing Workshop, who read its first pages and encouraged me to carry on; Amy Fox, who remains my most trusted editor and who is perhaps most responsible for the fact that my first novel, while still imperfect, is as sure-footed and well structured as it is (and whose abiding friendship means even more to me than her editorial talent, which is saying a lot); Melissa Kantor, who, in a few quick conversations—often during stolen moments at baseball practices or other activities our sons were attending— gave me invaluable advice about how a novel actually gets finished; JillEllyn Riley, who gave me spot-on editorial feedback when I needed it most; and Karen Sherman, who was the best copy editor ever.

No one, however, spent more time or dedicated more energy to the creation of this book than my friend, editor extraordinaire, and cofounder of She Writes Press, Brooke Warner, who talked me down off cliffs when things were progressing slowly—or not at all—and celebrated with me at every breakthrough. Brooke is fair, patient, hardworking, and visionary, and I am so honored to have her as my partner in the exciting publishing venture of which this book is a part. Same goes for Crystal Patriarche, who has made She Writes Press a part of the SparkPoint family, and whose leadership I know will take us far. I will also be forever grateful to my agent, Erin Hosier, who believed in me years ago when I brought her the manuscript for my first book, the publication of which truly changed my life. Erin enthusiastically championed *Wishful Thinking* in the marketplace and landed me a deal with a major publishing house. It says a lot about her unselfish commitment to her authors that when I chose to publish with She Writes Press instead, she supported my decision completely.

Writing is a lonely endeavor, requiring hours of solitude and the willingness to write even when it seems nobody in the world cares that you are writing but you. (Which is pretty much true.) I would never have finished this book without the communities of writers I have either founded or been invited into; from them, I got the inspiration, advice, friendship, and wisdom I needed—and will always need—to sustain me. Thank you, first and foremost, to the passionate, generous, indefatigable members of SheWrites.com, who have cheered me on and guided my path from my very first "Gone Writing" post through to the end. Thank you, too, to the New York, London, and San Francisco Salons of Women Writers, the authors of She Writes Press, my fellow residents at the Hedgebrook writers' colony, and my fellow board members at Girls Write Now. It is impossible to individually list all the women who have impacted my life through these organizations, but I would be remiss if I didn't single out Deborah Siegel, my cofounder at SheWrites.com and a consistently loving, intelligent presence in my life; Nancy K. Miller, my cofounder of the New York Salon of Women Writers and one of my most cherished mentors and friends; and Maya Nussbaum, whose tireless advocacy of the girls of Girls Write Now reminds me daily that writing is hard precisely because it is so important.

Thank you to my family, and especially to my parents, whom I have relied upon in recent years in ways I'd never have imagined possible as an adult until I went through a divorce. Special thanks also to my sister, Kimberly, who read an early draft and helped me fine-tune the world of Jennifer's work. I am grateful to my friend Naseem Zojwalla for her early read, and to Sidney Perkowitz, professor of physics at Emory University, who bridges the worlds of science and art in his own endeavors and helped me to bridge them credibly in this book. Josefina Pierre-Louis is my family's caregiver and an indispensable part of my life; she has also been like a sister to me and will always be a dear friend. Matthew Kaplan was perhaps the biggest surprise of the years spent writing this book. When I started *Wishful Thinking*, I couldn't imagine falling in love again. When I finished it, Matthew was sitting across from me in a coffee shop, holding my hand. He is my emergency contact person. I hope I will always be his.

Max and Jed, there are no words. You have followed my progress with this book from its inception, enthusiastically discussing every aspect of it with me over family dinners, from the process of revision to the ins and outs of the book business. You are good, loving, precocious, hilarious, beautiful boys, and while you are still works in progress, I already know that raising you is the best and most important work I will ever do in this world.

And finally, Diane. Before there was Diane Sexton, there was Diane Middlebrook—biographer, poet, teacher, and beloved mentor to me and countless others lucky enough to have known her. It is the real Diane's voice, style, brilliance, fearlessness, and tenderness, too, that gave life to the Diane who sparkles and strides across these pages. Hearing her voice in my head as I wrote was no substitute for her presence in my life, but it was a kind of joy. One of the hardest things about finishing this book was letting her go. But of course I will never do that.

WISHFUL THINKING

KAMY WICOFF

Reading Group Guide

reading group questions and
topics for discussion

1. At the beginning of the book, Jennifer says that when she was a girl, she dreamed of being two people when she grew up: a stay-at-home mom and the president of the United States. Now that she is grown up and trying to balance her life as a working mother, she feels the need to be multiple people more than ever. How much do you think this is pressure Jennifer is putting on herself, and how much do you think it is pressure she is getting from the outside world?

2. When Jennifer realizes she has lost her phone, a deep dread and prickling panic overtake her (later she discovers there is a word for the fear of being separated from your phone: nomophobia), but a part of her feels liberated from her "digital ball and chain." How do you think these dueling feelings play out over the course of the book, and what do you think the author is saying about the way people use smartphones in modern life?

3. Early in the book, Jennifer relates that her new boss, Bill Truitt, came to city government on a mission to impose what he calls a "private sector work ethic" on her department, including longer hours and more emphasis on in-office "face-time." To Jennifer, this means not only making the fact that she is a single mother all but invisible when she is at work, it means being expected to work as though she has a wife—"the kind of wife even husbands didn't have anymore." How does Bill's notion of the "ideal worker" impact Jennifer and Alicia? Tim? How would it impact a man working for Bill who had children and a wife who also worked?

4. On page 27, Jennifer composes a "somewhere there is a woman" e-mail to her best friend Vinita. The theme of these e-mails and texts between the two friends is the mythical woman who has, and does, it all, whose perfect life (as advertised on Facebook), haunts them. Where do you think Jennifer and Vinita get their standards for what makes a "successful" woman? How do those standards impact the way they evaluate their own lives?

5. When Jennifer opens the app, she sees the tagline *An App for Women Who Need to Be in More Than One Place At the Same Time*, and describes it as the most alluring tagline she has ever seen in her life. Not believing the app is real, she books an appointment to go to her older son Julien's guitar recital, something she was otherwise going to miss. What would your first Wishful Thinking appointment be? How many times could you have used the app in the last twenty-four hours?

6. Jennifer's ex-husband, Norman, all but abandoned her and their two boys in the years immediately following their divorce. Now he is back and asking for 50 percent custody, a request that outrages Jennifer. In what ways do you think Jennifer is right in her response to Norman's request? In what ways is she wrong?

7. Why do you think Dr. Sexton agrees to give Jennifer the app?

8. Dr. Sexton explains to Jennifer that the app operates by creating a wormhole. Did you feel the science behind the app was compelling/believable? How did you feel the science either enriched or distracted from the story?

9. Jennifer is thrilled to pick her boys up from school, but by six o'clock, cleaning her apartment is more appealing than continuing to play with them. Jennifer is aware of this paradox: sometimes the *idea* of being with her children is better than the actual experience of it. If you are a parent, have you ever felt this? If not, have you observed a similar paradox in other parts of your life?

10. How does Norman's falling in love with someone else effect Jennifer? Are Jennifer's children the emotional center of her life? How does that impact her and her boys?

11. In Chapter 13, Dr. Sexton relates her story to Jennifer, including the reason she is no longer affiliated with a university—a professor at the university she left suggested that women were unable to compete with male scientists because their interest in child-bearing during the years physicists typically peak (early twenties) was a hindrance to them. This incident is fictional, but in 2005, then-Harvard president Lawrence Summers suggested that there were fewer women in science because a) fewer women were willing to put in eighty-hour workweeks; and b) there are innate differences between women and men that impact scientific ability. How do you think other characters in the book—Bill, Vinita, Susan, Jennifer—would react to these kinds of arguments?

12. Jennifer and Vinita have been best friends since college. But in recent years, Vinita's marriage to a wealthy investment banker, in stark contrast to Jennifer's marriage to a struggling actor, has created a gap between them that neither has ever explicitly talked about. At Jennifer's surprise party, however, when Vinita angrily confronts Jennifer about her use of the app, it comes out: Jennifer

doesn't feel Vinita's experiences with "juggling" work and family can be compared with her own because Vinita has so much money, and so much help. Is this fair?

13. When Alicia discovers Jennifer is using the app, Jennifer tries to excuse her behavior partly by suggesting the app could help the women in the public housing projects they serve—a suggestion that outrages Alicia. "[Your idea is] to throw a bunch of poor women through a wormhole every day so they can take care of their children and collect their welfare checks at the same time? *Time travel* is easier than passing affordable child care?" Upon hearing this, Jennifer, stung, reflects that she has always hated the "every-person-for-herself" attitude that isolates and blames so many of the public housing residents she works with, and yet she has just suggested that in order to address the multiplying burdens they face, single mothers should multiply themselves. When the demands placed on you, at work or at home, seem too much, is your first instinct to blame yourself? Or to challenge the system that produces those demands?

14. When Jennifer is contemplating the effect the app has had on her life, she asks herself: *When you can do anything all the time, what does anything you do mean anymore?* To what extent do the choices people make about work, life, and love, and how much time to invest in them, have meaning because choosing one thing inevitably means sacrificing something else? Are Jennifer, Alicia, Vinita, and Dr. Sexton equally free to "choose" between career and nurturing relationships, for example, or is the degree of choice each woman has dependent upon her circumstances?

about the author

Photo credit: Elena Seibert

KAMY WICOFF is the best-selling author of the nonfiction book *I Do But I Don't: Why The Way We Marry Matters*, and founder of one of the world's largest communities for women writers, www.shewrites.com. She is also founder, with Brooke Warner, of She Writes Press. She lives with her family in Brooklyn, New York.

To learn more about Kamy, as well as the real music and the real scientists behind Wishful Thinking, visit:

www.kamywicoff.com

SELECTED TITLES FROM SHE WRITES PRESS

She Writes Press is an independent publishing company
founded to serve women writers everywhere.
Visit us at www.shewritespress.com.

Play for Me by Céline Keating. $16.95, 978-1-63152-972-6. Middle-aged Lily impulsively joins a touring folk-rock band, leaving her job and marriage behind in an attempt to find a second chance at life, passion, and art.

Vote for Remi by Leanna Lehman. $16.95, 978-1-63152-978-8. History is changed forever when an ambitious classroom of high school seniors pull the ultimate prank on their favorite teacher—and end up getting her in the running to become president of the United States.

Royal Entertainment by Marni Fechter. $16.95, 978-1-938314-52-0. After being fired from her job for blowing the whistle on her boss, social worker Melody Frank has to adapt to her new life as the assistant to an elite New York party planner.

Warming Up by Mary Hutchings Reed. $16.95, 978-1-938314-05-6. Unemployed and depressed former musical actress Cecilia Morrison decides to start therapy, hoping it will get her out of her slump—but ultimately it's a teen who cons her out of sixty bucks, not her analyst, who changes her life.

A Tight Grip: A Novel about Golf, Love Affairs, and Women of a Certain Age by Kay Rae Chomic. $16.95, 978-1-938314-76-6. As forty-six-year-old golfer Jane "Par" Parker prepares for her next tournament, she experiences a chain of events that force her to reevaluate her life.

Shelter Us by Laura Diamond. $16.95, 978-1-63152-970-2. Lawyer-turned-stay-at-home-mom Sarah Shaw is still struggling to find a steady happiness after the death of her infant daughter when she meets a young homeless mother and toddler she can't get out of her mind—and becomes determined to rescue them.